THE LAST TRAIN TO KAZAN

Stephen Miller was born in the USA and now lives in Canada. After graduating from Virginia Military Institute in 1968, he moved to Vancouver to concentrate on creative writing and theatre, starting as a stage carpenter and working his way up to becoming an actor and scriptwriter. *The Last Train to Kazan* is his second novel.

Visit www.AuthorTracker.co.uk for exclusive information about Stephen Miller.

Also by Stephen Miller

A Game of Soldiers

STEPHEN MILLER

The Last Train to Kazan

HARPER

Harper

An imprint of HarperCollins*Publishers*
77–85 Fulham Palace Road,
Hammersmith, London W6 8JB

www.harpercollins.co.uk

This paperback edition 2007
1

A catalogue record for this book

978 0 00 719123 9

Set in Sabon by Palimpsest Book Production Limited,
Grangemouth, Stirlingshire

Printed and bound in Great Britain by
Clays Ltd, St Ives plc

For St Elmo's daughter

Moscow

July 1918

The first bloody summer of the revolution – and the Bolsheviks are losing. White forces are pushing towards Moscow from all points of the compass.

Forced to make a separate peace with Germany, the Red leaders are loathed by the Allies and many of their own supporters. Terrible atrocities occur each day in the name of freedom, in the name of the workers, in the name of God. The Revolution hungers for money, for bullets, and for credibility among the proletariat. As Bolshevik support wanes, one of the only cards left is the Imperial Family – Tsar Nicholas, the Empress Alexandra and their children, initially under house arrest at Tsarskoye Selo, then moved to the remote Siberian town of Tobolsk, and soon to be moved once again.

These re-locations are justified to the Romanovs as being necessary for their own protection. It is plausible; after all, there are millions who blame the Tsar for all their misfortunes – for their failed war, for their poverty and their ignorance, for the dream of a workers' paradise that appears to be stillborn.

Now in this darkest hour of the People's Revolution, the

Romanovs have become a commodity, their value rising and falling on an informal exchange between realpolitik and monarchist nostalgia. Among the several contending forces, some want to rescue the Romanovs, others want to kill them, but all want to use them in some way.

They are seen by everyone as a lever.

And no one knows their fate.

'Even if the Imperial Family is alive, it is necessary to say they are dead.'

ROBERT WILTON, *Journalist*

1

Pyotr Mikhalovich Ryzhkov walked across the bright Neglinnaya Prospekt to the Hermitage restaurant. He was dressed in a brown suit, his least shabby, and carried his fedora in his hands since it was too hot to wear it. Moscow was stifling, a spider's web of streets that radiated from the river and ran uphill, spreading above the Kremlin and the old wall of the city until they intersected the ring of gardened boulevard just next to the restaurant.

He was pretending to be a poetic soul, musing on beauty and lofty thoughts during the tram ride up from Tatarskaya. Yes, a poetic soul – a translator and valued member of the French embassy staff. A Russian veteran of the Foreign Legion, caught up in the Western Front war, and newly posted from Paris to Moscow on account of his background. Well . . . if anyone checked, that much was true. Translating? Yes, he actually did some translating, but mostly it was to explain to this bosses what a particular scrawled message might mean, or to interpret a phrase taken from a stenographer's transcript of an intercepted telephone call.

What he really did for his salary, and purely because he had very little choice in the matter, was organize a short string of informants, both in and out of the Bolshevik government, who sporadically provided information to France. And, since everything was in chaos, the Bolsheviks suffering from factional disputes, there was no shortage of recruits. Ryzhkov did not have the privilege of selecting most of his sources, and therefore he was expendable. He knew all that. He was more than painfully aware that he was one of the only experienced agents working for the French, but precariously out on the point, with no uniform, no credentials.

But now perhaps he had somehow actually grown into the skin of a poseur. His life had been a lie for so long, and his deceit tested by enough challenges, that pretence and play-acting had been annealed into his being. If he were to be honest, he would have to admit that he fought almost every day to remember who he really was. The only way out of it all was to either win or surrender – not really much of a choice, he was thinking.

And then he saw the man, the same one he had seen in Theatre Square, waiting by the tram stops.

Paranoid, he thought. Occupational disease. After a while you saw the same people all the time. True, Ryzhkov had a great memory for faces; the man could be someone he'd seen before, outside on the street, in a café. Just an ordinary citizen en route to – where, exactly?

Don't think about it. Go on as usual.

And so he did. Musing about the city. Poetic soul.

He waited until the tram stopped, swung out of the seat and down onto the wide sidewalk and walked past the fence to the entrance to the park.

Test them, he was thinking. It could be an exercise, so test them. Do nothing out of the ordinary, but test them all the same.

He stopped, checked his watch. Ah . . . early. Stroll around, have a smoke. Admire the church in the far corner by the little pool that they'd built into the park. Yes, yes, a beautiful day. Pose as a happy man; tip your hat to the ladies, smile at the children. A nobody, a clerk-translator on his day off, going to meet his friend at the popular restaurant. Half way around the pool he checked his watch again, made a new decision and turned around.

Ahead of him two men casually stopped and fussed for cigarettes in their clothing.

He walked faster now, heading back to the restaurant, up the steps. Under the new administration the Hermitage was a 'people's canteen' and, reservations being an affectation of the upper classes, service was strictly by queue. But one still had to pay, and there were only two couples waiting ahead of him.

He was directed to his table. Made a show of waiting for his friend. Ordered a glass of *konyak* and then went to the bathroom. In the farthest toilet he reached behind the tank and found the little magnetized box, pulled it away, opened the cap, took out the rolled cigarette papers, capped the box, hid it behind the tank in the horizontal position, flushed the toilet and, still holding the paper in his fingers, went out to the sinks. No one. A flush in the corner stall; at nearly the same moment the door to the washroom swung open and an older man entered fumbling with his pants buttons. They wouldn't try to take him in the restaurant itself, he was thinking.

He washed his hands and went back to his seat. The papers were in his pocket now. He sat and waited for his friend, nursed his *konyak* and tried to work out what to do.

They could have him any time, this government. Why now?

Outside men and women walked in the empty park, admiring the straggling gardens, looking at their own reflections in the windows. The old restaurant was not even half full. There was nothing on the menu but soup and eggs. The eggs cost 150 roubles.

Ryzhkov caught the waiter's eye and asked to use the telephone kiosk. Inside the kiosk he took out the papers and looked for a place to hide them. The seat was made of leather gone ragged and built into the wooden cabinetry. A strip of moulding on the inside rim of the seat was loose and he flattened the papers out on the marble shelf in the kiosk, slipped them beneath the wood and banged it tight with his fist.

There was no answer to his telephone call. He thought about telephoning the embassy, calling Merk to rescue him, but the new government kept records of all calls at the district switchboards, and if they were going to take him it would be soon now . . . when he left the restaurant.

So he went back to the table. Sat, fuming, for a few more minutes. Angry, letting his nerves out a little. Everything was plausible, so far. But there was nothing, nothing, nothing to grab onto.

Suddenly his anger overwhelmed him. He sat for a moment and broke out into a sweat, his face gone red. Outside, lingering at a lamppost, the man on the tram was given a light for his cigarette by a total stranger. They stopped to exchange a few words and then parted.

He'd waited long enough for his imaginary friend that was never going to come. Abruptly he was standing, shrugging at the waiter, who shrugged back – not an unhappy man. Happy to have work that put him close to a little food now and again, a life indoors under wide ferns and palms that softened the glare through the huge windows. Not a bad job in the middle of a revolution with winter coming, Ryzhkov thought.

A breeze riffled through the leaves from under the awning. He went down the steps. Now he was being a man who suddenly had time on his hands. He walked to the tram stop and waited. There was no point in even looking around now. He knew.

4

He took the tram as far as the Theatre, then got off and wound his way through the old market, shopping for a few items. It would give them a few more places to check, if they thought he'd dumped the package. Test them. Fight back, he told himself, still angry, frustrated. Blaming himself for never saying no, for thinking that coming back to Russia would mean that he could do something, change something. Find whatever it was he'd lost.

He'd been on the little street a thousand times. It was across and behind the Kremlin from where he'd grown up – his father's second house on Gazetni Street. They'd moved there to be close to the university where the old man had sometimes worked. Ryzhkov had gone to the Alexander School right in the centre of the city. It was one of the only good times he could remember.

He picked up the tram again, following one long strand of the spider's web past the Ilynskaya gate and the Church of Transfiguration. Four years of war and revolution had leached the life out of Moscow; the trees had slowly vanished for fuel in the winters, there were no more dogs in the city, they had all been eaten. Money was of dubious value, the prices fluctuating daily; the best way to 'buy' something was to barter for it, preferably with food. There was a brisk market in bootleg vodka and schnapps. Men sold it in home-made tins on corners. The Bolsheviks had posted strict proscriptions on alcoholism, but the people had ignored them.

They would take him soon, if they were going to take him at all, and since there was no escape he gave them time to organize. He might as well make it easy. He had no stomach for a fight. At the next stop Ryzhkov got out and walked up the hill behind the Kremlin onto the wide plaza.

Above him loomed St Basil's, famously named for the saint who was supposedly watching over Moscow and protecting her citizens. Appropriate, he thought. He went inside, admired

5

the frescos and the ikons of the saints. The cathedral was cool in the hot summer day, and Ryzhkov walked into one of the chapels, stood in front of the array of ikons, and, more as a test for himself than anything else, tried to pray.

It didn't matter that no prayer came. It didn't matter if he was killed. He'd long since given up worrying about death. Like all the men who'd lived through the trenches he'd only prayed that death might come quickly. A little mercy, that was all.

There was no more time, he thought. He saw a man who had come in behind him and was waiting there, hat in hand. Another was standing just at the outer doors. Both of them were young but looked like they might know what to do. He turned to leave and they followed him out onto the steps.

Below him two carriages had drawn up and four other men were waiting.

'Bonjour,' one of the men said. They were laughing and it was too late to run.

From sleep. Dark and vast; adapted for survival so that one part of him was lost in the void, while the other heard the step of the guard in the corridor; the change of the shift, the scratch of a match, the exhale of tobacco. The scattered snap of the gunshots in the courtyard.

He would never have a whole sleep again, Ryzhkov knew. Along with millions of other men, he had adjusted to it. Lying there in a daze, you could at least gain some rest. Besides, if you really slept you might have dreams.

Ryzhkov knew his jail; he had walked past it a hundred times as a young man in Moscow, been into the offices with his father back when it had been the headquarters of the Anchor Assurance and Lloyds of London. Now, it was known by its street address, Bolshaya Lubyanka 11 – newly transformed into the headquarters of the the Extraordinary Commission – the Cheka, the Bolshevik secret police.

It was summer, but the cell was dank. Lit by a window that itself was bisected by a new wall that the revolution had thrown up, red bricks with sharp crusts of mortar that had oozed out of the gaps. Maybe six feet wide and twice as long to the cold outside wall; a thin flea-infested pallet and a bucket.

At first all cells were the same, he thought. And then, once you'd spent enough time fantasizing about escape, or trying to find tiny hiding places to store your pathetic contraband items – a pencil stub, a nail, a fragment of tobacco that had been filched from under the door and saved in hope of a wayward match – you realized that each cell was an individual, like people with their own personalities. There were the impassive ones who'd been wrenched from the soft life and burned down to an austere essence; cruel cells, like people who could watch you die rather than sacrifice a single tear; the cells that kept their dark stories to themselves; cells that couldn't stop screaming.

It had been three days and he was still in the clothes he had been arrested in; there were no uniforms for the prisoners. You were interrogated, then executed in whatever you were wearing when they picked you up; the last set of clothing you wore became your shroud.

He'd had one long session on the first afternoon. Just questions, no side talk. First one Chekisti, then another and another until there were four. They didn't bother identifying themselves.

They knew all about him and his attachment to the French intelligence networks once he'd come back to Russia when Kerensky's Provisional Government granted amnesty to all the politicals. He was openly working at the French embassy and it wasn't a great leap of detection for them to bring him in.

He sat there handcuffed to his chair and gave them all the obvious answers. One of the men wrote it all down. Testimony. He took his time and was careful. He was a translator, an embassy employee. He wanted to be put in touch with the Ambassador's office, and he wanted the services of a legal representative. All the time he was answering he was trying to work it out.

Something had cracked, something under the pressures of civil war and counter-revolution had pushed events into an emergency. Events had obviously overrun whatever immunity he might have possessed as an employee of the French. It could be a change of plans on high; there was a faint possibility he could be some sort of bargaining chip, or maybe the French had given him up to the Cheka for some favour.

He would never know, and, whatever it was, the world had moved on. He was not a prize catch, there was nothing he could divulge that would make the slightest difference to either side. He thought it might possibly be that he was only being kept alive because of a clerical error.

In semi-sleep he heard the laughing guard coming along the corridor, his stick banging against the doors. Ryzhkov stood, his knees paining him, bladder full, every muscle gone stiff, reluctant. The stick approached, crossed his doorway and continued along the hall. He counted the doors. Three until the end, and then the guard turned back down the line, peering inside to check that everyone was alive this morning. The grill slid open. Ryzhkov looked into the watery blue eyes, the shock of blond hair.

'Ah, good morning, Monsieur Ryzhkov,' he called out. 'You're looking thinner, but why waste food on the likes of you when the people's army needs nourishment, eh?' Of course the guard didn't know any of the details of his case, it was the only advantage Ryzhkov had over the boy.

'I'm wondering if you have heard the latest news, that everyone on this corridor is to be executed. Did you know that? Only a matter of days, I'm afraid,' and then the little laugh as the grill slid shut. The story continued to the next chamber. '. . . morning, Monsieur Swetovsky. Yes, you heard me correctly. We're cleaning out all the dead wood . . .'

Ryzhkov walked the length of the cell, urinated into the bucket, and then returned to the door. The guard's hearty greetings were still echoing down the hall. From somewhere there was the scuffling of boots on the tiles, a protesting voice, the sudden sound of metal against metal. It meant they were taking someone out. Now he could no longer hear the laughing guard; his cheeriness had evaporated. The men who came to take you were solemn when they did it. For them it was just a grim task, getting a physically reluctant creature from point A to B. More clatter along the corridor, the closing of the door, and then, finally, the laughter of the guard returned.

Ryzhkov walked the length of the cell a hundred times, folded over the mattress and sat on it and waited while the guard came at last to his door, slid the morning meal through the hinged gate. 'There you are. A waste, if you ask me, since you're going to die soon.'

'Thank you very much,' Ryzhkov said, rolling off the mat, dragging the plate across the floor and, hungry now, sipping the soup out of the tin before attacking the archipelago of cabbage marooned in the centre of the dish. There was a tiny sliver of something that looked like meat, or perhaps it was a stick of wood, a fragment of a cooking spoon or a ladle. It didn't matter; he ate it.

The guard had developed an attachment to him. Perhaps because he was a mystery and Ryzhkov hadn't offered the young man anything. A polite mystery, because that was the only way to deal with jailers. You couldn't intimidate them, or abuse them. The only thing you could do was wait. There had been one revolution that had put him here, maybe another would free him.

The boy sat outside on a stool that he'd hauled down he corridor, taunted him with questions. Perhaps he saw it as a way of educating himself by studying the enemy, just as an apprentice angel might study a lesser demon. 'I don't understand you,' he said to Ryzhkov. 'You claim to be a revolutionary? That's absurd. How can you say something like that?'

'Absolutely.' Ryzhkov was trying not to bolt the cabbage. It was all he would get until the evening, and as for activity, it was just about all he would do, unless using the bucket or strolling from wall to wall counted.

'You claim that you are a clandestine operative. For the revolution also?'

'I claim nothing. I already told them everything, and besides, it's none of your business, is it, comrade?'

He laughs. 'No, it's not my business. But since you say you're a revolutionary, then why are you here?'

'There are many varieties of revolution, comrade. Why are you here?'

'I'm here to detain and execute vermin like you. I'm killing capitalist rats, that's what I'm doing.'

'Ahh . . . Well, I'm not a capitalist, if that's what's worrying you. I have nothing, own nothing. Nothing at all. Never have. Not for a long, long time.' Idly he wondered whatever had become of the apartment he had once owned in Petersburg. Probably a flophouse for deserving peasants.

'I love to kill people like you. I am good at it,' the boy said, unable to take the laugh out of his voice. 'I have been recognized for my efforts. I'm to be given an award for diligence and valour.'

'I thought there were to be no more medals in Russia?'

10

A pause while the guard thought it through. 'That's correct. Correct. No classes. Only levels of achievement, literacy, health for all, an end to drunkenness and debauchery. All the things that we have been lacking. Now they are within our grasp. Only a little more cleaning up to do. Only a few more vermin to kill . . .' The laughter again. Forced. Ryzhkov slid the plate across the concrete floor and through the little hinged opening. 'Now we are on the verge of attaining all the things we've been lacking, comrade Ryzhkov. I call you "comrade" because deep down I do believe you can be saved.'

'With the grace of God.'

'Don't tell me you believe in that garbage.' The laugh spluttered out in the corridor. The plate was abruptly swept away, the doorway flaps closed.

'Perhaps I am simply hedging my bets.'

'The church! Those are the ones responsible for all our undoing, moaning and groaning about an afterlife. People like Rasputin. If you're one of them, you really do deserve to die.' He spat and walked away.

Ryzhkov dozes. Although it is not dozing really, more like staring at the plastered wall until he falls into a trance, reliving the choices that led him first to the Okhrana, then to the fugitive life, then to the trenches, on and on, through all his life's mistakes. While he is so occupied, there are new boots clacking down the corridor. A door is unlocked, thrown open. A man, screaming, jerked free of his own particular trance, is hauled out and away. A Bolshevik voice recites an 'official' proclamation of death. Another door is closed, and a few precious moments later . . . a splattering of gunfire.

And then they come again.

Ryzhkov is bolt upright now as the boots crash through the door, down the corridor. And he stands, stands as he has been taught at the precise centre of his cell, which now . . . he no longer wants to leave. Now it has become a place of safety. Home.

The door is wrenched open. Three toughs, and behind them is the laughing guard, the smile spreading across his wide blond face. 'One less *burzhui* to deal with. One less parasite. I am going to be crying big tears of happiness! Oh, catch him!' This last because Ryzhkov has fallen, either because he is weak from the rations or because he is terrified, or because after all of it – after all the times he has cheated death – this . . . this . . .

This is all happening too quickly. In front of him the tiled corridor, filthy since the guards of the Red Army are no longer compelled to perform menial jobs that soldiers normally perform. They bull along it. No one gets in their way; there are, after all, no officers to carry out inspections, to criticize the polishing of boots, the crease in one's trousers . . .

They go now from A to B, but he is not walking. The strong young sons of revolutionary Russia are dragging him along. Ahead of him the guard, eager to help out, throws open another steel door.

' . . . revolutionary council decision to extract the penalty of death in payment for a lifetime of parasitic activity, of conspiring with the forces of the capitalist enemy, it has been determined that one Pyotr Mikhalovich Ryzhkov shall be immediately . . .'

A short series of steps, one two three, yet another steel door, remarkably heavy doors for an insurance company, but necessary now that the enemies of the people have begun to be filed away in the basement offices.

A sudden breath of cool air – a diagonal of shade crosses the courtyard. There is, he realizes with horror, a guillotine set up at the very end of the courtyard, and if that was not enough, a gallows, newly built of stripped logs still sticky with resin. But Ryzhkov is being dragged past both of the machines to a wall speckled from gunshots gone awry. A slime of blood is slowly making its labyrinthine way between the cobbles towards a drain. There is a hose there and a quartet of terrorized cadets still in their old Corps des Pages uniforms, tattered and filthy, shackled, with bruises on their dirty faces, sooty and tear-stained. Mere boys kept there to watch and remember, to wipe things down and at the end of the day to take it up the arse.

His bowels loosen. His eyes are stinging. Everything seems beautiful, beautiful. The sun slicing across the courtyard, the guillotine standing erect and waiting for a more distinguished neck than his.

The official voice has finished its litany of his crimes. He is thrown to his knees. The soldiers work the bolts of their rifles, two bullets are chambered. Only two! Soon they will even economize on that, he thinks.

He goes inside himself. A man in a suit has walked up directly in front of the soldiers. After a moment Ryzhkov becomes aware of the man's shoes in front of him. The guard's disbelieving voice protesting; even in disappointment he can still laugh.

The infantrymen retreat a few steps and someone grabs his hair and lifts his face up to the sun. It is the guard, cheated out of the punch line to his joke. 'After they ask you a few more questions, then we're coming back outside and finish you.'

They light up cigarettes as he is led across the courtyard under the shade of the pine-scented gallows, through a yellow doorway and down another short corridor. Then they spin him, and push him face-first into the wall of an office, unmanacle his hands, and order him to sit.

In front of him is a plain table, and behind it a second chair. He realizes his pants are soiled, from blood, faeces, urine . . . his own or someone who has gone before him, how could he tell? The room is gorgeous, he thinks. Paradisiacal. A lovely large room, luxurious and clean. With a single window high in the wall, made of glass that has been manufactured with wires inside it.

Shatterproof.

A knot forms in his throat, and he sobs one more time, involuntarily, like a hiccup. Saved, he thinks. Saved at the last moment. Like Dostoyevsky. Saved by some quirk, some whim. Given a few moments more of life, all because of some niggling little detail, some minor bump in the roadway of revolutionary progress. Once it's all cleared up the guard will get his laugh back.

Maybe it's a dream. Maybe he has already been executed . . . and this 'little room' is just a way station? A limbo, an office of final accounting where he will be called to explain the many mistakes of his life. If he gets the answers right, perhaps there will be angels and virgins, an old man with a white beard and a gilt-covered book turning to a page inscribed with his name.

Still, he was ready, he thinks. It has taken so long, after all. A lot of pain. Too much pain, and eventually you just . . . give up. And he was ready (still, it was too quick!), truly ready to meet his maker, to slide into that great dark pit of the unknown, or just to cease, whichever it would be . . .

Kneeling in the blood and vomit, he was ready, and he is ready even now. The salted crust in the corners of his eyes, that's something he can wipe away. The clothes can be cleaned. He will catch his breath soon. The blood will clot. That sob will stay contained somewhere between his guts and his lungs. All of that can heal, even his memories will be papered over with whatever pattern his brain can come up with in order to keep him sane.

Meanwhile there is the beautiful room in which he now lives.

Voices in the hall. It is an ordinary door, with an ordinary lock. The smells in this part of the prison are different. Paper, vinegar. Everything is cleaner, less fearful. The hallways have been mopped. They obviously don't use buckets to do their business in this wing. Is that music playing in the distance?

The efficient sound of shoes in the corridor. A quiet few words, and then the sound of a key turning the lock.

And . . . in walks the dead man.

2

The dead man was Velimir Zezulin.

For a moment Ryzhkov was frozen. Stunned, he coughed in surprise, jumped up and got almost half-way out of his chair. He had not seen Zezulin for . . . almost four years to the day, and on that occasion Zezulin had been drunk. Dead drunk.

Later, the last image he'd seen of Zezulin was of their portraits, along with Konstantin Hokhodiev and Dima Dudenko, printed on St Petersburg police fugitive warning handbills. Maybe no one had recognized him, since the photograph, taken from Zezulin's ancient Okhrana identity card, was so out of date. Together the four had been sought as murderers of Deputy Minister of Interior, Boris Fauré. What was deliberately not said on the posters and handbills was that they were also suspects in the abduction and murder of their own superior, General A.I. Gulka, head of the entire Third Section.

Somehow he had survived and was now back, a new Zezulin, brisk as a wolverine. Moving with assured fluidity, a solid man with energy held in reserve. He came in, closed the door on the sentry, and sat. Their eyes locked for a moment and then Zezulin pointed to the ceiling and gave an almost imperceptible shake of his head.

Ryzhkov was suddenly very tired. He found that his head was bobbing from side to side, saying no, no . . . Zezulin must be dead, he had to be dead, as dead as Kostya Hokhodiev, or as vanished as Dima. Surely he'd been killed, since he must have been caught. Of the group, Zezulin was the only innocent and he'd had no warning, so they must have taken him. Zezulin would have been their only prize, so they would have tortured him, and, since he knew nothing, they would have tortured him some more. Eventually they would have shown him the papers, various authorizations Ryzhkov had cadged from him when he was in an alcoholic stupor.

But here he was. Alive, with Ryzhkov's file in his hands.

'Citizen Ryzhkov. You will answer the questions I put to you, do you understand? You should understand this by now, given your dossier. You have been interrogated many times, I'm sure you know all about these procedures. Yes, you understand? Correct?'

'Yes,' the sound came out of Ryzhkov's mouth like a whisper.

'You will be entirely forthcoming.'

He nodded.

'Your name?'

'You know my name . . .'

'I do, indeed. But you are going to confess it. You will give me the details of your life, your Okhrana training, salient events of your career as an employed thug within the Tsarist political police, the identity of your supervisor, other personalities in your section . . .'

'That was a long time ago,' he said wearily. And it was true. Several lifetimes ago, so remote as to be unreal. A life mulled over, dissected and regretted so many times that

17

there was no honest version he could give. He just shook his head.

'Your name is Ryzhkov, Pyotr Mikhalovich, I know this from your file. This is your photograph from your identity card as a member of the Tsar's terror police. These are your evaluations, your recruitment letter, your grades at the gymnasium. I have everything. We have known about you all along.' Zezulin's voice had begun to rise, then he bit it off. They looked at each other for a long moment. 'I am sure you can remember a great many details. Do you remember, for instance, the name of your Okhrana supervisor at the time?'

With an almost involuntary shrug, Ryzhkov shook his head. What was he supposed to say? Everything was whirling. He felt the sharp curl of nausea, swallowed to keep the world upright.

'Can't remember? I'll save you the trouble. His name was Zezulin, Velimir Antonovich. Like you, a paid butcher for the Tsar, the head of a death squad. A terrorist and probable double agent. You will be interested to know that he was executed in the first days of the revolution. This is his photograph. You remember working with this man, don't you? Admit it.'

Ryzhkov's head jerked up. He was looking at a photograph of a dark-haired mask, staring at the camera, as dead as a fish. It could have been anyone, anyone at all. An anonymous face, someone off the street. It vanished back into the dossier.

'Good. You signify that you knew him, fine. Now we're getting somewhere. Do you want a cigarette? Some water? You don't look that well. Perhaps we'll have some food brought in. Do you feel like answering any additional questions or would you like to go back to your cell?'

Not only had he changed his identity, Zezulin had taken on a completely different personality. Gone was the slovenly drunk, the slurred voice, the fragmentary memory. Now, instead of staring out the window at the street outside their section house, his eyes were locked on Ryzhkov, the hypnotic glare of a poisonous snake deciding exactly where to strike.

'If I blink, you die,' Zezulin said softly across the table – the voice of a parent explaining an unpleasant and complicated reality to a child. Ryzhkov suddenly realized that fresh tears were running down his face. Lost, lost again. Life was just a vortex of loss . . . He shrugged again; it was all he could do – make the gesture reserved for cowards or those who couldn't think of a quick comeback.

'Fine. Please, you will tell me about your work with the French Secret Service. In 1914 you escaped and travelled to Paris . . .' Zezulin had relaxed somewhat, the eyes were softer. 'You do know that I have all the travel documents.' Zezulin fussed through the dossier. 'Yes . . . You went to Paris, you were recruited into the Foreign Legion, served here and there, and then at Verdun, and from there – '

'I knew . . . languages, so I went to the signals.'

'Yes, yes. I'm sure it was all very helpful, listening to the Germans in the trenches . . . help the artillery find their targets. Then you were wounded, court-martialled . . .'

'I was paroled.'

'Paroled, yes. I know all of this. But they had something on you, so they made you come back to Russia and work for the French. Don't feed me this translation nonsense. We had you followed. It's all right here.' The wolverine's paw slammed down on the dossier. 'So. You can't run any more.'

'No.'

'Cigarette?' Zezulin put a box on the table. 'Tea?'

Ryzhkov reached to take out the cigarettes. Zezulin watched while he fumbled with the box, dropped it, dug out a cigarette, dropped it too, and finally gave up and left it on the table, unlit.

'Here it is,' Zezulin said. 'There have been a series of decisions regarding persons like yourself. Chickens. Chickens who serve the farmer . . .' Zezulin began. 'People like you, who under the former government were responsible for heinous crimes. Killers, thugs, terrorists. Some of them are psychologically distressed. Well, that's understandable, so many have had it hard what with the war . . . but my biggest question is why? Why did you come back, Ryzhkov?'

'I didn't have a lot of choice.'

'Mmm. But why did you decide to throw in your fate with the French? Do you like their cooking? Their certain something? I mean, a man like you made it out of the trenches, you performed with a certain amount of gallantry. Millions have performed such things, but you did more. A lot more. You're a warrior, Ryzhkov, a spy. A man who survives. Survives beyond the limits of most men in the business. You don't love it. You're not obsessed with the enemy, it doesn't seem to make you happy, but here you are. Back home. The question is why? What do they have on you, eh?'

The question hung in the room. Ryzhkov tried to look him in the eye but failed.

'Tell me. What is it? Who is it?' Zezulin's hand wavered, settled on the dossier and the thick fingers began to pat it, like a baby he was trying to burp.

'"Mother, dead. Father, dead. Brother, died as a child . . ."' He looked over at Ryzhkov and shrugged. 'You didn't come back to Russia because you're in love with the rooftops of Paris, and you owe them something. You already took your revenge, I suspect. No, you came back for a fellow human being. Maybe your wife? Mmmm . . . I don't think so. You hadn't lived with her since 1912. It's not her. She's safe in Portugal, the last anyone cared. So who is it, Pyotr?'

Ryzhkov looked up at him. He just wasn't a good enough actor.

'Was it her?' The photograph slid out of the dossier like a knife stroke curving towards his chest.

Vera Aliyeva curled to a stop, looking up at him.

It was a commercial portrait. Something she had commissioned for publicity in Petersburg. Shot with soft gauze and a backdrop meant to suggest clouds. In it Vera was innocent, looking aloft at some more radiant possibility. So young. A century ago.

'What about that, Monsieur? You say you don't have a choice? You didn't get to choose? Oh, I'm sorry about the unfairness of everything. That's what the revolution is all about, of course. Rectifying things. By the way, did you know that Lena Hokhodieva is still alive?'

He could not help but look up. Kostya's wife had been dying with cancer, almost a complete ghost when Ryzhkov had last seen her. 'No.'

'Yes. She's made a complete cure. It's a miracle. Defied the gods. She's fat, you wouldn't recognize her. Good for her, eh?'

'Yes.'

'It's just luck, Pyotr Mikhalovich. Someone has to be found to do certain things. You're not the first person who is a victim of a government or . . . governments, or the lack of them. It won't buy you any special favours around here.' Zezulin was smiling. 'Someone has to do these things. It's bloom or die, eh? And while you don't care about your own death, maybe you'd even welcome it, you would care about someone else's . . . about this woman here.' The finger gestured towards the photograph; a cheap thing, unmistakably banal, bound in a yellow pasteboard frame with an advertisement for the Nevsky Prospekt photographer she'd charmed into giving her a deal.

'Ah yes. Good. You have indicated that you recognize her. Excellent. Once more we are getting somewhere. Now we

21

have decided to be grown-up friends and we've put down our last secret, eh?' Zezulin was saying. The voice of a happy man. 'I'm so sorry, but you can't keep the picture.

'Look, my friend,' Zezulin leaned in close. There was the smell of pickles on his breath. 'This is not some common theatrical, this is not boys playing games in the barracks. This is real.' He patted the dossier on the desk. 'We both know you're going to do what I say. I can use you to kill, or I can use you for bait. Let's not waste any more time. These are the trenches too. I know you have courage, and all that.'

'And this is all for the people?'

'Yes, yes, the people, of course. But because it's all secret, they don't know it.'

'And if I don't do what you want?'

'It won't be the first time I've misjudged someone, eh? So, we'll take you out and shoot you, and of course you have no need to worry about the future of –' he patted the dossier, '– your friend. Right? You were Okhrana, you know how the levers work.' He settled back into his chair.

'But if on the other hand you go out and be the ruthless secret policeman I know you can be, then I can give you more information about certain persons, if that is what you are interested in. You know? That's the carrot. Death for you and your loved ones is the stick, eh? Well . . . no offence, we're all under threat of death. That's what terror means, brother. Welcome. As you can see, the inmates have taken over the asylum. Come in to my personal padded room.'

Ryzhkov willed himself not to shrug. 'I suppose if I have to work for someone I'd prefer to work for the people, in the asylum or out.'

'I knew you would see the logic of it. Here, let's take those off.' The soldier moved forward to busy himself with the key.

'Look, ah . . . comrade . . . What shall I call you?'

'Comrade is fine for now.'

A few minutes later they were taking a stroll through Cheka headquarters, even stranger corridors offices that led to waiting rooms that led to cells and interrogation rooms. A dormitory wing that exited onto a garage.

'Just for your private information, Pyotr, the existing intelligence apparatus of the People's Government is like a . . . choppy sea,' Zezulin expounded. 'The great Romanov ocean liner has sunk and now we are all helpless in the expanse of stormy ocean. For just a moment you see a survivor, you encounter them, and then another moment they are gone. The winds have carried them far away.'

'Yes.' Ryzhkov sighed. Walking along without the manacles, he didn't know what to do with his hands. His arms kept involuntarily trying to come together over his fly. They walked along past stables, a garage, a shed where they stacked the firewood. Somebody was making telephone calls, couriers were running in and out. And always the telegraph chattering.

'One has to make the most of every moment and every relationship. Moscow is a hotbed of spies and rumours. You wouldn't believe it, Pyotr. Innuendo, fabrication, conspiracy . . . Around here everyone is supposed to keep quiet. There are layers and layers of secrecy, but the personnel? They're all new, all of them think they are running the revolution all by themselves, everyone wants to be a hero, and everyone talks.'

They crossed into a second courtyard; beyond was a gate, a big loading door that opened onto Sofika Street and freedom. Wagons, people going by, fanning themselves lazily against the heat of the summer's day.

'So this is what I know . . .' Velimir Antonovich Zezulin said, offering Ryzhkov a cigarette.

Zezulin was on a short leash to hear him tell it. Noskov was his new name, Boris Maximovich. 'Nice, eh? I forget where I picked it up.' Once he had wrung himself out and cleaned himself up, he'd discovered that he could still function. He'd regrown his tendrils and in the process his attention had been . . . well, somewhat heightened. He'd sensed things, many things in his newly sober state that he would have missed in the bad old days.

And worse was coming. 'The revolution, to be honest, is not going that well. The Allies are hungry and on the attack. The Czechs are the immediate problem.'

'Czechs?'

'Quite a few, fifty, sixty thousand taken as prisoners from the Austrians. Most of them are deserters, they wanted to cross over and fight against Austria for the freedom of a new Czecho-slovak country. You can lay the blame at their feet, if you want.'

'So what was the problem?'

'They were on the trains in the middle of Siberia, but it seems they made their own little revolution, and now they control the Trans-Siberian railway. To them you can add the Japanese, inscrutable as always, but always ready to make off with the riches of Siberia and put themselves in an even more dominant position over China. They've sent their soldiers into Vladivostok. Of course the Americans, the British and the French are involved. The Canadians are involved . . .'

'It's a civil war.'

'Very good. I see you have been reading the newspapers. Which brings us to our masters, the Germans, the people who have everything and want more, eh?'

Ahead of them was a disturbance, men shouting at the end of the courtyard. A shot rang out and Ryzhkov saw they had brought a man out for killing. Four guards, and another team of four for the truck. They must have made him kneel but then the shooter had mis-aimed and only wounded the prisoner, who was trying to crawl away as the blood spurted from under the collarbone. One of them stepped forward and put his rifle close to the man and pulled the trigger a second time. The sound of it and the slap of the prisoner's head on the cobbles brought everyone to the windows. The killer was blushing furiously.

'Regarding the Germanic menace, our leaders, Comrade Lenin, Comrade Trotsky, they do what they must. They are between the hammer and the anvil. Also there is pressure from within. Among us Bolsheviks there are factions within factions, wheels within wheels, masks behind masks, you get the idea. Lately we have been taking steps against these enemies beneath our own roof . . . as you see.' They stood there smoking and watching the execution squad at work. It was a woman they next led out. Her thin wail came to them on the summer breeze.

'Honestly, Pyotr, the problem is knowing which revolutionary tiger to back. Guessing as best you can who will come out on top in the internal struggles, or what might be going on beneath the surfaces. So all of us, we're being put in a situation where we need to protect ourselves.'

'So as better to serve the people.'

'Yes, yes, yes, and so on.'

The bullet, the clashings of the bolts on the rifles. The men bending to their work. The motor started up and the guards climbed in. He didn't think it meant that she'd be the last one they killed for the day. There was always another truck waiting.

'These much-vaunted personalities . . . privately I know they are acting strangely. Trotsky is curious. Dzerzhinsky is irritable. Comrade Sverdlov in his capacity as secretary to the Central Committee is the most overworked, and Comrade

Stalin is nowhere to be seen. Necessarily, Comrade Lenin is constantly in touch with all sorts of people, the Germans and a lot of others as well. We are in Moscow, this is the centre of the world stage at the moment. Just so you are aware, Ryzhkov . . .'

'So what's this all got to do with me? Why did you save me? What do you want, comrade . . . Noskov?'

'Yes, good. You remembered. I'll tell you what I want on your way to the barracks. You're Cheka now. We have to start a brand new file on you. We're in a hurry, but let's quickly get you cleaned up and into better clothes. Nothing too bourgeois, however,' Zezulin said as they walked out of the prison.

Woozy from the sudden intake of food, Ryzhkov floated deliriously through the Cheka baths, a somewhat cramped facility, and made an effort to stay awake during Zezulin's recital while he tried on some newish clothing that had been obtained for his use.

'As you probably know, last year the Imperial Family was moved from the old capital –'

'Petrograd.' Ryzhkov said. The word would never sound quite right on his tongue, patriotic as it was. It would always be St Petersburg for him. 'Yes, I remember that. That was done secretly.' He almost laughed.

'Yes. Typical of secrets in Russia, everybody knows everybody else's. Blinded by clouds of secrets, no one can recognize the real ones. At any rate, they were, yes, moved. The architect of this scheme was the unfortunate criminal Kerensky. He did it either because he was afraid the advancing Germans would capture the Tsar, or because he realized that possession of the Imperial Family might be an advantage in hypothetical negotiations,' Zezulin muttered and shrugged.

'Where were they moved?'

'To hell and gone. Into Siberia. The town of Tobolsk, district capital, just beyond the Urals. I have never been there, of course, and I don't know anyone who has. No, that's not true. Rasputin, he was from a town on the Tobol. That's the name of the river. There's no railroad, they come down and get you there by steamer. Last year someone in the Provisional Government decided that Tobolsk was far enough off the face of the earth to be safe, so they loaded the Romanovs onto the train, pasted a Japanese Red Cross banner on the sides, kept the shades drawn when they went through the stations. Still, there were crowds waiting to throw flowers at them when they got off the boat. Big secret.'

'Fine.'

'They had their friends follow and take up residence across the street. They had their books, personal effects, their dogs. And they obviously must have taken some valuables with them. We have lists, of course, but lists, being what they are, never include everything.'

Ryzhkov was studying himself in the mirror. Still in reasonable condition, he thought. Newly shaved but not shorn. It would take some time for his weight to come back. He fit his simple suit well, the kind of thing a clerk might wear to and from his office: a shirt that was worn but free of actual holes, a homburg that made him look like an idiot, and that he resolved to get rid of as soon as possible. Only the shoes were out of place. Not a clerk's lace-ups with mandatory shiny toe caps, but heavier workman's boots. Still muddy from use. Shoes made for walking, and heavy socks to match. They sat on a low stool beside the mirror. Zezulin had recommended them.

'Then in April, as soon as the ice broke and they could get a steamer back downstream, they were moved again, this time to Yekaterinburg,' Zezulin said.

'Yekaterinburg? Why there?'

27

Zezulin shrugged. 'Different people say different things, but you might think of it as a philosophical tug of war, a jurisdictional dispute. The city of Yekaterinburg is held by the Ural Soviet, a very committed bunch of hard-working, hard-drinking miners, men who have spent their proletarian enslavement toiling for the mineral barons. They have grievances. They pulled the hardest, got the least, etc . . .'

'All right.'

'And, as far as anyone knows, that is where they are now.'

'Yekaterinburg?'

'Unfortunately Yekaterinburg is an unfashionable city, but revolutions bring hardships on us all.' Zezulin stepped in front of him and tugged on Ryzhkov's cravat, trying to get it straight. 'A great many people would like to possess the Romanovs. Several persons in various countries have offered them sanctuary. Unofficially, of course. And, naturally enough, sums of money are mentioned. We're not sure exactly. It's all secret. Remember these are aristocrats. People with the best pedigrees have persuaded all their friends to lend a hand. The British, who are always into everything; your masters the French; all sorts of people are coming up with rescue schemes.'

'So . . . bribes?'

'Of course, it takes the form of bribes, payments for some sort of safe passage, a definite possibility, but also . . . some of these same people, people of the bluest blood, are ready to pay for a guarantee of the Tsar's death. That way they could take over the throne for themselves, right? You can be sure money is at the root of it. We know of substantial deposits in foreign banking houses. Call yourself a Tsar in exile? It might not be a bad job for someone with the right qualifications. Worth fighting for, worth raising an army, hiring a few strong men, I'd say.' Zezulin smiled again. His

28

hand grasped Ryzhkov's sleeve, turned him so that he could get a better view of the latest parody of himself.

Zezulin had gone serious. 'You'd better know that at this moment Czech legions are threatening Yekaterinburg. They may have already taken the city, we don't know. The telegraph links to the city have been sporadic at best.'

'So no one knows exactly where the Romanovs are?'

'Correct. That's what you're going to find out for me – you're going to Yekaterinburg and you're going to find out where they are and how they are. You are going to report that information back to me. You are going to pay particular attention to their security and whatever possessions, and if it comes to it you are going to safeguard them and wait for instructions.'

'Oh, that doesn't sound like much. You've got to give me some help. Who do you have there?'

'The Ural Soviet, if they're still in the district.'

'If you can't get anything in, how am I supposed to get anything out?'

'Your contact in Yekaterinburg is a man named Nikolas Eikhe. He's a metalsmith there. He lives on the edge of the city – it's small, he won't be hard to find. I'm sure you will do what you can. I have faith in you, Ryzhkov.'

'I only get him to help?'

'It all depends on what you learn. If you don't learn anything, I'm not going to be able to get you anything, am I? Come on, spare me.'

'I'm doing this for the people, I suppose.'

'It goes without saying. That's good enough,' Zezulin said to the tailor. He steered Ryzhkov out and back up the steps, still in a hurry. 'Are you tired? Don't worry. You'll get a good sleep very soon.'

At the top of the steps they hailed a *droshky*. Zezulin made the driver raise the top even though it was summer, and then took them on a hurried tour of Moscow, while looking over his shoulder constantly. When they had looped back on themselves three or four times, he ordered the driver to pull in the entrance of a hospital past the Krasniya Gate. They walked right through the grounds and out the back to an adjoining street. At the corner there was a second *droshky* pulled up. The driver got out and held out a rucksack and an oiled packet tied with twine. Sticking out of the rucksack was the corner of a loaf of black bread and what looked like wilted turnip greens. Zezulin took the packet and handed it to him.

'This is your pass to travel on the railroad, and your Cheka identity papers, your red card. When you meet who you think is Eikhe, you say this: "Have you ever been to Brazil?"'

'You're joking?'

'"Have you ever been to Brazil?" "No, but I love the beach." Got it?'

Ryzhkov stood there for a moment. Nodded. 'Yes, I've got it.'

'Good. Eikhe will give you any assistance you need. You can communicate through him back to me. The details are in the envelope. Burn it after you've read it and memorized everything, please. If you get caught, it will be revealed that all these are, of course, forgeries.'

'Thank you.'

'Yes, it's all very secret. Get there as quick as you can. If the Whites take Yekaterinburg you'll have to transform yourself back into Monsieur Ryzhkov and give them whatever passwords you've been trained to use back in Paris. Then you'll be on your own until you can get back here. Go. Your train is on track 4, you'd better hurry, and may God be with you and cause the enemy to believe your stories.'

3

The Kazan station – he'd been there dozens of times, but now it had changed. A ring of soldiers at each entrance. Machine guns, sandbags. Zezulin pointed the way and then vanished behind him. He walked the last few yards himself, out from under the shade of the trees, across a bed of flowers that had yet to be trampled.

It was crowded there, and it only enhanced Ryzhkov's impression that he was being drawn into a great throat, sucked out from the sun into the blinding darkness – a place of screaming whistles and shouted commands in a dozen languages echoing beneath the great chambered roof. Into the dark cavern with not even time enough to feel what it was like to be a free man in Moscow, as if there were such a thing.

A Red Guard asked for his papers. He showed them and was moved right along to a sergeant seated at a desk at the head of the stairs. It was like a conveyor belt for people with the correct documents, and he kept moving the entire time. No one even really touched him. When they saw that he was Cheka, and only interested in speed, it got them all jumping. He passed through a mass of bawling refugees, a sergeant running along with him for half of his walk, checking his papers on the fly, and doing everything in his power not to salute. The Cheka was just like the old Okhrana, Ryzhkov thought, only with different uniforms. A black leather raincoat instead of the cheap rubberized canvas ones he'd worn as a plain-clothes *gorokhovnik*. The teams had changed; the flags had shed their blue and white colours and evolved into revolutionary red; the double-headed eagles had all been knocked to the ground. You walked along and counted the blemishes on architecture throughout the city.

The sergeant fell away and he arrived at track 4 and his carriage, climbed in to find his compartment, which he had all to himself for a time. He wondered why he was getting such deference and then looked at his identity papers. They'd made him an inspector with the internal unit of the Cheka. Rank of captain. Obviously doing something important since he was travelling alone with a single rucksack.

He pulled down the shades, put the rucksack on the seat opposite and looked through it, found the pistol they'd given him, an ugly Mauser. Read his instructions, a sentence of brief gibberish, a simple cipher system that he could use, a cable address, NOSMOC4, and a wireless address which would probably be useless.

He put everything away and raised the shades. At the very far end, a hospital train had emptied and was being swabbed out. There was a whistle, a porter ringing his bell. With a tremble and then a lurch his train began to glide out of the station and he looked out the window to watch the great vaulted ceilings slip away and give over to sky.

Another Chekisti came past the door, then backtracked, checked the number of the compartment and came in. His name was Sudov. Ryzhkov had a good look at him and found him pathetically young. Working hard on his first beard, a little trill of red hairs over his lip. He was going out to his first assignment, to assist the commissar in Perm. He deferentially made room so Ryzhkov could put his feet up, and they talked.

Sudov was from Petersburg. There was no food there at all, he said. Perhaps now, in summer, but back in the winter there had been no food. The boy had loved it there, the skating games in the winter, the American hills – a kind of artificial sledding ramp that had been set up on the Field of Mars, girls with rosy cheeks, the bonfires. His favourite time.

'Did you ever go to the Komet?' Ryzhkov asked him.

'Where's that?'

'It's a night club just off Sadovaya Street. They did plays there before the war.'

'No, no, I don't know it. I was too young, my parents would never let me.' He smiled. 'I went to the Peaches Club, though. That was a place for good times.'

Listening to young Sudov Ryzhkov fell into a long slow dreaming. With the outskirts of Moscow slipping away, the train rocking between the switches on the way out of town, dreaming about Vera and the old Komet club and all of it. That one single good year, their only year. When Ryzhkov fell into sleep the boy was still rhapsodizing about the quality of chocolates you could by at Eliseffs on the Nevsky Prospekt. 'Perfection,' he said. 'The very best, like no other place on earth.'

Outside the window is Russia. The summer sun burns down to a cloudless sunset that fades to green, passing into the red dusk, the night air rising that sets the trees, the laundry the women have hung out, the dried straw along the side of the roadbed, all to waving. A great warm wind rises out of the earth, and when the train stops you can hear it moaning through the windows. The train itself, a place of eerie sighs; the soldiers writhe in their lonely torment, clutching their genitals, pushing their companion's shoulder away, and grumbling in their sleep.

Ryzhkov passes from dreams to wakefulness in a long series of bumps and jars, knocks and shudders in the night that spark his worst anxieties. Somehow it is more fearful because he is too comfortable; relatively warm and reasonably fed in a time of famine, but unable to sleep, his character out of synchronization with his fellow travellers.

The train is filled with companies of Red Guards being rushed to the front. Ryzhkov, wandering up and down the train in his boredom and to relieve his stiffness, finds himself moving along, looking at the faces of the guards as the sun rises, glaring sharp and bright, causing the men on that side of the car to grope for the shades and turn their faces away. But none can fully escape because the track curves all the way to Nizhni Novgorod, and the fortunes of the sun are always changing.

He is at the head of the carriage when he meets a corporal in the buffer between carriages. The corporal is smoking and talking to a man who has taken off his shirt to shave. They both fall silent as Ryzhkov passes through.

'Did you hear anything?' he asks them.

'All this lot are being sent up to hold Perm. This might be the last train.'

'It might,' says the other.

'So the Whites, they're almost at Yekaterinburg?'

The corporal shrugs. 'The big battle is going to be in the south. I heard it from the commander,' the man says, and pushes forward a cigarette.

'Thank you very much, comrade. Where are you two going, then?'

'Well, we're to get off earlier, at Kazan, but . . .' The corporal turns to the second man and they both shrug.

Ryzhkov decides to be what is expected, he smiles, bows to the corporal.

'Well, the Czechs are fast, but we're fast too,' he says and they turn and look out the window. The train has begun to put on speed. They should be in Nizhni by the end of the day. All of them racing down the tracks, trying to staunch the wound to Bolshevik Siberia.

'What about you? Where are you going, comrade?' the man asks.

Ryzhkov points to the head of the train. 'All the way to the end,' and moves along through to the next carriage.

Back in his compartment he inclines his head towards the window. In the far distance is the silver curve of the river that leads towards the ancient river city of Nizhni Novgorod. As the train leans over against the banking of the tracks, Ryzhkov's view is taken away from the horizon and drawn closer to the sudden clearing of a new woodlot – a flare of pale wood chips and peeled logs. Then the little nub of civilization reaches its limit at a tangle of fencing, and is swept away, and as the carriage levels he sees a thick man standing there tending a wide patch of burning grass, shovel in hand, trying to corral the fire he's started towards a ditch.

4

Amid the activity of the Supreme Command headquarters, only one man was in repose: standing quietly in the shadows awaiting the Kaiser's arrival was Admiral Paul von Hintze, newly appointed Minister of Foreign Affairs. He had been in the job less than a month, and he was tired. There had been little or no time for sleep since his appointment.

Among the staff officers and aides there was an air of controlled yet feverish anticipation. It was the fourth and final attack of General Ludendorff's great strategic offensive – or the 'Kaiser Offensive', as the newspapers would have it – designed to smash through the trenches and the wire, break the will of the French and British, and force a peace on Germany's terms, before the Americans could arrive and save the day. The great opening bombardment was set to begin at midnight.

At the centre of the room was a large map of the Western Front, and from his position von Hintze could see the coloured ribbons that demarked the great scar that ran down the centre of Europe. He took grim satisfaction that all the ribbons were in French or Belgian territory. Ludendorff's first three attacks had been successful, but how could one advance across Europe, push to within fifty miles of Paris, withstand every counter-attack, and still not be victorious? Von Hintze knew that the answer lay off the map . . . in the Atlantic where the British were blockading Germany and starving her into submission. The first three waves of Ludendorff's attack had washed across the fields of France and Belgium, and then . . . simply run out of energy. There were no coloured ribbons to represent the hunger of the soldiers, the fatigue and desperation that sapped the will of the most ardent warrior.

There was a sudden movement at the large doors, a command, and every military man in the room snapped to attention as the Kaiser entered. He was, on this night, dressed immaculately, in the uniform of the Supreme War Lord. In his withered left hand he clutched the hilt of his sabre, in his right a Field Marshal's baton.

For a moment von Hintze was struck with a pang of pity for the man. While they were almost the same age, and distantly related, psychologically they were opposites. Wilhelm had grown up conscious of his deformity and the need to both hide it and compensate for it. Embarrassed and terrified by his own inferiority, he had developed an arsenal of strategies to deflect any crisis, erase every slight, and expunge every weakness from view. As an emperor ruling by divine right, it was inevitable that Wilhelm would adopt the pose of the hyper-masculine War Lord, but Von Hintze, with his naval background and his experience as a diplomat, was adept at reading men's motives. He did not consider himself a politician by any means, and had always preferred to work quietly, if possible behind the scenes.

As the Kaiser entered the room, his mood seemed ebullient. He smiled at the field officers bowing to him, but von Hintze knew that if today's attack failed, or if any news arrived in the evening that hinted at a setback, Wilhelm could easily be plunged into paranoia and angry depression. Among the intimates of the Kaiser his quirks and preferences were common knowledge, but now von Hintze studied the man closely, for in his new job as Minister he would have to orchestrate miracles.

He made his way across to the great map and approached the Kaiser. Wilhelm saw him and manufactured a smile that could not quite mask his wary look. Von Hintze bowed stiffly, then moved closer. 'If I might have a word with you, All Highest.'

'After we start things, I hope,' said the Kaiser glancing towards the map. He had come to headquarters to mingle with his generals; the presence of von Hintze could only mean a fresh problem, the kind that could not be solved by howitzers.

There was the muted buzz of a field telephone from the desk just in front of them. Ludendorff looked up and said very quietly, 'The attack has begun.' The Kaiser raised his baton in salute and a ripple of applause spread through the room. For a moment afterwards there was a silence that hung in the room, as if they were all holding their breath, then the magic vanished as a series of telephones buzzed into life.

'How long will the bombardment continue?' the Kaiser said, his sharp voice cutting through the din.

'A full hour, Majesty. Eight thousand guns, the largest bombardment of the war,' said Ludendorff with pride. Looking at him von Hintze could not tell if he was smiling or not.

'Excellent. The largest! Well, well.' The Kaiser turned to von Hintze. 'Perhaps this is a good time then?'

'There's plenty of time. Your car is waiting, Majesty.' Ludendorff had laid on a visit to an observation station. It was a particularly clear night and the Kaiser would be able to watch the pyrotechnics as the bombardment progressed over the Allied lines guarding Rheims. It would also serve to get the Kaiser out of his hair, keep him happy for a while.

'Yes, I understand, but there are other matters.' Von Hintze reached around and guided Ludendorff by the elbow. 'Please, All Highest, if we might . . .' They began to walk away from the map table into the shadows, and von Hintze lowered his voice. 'It's information about the . . . special case.'

'Ahh,' said Ludendorff, 'the special case, yes, of course.'

It seemed to Von Hintze that the Kaiser's face suddenly became stricken. 'Yes, yes . . . very important. Very good, Hintze. Is there any progress?'

'At the moment there is a crisis, since the Czech deserters are approaching the city. What action to be taken is a question that finally only you can answer, All Highest.'

'Ahh, please, no,' the Kaiser said, shaking his head. Everyone knew that he hated to actually take a decision. His normal reaction would be to bluster and threaten, then he would inevitably vacillate, and then the postponements would start.

'First, Majesty, as to the disposition of the special case, the British have said no.'

'Then there is no option left,' Ludendorff intoned.

Wilhelm turned and glared at him, shook his head violently. 'The British will change their minds when they see a sure thing in front of them. They always do.'

'Among the British, the war has been unpopular, particularly among the working classes. Any gesture of support to a monarch, even one as benevolent as your cousin Nicholas, would inflame the various Socialistic elements within the country. In short, they are afraid of repercussions, Majesty,' von Hintze said. Having Ludendorff there made it easier to be direct.

'Yes, but didn't we talk about that?'

'Yes we talked, but it doesn't change anything,' Ludendorff said, turning to glance back at the map table.

'Yes, Majesty. We spoke specifically about the idea of a change of identity, of anonymity, but –'

'What's wrong with that? You're not going to tell me it's impractical. Come on, von Hintze, of course it can be done.'

'It is very difficult, Majesty,' he said quietly.

'I see what is happening. I am not going to abandon my own flesh and blood to the mob, eh!' Wilhelm said. His voice had risen. A brace of staff officers looked over to them, and then nervously away. 'What would I be then? A coward? Well, I may be many things, but I am not a coward like my British cousins. When I save the family, then they'll thank me for it. Wait and see,' the Kaiser said. Angrily he made a stomping motion with his foot.

Von Hintze looked over at Ludendorff, waiting for him to chime in, but the great strategist only rocked back on his heels and gazed at his staff officers moving about the table. As usual the army was leaving the real problems up to the civilians. For an uncomfortable moment the three of them stood watching the cadets pushing pins in the map. The room was a hive of whispers, the slithering of memoranda crossing the blotters, the scratch of pens, the ratcheting of the telegraph that pierced the room whenever the door opened.

Von Hintze took a deep breath and began again. 'Unfortunately Yekaterinburg is on the point of being surrounded and it may already be too late.' The Kaiser in his agitation had walked out into the light. Von Hintze looked at the grey eyes, tired and flecked with bloodshot from fatigue and strain.

'I know what you are saying, gentlemen, but back when this plan came up, when the idea was first presented to me, everyone was happy, everyone was happy to give me certainties. We spent a million pounds –'

'Half a million. The first payment only, All Highest.'

'And we still don't have anything to show for it?'

'It's worse than that,' Ludendorff started.

'Here's the latest telegram, All Highest,' von Hintze said, fishing it out of his pocket and handing it to the Kaiser, who held it up into the light.

'Bloody, bloody . . . What the hell does this mean? "Awaiting shipment all pelts. Seven boxes. Will transport on receipt."'

'He's posing as furrier's agent.'

'Ahh.'

'He would be told to cancel the order.'

'My God . . .'

'Lloyd George is afraid of a similar revolution as has befallen Russia. That's the reason for the British refusal. They were quite clear about that. Truthfully, Majesty, an upheaval is a real possibility, even I am forced to admit.' For the first time when Wilhelm rounded on him, von Hintze made himself keep speaking. His hand was trembling. He pressed on.

'If we go forward with the scheme, and even supposing we save the family, if it somehow becomes known, the public response —'

'There will be no talk of a revolution in Germany,' the Kaiser insisted. 'It's absurd! Not when we're winning!'

For a moment von Hintze stood there. His eyes wandered to the great illuminated map and then back to the Kaiser. There was no effective way to get through to the man that today's attack was in reality Ludendorff's last desperate gamble.

'It doesn't matter about the talking of revolution. You can forbid all you want and there will still be talk in the streets. It's clear. You can't have that family here. You can't have them in Germany,' Ludendorff said, his gaze swivelled on the Kaiser.

'I cannot abandon my own flesh and blood. I will not do

it!' the Kaiser hissed. The force of it bent him over at the waist. Across the room he saw the bulk of Hindenburg shifting in his chair. He had a field telephone headset hanging around his neck, and he took it off and handed it to his aide.

Von Hintze jumped in. 'Even if we were able to go forward, there's so little we can do, Majesty. With the approach of the Czechs the wires are severed in places, and any communicating takes longer and is less secure.'

'So, he will have not received his orders?'

'He does not know whom to contact, Majesty, and under the pressure of events it's likely that the revolutionists will execute the Tsar.'

'It's probably already happened,' Ludendorff sighed.

For a moment the Kaiser looked at him blankly. 'But . . . our agent, he will still continue with the mission, won't he?'

'He will await instructions, Majesty.'

The Kaiser looked at him. 'You mean he will wait there, surrounded? My God, who are these men?'

'They are soldiers, the same. They are all soldiers,' Ludendorff said flatly.

'A very unusual breed of officer,' said von Hintze.

'My God,' the Kaiser said. His eyes were full of tears, and he wiped them away with his sleeve. 'I'm giving him the Pour le Merite! Who is he? At least I want to meet his family and give them my thanks for producing such a noble son. He signs it "Todmann" – that's only his code name, yes? Well, I know you're not supposed to tell anyone, but . . .'

'I can tell you very little about him. Colonel Nicolai keeps it all secret. He has a designation number, 3J64-R,' von Hintze said, looking at a paper. 'The R is for Russia, so –'

Wilhelm reached down and pulled a blank order form from one of the staff officer's desks, bent to his pen. 'What is it again?'

'"3J64" is good enough.'

The Kaiser scribbled out the order to grant 3J64-R, whoever he was, the honour of the Pour le Merite, and the benefits that would go with it.

'I tell you, if we had a hundred more like this one, you and I would be having lunch in Paris this afternoon,' Wilhelm said, looking up at Ludendorff. 'And I tell you, I can't bear to think about Nicholas being hanged in front of a mob in Red Square. I can't allow such a thing,' he said to him.

'Do you want to be in Nicholas's situation? The British aren't fools. They see the danger. Spend all this . . .' He waved an arm back at the room of staff officers. '. . . to win a victory, and throw it away by saving your cousin?' Ludendorff said, outrageously direct. He was exhausted, von Hintze saw. 'You can't allow yourself the luxury of saving them . . . All Highest,' Ludendorff said. It was impossible to tell whether he had nearly forgotten to add the honorific at the end, or if he was being sarcastic.

Wilhelm looked at him for one long withering moment. Then he returned to writing out the award order. Von Hintze realized that after all their talking the Kaiser had still taken no decision about the 'special case'.

'Should I be so fortunate as to make contact with him, what should I say, All Highest?' he said, looking at Ludendorff, who sniffed.

'If he's surrounded what can he do? Tell him to stay in place and wait for instructions,' the Kaiser said angrily. 'When we prevail,' said he added, signing the order, 'then there will be negotiations, and if we have custody of the Imperial Family, then, you know . . . a secret overture might be made. It would be in everyone's interest to be discreet. They say Nicholas is a butcher, they say I'm a butcher. If Jesus were Kaiser they would say he was a butcher. It's just more Socialistic agitation. Cowards!' the Kaiser snapped.

'Good,' said Ludendorff, turning and leaving for the table.

He intercepted von Hindenburg and waved him back to his seat. There were more telephones buzzing now, and cadets were adjusting unit designations along the jagged lines that ran across the great map. Covered by the gigantic barrage, their storm troopers were advancing to encircle Rheims.

'You know, they don't understand,' the Kaiser said to him. 'It's the hardest, the most excruciating duty for a War Lord. To consign brave men, the very life's blood of the Fatherland, to send them out to their death. At the same time I am unable to help my own poor family.' He shook his head. For a moment von Hintze thought he might be weeping.

'And this one,' the Kaiser said, waving the slip of paper that would grant 3J64-R a life-long pension. 'This "Todmann", he's just an unknown man. A solitary, faceless, nameless human being. We've asked him to accept a life of shadows, to accept torture and an anonymous death if he is discovered. This man is a martyr,' the Kaiser said, pressing the paper into Hintze's hands. 'The bravest of us all.'

An aide had stepped up. He held the Kaiser's long cloak. It was to shelter him on the drive up to the observation post where he would be able to see the artillery. The Kaiser put on his *pickelhaube*, adjusted the strap beneath his chin, turned to allow the aide to settle the cloak about his shoulders.

'There's no room for weakness,' the Kaiser said to von Hintze. 'If you're still having qualms, Herr Minister, get over them. Anything else can wait,' he said sharply and moved towards the door. A command was shouted, the staff officers briefly fell silent, came to attention, and once the Supreme War Lord had left they went back to their maps and telephones, managing the attack that was designed to bring victory to Germany.

5

Everything is ready. Everything is more than ready. He has paid out monies, arranged for transportation. Not wanting to go any further than that. The city is an uproar. A panic. A good time for anyone to be leaving.

The date has been decided. He has sent his confirmation, but the wireless receives nothing. Accordingly he has made the walk up the long hill to the station, dressed as well as he can, waited in the queue for what seems like hours, grown frustrated and then realized that it would be far better to pay for a boy.

And this is what he does, finding one of the wretches that wait just outside the station so that they will not be run off by the one of the Red Guards assigned to patrol the entrance.

'I need a courier. Who's the best?' Making it like a challenge, the kind of thing boys of a certain age prefer over all others. Putting on a smile to dazzle them. One tough on top of a luggage cart doesn't flinch. 'It might be difficult,' he says to them, still smiling, 'but I'm in a hurry and don't have a lot of time.'

'Two kopeks,' they are all shouting. The little ones cluster around his knees.

'I am having dinner with a special person. She needs consoling.'

'If you want the receipt, it's extra,' says the tough.

'No, I don't know where I'm going to be. You keep the receipt and I'll come back for it.'

'It's still extra,' says the boy, and the little ones look around, willing to do whatever he tells them for less.

He looks at the boy's eyes. Not unattractive. Good enough. Big enough to know what getting hurt means. Now all the little ones have shut up.

'Fine, then,' he says. 'You.'

They move into the corridor and he finds a counter and the forms. He writes the message, changes his mind in mid-sentence and tears up the form and starts again.

The boy reaches into his pocket and takes out a tin box, something once used for pills. He has a cigarette stub in there, and begins to dig for a match.

'Here,' he says, and gives the boy his cigarette case. Turns back to the writing.

'Sometimes the best-laid plans go all wrong, you understand?' he says to the boy.

'All the time,' the boy says, carefully closing the case, turning it over in his hands, feeling the warmth of the silver. Expensive, the boy will be thinking. Nice, but something that's been around, a dent here, a place where the silver has rubbed off at one corner, as if it had been dragged along the ground. He holds out his hand and the boy gives the case back. The touch of a smile.

They are equals now.

'The important thing is not to panic. Not to lose your head, eh?' Looks over at the boy and smiles. He straightens up from the counter top and gazes down through the doors out to the open square.

Tonight, he thinks. Certainly, it will be tonight, he is thinking. The Bolsheviks are packing up and leaving town, the better to make their stand on the Volga. Everyone is trying to get out of the city on the last train. Those who've kept back a little are even trying to bribe their way out of town.

If you are going to run away, he is thinking, you should resemble as much as possible someone who is running away. Someone with something to save, something to protect. It's victims who run away.

He tears up the form again. Starts over.

SPECIAL SALES #R4-0B3
READY TO PURCHASE SEVEN. ADVISE REGARDS DELVERY SOONEST.
TODMANN

He signs, and folds the form in half. 'I'm going to give you a rouble extra, eh?'

The boy frowns, looking at him, surprised that this supposed sophisticate has revealed himself to be a far bigger fool than he has suspected.

'But it's not for you, it's for one of the operators in there, eh? Go in through the door and give him the note. For that much it goes to the top of the queue, yes?'

'Yes, of course.' The boy actually smiles.

'Thank you, and here, soldier. Take another.' He opens the silver case and gives the boy another cigarette, wondering if he's the kind to rush through things or make them last. 'I'll see you later,' he says.

'Fine,' says the boy after a moment. A good boy. Good eyes. Strong and hungry.

'I'll be back for the receipt. I need it for business, so make sure you keep it. Keep it safe in your little box, eh? If they reply, I might hire you a second time, eh? So, go on, then,' he says, and watches him walk down the corridor, jump the line, take his cap off as he pushes into the telegraphers' cage and, good boy that he is, do exactly as he's been told.

6

Everything changed in Perm. Ryzhkov watched the soldiers as they suddenly emptied out, and there was the first delay; a full half-hour while they watered and fitted an extra tender. The wires were down and no one knew if they could re-coal at Yekaterinburg yard.

He walked around the city, stood there watching the Kama running low between its embankments, used his Cheka credentials whenever he needed, and poked his nose into everything. Dropped in on the commissar and let him know that he might have important communications from time to time, looked the man straight in the eye. Watched the wheels go around even as he agreed. Special handling, then. Absolutely.

They got going again at dusk. He managed to requisition a loaf of bread at Cheka mess, which was a long room in the basement of a therapeutic school with kitchens at the end and steaming soup pots. Then in the night the train had slowed, and stopped intermittently – the entire journey elongating from a normal eight hours to two days and counting.

The weather had changed, becoming wetter. It began to rain in the night, and it was in some grey late July hour when they finally arrived, passing through a hurried line of barricades the Bolsheviks were throwing up at the village of Kungur, where the road to Moscow intersected with the rail-road – an important little place, for if the Czechs overran it they'd be one step closer to controlling the railroad all the way to Viatka, and that much closer to joining with British and American forces advancing south from the port of Archangel.

And if that happened the people's revolution would be surrounded.

They were losing, Ryzhkov saw. The train was completely empty in the last stretches, not a good sign. It appeared that there were no reinforcements rushing to help the Ural Soviet and the people of Yekaterinburg. And, even with the fresh troops he had been travelling with, it was obvious that there would be no strong Red defence of Perm. It was just the mathematics – there weren't enough trained Red fighters to stop the Czechs. No horses to speak of, no artillery.

No hope.

'Where's this?'

'Yekaterinburg – but there's two stations. They are trying to decide. They might not be able to get into the city,' one of the conductors told him.

The train, which had been creeping along, slowed to a halt some distance outside the first stop, a rural station on the way into the city. Manning the watchtowers beside the road were factory workers, with red rags tied round their sleeves, while below them a mass of wounded Bolshevik infantrymen waited for evacuation. The only station was hardly more than a tiny loading dock, and a telegraph shed at the crossing of the Moscow road.

The conductor came back and said they wouldn't be going into the city to the central station. Too dangerous. In the distance there was a sudden crash of an artillery explosion, and Ryzhkov shouldered his bag, stepped down out from his carriage and started walking down the tracks to the crossing.

There was another ripple of artillery rising up through the hills, a long distance away, but still his shoulders hunched and his stomach went light. The little station had been blacked out except for a single shielded light. The artillery had given him the shakes, and all he'd wanted to do from the moment he'd got out of the train was run away as fast and as far as he could.

Find the Romanovs and then get out, he told himself.

Places are either good, or they are bad. Yekaterinburg was bad, a city in chaos, stupefied, not knowing to whom it should pay allegiance. Ryzhkov's first view of the city was from the back of a automobile-tyre-shod cart that was being used as an ambulance back and forth to the crossroads. There was plenty of room going back. The driver was careful to explain that he'd been recruited by the local soviet when Ryzhkov flashed his Cheka book at him. 'It's fine. I don't care which side you're on,' Ryzhkov told him.

'The city is clearing out, you see? Everyone is scared.'

'Sure.'

'There's only a couple of your boys left.'

'I'm not staying long either.'

'For the best, I think.'

They wound their way down the Moscow road, passing the little farms that had been carved out of the birches, slowing to cross the bogs that lined the low parts of the road. Beneath the trees it was wet and the driver pulled the awning over them, so that all they could see were the hocks of the two ponies that were pulling them into the town.

The road widened out as they came down through the populated heights of the city sloping down to the river Iset. Looming over the huts and outbuildings were the first of the larger wooden houses with the usual traditional accoutrements, ornate filigree under the gables and around the doors, painted shutters, saw-cut banisters and sharp picket fences surrounding yards which once had been carefully tended. Then came the first of the really substantial buildings, built with brick and a lot of stone, since the Urals was an ancient mining region.

Precious metals had been quarried out of the mountains for centuries; iron for cannons, gold for money, platinum for jewellery and coal for steam engines. The city had been created by Peter the Great to honour his bride Catherine, and to serve as the gateway to Siberia, a region vast beyond belief, containing too many time zones and nationalities with customs that were utterly foreign to most Russians. In addition to the administrators and bureaucrats based there, Yekaterinburg had become a city of miners, lumberjacks, railwaymen and metalworkers. There were smelting plants, foundries and metals factories ringing the city and spread across the long slope down to the lake. The lake itself had been dammed in the distant past and now it was rimmed with vacated mansions and idle fishing boats.

The city was quiet. Supposedly the revolution had been particularly vigorous in the Urals. An industrial region with a tradition of exploitation had given rise to a hotbed of workers' agitation, and the mines and factories had been quickly shut down by the expedient of sabotage. The most committed of the workers had already been subsumed into the Red Army and the city was in the process of being inherited by those too poor to run away, those who longed for a Bolshevik defeat, or those who had merely waited too late.

Ahead of them were the first signs of life: two men smoking beside an open door, a woman with a chicken under her arm moving protectively down the sidewalk, two ancient men harnessing a dray.

'What is that?'

'Oh,' said the driver. 'That's the Church of the Ascension.'

'No . . . *that*, beside it.' There was a high barricade made of cut logs like a fort in an American wild west film.

'Oh, that's the Special House. It's where they killed the Tsar,' he said, turning at Ryzhkov's sudden reaction.

'Killed them?'

'So they say.'

'When did this happen?'

'Three days ago in the night. Killed the Tsar and his son. The women have been taken away.'

'You know this? You saw them go with your own eyes?'

'They are killing the entire family, so some say.' The driver shrugged.

'Do you mean Grand Duke Michael Alexandrovich?'

'Him, too, the Tsar's brother. They killed him in Perm last month, everyone said. That came to the telegraph. But then we heard at the hospital that he and his driver got away.'

'There are too many rumours. I'm trying to find out what really happened.'

The driver arced his head in the direction of the house. 'The Tsar is dead, I think that is the best guess, but –' nodding towards Ryzhkov's breast pocket, '– you should be able to find out, eh?'

Ahead of them was the confluence of two monstrously wide streets. The driver drew up outside the American Hotel. It was still draped in red flags, and there was a knot of Red Guards there making a show.

He walked up the stairs off the street, showed his card and went inside. In the wide saloon that opened off the lobby three men were hammering and nailing tables together. Otherwise the building seemed vacant and littered with the obvious markers of defeat. Two clerks were crossing down

53

the corridor with boxes of files, en route to the furnace in the ballroom. A third clerk knelt beside the furnace blowing and cursing at a smouldering mound of paper. He stopped one of the young men with his magic red book and asked for direction to the Cheka office.

'You're too late, sir. The building is being abandoned. I'm burning the last of the pay records right now, and then I'm on my way.'

'But Cheka headquarters is here in the hotel?'

'Oh yes, right down that hallway. Room number 3, sir.'

He walked down to the room. The door was open. Number 3 was a large rectangle, a small cloakroom at one end. A sofa. A pair of desks. Several broken lamps. Fragments of paper and carbon flimsies spread across the floor. Another boy walked past him with a broom and began sweeping them up into a pile. An inkwell had turned over and black footprints had been tracked into the Turkish carpet.

'Where have they gone, do you know?'

The clerk shrugged and did not meet his eye. 'Back to Moscow, comrade . . .'

Ryzhkov crossed the office to one of the desks, looked in its drawers and found a Yekaterinburg city directory there. It listed all addresses, and those with telephones were printed in bold. There was only one Eikhe in the book – No. 2 Kushok Lane.

'Do you know where Kushok Lane is?' he asked the clerk.

'Right on the other side of the city, in the direction of the Trouchenko foundry.'

'Too far to walk?'

'Oh, yes.' Ryzhkov watched him crabbing the papers into a ball, stuffing them into a mail sack.

'Where is the local soviet?'

'Besides right here, you mean?'

'I need to talk to someone with responsibility.'

54

The clerk made a doubtful face. 'Either at the municipal hall or at the civic theatre, I'd guess.'

Ryzhkov walked out of the American Hotel, past the young guards who were not quite sure what they were guarding, down to the street. The ground sloped slightly towards the area around the dam, and he kept going until he came to the municipal hall, an old building that looked suddenly out of date and in the process of being abandoned, its doors thrown open and two anxious Red Guards still lingering outside. A motor car and a truck were idling there, ready for a final run to the station.

He asked directions, and across the park he caught the Number 14 tram which was still running, and which carried him some dozen blocks past the sprawling and dead quiet Selki factory and let him off at the last stop.

From there Kushok Lane was only two blocks, and he stepped out into the muddy street and began walking. On one side of the street was a row of workers' houses that had been arranged diagonally to the street, climbing the low ridge with a fine view of the city beneath. There were children playing in the worn expanses in front of the houses, running around the fruit trees that had been girdled with octagonal planters for protection.

No. 2 was a semi-collapsed ancient wooden house, the logs darkened to blackness with soot, weeds grown up and died in a tangle around the foundations. A wide canvas tarpaulin that had been rigged up to shade half of the house, where a woman was butchering what Ryzhkov recognized to be a goat.

'I am looking for Nikolas Eikhe,' he said to her.

She turned and gave him a long look, taking in the suit – now truly shabby – the thick shoes, the rucksack with the leather raincoat rolled into it. 'He's not here.'

'Ahh . . .'

'What's it about?'

'I need to speak to him. It's important.'

'He's not here, Excellency.'

'When he comes back, maybe you can give him this.' Ryzhkov set the rucksack down, groped in the pockets for some paper. All he had was an envelope with his train schedule written on it. He wrote 'Ryzhkov, #3 Hotel American.'

'Shall I say what it is concerning?' the woman said. She was busily scrubbing out the great cavity that had been made by extracting the entrails of the animal.

Ryzhkov looked around the little street. The houses here were much older than the workers' factory houses at the end of the block. 'Eikhe is a German name, isn't it?' he asked.

'Yes, the family were Volga Germans. Here since the 1700s, so he claimed,' the woman said. She was older, but still strong, with her hair bound up in a series of towels that made her look like some sort of peasant queen, wearing a large apron, her sleeves rolled up to her armpits.

'I just want to talk to him, and I want to talk to someone who can put me in touch with the soviet.'

'They're all gone,' she said with finality.

'You're sure? There has to be someone around.'

'They're gone. I'm sure.'

'What about his friends? Maybe someone knows where I can find him.'

'He doesn't have any friends,' she said flatly.

'What about the Tsar?'

She looked up at him, shook the bloody rag out and dumped it in a dish beside the table. 'All of them are dead.'

'How do you know?'

'Oh, everybody knows it. It happened at the weekend. I know one of the women who mopped up the blood.'

'Who was that?'

'Just a woman. Someone I know. Look, they're dead,

comrade. When he comes back I'll give him your message. What does it say?'

'Ryzhkov. Number 3, American Hotel.'

'Is that where you're staying?' Her eyebrows went up at the cost of it.

'No. It's just to let him know who I am. You make sure and tell him. It's important. And I'll come back, eh?' he said, jabbing his finger at her.

At the bottom of the hill he waited to catch the tram, but gave up and walked past the long façade of the factory into the city. There was another distant crash and Ryzhkov realized that the artillery had stopped for some hours and only just begun firing again. A few minutes later an automobile blew past him with several Red Guard officers packed into the seats.

When he had walked another block, at the corner he could see a stream of citizens entering the Civic Theatre. The fast car that had passed him on the slope was sitting there, with steam coming out of the radiator cap. Several carriages and military wagons were drawn up in the lane and soldiers were milling about the entrance. Ryzhkov let himself be funnelled through the great doors to the theatre with everyone else. The windows had been thrown open and the curtains pulled shut against the sun. The whole room was a stew of dust motes and muttered conversations.

He found himself standing in the aisle at the back of the house. A squad of soldiers marched in, split into two ranks, and half of them passed right behind him, eyes alert and looking around for assassins. They went down the aisles and took positions with their rifles at rest at the foot of the stage.

Immediately a man came out from the wings, clutching a yellow sheet of paper in his hand. He was in his thirties, with dark hair slicked back and combed neatly behind his ears. He had a pince-nez that he wedged onto his nose and he moved to the centre of the stage and began to read before half the crowd noticed he was even there. He had to wait for the room to quieten and then began again. His voice was light, and someone called from the back rows for him to speak up.

'My name is . . .' It was still noisy in the room; they were letting people come upstairs onto the balcony and they were all still talking, not aware that the show had begun. The man backtracked yet again.

'My name is Fillip Goloschokin, military commissar of the Ural Soviet, and I announce today that, by order of the regional Ural Soviet, in the awareness that the Czecho-Slovak soldiers, those hirelings of French and British capitalists, are now close at hand, and in view of the fact that a White Guard plot to carry off the whole Imperial Family has been discovered, and that all the old Imperial generals are in it with them, that the Cossacks are also coming, and they all think that they will get their Emperor back, but they never shall –' His thin voice hung in the hall. 'We shot him three nights ago!'

There was a pause. Goloschokin repeated the last line again and looked off stage. Someone was speaking to him, but the words were distorted.

'Three nights ago!' Goloschokin repeated, and walked off into the wings.

The theatre was immediately filled with a torrent of conversation. A great crash of applause began which was almost immediately stifled by a series of shouts. Several women were in tears and were being assisted by their friends. 'Where is the body?' someone screamed from the balcony over and over. A group had rushed forward and were being held back by the young soldiers who had lifted their rifles to the ready and were guarding the two approaches to the stage. There was a rush for the exits.

Ryzhkov joined the flow out onto the street. The military trucks were already speeding down Glavni Prospekt in the direction of the station.

Now that Goloschokin had gone with the rest of the Ural Soviet and all that was left was the echo of the official announcement, Ryzhkov thought he ought to make for the station and telegraph NOSMOC4, but what would he say? The announcement would be wired back to the Kremlin by the Ural Soviet themselves; everything else was rumour.

He walked along the embankment of the pond that occupied the centre of the city, heading for the station. All around him people were moving, like ants that had been driven out of their hiding places. Several lorries rushed past him, and people ran across the street, hurrying to hoard anything that their fantasies suggested they might need before they dashed off to crouch behind shuttered windows.

At the station he wrote to Zezulin:

NOSMOC4 – MOSCOW
RUMOURS EVERYWHERE. OFFICIAL ANNOUNCEMENT BUT NO
PROOF. CANNOT FIND E. WILL CONTINUE.
RYZHKOV

The telegrapher shook his head, but a wave of the Cheka card drew a grimace and Ryzhkov's telegraph form moved to the top of the queue. Steam whistles startled the birds, and the last of the trains were pulling out, heading west for safety.

He walked out of the station, out onto the wide expanse of the square. The wind was blustery, the sky had cleared and the sun was drying the puddles into crusts and sending the flies buzzing out of the gutters. The wind abruptly changed direction and in the distance he could hear gunshots in the hills. In front of the station the square was completely vacant. The Red Guards had vanished, and everything had fallen into a sudden silence.

He headed back into the centre of the city, tore up his Cheka card and travelling documents and dropped fragments into each gutter that he passed by, paying particular attention to the identification page and his photograph. If Eikhe was in town he had probably gone to ground; anyone with connections to the local soviet would either try to escape or go into hiding. He decided to keep the coat, it worked well in the weather, and he might need it again if he ever wanted to get back to Moscow.

When he got closer to the market he walked down the lanes looking into the garbage until he came out with a reasonably clean section of newspaper. He sat down on the steps of the Municipal Hall, folded the newspaper into a long strip and braided it around his sleeve to make an armband.

Then he took off his hat and mopped his brow, took a deep breath and waited for the first Czech cavalry to arrive.

7

Ryzhkov had actually fallen asleep there on the steps when the first cavalrymen rode into the square. He jerked awake and stood up to watch them. They came into the city with the arrogance that men on horses always carry with them, when they are armed to the teeth and don't care about those in their path. With their entrance it was suddenly their city and not the Russians who'd resided there.

A clutch of nervous supplicants had gathered at the front of the building, the ones who were most frightened or angered by Bolshevik rule, the ones who'd been dispossessed of their little local empires. The rest of the square was empty. When the Czech cavalrymen saw them they rode over, called out some gibberish which no one could understand, cantered about the square for a few moments, and then tore off looking for the station. There was some laughter from those who were waiting, and one of the men spat out into the street.

A few moments later a military truck pulled into the square and a squad of infantrymen leapt out, their purpose to seize the Municipal Hall. As the soldiers moved up the steps one of the civilians forced a bottle of home-made vodka on a dark Czech, who took it with his pals, all of them laughing at the Russian with his hat in his hand. They went inside and left one of their squad to guard the front doors.

Already more people were creeping out from behind their doors. A few shutters on the apartments on Glavni Street were thrown open and people had come to their windows to watch the Czechs busy at occupying their town, and wondering if they might get something out of it. Half an hour later a young lieutenant came out and began collecting the details of the now sizeable group that had fetched up there at the steps.

When the lieutenant asked him who he was, Ryzhkov leaned close. 'I am an agent of the government of France. I need to speak, confidentially you understand, with the military attaché,' he said, and then shrugged to show he realized how fantastic it might sound.

The young man looked at him steadily and the stenographer he'd brought out with him stood there, his pen suspended over the ledger. 'I'm sorry, I have no identification, I had to burn it, ' Ryzhkov said, adding a smile.

'Very well,' the lieutenant said slowly, and called two men over to take him to jail.

They took him straight through the Municipal Hall to the rear entrance, down another set of stairs to a waiting prison cart. There were three men already in it, chained to a long rod that was built into the wall of the van. One of them was dressed in formal attire, as if he were attending an official function; another was a Bolshevik soldier in uniform. There was a bloody bruise over his cheek, and he had been injured inside, because every movement of the cart made him wince and draw a tight breath.

They waited, watching through the grill the soldiers come and go. In a few moments they were shoving another man down the stairs, the doors were wrenched open and they tried to push him in. He was screaming at them, grabbing at the door handles.

It was a misunderstanding, he said. Everything was a misunderstanding. The Czechs began to kick him. A prominent person was on their way to vouch for him, and afterwards he would show them the city. They kept kicking him until he gave up shrieking and when they locked him to the rod he sat there, sobbing and sweating, his suit pulled open, clutching his hat in his manacled hands. Then they were off – lurching around behind the hall, down a lane and into the wide street where he could see industrious Czechs erecting barricades at the major intersections.

They were organized, the Czechs. They were still in their units, had only been able to rely on themselves throughout the war and their imprisonment once they'd deserted into Russia from the Austrian army. Now they were running things, and they knew how to do it, Ryzhkov saw. Squads of soldiers were moving through the streets, pounding on doors, requisitioning everything they needed, buildings, firewood, food, animals and people for the greater glory of the White cause.

They rounded a corner and jerked to a stop at the jail. There were several of the old city policemen there. Some of them had worked for the Bolsheviks but had held back their pre-revolutionary caps or jackets, and as members of the reconstituted constabulary they had put them on over their ordinary clothing. Now they were generously helping the Czechs to get things up and running. They went about their jobs with the kind of alert efficiency and overblown enthusiasm that a man will display when he thinks he might be fired before lunch.

By the time Ryzhkov made it to the holding rooms, they seemed to know all about him, and he guessed that the lieutenant must have sent word ahead by field telephone. He was separated from the rest, locked to a bench, then unlocked and given over to an officer who appraised him with a slight smile, and, with two other warders, walked him down to the cells.

The first cell they'd tried was already occupied, so they put him in a larger room, meant for four, but now seemingly dedicated to Ryzhkov alone. His manacles were unlocked and a few minutes later they brought him some bread and kvass. While he ate, the officer came back and watched him.

'You say you're a Frenchman?' The Czech's French was accented but understandable. The cadence was like a schoolboy's. Maybe he just wanted to practise.

'I'm Russian. I was Okhrana, then I was in France through the war.'

'Ahh . . . with the Legion?'

Ryzhkov shrugged and nodded. 'I work for the French now,' Ryzhkov said.

'Well, we all work for the French. They are in command, after all. Or at least that is the latest fiction.' The Czech smiled, and looked down the corridor for a moment. 'The Conte should be in soon. He'll see you, but you'd better have the right answers, *mon ami*,' the officer said, and drew a finger across his throat. 'If you're the real thing we'll find out. If you're lying . . . well, tell them in hell that I was a charitable man, eh?' The officer stooped and slid a pair of cigars through the bars and set a box of matches on top of them. 'Just don't start any fires.'

'Thank you. I'll be careful.'

Ryzhkov finished his food, and used the toilet in the corner. Went over and picked up the cigars, and had just taken off his shoes and collapsed on the lowest of the iron beds when the guards were back again.

They were measuring him now, watching an ex-Okhrana

brought low; the kind of man they'd all heard about come into their world at last. He didn't look like so much, not so tough, they would be thinking. Look at how things had come round! Here he was, finally in the cell he and his kind had always deserved; even someone working for the Whites would think about the Okhrana like that, the legends of their brutality had been so notorious.

The two guards stood silently while he extended his arms to be locked together, then, supporting him on each side, they conveyed him back upstairs. They used a passage that was narrow, originally intended for servants in the distant past before one of the Tsars had had appropriated the building for a courthouse and jail to house the enemies of the state that had evolved in the dark mines far below.

Everything so far had been a prelude. Dramatic enough, but only bluff and process, and maybe he had been lucky enough to push his execution a little further into the future. His real worry was that, in exchange for his life, what could he give them? In Moscow he had asked Zezulin about it, because it was almost certain to come up.

'Yes, yes, yes, but if you give something to them, Pyotr, what will you do after that? You give it, then it's gone, then you're nothing. Besides, things are changing daily. No one is predicting the future. That's for fools. You want to give them something? What? Strategy, tactics? Names of agents and traitors? How did you come by all that? No, no. You're *running away*. You're terrified. You don't have time to put together a nice present for the Czech counter-intelligence. You're scared and in a big hurry. You can tell them the whole truth if you want, if you think they'll believe you, but just do your job for me at the same time. Try to act like you mean it. Do you think you can manage that?'

So he had nothing.

An area had been carved out of the offices upstairs; it

looked like the kind of room a school headmaster might have as an office. There was a furnace in the corner, and in the 'beautiful' corner opposite a collection of empty shelves with holes in the plaster where the icons had been stripped away by the Bolsheviks and not yet restored by the new government.

A sergeant supervised the seating of their prize; a few minutes later he heard voices, and an officer came in. The guards left, closing the door behind them. Ryzhkov nodded, and said 'Good afternoon,' although it was still morning.

The door opened and a secretary came in. 'All right, tell us your story,' the secretary translated. Then the questioning began, and curiously it relaxed him.

'Tell him,' he said to the secretary, 'I'm only trying to get out of here. I was working for the French in Moscow, the Reds caught me, I was released for a few hours and I ran. I had papers but I destroyed them. I'll tell you everything I know, but it's not much . . .' It went on and on, and he told it flatly with as much dignity as he could muster. The more he talked, the more it sounded like blather. Even the secretary was looking at him with a smirk. At the end there was a silence and he tried to pick it up by telling them about his recruitment by the Deuxième Bureau and his work in Paris, but sitting there looking at them he realized how absurd it all sounded.

The officer sniffed, shook his head, flicked the remains of his cigarette out of the window and looked out on the courtyard below. On the breeze in the warm summer day were the sounds of military commands, the clashing of rifles being stacked on the cobbles, the sounds of gulls being startled from under the eaves, angry at the intruders.

'Come here,' the officer said in passable Russian, and Ryzhkov got to his feet and shuffled over to the window. Across the courtyard a wide gallows was being set up. It looked like something standard, from a kit. Struts and braces that a section of men could load on the back of a lorry and screw together as needed.

'This is civilization now,' the officer said. His voice was quiet. Purring. The accent unusual. 'This is what we have come to,' he said, looking around at Ryzhkov. They were about the same age, he realized, but the officer was immaculate – his moustache flecked with grey, the eyebrows dark and even, the eyes light blue and steady, the complexion a little darker, with golden tones rather than pink. A smile. 'So, you have been telling us the truth today, signor?'

'Yes, Excellency.' Ryzhkov almost reflexively bowed as he said it.

'Well, you've certainly had a very turbulent time. It's quite a story. Worked for the Okhrana? Ran away to France? Fought like a tiger, and now you're here. "Released for a few hours," did you say?'

Ryzhkov nodded and a 'Yes, Excellency' escaped his lips like a whisper.

'You'd better tell me if you're lying, yes? It's so much better if you tell me now, much better instead of me finding out later that you've been untruthful, eh?'

'It's all the truth, I swear it.'

'Swear?' the man said, almost laughing. '"Swear to God", eh? It's all true and you want to live? Live a long and happy life, work, have children, a little home. And maybe do something, something useful here in town . . .' The officer gestured and simultaneously there was a metallic clang as the workers outside tested the gallows trap. The gulls took off again, a chorus of shrieks echoing in the courtyard, wheeling overhead. There were the dim sounds of laughter, the men congratulating themselves on a job well done.

'Well, maybe you're just hungry, or maybe you're truly a French agent. I'm checking on that part of your tale right

67

now, but since you want to be helpful and you have no choice I suppose I can put you to work, now that you understand the circumstances.' The officer turned, looked out at the gallows and then lifted his hand to his neck and made a garish death's face – tongue lolling out, eyes rolled up. Like a schoolyard clown. Then he laughed and went back to the desk.

'All right then . . .' The officer spread his hands out on the surface of the desk, leaned back in his chair, a smile flirting with the corners of his mouth. 'I am Conte Captain Tommaso di Giustiniani, and for the moment I am head of counter-intelligence in Yekaterinburg, and your saviour. And now that we've both washed up here in this . . . enthralling little city,' he said with that slow smile, 'there is really only one great question to answer: Where's the Tsar? Yes? It is all very puzzling, and, since you are so devoted to the truth, Ryzhkov, perhaps we can find it together.'

8

The first train arrived just after four carrying the head-quarters of White General Golitsyn, his deputy, Major de Heuzy, and several cars of hangers-on and support staff, a *melange* of diplomats, spies, adventurers, journalists, disgruntled fugitives and commercial opportunists – a population made up of the lowest forms of life, all of them hungry and in search of food and lodging.

By afternoon the citizenry had reclaimed the streets and the city was suddenly busy, swarming with all varieties of blue-uniformed Czechs, the officers striding possessively through the shopping district, all of them demanding service and willing to pay, although it was in paper roubles that had been over-stamped by the White Kolchak-led government, or in letters of credit that no one could understand. There wasn't really any choice: if you had something they wanted you could either sell it for the pretend money or they'd just requisition it.

Over dinner the details came out. Ryzhkov was fed lavishly at the Fez, a restaurant across the square that had immediately been taken over as the officer's club. The room was not crowded, they were eating between hours. A troika of

Czechs held serious talk over cigars in the corner. The waiters came in and out, resetting the tables, tidying up for the dinner hour. Giustiniani had taken one bite when he began laughing at the quality of the cooking.

'You know,' Giustiniani said haltingly so that he wouldn't choke, 'I have been all over the world, based in some lovely cities. Everywhere, in every port there is at least one reasonably decent restaurant.' His fork stirred the concoction on his plate. It looked like a small steak of some kind smothered in a brown camouflaging sauce, and potatoes that had been mashed and blended with cabbage beside it. Ryzhkov couldn't decipher it either although it hadn't stopped him from wolfing it down. 'Every port brings people in, you know, from elsewhere. New blood, strangers with new ideas – fertilization,' Giustiniani continued wistfully, took a sip of wine and winced, shook his head and pushed the hateful dish away.

With nothing to fill his mouth, Giustiniani was free to tell his life story while Ryzhkov ate, and so began a poetic and amusing saga of olive groves and grapevines and cypress trees.

Tommaso di Giustiniani was a submariner in the Italian navy who had surfaced just in time to be sent to Russia to help the Allies quell the worldwide revolution. He had ceased to refer to himself as nobility, dropping the 'Conte' and shortening his name. 'The family is . . . well, it is not what it was,' he said by way of explanation.

Giustiniani liked to entertain and he liked to talk, and he had, apparently, all the time in the world to do it. But Ryzhkov saw him for a man who preferred being underestimated, preferred to conceal his true strength inside. You didn't go down in those tin cans if you didn't have the black space inside you somewhere, and you didn't last if you didn't know how to handle men. For Giustiniani, dropping his noble connections was an obvious first step; a title and estates were

70

worthless when pressure was cracking the hull, or when the destroyers were trying to find you, and all the crew knew it. Ryzhkov wasn't an expert on the Italian underwater boat service, but he knew that all such machines were fantastic creations that used the most expensive materials in their defiance of the seas. Thus, despite his old-world charm, the lazy smile, the unmuscled gestures, Giustiniani was a modern man.

The brandy came, and by that time Ryzhkov had grown sleepy and drunk. Giustiniani signed the chit and they moved into a large room that had been converted into a lounge and attempted to play billiards on a threadbare table. 'There is no felt, eh? No felt in Yekaterinburg at all. There is a felt *shortage*,' Giustiniani said, missing a shot.

At one point Ryzhkov found himself gazing at two billiard tables, the visions overlaying each other at angles, identical balls swimming in the sea, and knew that he was very, very drunk. He tried to snap back to sobriety because Giustiniani was talking about the Romanovs.

'Everyone says they are dead,' Ryzhkov said.

'Everyone says a lot of things. Everyone says that Nicholas and Alexandra were seen in Perm yesterday morning. Everyone says that our advance party stole them away just before we took the town on Tuesday accomplishing this with such stealth that no one actually saw them. Those kinds of witnesses we have plenty of. All we can be certain of is that the Imperial Family has vanished since last weekend. And their property also,' he added with a smile.

'What do you want me to do then?' Ryzhkov said. They were both standing there looking at the billiard ball. Giustiniani stared at him for a second, then reached out and swept it into a side pocket.

'I want you to go and get cleaned up. We're expected at an orgy.'

* * *

Cleaning up meant splashing cold water on himself in the shower at the military quarters that Giustiniani took him through, a quick shave which was frightening because of his inability to see his own face clearly, then more frightening when he finally came into focus. A rinsing of his mouth with mint water, and then Giustiniani was there at the door, looking as fresh as a spring day. They journeyed through the streets by hired cab, the driver being all too happy for the fare.

By the end of the night Yekaterinburg had been transformed into a town gripped by a fever as powerful as a gold rush. The people were manic, like inhabitants of a desperate new boom town – everyone simultaneously trying to ingratiate themselves with the winners and queuing up for transit passes to Vladivostok.

Outside the Hotel Palais Royal there was a fist-fight in progress, and soldiers stood about listlessly leaning on their rifles, smoking cheroots and waiting for the combatants to tire. The foyer was crowded with women negotiating terms and conditions with various suitors, and the stairs were threadbare and treacherous, owing to the increasing lack of illumination the higher one climbed.

It didn't seem much like an orgy to Ryzhkov, at least not in the imagined Roman sense. It was held in the ballroom of the hotel, supposedly one of the city's finest, and was crowded with sweating matrons and men holding their hats in their hands, everyone seeking approval, affection, a little cash, a passage east – easily the most prised item – or a position in the new government of Admiral Kolchak.

The ballroom itself was an elongated chamber with high windows at one end that looked over the city, giving a view of the stream that ran down to the lower Iset pond and the fishing docks at the head of the lake. There was a balcony there and the doors were thrown open, but this did nothing to dispel the cloud of tobacco smoke and the ladies' heavy perfume.

It was a curious mixture, a large number of Czech officers of various ages and a few other uniforms, most of which Ryzhkov could not place. Giustiniani was well known, it seemed. He kept Ryzhkov with him, introduced him to all as his 'aide', and otherwise ignored him. Ryzhkov excused himself and took air on the balcony. Refused all drinks and tried to sober up.

It was not to be, however. Giustiniani would find him on his next orbit and take him across the room to meet some other governmental dignitary or eminent military figure. The Czechs had acquired the Russian habit of commemorating everything with a vodka toast. And so it went, Ryzhkov losing count of how many times this occurred.

The whereabouts of the Romanovs was on everyone's tongue. The consensus agreed with the announcement he had witnessed – that the Tsar was dead and the family removed to a 'safe place'. The announcement had also been published on a broadsheet that had been pasted up around the city and recovered by the Czechs. Still, there were no bodies, and no eye witnesses to the Tsar's execution, since the executioners had fled the city, presumably with the Romanov women and servants in tow.

'But the worst sin is that there is no champagne, none whatsoever. The Bolsheviks drank it all!' a man was screaming at him. He was flanked by two red-headed women who hung on his arms and offered their cheeks to Ryzhkov. One woman had torn her dress and her heavy breasts were exposed. She made fluttering attempts to cover herself, and then gave up.

'What is this, then?' Ryzhkov said. They had forced a bottle on him.

'Vodka! Made locally. You mix it with lime juice and fizzy water from the springs! Goes down good, eh?' the man shouted. A band had begun playing but they were as drunk as everyone else and the music wheezed and swerved through

73

the tonal spectrum. Ryzhkov put his mouth to the bottle and drank the *faux* champagne. At least it was cold, with an antiseptic taste that seemed somehow more healthy than the punch that had been served but had now run out.

'Come on now,' the second of the redheads said to him. 'You're good for it, eh?'

Ryzhkov didn't know what she was talking about for a moment. The other two were dancing. The music was just an unstructured wailing, all out of beat and synchronization. The woman was kissing him now, and pulling him into the shadows. The room was emptying out, and filling up again. They had taken over the whole hotel. He found himself in a corridor with a group of other officers, the uniforms too confusing to place. The doors were open and the true orgy had begun in the opened-up suites.

'We may die,' the redhead said into his ear. 'We may die at any moment.' She pulled him into a room. There was another couple on the floor, but it didn't matter. Her hands were on his fly and he had thrown his coat on the floor. They wrestled on the bed with the other couple groaning beside them. He hadn't had anyone in a long time, and now she swam before him, her breasts wobbling as he tried to thrust himself into her, her face looking up at him, imploring him, gripping him by his buttocks, lunging up to snatch a kiss. The other couple had finished and were standing there laughing. He saw that she was talking with them, having a conversation in the middle of his efforts. '. . . not much . . . not much at all,' she was saying. After a moment she pushed him away.

'Too drunk,' he muttered, and the woman slapped him. For a moment he saw white, reeled backwards and made a fist, flung it at the woman, but she had already got up. Then he was on the bed, his face pressed into the hot blankets, while the other man hurled abuse at him. The other woman

74

was laughing as the redhead complained to her about his quality.

He staggered to the door but didn't make it. Vomited across an armchair, stood there clinging to it and coughing and wiping his mouth off on the antimacassar. There was a bottle and he took a drink to wash his mouth and spat it out on the floor. From the doorway he could see that more people had arrived. The fun was continuing. A girl was slumped against the panelling and crying. He stood there, supporting himself in the doorway and watching her. She was thin, blonde, and her hair had been cut short and frizzy. Her eyes were puffy and streaked where the kohl had run. She looked terribly alone in the middle of it all, absently beating the wall with her silk scarf in one hand, and holding the other to her mouth to stop the sobbing. She looked up at him and then started crying all over again.

They met in the centre of the corridor. Others were walking around them. It was like being an island in a river of drunks. She pressed her face into his jacket, sobbing, then looked up at him. The only beautiful woman he had seen all night long, he thought. The only honest thing in the city. She pressed her lips to his mouth and pulled him to her, strong for such a thin girl. He felt himself growing hard and she reached for him and they had each other there on the edge of the sofa, against the wall, everything happening at once, a quick little hurricane of lust and hands slipping over fabric and flesh, the bones of her back, her legs trying to reach around him, her face pressed into his neck, and his into the spikes of her hair. The smell of flowers.

It was over as quickly as it had started and they clung to each other while everything was ebbing away. She said something that he couldn't hear because of the noise of the lift just down the hall opening and closing spasmodically as each new drunken troupe tried to line it up with the floor.

Then suddenly she pulled away and was gone, not even a look back, and he was there, still in the river, fumbling with his clothing and not feeling better, not feeling any better at all.

He would leave, he thought. He would just walk to Vladivostok if that's what it took. No one would miss him in this chaos. Zezulin would assume he'd been killed, probably wouldn't waste the effort to take revenge on Vera. The world had already gone to hell. All that remained was the burning.

He staggered towards the stairs, and met the man who'd been in the room with him. There were words, Ryzhkov couldn't hear them or understand. It might have been a different language. He punched the man hard in the chest and he stepped back and slid down the wall, groaning. Everyone around them laughed. At the landing he saw Giustiniani coming up.

'I've been looking for you,' he said. 'This is Judge Nametkin, he's in charge of our investigation.' Beside Giustiniani was a portly man, deep into his forties, a bald head that someone had written upon with lipstick.

'Hello,' the man said. Large grey eyes looked up and smiled at him lazily.

'This is Ryzhkov, our new detective,' Giustiniani prompted and Nametkin extended his hand. 'We're going over there right away. Might as well get started, eh?'

'Where?' said Ryzhkov, and realized that he'd only made a noise, not a word, so he repeated again, 'Where-are-we-going?'

'Don't worry, you'll find out,' Nametkin said, forming his words with equal precision. 'Should we walk? What do you think?' he asked Giustiniani, bracing himself against the wall.

'Mmm . . . a cab, I think. The government is paying after all,' and they both laughed. As they went down the stairs, a man approached Nametkin and blocked their descent. His face was dirty, rat-like.

'You want to see Anastasia, comrade? I'll take you to her, but there are necessary fees –' Giustiniani batted him away and he collapsed on the stairs and began to cry. 'I have them, I have them all! On good authority!' he shrieked behind them as they escaped to the foyer.

'Loyalty,' Nametkin was saying to Giustiniani as they got into the cab. 'Loyalty is a porous, negotiable thing. This is the White world. You can believe in the virtues all you want, but where are you going to put your money?'

'Exactly. Money,' said Giustiniani. Ryzhkov took the seat in the back, feeling sick all over again.

'It's the worst of the worst. Who do you think is going to win? That's the basis, the entire basis . . .'

'Exactly. Basis.' As they rolled through the city Nametkin began to snore. Giustiniani leaned forward, said something to the driver, and they turned back.

'It's no use. We're all in. We'll do it tomorrow,' he explained to Ryzhkov, who had no idea, no idea at all what they were doing, where they were going, or why.

As the cab drew closer to the barracks he saw the girl he'd had in the hallway. She was walking along in the same direction, still trailing her scarf in her hand. When they passed her he looked back and saw that her face was washed clean, her chin high, and that she looked over to them for a moment, then looked away.

Straight ahead up the street, not caring about the men in the carriage, what they thought about the world situation, or anything they might claim to understand.

9

Propas, the chauffeur, roused him out of bed. It took some work. Ryzhkov was hung over, sick, and his head was pounding so that he could hear it. Another man was waiting while Ryzhkov, making certain of his hand-holds, climbed into the back seat. The man watched with a disgusted expression, waited for him to swing his legs inside, slammed the door and got in the front. The car was huge and painted field grey and, in places, a paler colour that might have been brown; brushstrokes done quickly, and the doors labelled in odd stencilled writing that Ryzhkov thought looked Chinese.

The man in the front seat turned out to be Ilya Strilchuk, the only remaining detective inspector who had been a veteran of the Tsarist Yekaterinburg police. When the Bolsheviks took over Strilchuk had escaped execution by hiding in the woods, but his wife and children had been murdered instead. He didn't turn around to look at Ryzhkov when he made his introduction, and he didn't elaborate on any of the details.

After Strilchuk's sad story, they fell silent. They were driving up a gentle slope, climbing away from the embankment and the historic centre of the city, the road curving to where it opened out upon a church and a wide square, which abruptly ended in a tall wooden palisade. The fence had been built of rough wood and newly cut logs, and a quartet of guardhouses were spaced along the opposite side of the street. Peeking out above the tall fence he recognized it as the house he'd been shown on the way into town.

'This is the place,' Strilchuk said, and the chauffeur set the brake. Strilchuk got out to help him, but Ryzhkov was conscious of his own dignity to the point where he made the effort to get out unaided. Giustiniani was at the front of the building, evidently waiting for them. The magistrate Nametkin was with him. They both looked just fine. The gate was opened by a boy in a cut-down artilleryman's uniform. He snapped to present-arms as they went through. Nametkin thought the boy was funny and kept nudging Giustiniani.

'Do you let just anybody in here?' Giustiniani said to the boy. 'There may have been murder done in this house, you know that, don't you?'

The boy shrugged spasmodically.

'This house is the subject of a military investigation. Everyone that comes is required to sign a register. Where is it?'

'A book, do you mean, Excellency?'

'Yes, yes, of course. A book. Can you produce it?' The boy turned and headed for the front door to search for it.

'Good morning, gentlemen,' Nametkin said. 'We need you to translate for our witness. How are you today, Ryzhkov? Hale and hearty?'

'I'll last the morning at least,' he said. 'What's this about a witness?'

'Just inside,' Nametkin said. They stepped into the foyer. The place was a mess. In the front room there was live ammunition piled on top of the piano. The floor was littered with leaves that had either been blown in or tramped in on the soldiers' boots and not swept away. Nametkin headed for the staircase. 'This first floor was the billet of the inner guard,' he said over his shoulder.

The house had been not so much destroyed as worn down. The upholstery on the furniture had been punctured and spilled out, the legs on some of the chairs had broken and the pieces thrown into the corners. Smells of food gone rancid, the filthy toilets, stale tobacco and sweat lingered in the rooms. 'The Imperial Family were confined to the five rooms above,' Nametkin said as they made their way up the central staircase, rounded the banister and walked into the hallway. Even with the windows open the house was stuffy.

'Up here the guards occupied the area beside the stairs, and the family lived behind these doors,' Nametkin said and waited for them to catch up. Giustiniani came up last, looking over his shoulders.

Nametkin threw open the double doors and Ryzhkov walked into the Romanovs' apartments.

He could see the rooms had been taken apart. Every piece of furniture had been moved about and repositioned, the cupboards opened, drawers tipped out and anything of value taken away. It looked like a building that had been repossessed by a series of particularly angry landlords and then abandoned. Underneath it all there was an elusive perfume that still lingered in the dust, in the fabric of the chairs and the bedding. It might be soap or something rotting just from being closed up in the summer.

Nametkin waved his finger at the mess. 'You and Strilchuk should get a list of all these possessions.'

'Yes, sir.' Strilchuk said. Whatever he said it always had that edge in his voice.

'It's part of the estate, I suppose,' Giustiniani murmured. He was standing at the windows. Ryzhkov saw they had been painted over with whitewash from the outside and then the sash had been nailed closed.

'Well . . .' Nametkin made a face. 'The Romanov estate? Until we have some evidence, I guess it must be assumed . . .'

Under a chair Ryzhkov saw a book. He stooped and picked it up: *Les Bienfaits de la Vièrge*. Inside was an inscription to Tatiana –

For my darling . . .

He slid it back onto the floor.

Around the room, nothing broken, no shards of glass. No blood. Just disarray and petty theft as the Bolsheviks had retreated.

'Ah, here's our friend,' said Nametkin. A guard walked out with a man whose hands were cuffed in front of him. They put him in a chair and Ryzhkov told him to tell his story while Strilchuk wrote it all down.

The witness was one Petr Matok, and he claimed to have been one the guards at the Ipatiev house. In Matok's version the Imperial Family had been brought to Yekaterinburg in two contingents: the Tsar, Alexandra and their daughter Maria came in April, then about a month later the remaining grand duchesses and the heir Alexei arrived and were taken to the Special House.

In the first week of July the Ural Soviet replaced the commandant of the guard with a Cheka officer named Yakov Yurovsky.

'Why did they do that?' Giustiniani asked them man.

'He was the man from Moscow,' Matok said, as if that explained everything.

'So it was orders from the very top, then, eh?' Nametkin said. Matok only shrugged.

'Go on,' Ryzhkov told him.

According to Matok, Yurovsky had grown up in Yekaterinburg and was an experienced revolutionary. He'd been educated, been a photographer, and had acquired sufficient medical experience to act as a doctor for Alexei on one occasion. Things changed with Yurovsky's arrival: 'Tthe broom sweeps clean,' Matok said. He was smiling a little now. No one was beating him up and he wanted to say the right things and keep it that way.

Yurovsky replaced almost all of the guards, dividing them into two groups with no connection to each other: an outer guard of local volunteers to police the approaches to the Ipatiev house where Matok worked, and a strictly isolated inner guard made up of imported Latvian riflemen whom he'd brought with him. The Latvians came with a reputation as reliable enforcers: only a year earlier they'd been the guns that secured the infant Bolshevik revolution.

With the changes the Romanovs gained some privileges while others were taken away. Father Storozhev and his nuns were forbidden from bringing their extra daily rations of eggs and milk. This lasted until one of the doctors protested that the heir suffered from malnutrition, and Yurovsky relented.

'But then it all changed, you see?' Matok said, his voice taking on tones of helplessness.

'Changed? How so?' Giustiniani prodded.

'With the Czechs, Excellency,' Matok said, reflexively bowing to the men standing there over him. Starting in the middle of July there was a sudden clampdown on anyone approaching the Special House. The Czechs were pressing their encirclement of Yekaterinburg, and when Yurovsky wasn't supervising the additional fortifications to the Special House he spent his time in the telegrapher's kiosk at the American Hotel asking Moscow for orders, Matok claimed.

'He was worried about being overrun?'

'Yes, Excellency. We all were worried,' Matok said, giving a little laugh and another bow.

Then, he said, only a few days later he'd heard the Romanovs had been executed in the night.

'Heard? Heard from whom? Were you here?'

'No, Excellency. I had been given leave. I would have been here, because when you were here you got extra food, and you know . . . I am always hungry,' he said. Matok looked up at them with big eyes. He didn't know if he'd told them enough to save his life, and from Giustiniani's expression the odds weren't good.

'So it was all Yurovsky's doing?'

'Yes, Excellency. All because of Comrade Yurovsky.'

Nametkin looked to Giustiniani, who sniffed. 'Take him back,' he said, and the guard pulled him up out of his chair and took him down the staircase. 'Well, to me it sounds like a fifth-hand story. "He wasn't here, he heard from someone else," you know . . . all these people come out of the woodwork,' Giustiniani said with a laugh. 'For instance, the Tsar is in Harbin – that's what it says in this morning's newspaper,' Giustiniani said, unscrewing a flask and holding it out to Ryzhkov.

'You want some other wild tales? There was a mysterious telegram received, there was a special armoured train provided by the British that arrived in the middle of the night, there is a secret tunnel connecting with the British consulate, there are mysterious strangers, black aeroplanes that land on the main street and then take off again a few moments later . . . and so on and so forth.'

Ryzhkov took a short sharp swig of what turned out to be brandy. Excellent brandy, he thought. He offered the flask to Strilchuk, who just looked at him blankly and didn't even move, then passed it to Nametkin.

Nametkin was searching his pockets. He came out with two pages and unfolded them. 'This is what we know . . .' Nametkin cleared his throat.

'This is from Gorskov, another of these guards,' Giustiniani said to Ryzhkov and Strilchuk.

'We will go by his notes,' Nametkin said, adjusting his spectacles. '"On the night of the 16th last, Yurovsky came up here with several members of the guard, and the Imperial Family were summoned to the dining area . . . There were trucks placed outside . . . "' Nametkin recited.

'Trucks so they could move them?' Ryzhkov said. Strilchuk looked over at him. Nametkin shrugged and waved the papers. '. . ."the Romanov women took a certain amount of time, but when they were dressed . . ." and so on. Some time later –'

'Didn't he say "forty-five minutes"?' Giustiniani's voice was one note above boredom.

'Yes, forty-five minutes later they were ready and then they were told that the Ural Soviet had decided to execute them. "They were immediately fired upon . . . "' Nametkin read, backing away, and turning to the dining room as if it were going to respond. For a moment they all looked around at the open cupboards and tins spilled out onto the floor.

'This is a box of hair,' Strilchuk said. He had found a cigar box and was hefting it as if to determine the weight. The box was stuffed with long curls of at least three different colours of women's hair. They all gathered around it. Giustiniani stuck his finger in the box and felt beneath the curls. 'Just hair,' he said.

'Hmmph,' Nametkin said, and returned to his papers. Strilchuk closed the lid on the box and placed it on an end table.

'". . . the Latvians opened fire . . ."' Nametkin read. 'It says that the Latvians immediately opened fire on the family, and at the end of it when they checked the pulses Anastasia was still alive –'

'In here?' Ryzhkov said. Nothing of the kind had ever

happened in that dining room, he could see. He looked over at Strilchuk who shook his head.

'– so they beat her with their rifles –'

'No, they didn't. Not in here,' Ryzhkov said.

'– "stabbed her thirty-two times".'

'Not in here,' Ryzhkov repeated.

'What, did he stand there and count?' Strilchuk said.

'The other story is that this Yurovsky took them down the back staircase –' Giustiniani put in.

'And took them into the basement room,' Nametkin said. Strilchuk walked out into the corridor, already looking for the exit from the dining area.

'Into a side basement room,' Nametkin said. 'Let's go and find that. The house slopes . . .'

'It's down here, I think.' Strilchuk led them down the narrow back staircase. At the foot of the stairs there was a portico and a set of four stairs down to wide doors, locked with a hasp and padlock.

'Christ,' Giustiniani said. He and Strilchuk went around to the guardhouse to see if anyone had the keys to the room.

Ryzhkov and Nametkin looked around the back of the house. There was a woodshed and a sauna bath, built downhill in the dried-out gardens. There was a smaller area to which the Imperial Family must have been recently confined, the grass worn away to dust, a series of chairs and a table made from a tree stump which still held a soggy newspaper and an oyster-shell ash tray.

'You know Conte Giustiniani was appointed to make sure we come up with the right answers to this whole enterprise.' Nametkin said to him.

'Really?'

'Oh, yes. General Golitsyn has his deputy, Major de Heuzy, watch Giustiniani, who watches me, and in turn I watch him. It's all politics, eh?' Nametkin said. He stood at the end of a little porch that had been built at the end of the bathhouse and looked around at the property. 'Old Ipatiev. It looks like he put together a pretty nice place for himself.'

'Yes, it looks like it would have been very peaceful at one time,' Ryzhkov said, imagining a garden full of grand duchesses running about. At the corner of the stockade was a large gate topped with new barbed wire. 'The trucks would have been brought in through there,' he said. The two of them headed up the hill; indeed, the entrance was chewed up, muddy from motor traffic in and out.

Giustiniani walked up with a ring of keys in his hand. 'He's just a boy, he can't read, he can't find the register, he just gives me the keys because I yell at him a little.' He fumbled through the keys.

'Look at this,' Nametkin said, pointing to the sheen of a cartridge case in the mud outside. Ryzhkov bent to pick it up; much stepped on, clotted with mud and sand. The brass case from a pistol cartridge; he put it in his pocket and stepped back to better appreciate the side wall of the house. There was a short stairway down to the basement doors, a single window looking out from what was supposed to be a storeroom, or perhaps it had once been a bedroom for a servant that had been added on.

Giustiniani had trouble with the lock and Ryzhkov stepped in to help; the old key to the door turned the opposite way. The door creaked open and they hung there on the threshold of the dark room, blinded a little because of the sunshine outside. They pushed the doors open wider to reveal a completely bare space.

And then he saw the bullet holes.

Obviously the shots had come from where they were now standing, their impacts clustered in the wall directly opposite the doorway. There were single holes and then a flurry of others. A lot into the floor as well – too many to count.

There should have been blood but there wasn't, so Ryzhkov walked over to the corner and got down on his knees.

'It's been cleaned, I think, yes?' Strilchuk asked, sniffing.

'It's all very tidy,' Nametkin said. Ryzhkov patted his pockets, and then asked if either of them had a knife. Strilchuk reached into his pocket and came out with a blade.

Ryzhkov used it to winkle a strip of moulding off the floor, a long piece that had come awry, shattered at one end by a bullet. It broke away and he picked it up and carried it to the sunlit doorway.

'Yes, all cleaned up,' he said, showing the dark band of blood to Nametkin.

'I suppose we don't want to take it apart just yet, eh?' Strilchuk said, looking around at the room.

'No, we can wait, but it should be sealed, eh?' Ryzhkov said.

'I wouldn't trust these people to seal a stamp,' Giustiniani said.

'How much blood is it, do you think?' Nametkin asked him.

'It's impossible to say. It's been well cleaned. When you get in the corner you can really smell it. Vinegar too, but there's the other smell. In this weather you can't get rid of that. And from the number of bullet holes, it's more than one person for sure,' Ryzhkov said.

'He says eleven,' Nametkin said, waving the paper at him. 'He says everybody.'

'Good God.' Ryzhkov turned and looked at the room, trying to imagine the press of eleven people gathered in there to be killed – the Tsar, the Tsaritsa, the boy, the four girls. Eleven?

'Who were the others?' Strilchuk asked.

'Their servants. Loyal retainers,' Giustiniani said in a voice that dripped cynicism.

Ryzhkov tried to imagine the scene. Eleven people, then. Plus, jammed in at the doorway there would have had to be the firing squad. A tightly packed little room. Maybe they'd been done in smaller groups. It would have been easier that way. He started to ask Nametkin about the other victims, but the prosecutor had turned and gone back outside.

Ryzhkov stood there for a few more moments, looking around the storeroom, the crazy splattering of bullet holes, the faint swirls where they'd mopped the floor with vinegar and sand, a sliver of broken threshold – the wood clean and yellow-brown. All of it lit by single barred, dirty window, and the flare of sunshine from the open door.

A collection of rosy shadows across the cheap wallpaper, the faint whiff of cleaning fluid and death.

The end of an empire.

The rest of the day was taken up with a parade of witnesses, a whirl of testimony and common police work. From birth it seemed to be a stuttering, confused murder investigation, pulled administratively between the Czech military under General Golitsyn, and Nametkin's bosses, the civilian 'government' – Kolchak's dictatorship with its green and white flag. Giustiniani added to the confusion by ratifying everything with a wave of his hand, keeping absolutely no paper record, and referring to Ryzhkov variously as 'investigator', 'secretary' and 'aide'. In practice Ryzhkov did whatever was required and additionally tried to provide anything Nametkin needed.

Besides Strilchuk, the 'investigators' were combined from what was left of the Yekaterinburg police, a sub-standard force of malcontents and traitors who'd found protection by banding together, and augmented by a detachment of soldiers.

Ryzhkov kept his eye on Strilchuk, who went about his work with a set jaw and a stare that never wavered. Giustiniani had also noticed his hard edge. By the afternoon Strilchuk had been moved to the front desk in the office and been given responsibility for coordinating the day-to-day logistics of the investigation.

In the afternoon Ryzhkov took a breather, walked out onto the steps, fished around in his pockets for a smoke, realized he had none, and cadged one off an officer who was standing there. Only a moment later Volkov, the young corporal who was filling in as their secretary, brought him back to the office to hear what a courier from the hospital had to say.

Apparently a Russian officer had turned up at the hospital and demanded to see the commander immediately. His story was that he'd been hiding in the woods, dressed as a peasant, near Koptiaki, a little town only four miles north of Yekaterinburg on the edge of the lake. Early on the morning of 17 July the villagers had been rousted out by Bolshevik guards from the hovels where they had been camped. They'd been told differing stories: the Czechs were coming, there was a dangerous demolition exercise planned for the area, all sorts of things. When morning came and the Bolsheviks had left, they all went back to the site.

When they got there they saw that there had been a fire, and when they poked about in the ashes they discovered charred clothing and several pieces of jewellery.

'Where is this place?' Ryzhkov asked.

'It's the Ganin pit. That's the name he told us, Excellency,' the courier said.

'Near Koptiaki,' Strilchuk said. 'Not far.'

'Do you know it?' Giustiniani demanded.

'Yes. It's a mine. They are all through the woods, here. An open mine where the coal is close to the top layer of the soil. The peasants dig them. You have to be careful in the woods. You can easily fall in,' Strilchuk said.

'Can you take us there?' Giustiniani pressed Strilchuk.

'Sure,' he said, not really deferring to Giustiniani in the way he said it. 'It's between here and Koptiaki. You cross the tracks –'

Giustiniani had turned on the courier. 'Where is this officer now?'

'Lt Sheremetevsky,' the courier said, reading from a piece of card, 'is on the way here, sir. The doctors could not keep him.'

'And the jewels, the various items, what was it exactly?'

'A jewelled cross and a brooch,' the boy read out loudly. 'They are now downstairs. We thought they should be put in the vault.'

Ryzhkov and Giustiniani went down to the vault to see the jewels. It was just as the boy had said: a cross and what looked like a jewelled pin, something a woman would use to fasten a scarf to her dress. Both had been wrapped and tied in butcher's paper.

Ryzhkov straightened, his entire body exhausted. His mind was dazzled with the details that were piling up in the case. After breaking down all the stories and trying to tease the truth from the rumours, it was obvious that Yurovsky was now the most wanted fugitive from White justice. Whatever had happened to the Tsar, Yurovsky had been in charge. He had last been seen leaving the city by motor car, about the same time Ryzhkov's train was dropping off its reinforcements for the Fifth Army.

They must have crossed, Ryzhkov realized suddenly. They might have actually stared at each other on opposite tracks, as Yurovsky escaped the White dragnet and Ryzhkov rushed towards it.

If he could get word back to Zezulin, Yurovsky could be picked up in Moscow. Zezulin could interview him to his heart's content in the bowels of the Lubyanka, and Ryzhkov's mission would be over. Maybe everything could be settled in one easy stroke. It was simple, probably too simple, but it was a chance. And if Yurovsky had managed to escape back to Moscow, perhaps he could too.

They went upstairs, sat in the shade on the balcony above the portico and waited for the lieutenant to arrive. Giustiniani was staring out at the filthy expanse of the square and humming.

Ryzhkov thought about the spray of bullet holes in the floor of the Special House's storeroom. A lot of lead for one emperor. The box of hair that existed for no apparent reason, that stuck out too. 'We'll go to the pit tomorrow, yes?' he said to the Italian.

'Oh, yes . . . We'll go there with shovels.'

They had been waiting for longer than an hour, and the squad of soldiers that Giustiniani had sent to find out why Sheremetevsky was late on his walk from the hospital (only two blocks) had still not returned. Giustiniani spat his cigar stub out into the street. From the corner a peasant stepped out and recovered it, bowing and smiling back at them, then rolled off down the street – bandy legs, filthy clothes and a knotted beard down to his belly.

'This so-called officer isn't coming,' Ryzhkov said to him, and Giustiniani looked around.

'Yes, I was thinking the same thing. He might not be real.'

They fell silent. Some men came by in a cart that contained a spindly cow, laid out and bawling, obviously ill from the way it was twitching. They got across the square just fine, but then two of the men had to move to the rear and push as the cart climbed the long rise up Voznesensky Prospekt.

It might not be real.

10

He was Wilton, he said. From *The Times*.

Not only the attention of *The Times*, but indeed the attention of the whole world was on Yekaterinburg. Yes, it was regrettable, like looking at an atrocity, eh? Looking at something that made you vomit. You got too close to horror and you recoiled. Sometimes the temptation to look away was strong, didn't they agree? The scene of the murders, the House of Special Purpose, he called it. The bedrooms were awash in blood, Wilton said. The horror was unimaginable. Of course the women, the young grand duchesses in particular, had suffered the most.

'Raped?' one of the men asked.

'Repeatedly. By the entire drunken hoard, then shot.'

'My God!'

'Perhaps they are better off . . .'

'Do you want another?' the waiter who'd been tending their portion of the bar asked Ryzhkov. By his accent he was Russian, but he'd picked up an odd ring to his voice. It wasn't French. Something else.

'Yes, thank you, comrade.'

'Comrade!' The man exploded in laughter. 'Hah! Yes,

here's to you – comrade! Comrades!' They all lifted their glasses.

The war was going well, Wilton said. He read every dispatch that came over the wire. White armies were attacking the Bolsheviks from all sides; Denikin and the Cossacks from the south, and now Kolchak and the Czechs from the East. Moreover the British had landed in Archangel and were pushing down the Dvina river from the north. Everyone would converge on the Volga. The Volga was the central highway of Russia. If only the Czechs could keep rushing forward, take Kazan and link up with the British, the Allies and the Whites would be able to advance and capture the ancient city of Nizhni Novgorod.

And from there they would have an open plain to Moscow.

'Say *fini* to your red fucking revolution, gentlemen. It's already as good as lost.' Wilton smiled and bounced on the balls of his feet. He was dressed in thick woollens even though the weather was still hot, a felt fedora on his head, face shiny with passion and sweat, and a smile like a gash in his skull. He insisted they all have a new drink he'd discovered in Paris.

'Ivanis!' he called across the room. He had to shout twice more before the bartender caught their eye and waved to him. 'He's the expert in these, boys. Ivanis! Make us one of those ones you did the other night.'

Ivanis came over to him smiling, a dark shock of hair falling into his eyes. Thin like a knife. 'How can I help you, sir?' he said.

'The bloody drink, that Sambo thing you did.'

'Yes, sir, right away.'

'Five of them, right? Give us the group rate, eh?' Wilton said, winking at them. Ivanis went to make the order. 'You can learn a lot from these fellows, eh? They see everything, hear everything. Somebody wants some information. Who do you ask, eh?' he said to Ryzhkov.

93

'How can I get in touch with the Ural Soviet,' Ryzhkov said. He'd gone by the house on Kushok Lane at the meal hour, but no one was there. He'd had enough to drink that he figured he might as well ask an expert like Wilton.

'That's exactly what I mean,' Wilton said. 'The American here is the only place you can get these things,' Wilton said, looking past them at one of the tables.

From there the evening went downhill.

The saloon in the Hotel American was subject to strange and hectic energies. Contingents of soldiers, adventurers, journalists, consular officers and employees would whirl through, collapse a while, then whirl out again. Among the saloons and salons of the city an ever-widening cruise had begun to develop. The streets in the still-warm nights were clotted with merry-makers and desperadoes. They clung to one another, floating from one watering-hole to the next in search of greater thrills, someone else to swindle, or just simple unconsciousness.

Ryzhkov had opted for the unconsciousness.

The Sambos finally came. They'd grabbed a table by this point and Ryzhkov was seated in his chair, leaning comfortably against the wall, sipping the concoction – a mixture of vodka, coffee and pepper, it took him back to Paris, where he had his first one, the drink having become the rage of the crowd at Café Cine where he pretended to work when Qirenque required. The drink itself was nothing special, only you couldn't sleep after, and Ryzhkov needed more than anything, he suddenly realized, to sleep.

'A member of the Ural Soviet,' Wilton was saying. 'Well, of course you'd love to put your mitts on one of them. If you get a lead, you call me first, eh?' he said, lifting his glass. 'God bless the Alsatians,' he sipped and murmured.

'And vice versa,' Ryzhkov said, rolling to his feet. He made his thank-yous and good-byes, excused himself from the table and walked, surprising himself at how stable he was, down the steps out onto the cool, dusty trough of Pokrovsky Street.

His rooms were lower in the city, around from the dam and up the rise a block and a half behind Glavni, a rather quiet neighbourhood, he thought. He liked the little rooms, the window under the slanted roof, the breeze that filled the house.

He climbed the stairs, let himself in, stripped off his clothing and lay there naked and drunk and unable to sleep, his world reduced to the rectangle of the window, the parallelogram of the thrown-open sash, the incomprehensible sway of the curtain.

He wondered about Vera, where she was, if she was safe. If she was alive. If they would ever meet again. She would like the little room, he thought. They could make a life together in that room, he thought. For a long time, the vision of them playing house kept his mind occupied. He fell into the dream easily, so hungry was he for it that he did not realize when he finally passed into sleeping, his last conscious thought an image of her, moving through the dances in an old cabaret at the Komet – something garish and lewd, something so tinged with fear and sex that it pushed back the frontiers of truth.

And dreaming of her there, he found it.

And slept.

'In Italia the phrase is "The fleas come out of the wall,"' Giustiniani said to Propas. It was late and the car was moving up the long curving street towards the station. He was dressed in his best uniform, the boots shined to a blinding gloss. Epaulettes, feathers, silver and gold braid. Everything but a sabre, which was technically an omission because he might need it in case he ever was required to step off his sinking submarine and surrender it. But since submarines didn't sink that way, and hating the damned thing because it always got in the way, he had left it back with the provost in Vladivostok. They drove along the side of the station, and down to a crossing.

'It's down here in the dark somewhere at the end of the yard,' Giustiniani pointed, leaning forward on the seat. 'Strilchuk is the night officer, eh?' he said.

'Yes, sir,' said Propas.

'What happened to Volkov?'

'He's at the baths, sir. Major de Heuzy asked for him personally.'

'And Ryzhkov?'

'At his flat, sir.'

'He is not. He's running around somewhere, doing his own extra investigations, sniffing around without permission.'

Propas remained silent.

'Whenever you find Ryzhkov, make sure he's up in the morning.'

'Yes, sir.'

'I'm going to be here for a while, I hope. At least an hour or two.'

'Yes, sir.'

'I'm going to visit a little flea. A very high-born flea, the Baroness Buxhoeveden. She has arrived in a private railway car she managed to secure somehow in Tyumen.'

They saw it parked on its own siding across the yard. A rusty green thing. Two of the windows had been boarded over. The light through the shades was golden from the candles.

'Looks cosy enough, sir,' Propas said.

'Ah well, I suppose she must make do.' Giustiniani pulled the latch and stepped down onto the gravel. 'When you come

96

back, if the lights are out you can go, eh? She's consented to an interview and a late dinner.'

'Excellent, sir. Good luck.'

Giustiniani smiled as he hit the steps. 'I assure you, Propas, luck has nothing to do with it.'

The Baroness von Buxhoeveden emerged from the jury-rigged rear compartment of the railway carriage she had been living in for four months.

Sophie was of medium height, in her thirties and still attractive, with a pleasant figure and a good bosom. Giustiniani rose as she took her seat on the somewhat threadbare sofa she had obtained in Tyumen for a song. She smiled at the Conte Giustiniani through tears that threatened to start afresh.

'And you can't imagine. You can't imagine the things I've heard. It frightens me. Honestly. It racks the soul.'

'We live in a completely unique time, signorina. This is the modern age. It is chaos.' Giustiniani poured them both glasses of a cheap port made expensive only by being port that had survived the long trip west of Omsk. He gestured to the décor of her carriage. 'Extreme hardships, danger. The world has grown hysterical. And as events have become unprecedented, so too have emotions.'

'Oh, yes, conte. I am so sorry. I'm weakened. This whole experience, it's been the worst thing in my life. Horrible. I'm incapable, I'm raw . . .'

'Of course. Naturally.'

'Dazed, please . . .' She wiped away a tear, reached for the glass and took it all in one gulp. 'Please,' she said, holding out her glass for a refill, a little laugh and a snuffling smile of triumph. 'It's good just to . . .' she couldn't finish the thought.

'That's better. Courage,' Giustiniani said, pouring, and they both drank. 'I am sorry to burden you with these memories, signorina, but you understand, Admiral Kolchak has authorized a full investigation, as one would in any homicide – or possible homicide.'

'There was a report that they were in Constantinople. There was a telegram read out –'

'I have heard a great many things, yes. It's important to hold on to hope, but there are a great many questions. Since you were one of those most intimate with the Imperial Family –'

'Yes, of course. Of course, I'll tell you whatever I can.'

'We can wait.'

'No. Tonight. I am up to it,' she said. That brave smile, her careful sip.

'Well.' He smiled, reached out and took her hand, rather in the manner of a doctor giving an honest assessment to a patient. 'Well, frankly, there are some questions about the Imperial Family's possessions.'

'Ah, yes. I understand. The modern world, you call it. It always comes down to money,' Sophie said, and the tears threatened to breach the dam again. She turned away.

'Some of these belongings have been retrieved, and must be identified. There were some boxes . . .'

'I'm sorry, dear commander. I cannot help you there. I know the girls had taken some of their jewels and . . . what is the word?'

'Hidden.'

'Yes, hidden them, sewn them in their clothing, you see.' She lets her head fall back, a careful touch to her bodice. It has grown very hot on the sofa all of a sudden. 'You see, we were separated after Tobolsk. I only watched them walking away, walking away down the track to their own carriages. For the last time.'

'I see. But they carried with them a substantial amount of jewels?'

'Oh, yes, I think so. In Tyumen a man came and took my deposition, a long list. Everything I could ever remember.'

'Excellent.' He allowed himself a pat on the arm and a long look into her very lovely eyes. 'You have been very brave,' he said, smiling, and very delicately reached up to touch her pouting lip. 'How did you know about their hiding of the . . . was it only the jewels?'

'Yes. You see in captivity all the regular money was confiscated or spent right away. All that was left was individual gems, taken out of their settings and sewn in. I know this from when I was there myself, and from talking with, oh . . . poor, poor Alix . . .' She gathered herself, turned to him and touched the centre of her dress. 'You can sew it, hide it in a button – like this?' She carried Giustiniani's willing hand to her breast. 'And it's safe there, or . . .'

Giustiniani looked at her. Sometimes honesty was painful, and sometimes passion overwhelmed reason. 'Please,' he said. His hand burned into her chest.

'Or in your underclothing.' Her face was red, tilted up, waiting so he could kiss her when he wanted.

'I see . . .' he said.

11

The pit was several versts out of town, off a long road that ran beside the railway tracks for some distance, then veered deep into the woods.

It had rained again in the night and the ground was muddy, the underbrush thick with birds and the sparklings of dew when the light slivered through the trees. Propas drove them in the huge 'Chinese car' with its stiff springs that tossed them about to the point of nausea. Ryzhkov sat on a narrow seat that folded down and faced the rear, its surface made of polished wood, so he was in constant danger of sliding onto the floor of the vehicle. Giustiniani kept his eyes trained out of the open window which had been detached and stowed in a pocket inside the door. The chauffeur sat in the front compartment and made conversation with Strilchuk. Behind them Ryzhkov could see a lorry with a detachment of Czech enlisted men, slithering back and forth in the ruts. It was too noisy for much conversation, nevertheless Nametkin would suddenly shout fragments of thoughts as sudden inspirations came upon him.

'Why so far?' was one of them, to which Giustiniani only nodded and spat a thin stream of cigarette smoke out into the refreshed atmosphere. Perhaps it wasn't real.

At length they turned off onto a narrower track. Giustiniani had to pull back from his window as the branches sprung through the opening; the car dipped precipitously, and Propas hurriedly jammed on the brake. It felt like they had crashed into a muddy stream bed. He set the brake, got out, edged his way around the front and made a face, then turned back to them. 'It's only just up the way here, but I'm afraid you'll have to walk, gentlemen.'

Giustiniani didn't even speak, threw open his door and started out. Nametkin sighed and followed. The truckload of soldiers wheezed to a stop right behind them.

The creek was really a muddy ditch that Ryzhkov almost jumped over trying to keep from ruining his shoes, but then slipped and went down on one knee into the muck anyway. It soaked his trousers immediately and he reflexively sprang up, cursing, reached out and grabbed a sapling, pulling himself up the little slope and back on to the road, which had now narrowed to little more than a path. There were tyre tracks all along. It had been used recently by other trucks and wagons, and there were deep pockets made from men's boots. The picture of its use came to Ryzhkov fully, instantly.

Ryzhkov had become a scientist of mud, a sort of Red Indian scout when it came to mud. He had come out of the war having lost his revulsion for mud and dirt, and maybe it was a welcome kind of knowledge. There had been much rain in June and July. It had soaked the soldiers on both sides, made them miserable, and kept the peasants inside their smoky huts. It meant a cold winter was coming, everyone said.

Beyond the lowest point in the road, the track immediately opened up onto a kind of field. Closer you could see several holes, open pits, spread across the clearing, at least half a dozen of them. Some had young trees thrown into them, protruding at odd angles. All across the surface of the field the ground was chewed up. There had been several fires set there. One obvious one, quite large, was just on the left side of the road, a great scorching of the earth, burnt grass and more mud, chewed up by boot prints and now dried.

There was a rustling, and he turned to see Father Ioann Storozhev. The priest had been one of the last non-Bolsheviks to have contact with the Romanovs; they had spoken four days before the night of the supposed execution. Ryzhkov watched the old man with his interrupted limping gait. One of the younger monks followed him with his head bowed, the old man already beginning a chanted prayer under his breath.

They had spread out, each of them following the maze of marks in the mud and grass, seeing it all fresh for the first time. Everything seemed to centre directly across the field at one of the larger pits. Just a square hole about the size of a large room. To stop the walls from caving in it had been faced with thick planks. Dark water nearly filled the pit. On the surface floated leaves, slime, insects, and a rainbow gleam of something oily.

'Someone used a rope here. See this?' Nametkin pointed out to anyone who was listening. And Ryzhkov could see he was right: a rope had cut a sharp groove into the wall of the pit, the topmost plank had been rubbed free of its algae and an orange blaze showed where the friction had done its work. There were recent gouges all along the rim of the pit, places where the grass had been kicked away. A thin tree had been broken off and thrown down into the water where it stood out like a periscope.

'It's not that deep, what do you think?' Strilchuk shrugged.

'Ten or twelve feet? We can pump it out, I suppose,' Ryzhkov said, still thinking about mud, water, death . . . Maybe it would never go away.

Giustiniani was some yards away, standing in a knot of

soldiers. He was using a shovel to stir around in the soggy embers of a fire. Ryzhkov went over to watch them. Giustiniani kneeled, combing his fingers through the black ashes and then pulling them back without really digging in, like a cat afraid to dirty his paws.

'Here we go,' Giustiniani murmured. A black plug separated itself from the muck and Ryzhkov saw a flash of light.

'It's a pearl,' said Giustiniani, wiping it clean. The fire had scorched it so that it was blue on one side, like a half-full moon. A soldier ran up; he was holding a fragment of cloth, something that used to be white lace.

'Where did you find it?' Ryzhkov asked.

'Just over here at the edge,' the man said, and they went off in a hurry, stepping around another near-invisible pit, to the place. There were a few sheets of soggy newspaper, faeces, some broken glass. It looked like the Bolsheviks had dumped their garbage there.

'This is what you do. Go around, around the whole place. When you find something like this just leave it, eh? Mark it, but don't pick anything up. We want to look at it first, yes?'

'Here's another, Excellency,' another soldier said, pushing back a bush. Tangled in the branches he saw a long strip of torn fabric – woman's clothing, good quality, judging from the lace around the edge.

'Make sure that nobody touches anything, eh. This is the same as a murder investigation, you understand?' Ryzhkov told the soldiers.

'Did they kill them here, Excellency?' one of the soldiers asked. The little group of men were all looking at him.

'Either here, or somewhere else, and then brought them here to dispose of.' For a moment they all looked around at the field, the abandoned mines, the wet grass. He pointed over to the big pit. 'Depending how deep it is, we'll start pumping it out, see what's down there, eh? Go look all around. Go slowly, be careful where you walk.'

'Yes, Excellency,' the soldier said.

Nametkin, Ryzhkov saw, was cradling something in an immaculate white handkerchief. He held it out to Father Storozhev. It looked like a crushed squirrel, something that had been left on the street. When Ryzhkov looked closer he could see a silver clasp. A small handbag.

The priest made the sign of the cross. 'Yes, it's hers – the Grand Duchess Tatiana's, her very own. I saw it many times,' he said. For a moment Storozhev's hand fluttered towards the artefact, his fingers brushing it, then retreating. He sniffed, then looked away from the muddy thing, staring out into the desolate field, a bewildered old man adrift within the last great tragedy of his life.

Nametkin looked up at him. 'Well . . .' he said, and then tried to fold the corners of the handkerchief over the handbag, almost like a shroud that was too small.

Over the course of the day more objects were found. The Czechs sent their detachments in shifts. A little camp was beginning to spring up at the least trafficked edge of the field. By noon a tent had been erected and the artefacts had been spread out on a blanket that the soldiers brought up and spread out. Food had been brought in and Storozhev told Nametkin the story of each object as it appeared. Ryzhkov went over to the table and slowly inspected the fragments of cloth. They had been soaked in paraffin and used to start the fires.

Every so often a brace of soldiers would run up with something between their fingers, held gingerly, the way you would hold something objectionable before tossing it into the trash. Other jewels had been discovered in the dried mud surrounding the pit and also in the ashes of the largest fire.

Because Strilchuk made everyone walk around it, a new track had grown up looping through the weeds leading to the tent and back.

The day wore on and it got warmer. Father Storozhev said his goodbyes and was driven back to the city. Ryzhkov took off his coat, hung it on a branch and worked in shirtsleeves with Strilchuk, the two of them taking turns raking through the debris. When he could, he took a few moments to try to get a picture of what must have gone on, trying to interpret from all the places where the Red Guards had pissed, shat, and flicked away their cigarettes; a smear where it looked like someone had vomited, empty and broken bottles tossed into the woods.

It looked like a party, he thought.

In the late afternoon there was a meal that was thrown together, only sausage and butter on stale black bread. A splash of cheap, sharp wine. He ate standing over the blanket looking at the evidence. Giustiniani came up beside him. 'This site is being taken over by the Officers' Commission,' he said. By that he meant that the Ganin pit area would henceforth be administered by the military investigation that was being conducted into the disappearance of the Romanovs, which was now running in parallel with Nametkin's.

'Is that good or bad?'

'Depends on what's found here, and that depends on how much water is in that mine, I would think. It means that I will be spending a good deal of time out here, and you will be running back and forth and telling me everything.'

'Fine, Excellency.'

'Please, Ryzhkov. Don't insult me. The biggest problem we are going to have is a logistical one. We have to actually dig this place up, wouldn't you say?'

'The pit, for certain.'

'What is it, Ryzhkov? What's wrong?'

'Well, it just looks strange.'

'Strange? I suppose it ought to. Personally I've never actually been at the scene of an emperor's murder before,' Giustiniani said and went away.

Ryzhkov sifted through the relics, the relics with no pattern. How did the jewels get there? Why were they burned, many of them? If the family had been killed, surely the Bolshevik guards would have stripped the bodies? But the items were found all over the field, in the fires, in the road, squashed into the mud by the pit wall, tossed into the woods. There seemed to be no reason to any of it.

He let himself go. Just walked aimlessly about the expanse, like a tourist in a foreign garden, waiting for the surprise, sniffing the air.

He found himself back at the large pit. One of the soldiers had taken off his uniform and was being lowered into the pit by a rope. In one hand he held a long stick that had been cut. There was about six feet of water, the corporal said, and from the scars on the planks it seemed that there had been an explosion – a hand grenade had been set off there, they thought.

It took until late in the afternoon before they finally got the machinery set up and began pumping the water out of the Ganin pit.

'It's called Four Brothers,' Strilchuk told Giustiniani.

'Four families couldn't make a living out of these holes.' Giustiniani looked around at the muddy field, shook his head and laughed.

'No, Excellency. It is called such for the four pines that used to grow over there by the road. Giants, they were.' In the low afternoon sun he could make out a set of gloomy stumps.

'They lived here when they worked the site, had their huts all around here, places for a garden, animals . . .'

Growing out of the weeds were the occasional shard of a house, crushed tins, broken glass. A rotten board with nails. You had to watch your footing. Across the field were places where the grass grew in patches where the tailings had forever blanched the soil.

'They would only be here in the summer, then they would go back to Koptiaki or the city.'

'I see,' Giustiniani muttered. The idea that he was standing on the bones of royalty didn't honestly bother him very much at all. Bones of aristocrats didn't impress him – he had his own. He'd been present at the funerals of plenty of aristocrats, held his aunt's hand when she died. Helped shoulder the bier of poor Aimone, his cousin who'd been crushed beneath his own carriage. If enough nobles died, perhaps only a few dozen, he might find himself crowned King of Italy. But for that they would have to find him first, he thought.

He sniffed and turned to inspect the machinery and scaffolding that the Czech sappers had thrown up over the pit.

There were a lot of mines around Yekaterinburg and a lot of pumps. The one that they had requisitioned worked off the engine of a lorry and a system of long belts that connected to the actual pumping mechanism. It was set up on a platform that the soldiers had nailed together there. A pair of black rubberized canvas hoses drooped into the black muck, arching with each pulse, the water spilling out a gallon at a time and carried out to the edge of the field along a ditch they had dug.

The mine was not nearly as deep as one might think, though it was too deep to work without ropes and ladders. Left unroofed, the rain and the water-table would fill the pit naturally, making it just deep enough to drown in.

He walked back to a tarpaulin that had been suspended beneath the trees, providing shade and relief from the occasional sprinkles. Major de Heuzy was there.

'This is a waste of time, you know that, captain,' de Heuzy wheezed. No answer was expected or necessary. As Golitsyn's aide he outranked Giustiniani. De Heuzy was a member of that circle of officers who were all bluster and authority with no experience of war except what had ended in failure. By reputation de Heuzy was a hopeless alcoholic, a conniver and a would-be spy, a man who had been shifted laterally through the worlds of military intelligence because nobody but Golitsyn could tolerate him.

'I was just thinking we might have to excavate this whole field, sir,' Giustiniani answered.

De Heuzy laughed. It was a cross between a loud bellow and a rumbling cough. 'The Romanovs are safe in Berlin as we speak. The whole thing is part of the same big conspiracy,' he said, winking at Giustiniani and making a fierce smile that showed his yellowing teeth. Odious creature.

'You have reports, sir?'

'Let's just say I've . . . heard things,' de Heuzy grumbled, and looked out at the work criss-crossing the field.

Giustiniani went over to the map table. Every artefact they had found had been plotted on its surface. He stared at it as an astronomer might contemplate the stars. Fixedly, the gridlines lacing the whole thing together. A matrix of death, torn cloth, broken bottles.

On the table beside him were large broken pieces of glass which had been recovered from two locations, both outside and inside the bonfire. He had put the fragments out on butcher's paper and was trying to puzzle them back together. Strilchuk had said they were hydrochloric acid bottles, blue-glass carboys that a strong man could carry two at a time, his fingers looped through the rings at the mouth of the bottle, counterweighted. He had seen them before; they were everywhere those bottles. They were used in the platinum process somehow, the acid binding with the soluble metals, and after they'd been extracted, the rest of it went into the river.

'Beautiful garden,' de Heuzy said.

'Yes?' Giustiniani looked up, his attention pulled from the vertigo of the site plan.

'A beautiful garden,' de Heuzy said again. 'That's what everyone would like, all mankind. Who can object to something like that, eh?' Giustiniani looked around. He had no idea what de Heuzy was talking about. 'And once they have it, what d'you think they'll do with it?'

'I have no idea, sir.'

De Heuzy laughed as if the answer was obvious. 'Poison it. Of course there will be good reasons. First it will be one thing, and then another. It's the holy garden of the people, but what the hell does that mean?'

Giustiniani looked around at the site, shrugged, speechless.

'Well, I'll tell you what it means. You take the idea of God, you become aware of it, you worship the idea, you become a disciple of the idea. You believe in God and the holy garden and then naturally you have to defend the idea, to lock the idea away from anyone who isn't an acolyte like you, yes? So that ultimately the idea becomes too dangerous to even contemplate. The very idea, you can't even have it any more! So, how do you unlock a God like that?'

Giustiniani let the corner of the map fall back to the table, gave up trying to do any work. Across the field the pumps abruptly coughed and stuttered into silence. The whole world seemed to ring in the aftermath. One of the soldiers was stripping off his uniform and preparing to be lowered into the muck. He saw Ryzhkov standing there, arms on his hips, waiting.

'Better go and see if they found anything,' de Heuzy said, waving him away.

Giustiniani walked away from the tents and out along the

path to the pit. All the men were clustered around the hoardings and peering over.

As he approached, they made way for him and he watched the soldier ease his way down the shaft, naked except for his boots. The muddy floor of the pit was covered with soggy embers, leaves and a long strip of cloth. The soldier reached down and hooked it with his finger, gathered it and put it into a basket that was lowered down beside him.

The Czechs were hollering instructions to him, phrases that Giustiniani could not understand, and the soldier used his toe to push against the wall of the mine so that the could swing out into the centre of the pit and grab at something. Giustiniani saw the target, something gleaming white in the muck, as the boy reached out and flicked at it. He missed, cursed and swung out again with another toe-tap, stretched out and grabbed the object out of the mud, held it aloft into the light. His faced creased with revulsion and he tossed it into the basket and called for his brothers to haul him up.

Giustiniani moved around to where the the soldier reached the top with his basket, and Giustiniani leaned forward to see the thing.

It was only a few inches long, eerie and wrinkled. For a moment he thought he was looking at some sort of petrified cat droppings, or a subterranean albino worm, but when the corporal picked up the basket and presented it for his inspection he saw that it was a severed human finger.

12

'The finger means nothing.'

'Unless it's the Empress Alexandra's.'

'It could be a man's, it could have been anyone's,' Ryzhkov said. He and Strilchuk had been up all night, and over a sodden breakfast in the bar of the Hotel American were trying to arrange their thoughts and theories about how the Imperial Family were killed and disposed of.

'All the testimony is contradictory. We have no real eye-witnesses,' Ryzhkov said.

'Yes, and there are no bodies.'

'Fragments, bits and pieces, the bloody finger . . .'

As part of their conjectures they had been trying to recreate the night of 16 and 17 July by analysing the actions of the inner guards. But there were no inner guards left in the city, so they'd fallen back on trying to create a chronology and a route for each of their second- and third-hand witnesses, and matching these with the movements of key persons in Yurovsky's inner guard of Latvians, with special attention to Yurovsky himself, but things still didn't fit.

'You knew this Yurovsky. He's from here?' he asked Strilchuk

'Yes, everyone knows Yakov Yurovsky, everyone of a certain age. I knew him, not very well, but I knew him as a boy. He left for Poland when I was fifteen. He came back to see his mother.'

'Maybe he has friends still living in town that we can interview,' Ryzhkov said, drawing with his finger in a splash of wine that was on the table, tracing diagrams between the plates, the ashtray and the general destruction on their table.

Strilchuk suddenly pushed his chair back, looked around him like someone who was lost, an alien being in a drawing room for the first time. 'You know . . .' he said, and then tapered off.

'What?'

'Well, you know, I am thinking that if I was Yakov and I am right here in my home town and suddenly things are growing very dangerous, I am wondering . . . did he actually get on the train that day when he left?' Strilchuk said.

Ryzhkov leaned back and stretched. He would need to sleep soon or he would be worthless. 'All right, so maybe he is in town, but didn't we have one of our witnesses say that they saw Yurovsky loading up cases into a car and then he and an aide drove out of town? And wasn't the story that they were forced to abandon their vehicle, and then they escaped at the second railroad station?'

'What happened to the car? I thought the car was famous for its reliability,' Strilchuk said.

'Which car was it?'

'It was the same one de Heuzy uses. Propas was the one who went out and drove it back into town and repaired it. Giustiniani uses it, everybody uses it. It's the big one,' Strilchuk shrugged.

'I think we should go and see our chauffeur,' Ryzhkov said.

Walking down past the Municipal Hall to the garage that

was built up next to the School of Mines at the corner of Glavni Street, they worked out the different ways that it could have gone.

Immediately after the executions Yurovsky had taken the Romanovs' valuables, contained in twelve cases plus a steamer trunk, and set out by motor car towards the central station, but instead veered off and took a different route – out of Yekaterinburg via the Moscow road. Somewhere along the route the valuables had been offloaded and the car abandoned.

Giustiniani's investigation had been operating on the assumption Yurovsky had returned to Moscow by rail along with the retreating Red Guards and high officers of the Ural Soviet. But on the days following the 16th–17th fighting was still going on in the forests around the city. The White armies were rushing around Yekaterinburg en route for Perm. As he was driving out of town, something might have happened; for some unknown reason Yurovsky might have been forced to stay behind, to hide somewhere in Yekaterinburg.

They rounded the corner of the school. Ahead of them was the long shed roofed canopy of the garage. It had been enlarged from the old stables of the building, swept clean of their original inhabitants, the horses banished around the corner to new stalls behind the General Post Office, and various awnings had been rigged to cover the motor pool that served the White units occupying the city. Ahead of them Propas came out, neat as a pin, even in the middle of a civil war. He was freshly shaved, and his undershirt gleamed white.

'Propas, was there petrol in the car?' Ryzhkov asked, walking past him under the canopies to the car sitting there in the yellowing light. It was huge, a creature of sloping fenders and battered running-boards, with various straps and cleats that had been added over time by a series of military mechanics. On the radiator was a badge of sculpted chrome that identified the car as being manufactured by the German company Neue Automobilgesellschaft, abbreviated as NAG.

'Petrol? Is there?'

'Was there,' Strilchuk said. 'When they found the car on the Moscow road, did it have petrol in the tank?'

'Oh yes, Excellency.'

'The car had just been left there?'

'Yes, sir. Abandoned. I cranked it once and it started up immediately. Good machine, this. Their little one won the Moscow to St Petersburg before the war. Very good rig.'

'And did you notice anything, any signs of violence? You've washed it, of course.'

'We wash her every other day, sir.'

'Was there any blood?'

'Blood? No, sir.' Propas made a face. 'The only damage, this door was broken,' he said, opening it and closing it again to show them how well it had been repaired. 'And also there was this . . .' he said, walking around to the rear and reaching up to push his finger through a single bullet hole, high in the rear panel of the great car, just below the lip where the leather seat was attached. 'That might mean something.'

Ryzhkov had borrowed a bicycle from Propas's garage. His legs were tired from the steady climb up the hill to Kushok Lane. He'd only decided to do it because there was no time. He was even prepared to flee the city that same night. The Romanov family had been killed, he was certain of it. All he needed to do was confirm it through Yurovsky and then he would be free to make his escape.

The plan, as far as he had one, all depended on whether he could make contact and bait Yurovsky into helping him. Once he'd reached Kushok Lane he waited in the woods until the lamps were blown out and the street was quiet. There was a moon, which was no good. No time, he thought, no time to plan, no time to watch or wait, or follow, or eavesdrop. Always no time.

He thought about whether to just go back to this rooms and do as he had threatened – use Giustiniani's police machinery to drag a net down Eikhe's street – but every day he waited put him further and further behind White lines, made it more difficult to get back to Moscow. He abandoned the bicycle and walked down the moonlit street, just like a normal person. Lit a cigarette. There were no dogs, he thought. Either lucky, or they'd eaten all the dogs here too.

At the corner he crossed the street, waited until he was out of view of the house, put the cigarette out, stepped into the shadows, kept watch down the rutted street to the corner of Eikhe's tarpaulin-covered slaughterhouse, while he planned how he would get there without being seen.

In the end he walked right out into the milky light. If they saw him coming he would be innocent. It wasn't until he got under the tents that he took out his knife. In the summer it would be hot inside, he told himself, looking for an opened window.

Around the back of the house he had his choice of three and a stump to climb up on, and, moving quickly, he was inside. Only a step or two took him to the front room with the woman, probably not even asleep, sitting up from her mattress.

'I just want to talk,' he whispered at her, crouching low and keeping his blade out of sight. 'I just want to talk to him, then I'll go.' She wrenched away, but he held her back, showed her the knife, and she froze, scared. 'I came by for Eikhe the other day. You're sure you don't have anything to tell me?'

'I told you what I knew. The Tsar is dead. That's the end of it.'

'Yes, that's what everybody says.' He let her go, and she

slipped heavily down onto the floor. He was moving towards the other room, the real bedroom where he thought Yurovsky must be sleeping, but there was no one there.

'I don't use it any more,' she said behind him. 'If you're still looking for this Eikhe, I think he went to Moscow when the Czechs took over. I doubt if you'll ever see him around here.'

'You're his wife?'

'I was,' she said flatly.

'So, what? He left you?'

'It's none of your business what happens between two people. Some things are still private, aren't they?'

'No, not really. I'll pass along this much: we think Yakov Yurovsky might have stayed behind,' he said, turning and looking hard at her. 'I'm looking for him. Where is he?'

'I'm not telling you anything.' Now the big woman was up, she started edging back towards her kitchen and the big knives she kept there.

Ryzhkov flashed the blade and she stopped in her tracks. 'I told you I needed to talk to someone in the soviet, I told you that! You want him dead?'

'Who?' she said.

'Don't,' he said, starting to get angry at her obstinacy. 'Everybody knows him, so we think he might still be in town. Someone is probably taking care of him. It's an emergency. What was it that you didn't believe?' Ryzhkov said to her, trying to keep his voice quiet.

'I don't know who you're talking about,' she said, but he could tell it was a lie.

'Yurovsky is in immediate danger. I have to meet him, to preserve his life . . . and to help him communicate with certain interested parties.'

'You're working for the Whites.' That was all that counted in her mind.

116

'Yes, I work for the Whites, but I work for the Reds too,' Ryzhkov said. 'Right now I'm working for you. I am Cheka. I was sent here because no one knew what the situation was with the Tsar.'

Once again she was moving back slowly, trying to get to her knives.

'No, don't . . . ' Ryzhkov shook his head. He didn't want it to end like this at all.

'The Tsar is dead. The family has been taken to a safe –' she started.

'Yes, I heard the announcement in the theatre. That was the very day I got here.'

'If you are who you say you are,' she said, 'then you should immediately return to your superiors and tell them that.'

'Were you there when he was shot? Did you see it?'

She just looked at him, then moved back out into the large open room that held the masonry furnace and its collection of pillows and household utensils. 'No, I wasn't,' she finally said.

'No?'

'Yurovsky told me about it.'

'But that's not really what happened, is it? It was a lot worse than that, wasn't it?'

'I'm telling you, that's what he reported to me. That's what was agreed upon.'

'But that's not what happened!'

'I don't know! How should I know? It was Yakov's command,' she said quietly. 'He picked his own guardsmen. So only he knows, I suppose.'

'Take me to him,' Ryzhkov demanded.

The woman gasped. It came out something like a cough and a growl. She reached back and pulled a cleaver out of the block. Ryzhkov just looked at her. She took two steps towards him and simply faltered.

'I don't want to kill you. I don't want to kill anyone ever again,' he said quietly. He could see her getting her courage up, coming forward again, bringing her arm up to swing. He wouldn't be there when she did it, but he waited and then took a step back, and when she started her downward arc he caught her arm, bent the knife out of her hand and threw her down on the floor. 'Sit down, before you hurt yourself, Madame Eikhe.'

'You bastard! Parasite! I think you're crazy, and you don't have any right –' she bawled.

'I don't need any right. I've got a gun, and I've got credentials from the Czechs and I'll use them if you push me. I'll have them tear your place apart, I'll have you hanged if I need to, but your job from this day onward, Madame Eikhe, is to put me in touch with Yurovsky. If he's here I can get him out, but I need to talk to someone who can confirm the executions. A witness, you know what I mean?'

'Yes, yes, I know what a witness is.'

'Good. I need to send back a report. A true report. I need to see the Tsar's grave. Verification. Do you know what that is?'

She looked at him for a long moment. 'Verification? Isn't that a fancy word for the truth?' she said, forcing an expression of innocence.

'I need proof. Proof of whatever happened. I need to make a report, and I am getting very tired of dealing with people like you,' he said, reaching out and tapping the woman twice on the forehead with his finger. 'And if you ever pick up something against me again, I'll kill you in a heartbeat,' he said to her.

'Christ . . .' she muttered.

'Now take me to him, so I can find out what I need and then get him out.'

'He can get out by himself!' She was in tears now, not

118

knowing where to go or what course of action was left open to her. Cornered.

'Listen to me. If the police think he's around here there will be searches. All down this street, down all the streets. Sooner or later he'll be found. If he fights he'll be killed. They've figured it out, do you understand?' Ryzhkov said. He held the knife up in front of her; the blade had been folded away. 'I'm not begging you any more. Time is running out, for you, for all of us. Get me to Yurovsky. Now.'

13

They had been keeping the commander of the death squad, Cheka Commandant Yakov Yurovsky, in the back of a rope mill around the southern edge of Lake Iset. It was a damp place, populated by rats scrabbling on the rocks, by bats and mosquitoes that hovered in the night air.

'It's up there,' Madame Eikhe said.

'When you want him, how do you do it?'

'If the light's on, it's safe,' she said.

'Fine. Go ahead then. Tell him. Then he can come out.'

'No, no . . .'

'Just do whatever it takes. You convince him. I don't have to prove myself. The Czech counter-intelligence will be happy to do that for me, and by then it will be too late. Tell him what I told you – either talk to me now, or by later today you'll all be hanging in the courtyard.'

She shook his head, spat, and then went ahead out into the light. Stood for a moment, fumbled in her pockets for a cigarette. A signal, Ryzhkov thought. Well, if that was the way she was going to play it . . .

He stayed there in the shadows and watched while the big woman fiddled with her matches, keeping one ear out for someone who might decide to run away across the rocks. Nothing. Maybe she was just nervous. Finally she walked up to the door and knocked. One, one, one, then three. The door opened a crack, her face was recognized, and she was allowed inside.

It was over now, Ryzhkov thought. He'd done all he could without torture or death, and if everyone did the prudent thing, maybe he would get out of it alive. For a moment, standing there in the dark, the memory of the caved-in street where he'd nearly died outside Malancourt came back to him. It was because of the wet smells down there by the water that he remembered that, he thought. There was the sound of someone walking inside, perhaps the sound of someone's voice rising. It was too faint to tell.

Then the light went out and a moment later the door opened. A scraping sound at the door and a figure stepped into the moonlight.

The man was about Ryzhkov's size, right at six feet, but heavier . . . walking slowly. Wearing a pair of working pants with one leg tucked back into his boots. He fiddled in his pocket for a moment. Stood there and loaded a pipe, turning around to show himself. Yurovsky looked different from his photograph and Ryzhkov realized it was because he'd shaved his beard off completely.

'I'm over here,' Ryzhkov said.

Yurovsky turned. There was the snap of a match as he lit the pipe. Plenty of time for a marksman waiting in the warehouses across the way.

'You wanted to see me?' Yurovsky said.

'Eikhe's woman told you everything?'

'The Tsar is dead, just like Goloschokin announced.'

'That's bullshit. I've been in the little room. I've seen the blood.' The woman had come out from the house; she could

121

have picked up a gun in there. Ryzhkov backed deeper into the shadows.

'You can tell him, I think,' Ryzhkov heard her say quietly. Yurovsky turned and looked back to her for a moment.

'If you say so, Veni. All right then. They're all dead.'

'All of them?'

'All of them. The Czechs were coming. We didn't have any way to get them out, there was a vote or something, and we did them all.'

'All of them? The girls too?' Ryzhkov said.

The woman made a sound. Almost a little laugh, a hiss. When Ryzhkov looked at her she looked away into the moon shadows.

'The boy?'

'Of course, the boy,' Yurovsky said. 'Do you think we are going to leave a Romanov behind to become a new Tsar? You think we want that disease to breed again? The Romanov family has killed millions. So now it's the hour for them to pay the price. How many do we kill if it's required? We kill them all.' Yurovsky said.

'We kill them all,' the woman echoed quietly.

For a moment Ryzhkov stood there looking at the two of them, ghostly in the moonlight. The tiny glow of Yurovsky's pipe.

'Then show me the bodies, comrades.'

'Go back to Moscow.'

'No,' Ryzhkov said. 'You're going to take me to the graves.'

'There aren't any graves. The bodies were burned. Burned to ashes,' Yurovsky said.

'You go back to your house and wait,' Ryzhkov said to the woman. 'He takes me to the place, then once I've seen as much as I need we'll all start on our way out of here. That's your chance, both of you. If you don't want it, you can stay here and wait for the Czechs. I don't care.'

122

It didn't matter, Ryzhkov thought. If he had to kill everyone he would. Then he would go back and report the atrocity to Zezulin: the Ural Soviet had panicked as the Czechs approached; they must have acted on their own. As commander of the guard, Yurovsky was responsible. Assuming he was telling Ryzhkov the truth, the entire Imperial Family had been herded together in a closet and gunned down. The pure horror of it would have been unimaginable.

But now it all had to stay a secret, Ryzhkov realized. Now that they'd had their blood revenge, the Ural Soviet had realized the magnitude of their crime. If the Czechs found the bodies and exposed the atrocity it would be a propaganda disaster: White journalists would show the Bolsheviks to be so brutal that they would murder women and children to keep themselves in power. So, they'd tried to cover it up by having Goloschokin announce that the family had been taken to safety. But if Giustiniani's investigation uncovered any more bones Yurovsky would probably pay with his life when he got back to the Kremlin.

He realized Madame Eikhe had gone inside and come out again with a rucksack.

'What's in that?' Ryzhkov asked.

'Last year's potatoes. The two of you might have to bribe someone,' she said. Yurovsky tapped his pipe out on the side of his boot, took the bag from her and slung it over his shoulder. 'You can take the trap at Gadekov's,' the woman said and went back inside.

Yurovsky looked at him for a long moment. 'Fine, then. We'll have to walk across the city to a sympathetic comrade's. Maybe we can get a ride from there,' he said, and started walking into the darkness.

Yurovsky waited until they were on the edge of town to make his move.

It was about what Ryzhkov had guessed might happen. He had been wondering why Yurovsky hadn't put up more of a fight back at the rope mill and why he'd simply agreed to show him what he needed.

Yurovsky tried to come at him from behind when they stopped the trap in a tiny opening in the underbrush, just a little trail that opened out into a clearing in the woods. The ground was wet there, muddy where others had taken at least a wagon through into a meadow. Perhaps a truck. In the low dawn light Ryzhkov could see where it looked like someone had been burning garbage.

And although he knew it might happen, still it was fast when Yurovsky made his rush. He sidestepped and rammed a fist into Yurovsky's midsection. He fell forward and into the wheel of the trap they had borrowed.

When Yurovsky tried to get up Ryzhkov was behind him and kicked him hard in the side under the ribs. He rolled over and found himself under the wheel with the pony starting to panic. After that it was a little chase, with Yurovsky scrambling to get out from the harness and Ryzhkov following him into the meadow. Yurovsky groped for his gun, but Ryzhkov had his Nagant out quicker. Yurovsky stumbled back and fell in the weeds.

'Give me the gun. Give it to me,' Ryzhkov said, standing over him.

Yurovsky waited there for a minute, breathing hard, not knowing if he was going to get a kick in the balls or a bullet in the face. Then he did as Ryzhkov said, slowly handing him the pistol and waiting while Ryzhkov tucked it back into his jacket.

'Now get up.' Ryzhkov watched him intently as he got to his knees, backing away in case Yurovsky went crazy again. 'While we walk back to the wagon you can try to convince me not to kill you, Comrade Yurovsky,' Ryzhkov said.

'Have you ever been to the mountains?' Yurovsky said.

'What?'

'The mountains. Have you ever been to the mountains?'

'Of course I have. Yes.'

'Ahh . . .' Yurovsky said. He was walking ahead now, his strength coming back quickly. The sky was rosy, the birds were filling the air with their chirps, their squealing. It looked like the start of a beautiful day.

'Look, Yurovsky, I do not know everything that is going on, but I have a little of the gift of clairvoyance, seeing the future, you know? I know the options, and you don't have any options. Your options are over. I can kill you, report back to Moscow that you liquidated the Imperial Family on your own judgement. I suppose I could take you back as my prisoner, but that might be more trouble than it's worth. The easiest thing would be to hand you over to my Czech friends and together we can spend some time listening to you talk about the recent past. Then you'll hang and I'll spend the reward money.' They walked on a few more feet. The pony was asleep, and stirred as Yurovsky drew close to her.

He stopped there, turned to face Ryzhkov. His face was twisted. Tortured. And for a moment he looked like a man who was suffering from a violent sickness and it took a second for Ryzhkov to realize he was on the point of tears. Now, looking at the gun, he began to go into a trance. Waiting. Waiting.

'Convince me, Yakov,' he said.

'The air is clean in the mountains,' Yurovsky gasped. 'Did you know that? The air . . .' For a moment Ryzhkov stood there watching the man, the gun riveting him to his muddy spot in the road. Watched and waited while he trembled.

'Look, you'd better just tell me everything. All of it. Everything.'

'I have been waiting for someone, you see,' Yurovsky said

as he dropped to his knees. 'I have been waiting for someone who knows about the mountains.'

'You mean that was your sign?'

'Yes. I have been waiting for him.'

'To get you out?'

Yurovsky sniffed, then shook his head. Looked up at Ryzhkov and then began to laboriously get to his feet. 'Oh, God . . . Fine, fine. I see. I see what's happening here.'

For a moment Ryzhkov thought he was gathering himself for another rush, and he took a step back onto the higher ground. 'This is the last chance. Tell me everything. Tell me everything and you live, Yakov.'

'No . . . fine. I apologize, comrade. Now I understand everything. I'll take you there,' Yurovsky said. He wiped his torn jacket sleeve across his face.

'What? This isn't the place?' Ryzhkov stepped back and looked over to the fire. Now it just looked like a heap of rags.

'No, no, this isn't the place.' Yurovsky was just standing there, hands on his hips, surveying the leaves on the trees. Ryzhkov walked down to him, handed him back his gun.

'Well?' he said. For a moment Yurovsky looked at him, and then he broke out with just a sad smile.

'Let's go, then.' Yurovsky turned and led the pony and trap out into the open meadow, circling it so they could get back on the road. 'So . . . I lose, you win. You are going back, you are going to report. You are going to have the proof you need for your master.'

'Our master, I think, comrade,' Ryzhkov corrected him.

'If you don't know about the mountains, I don't think we share the same master, so . . . No, if your mission is to see what's left of the Romanovs, I'll show you what's left of the Romanovs.'

They climbed back into the trap and lurched back up

onto the Moscow road in the direction of Koptiaki. Yurovsky backtracked and turned down an earlier turn-off, just an opening in the cover and a rutted track over a rock-filled ditch, then a serpentine trail that ran even higher, past a few isolated houses and later some abandoned hulks in the forest, towards a low bluff into which a mining concern had once thrown up outbuildings around the shaft's opening.

At their approach, two emaciated Red Guards came out of what Ryzhkov guessed had been an office built into the rocks next to the mine. As soon as they recognized Yurovsky they slung their rifles and began walking down to meet them.

As they got closer to the buildings Ryzhkov could see into the opening of the mine. In the shadow of the open shaft there were chairs set up, a bench and a crude table made from boxes. Seated there beside it was a desperately thin man propped up, sweltering in the heat with a blanket over him. A girl, her head covered in a scarf like a nun, melted back into the darkness.

Yurovsky tossed down the bag of potatoes to one of the soldiers. 'We didn't know we'd be coming, Vassili.'

'My Christ,' the guard said. 'You know we're all starving here,' he moaned, holding the bag up for his partner to see.

Behind the guards, a third man had come into the office and was looking out at them through the windows, his ghostly face peering out like a child who'd just woken up and found his parents gone. Everything odd and puzzling, but pleasant enough in a fairy-tale way.

And then –

Through the filthy glass Ryzhkov got a clearer look at the man. Enough to recognize him. Shorter than he'd remembered, the hair longer, thinner and more unkempt, the famous blue eyes watering into a rheumy grey. Something was different, and he stared at the man's simple face, a boy's face that had desiccated into something incomparably older, weary and befuddled.

And then he realized that the Tsar had shaved.

14

Ryzhkov hung there, paralysed. He watched as the Tsar retreated into the shadows, then saw that he was making his way through the mine office towards a side door that opened onto the shaft. As Nicholas came through the door his bearing began to change, his back became straighter, he had his hands in his pockets. It was him. Casually he strode out towards the trap. Yurovsky suddenly moved forward to intercept him.

'Good morning, Commander. Is there is no food?'

'I'm sorry, sir,' Yurovsky said, making a little flinching motion in his torso, a sort of half-bow. 'We were detained. This is just a short trip. I'll return with the ration tomorrow.'

'Is this our man?' The Tsar was moving towards him, hand outstretched, the beginnings of a smile. Ryzhkov took it. A surprisingly hard grip, with calluses.

'No. I'm afraid that –' Ryzhkov began to explain.

'We'll know more tomorrow, unfortunately,' Yurovsky cut him off and began to steer the Tsar back towards the office. At the corner Ryzhkov could see that two of the grand duchesses had gathered – Tatiana, whom he recognized, and one of the younger ones, Anastasia he thought she must be. They met their father there and went over to the old man in the chair who, Ryzhkov realized with a shock, was Alexei, the heir.

At the corner Yurovsky left them, then turned back, an expression almost like embarrassment on his face. Ryzhkov leapt down from the trap to confront him. 'All right, comrade,' he said, trying to make his voice quiet, but having it unsuccessfully turn into a growl. 'Perhaps you'd better explain a few things.'

'Over here . . . and let's walk.'

'I thought he'd been killed.'

'It was a plan, a secret plan.'

'To have them escape?'

'In a way, yes. To make it look as if they had been killed in the cellar. They are to be exchanged.'

'Exchanged? You mean as prisoners of war?'

'Well, no. Something like that, I suppose. You must appreciate that I do not know everything.'

'Well, just tell me what you do know,' Ryzhkov said. Reaching out now, pushing Yurovsky on the chest. One of the guards looked over and saw them, tensed. Ryzhkov took his hand away. They turned and walked on so they could talk confidentially.

'Look, it was a piece of theatre. We were to create the illusion that the entire family had been executed. We divided them from the servants. No one knew anything, everything had to be kept from them. They were smuggling notes in and out all the time using the nuns and the priests, so we didn't even have their cooperation!' Yurovsky's voice had taken on a desperate, almost wheedling tone, as if he were trying to solve a difficult problem posed by a severe head-master. 'I had trucks brought around to cover the noise, and the ones who were to do the shooting were specially selected. On the night –'

'Which night was that?'

'The Tuesday, the night of the 16th. We brought them clothing, things to use to make their disguises. The girls were to dress as nuns, the Tsar was a common peasant. I made him take off the moustache. The women had to cut their hair – the bitch was irritable as always,' Yurovsky said looking back up to the shaft. There was nobody out there now. The guards had made them all retreat into the darkness.

'What about the boy?'

'Oh God, the bloody boy. He's the worst. You have to carry him everywhere. He is always whining, playing jokes, criticizing everything. Devious little brat. A living headache, comrade.'

'So . . . it was the servants that were killed?'

'Yes,' Yurovsky said, growing quiet, staring at nothing for a moment. 'Yes, they were taken down to the cellar. We told them they were waiting for another truck to arrive. We got the royals into the first lorry and out onto the road. Once we were outside the walls the shooting could begin, you see? We didn't want to panic the Romanovs any more than they already were. They were told the servants would follow. They still think that.'

'They still don't know?'

'No.'

'What *do* they know?'

'They think someone is coming to take them to safety. That was the plan.' Yurovsky suddenly seemed to slump. His face was pale. For a moment Ryzhkov thought he was going to faint. 'That is the last part of the plan. They are supposed to be taken away, given new identities, you see?'

Ryzhkov looked at him for a long moment. 'I think I see a lie.'

'No, no, comrade. I assure you. This plan had authorization. It has to be totally secret, don't you see? If Goloschokin and the others in the Ural Soviet found out, can you imagine?

They would have taken over the Special House, the family would have been butchered. Somewhere, by someone, it was decided they were worth more to the revolution alive. They could be being ransomed. I don't know that for a fact, I'm just guessing. At least, that is what I think is happening.'

'You don't know?'

'Of course not. I don't know everything. I'm just doing my part, as I assume you are.'

'What about this person, this man who knows so much about mountains? Where is he?'

'I sent a telegram when I was ready, that it was to be the 16th. Everything was in a rush because of the Czechs. Then the next two days I go and wait for confirmation. If confirmation comes, that is good. If there is no confirmation, still we are watching the place of contact.'

'And?'

'No one comes.'

It wasn't surprising, Ryzhkov thought. Anything could have happened as the Czechs rushed ahead. A lot of messages had been missed when all the wires had been pulled down in the days before they took the city.

'So I have a message sent out by courier. That will take longer. But still no one comes. Except for you. And you don't know about the cleanliness of mountain air, comrade.'

'No . . . I just stepped into this. Now what?'

'You tell me. I thought that was what you were doing here, taking over the mission. Please, be my guest, comrade. I welcome any constructive suggestions.' Across the little road the two guards were dividing up the potatoes. Yurovsky turned and saw his gaze. Shook his head.

'And it hasn't been easy at all. They are terrible prisoners. Always complaining, always wanting medicines. Putting on airs. They still don't realize the danger. And they eat. My

God, how they eat.' He shook his head wearily, stood there watching the guards wrangling over the poor little bag of potatoes. 'I have to go back,' he said and looked up at Ryzhkov. 'Unless you think we should kill them?' Yurovsky's face was blank.

Maybe it was another test, Ryzhkov thought, something more important than knowing about mountains. He must have shaken his head or made some kind of sign, because Yurovsky continued.

'They cooperate after a fashion. Romanov is OK. He likes to do the chores and we let him. The bitch stays in her bed and complains. The boy sits there in his chair and whittles. The girls, well . . . they're pretty enough, I suppose. The little one likes to play jokes that aren't very funny.'

Yurovsky walked a pace or two up the hill towards the mine, then turned back. Lost. 'I suppose we could just let them go. Just, you know, just let them wander off. Sooner or later someone would find out who they are. Kill them, rape them. Justice would be done, in the end. When we get back to Moscow we could say they were stolen or that spies had helped them escape,' Yurovsky said in a voice like a dreamer. They were both very tired, he realized.

'No,' Ryzhkov said. He went over to the soldiers and took the bag out of one man's hands, swept the food into it, gave the men two potatoes each, and tossed another to Yurovsky. One of the men started to go for his rifle, but stopped when he saw the look in Ryzhkov's eyes. The guards were probably just as frightened as their prisoners. Red Guards looking to change their colours if the Czechs got any closer or found their hidden mine.

'You're going back and getting rations, right?' Ryzhkov said to the guard, who looked at him blankly and then turned to Yurovsky.

'If you wish, comrade, we can certainly assign Igor these

duties. You're in charge now, I'd say,' Yurovsky said loud enough for the guards to hear.

'Good. Then, get a lot, Igor. I don't care what you have to do – steal it if you have to.'

'We've already tried that,' Yurovsky said dryly.

'There's a little village, Excellency . . .' one of the guards began, looking down the road. They'd already started to defer to him.

'We need more than this. This isn't even enough for a day. Get whatever you can, and come back at first light,' Ryzhkov said. He dug in his pocket and handed Yurovsky back his revolver. The two guards had started to gnaw on their potatoes. Ryzhkov took the bag and started walking up to the mine.

'I have to see my wife. She's about to have a child,' the guard named Vassili began to complain.

'Fine. Igor, you take him with you then. Both of you get whatever food you can, see your wife, then find your way back here in the morning,' Ryzhkov said.

'Sure,' said Yurovsky. 'They can bring back wine, pheasant under glass, cakes, cookies, whatever can be scrounged up.' He was smiling. 'Tell me, comrade, while the two of them are plundering the city, what are we going to do?'

'You're going to pray, and I'm going to think,' Ryzhkov said.

He left them and went up the slope to the shaft opening, then through the little door into the office. Everything was dusty and abandoned. The table had been cleared and a hand of solitaire laid out on what must have been a foreman's desk. Ryzhkov suddenly realized how tired he was. All he wanted to do was stop, to sleep, to be done with it all. Down below him Yurovsky helped the guards climb up into the trap, took the pony by its halter and slapped it on the rump to start them on their way down the narrow track towards the city.

There were voices coming from inside the building and Ryzhkov moved into the warren of rooms. The office had been built flat against the bluff; it was a long narrow room so that anyone entering or leaving the main shaft could be observed and accounts kept. The sleeper ties for the mine railway were still in place but the tracks had long ago been torn up and used elsewhere. Everywhere was the dripping sound of water percolating through the soil above the shaft; the water had seeped down the walls and made strangely shaped stains on the plaster.

Behind the office was a larger room, with a series of long shelves, empty now of whatever equipment, tools or parts they must have once held. A series of bedspreads and tarpaulins had been strung up to curtain off the area. A lantern was lighting the gloomy space. Behind the curtains he heard a woman's voice. He coughed in warning and the voice quietened, there was a shadow against the curtain and one of the grand duchesses peered out, her hand grasping the canvas as if to cover herself. Ryzhkov could not see her in the gloom.

'I have to check on the prisoners,' he said to her.

'Everyone is fine.' She retreated a little now, actually pulling the curtain partially across her body.

'That's good.' He stood there for a moment, saying nothing.

'Are you the one who is going to take us away?'

'No.' Even in the shadows he could see her slump. 'Something's gone wrong. I don't know the details.'

'But it was arranged!' a second voice complained from behind the curtain. He moved under the curtain and the girl reflexively pulled back. A pair of camp beds had been set up and Ryzhkov saw a woman reclining there. She was covered in blankets, and her hair was piled within a bizarre cloth hat, something almost like a turban. Ryzhkov realized he was looking at the Empress Alexandra Feodorovna.

135

'Whoever was coming for you is late, or else . . . they're not coming at all. We're working on it.'

Alexandra made an angry sigh of exasperation, turned away and pulled the covers around herself more closely. Ryzhkov left the little tented bedroom and walked back deeper into the cavern that opened out onto the shaft. Now the light was brighter, and at the mouth of the mine he saw the other Romanovs gathered around a makeshift hearth. The terribly thin Alexei was doing his daily exercises, walking, supported on the arm of one of his sisters. The Tsar, watching a pot of water on the boil, he looked up as Ryzhkov approached. 'We have tea,' he said almost helpfully.

'Thank you, no.'

'It's the one thing we have enough of,' the Tsar said with a little laugh. Beside him one of the grand duchesses looked up and gave a small smile. The Tsar shrugged and then went back to tending the little fire that he had going.

Ryzhkov stood there watching them. Alexei had walked out into the sunlight and now had turned and was heading back in their direction. He had a limp, a sort of little hop that he made when he shifted his weight from one leg to the next, like a horse with a bad hoof.

'Can you travel?' Ryzhkov asked the Tsar.

'Yes, we're ready. At a moment's notice,' Nicholas looked up at him with hopeful eyes, the wide mouth breaking into a smile. With his moustache shaved for anonymity he didn't look like his pictures. Without it he looked stupid and shy. Older than Ryzhkov remembered, and thinner. Worn down. Ryzhkov had seen it a million times, that expression. Playing up to the jailers. Everyone did it; he had done it himself. Reflexively, without thinking, he made a little half bow, and the Tsar did the same, stuck out his hand. They shook. That was something new he'd learned how to do, Ryzhkov thought.

'Are we to be leaving?' the girl said.

136

Ryzhkov didn't know how to answer. He didn't want to give them any false hope. 'I don't know. Perhaps. Whoever was to make contact with us has . . . well, they were detained, or . . .' He didn't know anything. It was all just speculation. 'Our plans are changing,' he said. The Tsar reached over and took his daughter's hand – to keep her from asking too many questions, he thought.

'If you'll excuse me,' Ryzhkov said and went out to the edge of the sunlight past where Alexei was making his laps. The boy caught his gaze and looked up at him with a proud smile. Almost surly, challenging. Ryzhkov nodded, and the boy went back to his painful hopping across the entrance.

The situation was not good at all. Yurovsky's part in the ransom scheme had been left hanging when the overall plan had crumbled somehow. Now what had been inherited was a rescue mission. There was no support; Yurovsky had only been able to round up a pair of fugitive Red Guards, no food, not enough guns. The Ural Soviet had dissolved or run away as the Czechs had taken the city. Contact by Moscow had broken down and was limited to the the risky adventures of clandestine couriers. Everyone was tired, angry, hungry. Terrified.

Ryzhkov knew that the exchange plan must have had its origins at the very top of the government. Lenin and the inner circle. It had been a desperate gamble, rushed into place and vulnerable to the threat of the attacking White armies. Exposure was fatal, so secrecy and deniability were critical. But in ways unforeseen, something had gone wrong: signals missed, instructions undelivered.

A sudden wind set the birch leaves to twitching, a rapid nervous shimmering atop the green and silver trees. Ryzhkov turned and looked back at the little cave where the Romanovs had now made their final palace. A thin plume of smoke billowed into the sunlight and Ryzhkov realized the Tsar was sitting there in the darkness, smoking and watching him.

He too must realize that their situation here was untenable, that right now they were a danger to anyone they came in contact with. It wouldn't read well, this last chapter of his great dynasty. The heroes were all gone, and the plot was coming to an end all too quickly.

Ryzhkov had known that long sinking feeling too many times and it always made him sick; your life slipping away and no appeal that was going to be answered from heaven.

It must be horrible for Nicholas to realize that he and his family were no longer valuable, that they had merely become an impediment to all parties, that sooner or later blood was going to be spilled, that time was running out for his children and his wife, and that everything was up to the stranger with the revolver in his belt.

15

He leaves her in the early hours, a sleepy perfume clinging to him even as he gains the street. Pretty enough, but even as a baroness she means nothing. Perhaps he may be underestimating her, and possibly she feels the same way about him. They are at best temporary allies, lovers of the moment. Personal conveniences, tools to be thrown aside once they've lost their edge.

Not for the first time he damns the man who laid out Yekaterinburg, a grid of outrageously broad streets, mud and mundane buildings, dull people with dull feelings and dull ideas. Not for the first time he wonders if he will die here, or be caught and imprisoned, then trotted out against one of these dull ochre walls and shot to death by some half-literate peasant. And not for the first time he decides that his life will not end that way, not if he has a hand in it.

He walks down Arsenyevsky Prospekt and cuts through the lanes beside the pond, working his way down the hill, until he reaches the hotel. Loman, his fellow bartender, is already there.

'Ivanis! You weren't in your rooms last evening,' he calls out, his grin punctuated by toothless pauses.

'No, I was entertained elsewhere.'

'Lucky boy.'

'Somewhat. Were you looking for me?'

'Florinsky's cousin was having a celebration. It's his grandson's christening.'

'Ahh.' Florinsky, their boss, would take any opportunity to have a drink.

'You're early.'

'I have nowhere else to go. Besides, the breakfast is cheap here.'

'Brune left out some food.'

'Good enough,' he says and goes in through the tradesmen's entrance into the kitchen. There is a bowl of soup and bread which he slices and shuffles around the darkened kitchen looking for butter. Giesa comes in with a bucket of sausage pieces and a smile. Sausage, so rare for these many months, has become available again thanks to the Czechs and their affinity for spending money. There will indeed be a breakfast served in the restaurant today.

'You're early,' Giesa says.

'I was hungry.'

'Save some for Oleg, he's coming later.' Oleg is one of the men from the outlying villages who supplies home-made vodka for the bar, one of several newly minted entrepreneurs who have sprung up in the wake of the Bolshevik retreat.

He has been working here long enough to learn the various swindles and schemes that Pavel Florinsky brought with him from Omsk when he took over the hotel. Part of it is the dilution of real vodka, the kind one might find in a bottle with a label, with whatever can be obtained on the cheap from a multitude of sources. Florinsky manages his business with diligence and a kind of Russian avariciousness that one cannot help but admire. A quality he has become more and more aware of since he has been east of the Urals, where it seems almost native.

He finishes the soup. It is not enough. For some months now there has not been enough, not enough food, not enough wine. Not enough pleasure or passion, or peace, or anything worth having. Maybe he is becoming a Russian, he thinks, marvelling at his own adaptation so far.

Giesa and one of the sleepy boys that work in the reorganized kitchen begin to feed the stoves. A samovar is bubbling on the sideboard as he walks through towards the bar. He throws open the shades and the sunlight comes crashing into the dusty room as he pushes open the windows. A little fresh air never hurt anyone. Perhaps he can get out of this god-forsaken place before winter. A man, a little tweedy fellow that he recognizes as an English journalist, waits impatiently at the door with a newspaper in his hand, his weight bobbing back and forth from foot to foot; his eyebrows rise hopefully through the glass, then collapse irritably when he is waved off. There is some time yet before the bar will open. Some decisions are not taken lightly, and Florinsky's rules are rules, even for an Englishman with a thirst.

He moves behind the bar and along its length. There are chores that must be done, and because of the required amendments to his plans it has become necessary for him to keep his job a little longer. Intending to stay in Florinsky's good graces, he bends to the tasks at hand – the washing of glasses, the emptying of the trash, the polishing of the ashtrays. Florinsky in his money-lust dreams of Yekaterinburg as the Paris of Siberia, and as best he can he has fanned those flames.

He unlocks the door and places the bottles on the ledge. When they are cleaned they will be refilled with whatever noxious mixture the peasants have dealt them this week, the quality varying from mediocre to poisonous, and blended to

141

the necessary proportions to achieve the profit required by Florinsky.

And there he is: Pavel Egoriovich Florinsky walking down the cobbled lane, heading for the back entrance. He carries a package under his arm, something wrapped in butcher's paper, another smile. Why are these Russians always so happy? Behind him a sweating peasant pushes a cart, a sort of barrow with two front wheels, and four large oil cans: today's haul of *faux* cognac, schnapps and even whisky, if one adds a little sugar and tea for flavour and colour.

'Good morning to you, brother,' Florinsky calls out to him.

'Good morning, Excellency,' he says. Florinsky likes being called by the title, it is sort of a game they play, he pretending to acknowledge the man's rapid rise in the business world, Florinsky pretending not to notice the mockery.

'Look at what I have found,' Florinsky says, pulling the package out and untying the paper. 'Old Oleg brought them in. Only ten roubles, can you believe it? Anya is going to love these.'

He spreads the paper open to reveal a pair of women's shoes, long in the toe with exquisite straps and shiny with what he realizes is a patterned silk covering over the entire upper. Embroidered golden threads in a little chevron at the toe.

'Aren't they magnificent?' Florinsky says, almost whispering, and looking up at him waiting there at the door, an expression on his face like an altar boy. 'Anya's going to really love me good when I bring these home.'

'They're too good to wear around this city,' Ivanis says.

'Oh, yes, I know, what with all the mud . . . But when we have guests, then they'd be perfect, don't you think?'

Florinsky passes the shoe up to him and he inspects it, the immaculate lining where, true, an aristocratic foot has visited, but not stayed long enough to wear down the silk or dirty the sole. They have hardly been used. There is no label, they have been made individually.

'Yes, these are excellent. Very high quality, Pavel Egoriovich. And only ten roubles? Really?' He smiles at the man's prizes and lets his eye travel over the shoe – a light, perfect thing that nearly evokes a laugh from him, the kind of artefact one does not see much these days. 'Where did Oleg come by something like this?' he asks.

'Oh, I don't know. Who cares? For ten roubles I'm not going to ask any questions.'

'He's probably got his fingers in all sorts of people's business.'

'It's the barter system, eh? No one really knows. Pretty soon a banknote with the Tsar's face on it might not be worth very much. And military money? I'd rather have something I can use for my own benefit,' Florinsky says, reaching to take the shoes back.

Ivanis helps Florinsky and Loman load the cans of home-made vodka into the locker and then continues about his business.

The real traffic will not start until mid-morning, and he congratulates himself for getting an early start on the day. It gives him time to duck out early, leaving word with Giesa that he will be back in time for the rush.

He walks down Pokrovsky Street and hires a little one-passenger *izvolchik*, waits until they get out of town on the Moscow road to ask the driver if he knows Oleg's village.

'It's just his house and his brother's, not really a village, Excellency.'

'But you could take me there, and back? I just want to see it?'

'Certainly, Excellency.'

'Fine, then.' He has the money, and settles back to memorize the route, up the rising ground, heading towards the heights that overlook the railroad, crossing it and continuing along a broad plateau that occasionally affords views through the trees of Yekaterinburg below.

The entire journey takes less than an hour. They finally arrive at an area that has been hacked out of the birch forest long, long ago, the stumps eradicated, the ground ploughed and harvested until it has been spent and even he can see has lost its fertility.

'This is Oleg's house,' the driver says. 'And that –' half turning in his seat to point to what looks like a weedy, sod-topped hill across the track, '– is his brother's. Shall I wait, Excellency?'

'Just a moment,' he says. Steps down from the little *izvolchik*, walks out onto the track. There are ruts in the road there, places where other wagons have come and gone. He looks at the ground casually, reaching in his pocket for a cigarette, pretending to stretch his legs while all the while studying the tracks. There have been automobile tyres, he sees, pressed into the wet earth, now turned to dried clay where the sun has baked their impressions. An automobile, way out here, imagine.

He allows his eyes to follow the muddy tracks as they climb and eventually curve and vanish in the trees.

'What's up that way?' he calls back to the man.

'Nothing, Excellency.'

'Nothing?'

'They used to mine for platinum in these hills, but not for some years.'

'Ahh . . . a mine, eh?' He turns to smile at the driver.

'Not just a hole, it was a going concern, but they couldn't stop the flooding.'

'Too, bad, eh? A loss of jobs.'

'Yes.' The driver nods, and then nods again as if to confirm his agreement. 'Yes, Excellency. These are hard times for those below ground.' He nods as if he cares, takes a final pull of the cigarette and flicks it away onto the dry road. 'Do you want to go up there, Excellency?'

'No, no, this is fine. In fact, I should be getting back to the hotel,' he says, climbing back into the cab.

Any reprimand waiting for him at the hotel means nothing now, and he has some things to arrange.

Once again his life is about to change.

16

Disgruntled, Yurovsky slept at the end of the shed, exhausted, falling into a rhythm of snoring supplemented with yelps and whimpers when he dreamed his unknown, terrible dreams. Ryzhkov stood watch, but it was the worst kind of sentry duty. Dangerously quiet, alone, but comfortable, lulled by the movement of the leaves, the call of an owl, the rising of the moon. What horror might happen on such a night?

He retreated to the office and found a place to sit where he could observe the rise of the approaching road, lost himself in his thoughts as the moon ascended, moving its shadows across the ruts, obliterating the stars with its creamy light.

The Romanovs stirred throughout the night. He heard a brushing at the threshold and turned to find one of the grand duchesses with a cup in her hand. 'Is there water?' the girl asked, her voice cultured and incongruous in the shabby industrial surroundings.

'I'll get it,' he said. The water was kept in a leaking canvas bag, something that had ordinarily been used to carry cooking oil, and now re-purposed to carry their water. 'There's not very much left. We'll go in and get more tomorrow.'

She came over and held the cup out for him to fill, took

it back out of the room without a word. He had just sat back down when she returned.

'Thank you,' she said.

'Oh . . .'

'My father knows you. From before.' She was standing there against the desk, looking out at the forest.

'Really?'

'He never forgets a face. He remembers everyone. It's amazing, really.'

'We were sometimes assigned to the guards. They would use us on the big days.'

'The big days, yes . . .' She turned and he thought he saw a smile, a little tilt of the head. 'They used everyone in those days.' Saying it like it was a long time ago. Well, he thought, maybe it was.

'I was Okhrana,' he said.

'Yes,' she said. And after a moment she sat on the desk, leaned back against the office windows, curled her knees up under her dress and made herself at home.

Ryzhkov shifted in his seat, a little uncomfortable. Not knowing what to say to her. Meeting the family meant confronting all his feelings for . . . for Russia, for the war, for everything that had come before. What do you say to the Tsar, a man that was born as near to God as any mortal could be? How could you express your feelings for the man or his dynasty, or his generals – a pack of dilettantes and scoundrels who had happily marched into war intoxicated by martial music and gold braid. Oh, maybe Nicholas had done all the supposedly honourable things. He'd saved France, so they had said at the time, by rushing a million peasants into the cauldron of Tannenburg – his army of ill-trained and criminally ill-equipped farmers diverted an entire German corps and prevented the realization of Germany's meticulous Schlieffen Plan. Shouldn't that be written on his ledger at the holy gates? All right, fine as far as it went, but for all the sacrifice nothing had been won, and war hadn't felt very noble when he was arse-deep in fire and mud at Verdun.

'How is your health?' he said, his voice sounding absurdly polite.

'Oh, I'm fit enough. I'm a horse,' she said with a little laugh.

'And your brother?' Even in the dark he could see her change of expression, as if her face had gone behind a cloud.

'He's very . . . ill. He has been for some time. I suppose it is an open secret.'

'Yes.'

'He has a good heart.'

'The Empress?'

The girl looked at him, a tight smile. 'She hasn't been called that for some time.'

'Your mother, then.'

'She will not be separated from my father, whatever happens. She will die with him if she has to.' For a moment Ryzhkov saw her directly, the absolute certainty of her young convictions. As if she were demanding that there at least be a few principles that she might yet hold on to in life – a brother with a good heart and bad blood, a wife totally devoted to her husband.

'Did you know what the plan was?'

'We know nothing. They just came and got us in the night, told us to cut our hair, put on these clothes. That's all we were told. That's still all we know.'

'So, now you wait.'

'Yes.' The girl looked away from him. The moon was bright now and the glowing light filtered through the dirty windows, bathing the two of them in its strange radiance. 'What did you do before?' she asked.

'In the Okhrana?'

'Yes. Was it difficult? Exciting? Chasing spies?' She was smiling and began to rock back and forth now, hugging her knees like a schoolgirl sitting around a campfire wanting to talk about ghosts.

'It wasn't anything like that. Police work. Drudgery most of the time. Just like taking out the trash.'

'Did you ever kill anyone?'

The question stopped him for a moment and he fought to keep his memories in order and tried to frame an answer. Ended up just shaking his head. 'We've been in a war for . . . years now. I was in France, so –'

'Was it horrible?'

'Yes, it was horrible.'

'Were you afraid?'

'All the time.'

Her face made a little expression, a down-turning of her mouth, as if she had tasted something not quite up to imperial standards. 'I don't think I would like to be a man.'

Ryzhkov laughed. 'I don't think I would like to be a woman.'

'No. You have it worse. You have to be a hero.'

'Well, you have to be the victim, you have to be beautiful, you have to have babies.'

'Yes, but still. To fight, to grow up knowing about guns and swords and . . . to have courage, to be expected to be brave at the drop of a hat. I don't think I could do it.'

'You could if you had to. There are a lot of brave women, millions of them. And bravery doesn't require having a war to fight.'

She looked at him for a long moment, and then leaned so she could see back through the door to where the others were sleeping, then turned to him and her voice dropped to a whisper.

'You know, it's very . . . strange. Very odd. How people

change. How I've changed. All this – these last years . . .' She made a gesture with her hand, a long arc as if to bless the mine, the little office, Ryzhkov, the gleaming trees, and all of Russia beyond. 'I don't know, but I guess that if things were like they used to be, I suppose they would arrange it so that I would be introduced to someone suitable, a prince, or something.' A little laugh, and she looked at him to gauge his reaction.

'A prince, yes.'

'Oh, nothing less would do! A prince on a white horse. A stupid boy with an old castle. I would have had that kind of life, and now . . .' Finally she shrugged, the face serious for a moment, and then she shook her head and her voice whispered its secret. 'But this . . . all this, I never expected. And because I never expected it, never even dreamed that I would be just . . . just an ordinary person, in that way, you see, it's exciting. It's . . . it's kind of an adventure.'

'I suppose.'

'It is! For the first time we're truly alive. Before we were just marionettes, we were just being who we were all supposed to be. "I am Grand Duchess Marie!"' she said in a theatrical voice, and the little musical laugh came to him in the moonlight.

'But still, it's very dangerous for you,' he said, trying to comfort this dreamy, stupid, beautiful girl, and maybe trying warn her too.

'Yes, I know. The Czechs, all these revolutionists, whichever way we go we are surrounded by thugs. White or Red, it doesn't matter. They'd rape us as soon as look at us,' she said and then looked over at him. 'Yes, I know about all that. I'm nineteen, I'm no longer a child. The world can be cruel, that's certain. I know. And we had plenty of attention on the boat down from Tobolsk, I can tell you. So I know how dangerous life can be,' she said earnestly.

150

'You should go and get some sleep.'

'I can't sleep. If I sleep I might miss something,' she said, and then the smile broke through again. She shifted on the desk, swung her legs around and scissored them back and forth for a cycle or two. Awake. He could not help but smile at her. 'Were you married?' she asked.

'I was, yes, for a time,' he said, amazed at how he was just sitting there answering all her questions as if he'd been given a truth pill.

'But she died?'

'No. She went to Portugal. That was a long time ago.'

'And since then no one . . . no one at all?'

'Yes, there was someone,' he said, suddenly wanting to go outside and patrol the perimeter, make sure the guard was awake. Take a leak, smoke. Anything to get out of there.

'She was beautiful?' she asked and kept on when he made no answer. 'She was! She was a spy too?'

'I'm not a spy. I wasn't a spy, at least. She was a dancer.'

'Ahh!'

'It's time for you to be in bed,' he said, half rising and trying to shoo her out.

'I'm not tired.'

'You should go. Go on.'

'Are we leaving soon?'

And at that moment Ryzhkov made the decision, the regret piling onto him even as he said the words. The way a man who has sworn off liquor returns to the bottle, the way a dog slinks back home to sleep beside its brutal master. Falling into it without any thought, planning or reason, and hating himself all the more. 'Yes,' he said. 'In just . . . another day. I have to get a car, something to carry everyone. Don't tell them. I don't want to get their hopes up.'

'It's our secret.' She smiled, jumping off the desk and coming up to him. For a moment they met there in the moonlight.

151

She grasped his sleeves, awkwardly. A little non-embrace. Still there was that smile.

'No one cares about us any more,' she said. 'You're the only one.'

'Go now.'

And she stood on her toes to give him an impulsive peck on the cheek, like you would kiss an uncle who'd just bought you a treat, turned and moved to the door, but stopped, spinning around at the threshold. 'Don't worry about Alexei. He can walk. I can help. We'll be ready,' she said, and even tossed him a mock salute.

And then she was gone, back into the darkness of the mine.

He stood there for a moment, almost reeling. Kicking himself for promising her anything, anything at all. He pushed open the door and walked outside, stood there in the brightness and rolled his head around on his shoulders to clear his mind. She was just a girl, a pretty girl who could speak French, and write poems, and appreciate all the finer things of life, part of a pretty family who'd run into trouble. Nothing unique in that, there were millions of families who were being shattered, children who were thrown into lives they had never been told to expect. There was more suffering, more spilled blood than the world could ever wash away. He had seen his share of it. Too much, and he didn't need to see more.

And it was there, while he was standing in the moonlight, when he really finally made his mad decision – to take them out himself.

Get them out of Yekaterinburg, over the Urals and back to Moscow. And then? Well, then whoever was in charge could do what they wanted: take the money that had been offered, send them on down the line, put them on trial, change their names, whatever. But then it would be over. He would have done what little he could. Yes, he would save them, and in so doing he would save Vera, and himself as well.

And then . . . then he would wash his hands of them. Wash his hands of the whole affair.

17

In the morning Yurovsky was irritable. 'I've always been one for the mornings. I always liked a good breakfast, and then hard work. I could work forever if I started out like that.'

'Making photographs?'

'Yes, or any of the other jobs. I was a natural worker. A happy slave. All you had to do was just feed me my hay, and I'd pull the cart all day long. That's why this is so . . .'

'Well, everyone's life changes, eh?' Ryzhkov said.

There was a whistle down in the trees, and he and Yurovsky stepped out in front of the office and waited. One of the guards was standing in the road, showing himself. He was carrying a pack and the bag that had been used for the potatoes the day before. When he saw them he began to trudge up the road.

'Shit, he didn't bring the trap,' Yurovsky spat. They met in the road at the edge of the trees. 'Where's the trap? How do you think we're going to get back?'

'There are police everywhere. Vassili has gone. They're rounding people up. I left the trap in front of a house down the street and didn't even go into his house.'

'Ahh.' Yurovsky looked over at Ryzhkov, a sort of sour smirk on his face as if the dragnet was all his fault.

'What did you bring, Igor?'

'I found more potatoes,' he said, smiling.

'Wonderful.'

'I found three cabbages, and –' The man's face brightened. '– and I got this from Tochev's widow. She's not eating.'

'What do you mean?'

'She just sits there.' He shrugged. 'She didn't need it, so I told her it was important and she just waved me off, so I took it.' He held out a lump of smoked pork. It looked like a burned ember or some sort of oddly shaped brick of excrement.

'My god,' Yurovsky said. 'A real treasure.'

'And my aunt fed me, so overall it was a good night.'

'Where is Vassili?'

The man shook his head. 'When he didn't show up, I went there. Masha, that's her mother, wouldn't let me in. She finally said they were gone.'

'So he's deserted,' Yurovsky said, spitting down on the trail.

'She's going to have a baby any minute. They couldn't have gone far.'

'Christ.' Now they only had one guard.

'He'll come back, I'm sure of it. He's a loyal comrade.'

'If he comes back I'll shoot him, and then I'll shoot you for letting him go.'

'Water?' Ryzhkov asked.

'Vassili was supposed to bring the water. I only have this.' Igor swung around to reveal a canteen strapped onto the rucksack.

'Christ in heaven,' Yurovsky muttered, then went back to examining the lump of pork.

'Well, you'd better go up and help the Tsar with the

cooking. You can make up a big pot of kasha and share it with them, eh.' The man looked up to the mine with an expression that almost bordered on the fearful. Even imprisoned, the royals evoked awe in their jailors.

The Romanovs took their time rising. The Tsar was first to show himself, busying himself about their pathetic encampment, smoking, pacing and waving his arms around in an attempt to get some exercise. He wanted to chop wood, Yurovsky had told Ryzhkov, but there was no axe. Yurovsky walked out into the woods and came back with some broken branches for the fire, and the Tsar retreated into the cave to boil water for their tea.

Ryzhkov walked off down the road a few steps. It was as if the ground was sinking away underneath his feet. Everything was vague. There were a million little problems that could get in the way. He must have been dreaming or drunk when had been talking to Marie the night before. An idiot. He had a hollow pit in his stomach from hunger. It was always worse when it was combined with inactivity or boredom. Then the stomach took over all desire from the brain and conspired to cramp and ache until it was given nourishment, like a child that would not stop begging.

Yurovsky had come down from the mine entrance. 'Did we come up with any big ideas in the night, commissar?' Yurovsky said, and then because he must have been able to read Ryzhkov's dark expression he spread his hands and looked away. 'Sorry,' he mumbled.

'What we're going to do, Yakov, is: we're going to take them out of here. We'll deliver them back to Moscow ourselves,' Ryzhkov said, standing there with his hand on the pistol. If either Yurovsky or the guard gave him any trouble he'd already decided to shoot both of them.

'Fine. How are we going to do that exactly?'

'You go back into the city. Find Eikhe's woman, go around

156

to the fishing shacks along the lake. Find some friends who will help us.'

'This was all the responsibility of my contact.'

'Yes, well, it's your responsibility now. We'll need everything, disguises and provisions.'

'Storozhev's monastery can be the safe haven.'

Ryzhkov looked at him for a moment. Not really wanting to involve anyone else, particularly the church who were sympathetic to the Whites, but knowing that they would do anything to preserve the Romanovs, and knowing that for the rescue they would need a staging ground. 'All right, the monastery, if we must.'

'Then I can go and find the boat,' Yurovsky said.

'And I'll get a car, something to pick them up here, all the maps.'

'And the passes, don't forget the passes,' Yurovsky said. He took a few steps there in the centre of the road, looking up at the trees, like a boy daydreaming. It was irritating as hell. 'So, I think I understand, commissar. We meet at the monastery, pick up the supplies, drive to the mine here, pick them up and head for the lake and the boat that I will have waiting. Then what?' Yurovsky smiled.

'We strike out south to the railroad and board somewhere before Ufa. I use my White credentials to jump the queue and we take the first train towards Simbirsk.'

'We go between the armies?'

'Yes. The Volga will be the hardest, when we have to cross from White to Red with the whole family. We can split them up if we have to,' Ryzhkov said. By the time they got to the Volga their food and money would be gone. By that time one of the armies might have made a counter-attack. By then anything could have happened. There were lots of opportunities to get caught and killed.

Yurovsky was looking at the ground, shaking his head.

'Well, we can't go back on the railroad from Yekaterinburg, can we?' Ryzhkov said.

'Not without an army.'

'Fine, then we head south for Simbirsk.'

'And then?'

'Then we cross the Volga . . .'

'This is getting better and better. Why don't you just tell me as we go? I don't think I want to know the details of the whole idea. It will just confuse me.'

Ryzhkov shot him a bitter look. 'I haven't thought of everything. We'll head for the railroad.'

'Sure, they give out free tickets all the time.'

'We'll use a pass.'

'For nine, don't forget. The girls, the boy, the parents, and us. Do you want Igor to come along? In that case it's ten. I don't think anyone would notice ten people travelling to Moscow on a troop train. Four beautiful girls, no one would notice them; the bitch, her face is unfamiliar –'

'Why don't you either help or shut up for a change.'

'Sorry.'

'I need to contact Moscow, let them know the situation,' he said.

'Veni can give it to one of her couriers, but if it's something as highly sensitive as . . .' Yurovsky turned and looked up towards the Imperial Family and their pathetic breakfast.

Ryzhkov turned and paced back and forth in the road. With the wires down he couldn't ask for instructions for Moscow or even inform them of what he was trying to do. They couldn't stay there guarding the Romanovs forever; sooner or later the secret of the mine would leak out. One of the guards who'd supposedly retreated back to Perm would be sure to let something slip, or complain, or get drunk and pour his heart out, or what was most likely – sell their knowledge. Time was of the essence.

'Let's go,' Ryzhkov said. 'We're walking back to the city. Go and tell Igor that we'll be back tomorrow, to have them up and ready for travelling, then he can go back home.'

'Yes, commissar.'

'Just do it.'

'Yes, commissar.'

Ryzhkov pulled out the pistol and shot a bullet into the ground at Yurovsky's feet. It caused him to jump back and slip on the gravelly road, and he fell on his backside.

'Don't play with me,' Ryzhkov said, his voice brittle as flint. He could feel the blood pounding in his temples, and his vision had reddened, narrowing on the man sprawled, staring up at him. It took a genuine effort as he slipped the pistol back into his waistband.

Yurovsky scrambled to his knees, stood up, red-faced and breathing hard, then turned and climbed back up to the mine. Igor had come to the edge of the shaft clutching his rifle, his hand on the bolt ready to chamber a round. Behind him, the Tsar walked up, stopping a few paces away, watching.

It was, Ryzhkov thought, nearly two miles down the winding road, splitting off onto narrow trails that Yurovsky knew from his childhood, to get to the outskirts of Yekaterinburg.

The two of them spoke little. Ryzhkov would issue instructions whenever he came up with an idea. Everything seemed mad to him. Yurovsky had lost his sarcasm and even made a few suggestions. It was not much of a plan and both men knew it. But, Ryzhkov thought, it felt good to make the decision. To do something, anything at all, instead of nothing; to at least strike back, even if you were striking back against a cloud of uncertainty and circumstance, armed with nothing more than a prayer for good fortune.

'I'll go through the trees up here. I don't want one of your patrols to pick me up, eh?' Yurovsky said, edging off the road.

'Anything goes wrong, I'll try to spring you if I can, but you're a famous fugitive. They've got your photograph everywhere. They were talking about a reward the other day. They'll catch you, if not today then the next day. They'll talk to you in a very serious tone, and after that they'll want to put on a real show,' Ryzhkov said flatly, watching his face.

For a moment Yurovsky seemed sad, like a young scholar who'd been expelled from university, then the chin came up and a look of defiance took over his face. 'How do you know I'll come back at all?'

'Where else do you have to go, Yakov? If the Whites find you, you're dead. Your only hope is to come back with me to Moscow and explain how you failed so abysmally and beg for mercy. From what I've been told, Sverdlov is an understanding fellow. I'll put in a good word, and you might get off with a dozen years of hard labour.'

'I know plenty people in the area. I could hide here. Others are doing it.'

'If you know people, then go and get us the guns. We can use the help, Yakov, but if I get to the monastery tomorrow and you're not there, I'll find you and kill you myself if that's what it takes.'

'Well, that's . . . very friendly.'

'Difficult times we live in, comrade.'

'Au revoir, then,' Yurovsky said and turned away. The two men separated and Ryzhkov watched Yurovsky until he vanished into the trees.

18

There were, Zezulin thought, a great many cable rooms. And probably a great many vaults contained within the shell of the insurance building now known simply as 'Lubyanka'.

The present cable room in which he found himself had grown up in the west corner of the Lubyanka headquarters of the Extraordinary Commission and had once served as a canteen for the insurance company's workers. It had the great advantage, Zezulin thought, that it was also plumbed with a small kitchen and a storage vault, a sort of shielded pantry, that afforded utter privacy.

To get to the cable room he had been routed through three layers of security. The first layer had been simple – he had been the recipient of a note from Kuzma Pauls, the man who managed it; he had reported to a man at a desk with a clipboard flanked by a bored-looking brace of Red Guards; and finally been passed through to a receptionist who operated a gate equipped with an electric lock; and then he was walking down the old corridors and into the surprisingly informal warren of the cable rooms and the coding section.

Pauls met him in the hallway and steered him through the cubicles and curtained-off work areas to the vault in the corner. 'You asked about Yekaterinburg, so that's what this is about, Velim – I mean Boris . . . Boris, ahh . . . what is it again?'

Zezulin, smiled. 'Boris Maximovich . . . Noskov. Thank you for remembering, Kuzma. And thank you for calling me. It could be important. Or perhaps not. You know.'

'Of course. Nevertheless, Velimir, we saw a great deal of telegraphic communication, hundreds of messages each day in and out of the city of Yekaterinburg just before the city fell to the White criminals.'

'Yes?'

'Then as soon as the Czechs came in the lines went down, of course. Most of these final messages were ordinary desperate communications, by necessity sent in the clear, or in simple business ciphers. Then there was a second category of messages – those from various consulates and embassies. Naturally the German embassy here in Moscow was the point of origin of several of these messages, and our young men and women here have been routinely intercepting and breaking their various codes, one after another as they change them.'

Pauls and Zezulin had known each other from before; Pauls was a walnut-skinned denizen of the bowels of the Tsar's General Staff building in Petersburg, a benign Jew hiding at the very centre of the empire's limbic region. Pauls had developed a stoop and watery eyes that were alarmingly cloudy for someone who stared at text for a living. The man had been, deep within his secret heart, a reformer, and then, as events pushed him, something of a revolutionary. Maybe Pauls had been forced to bargain for his life when he flipped over to the Red side. It was not an uncommon story, Zezulin thought. Rather like his own. 'Good work, comrade,' he said.

'Oh, yes. Thank you very much. We're very accomplished down here. Now, this latest is a message to one fellow but it's in a special code. Not the hardest to crack, but something that isn't just for the ordinary man in the street, eh? So, to summarize, we have messages to him, these in the months of April, which from our conversations I gather is an important month . . .' Pauls let it hang.

Zezulin had not told him very much about his interest in the fate of the Romanovs, and certainly nothing of his motivation. The two of them operated from a position of mutual respect based on favours owed, a history of commerce in secrets both major and minor. Zezulin had not always been a good secret policeman, but he had been an honest one with his fellows. And Pauls was the same.

'Yes. This is fine,' Zezulin said. 'But I thought everything stopped when the lines went down. How did you come up with messages to him now?'

'Let's theorize,' Pauls said. 'He might have a wireless, but maybe it's broken, maybe he's afraid to put up the antenna, maybe it won't reach, who knows? But what we do have is this most recent message to him.' Pauls put a yellow sheet of paper on the top of the filing cabinet.

TODMANN
PLANS REJECTED. NO FURS REQUIRED. LIQUIDATE
ALL STOCK. CONFIRM BERLIN SOONEST.
SPECIAL SALES #R4-0B3

'So, fine, this is a business message, sent to our Herr Todmann, something that seems totally legitimate,' Pauls said.

'Another "sales agent"? I don't know about legitimate.'

'Sure, sure. That's how he's covering his identity, he's a commercial traveller. Somebody's agent, and now he's caught out there in the midst of a civil war. Oh, my God. Still, business must go on. So they normally use the embassy to send their messages, these furriers. Who knows? It's done all the time, supposedly. They have accounts they keep, business services, all sorts of attachés who are willing to help save a poor honest German salesman lost in Siberia. We don't know who they are exactly, there's no company name.'

'So?'

'So, what's different is that this wire was sent via diplomatic code to Sweden, and then to Portugal.'

'They're trying to get it –'

'Yes, right. We couldn't follow it after Lisbon, but you would assume that they were sending it to Yekaterinburg, embassy to embassy, who knows? All around the world to Vladivostok, and so on, so that he will receive it through the White side.' Pauls looked at him with the wet little rivulets in the wrinkles that surrounded his cloudy eyes. At the rims the skin was purple like a fig.

'Special codes, sending a message all around the globe, I think they don't do that sort of thing just for anybody, eh?'

'No,' Zezulin said. 'So when did they send this message out to this Todmann?'

'Middle of July. We didn't really get going around here until May, so the whole record on these two addresses is perhaps spotty. So maybe is this something that will help you?'

'Oh . . . it's fine. It's good, Kuzma.'

'I've gone back and dug out everything we have on this fellow. Do you want to take a moment and go through it all?' Pauls held up the folder; splayed from it were a half-dozen other yellow sheets.

'Yes, thank you.'

Pauls closed the vault and Zezulin was alone within the chamber. It was quiet and dry in the room, warm from three lamps set into the ceiling and the asbestos insulation that had been built into the walls. Nestled in the racks that had

164

once held canned goods and kitchen gear were locked file boxes, standing from floor to the height of a man. They all were marked with a number that had been painted on their faces and nothing else. There was no key posted on the walls. They could have held anything.

Dividing the vault was a lower aisle of three cabinets upon which someone had placed a tabletop. Zezulin opened the dossier and spread out the deciphered telegrams across it.

Todmann had first appeared to the Cheka in an ordinary telegram from Yekaterinburg in April 1918:

> SPECIAL SALES #R4-0B3
> FURS ARRIVED. PREPARING VENTURE. AWAIT RECEIPT.
> TODMANN

The telegram had been received and processed by the Germans. Two days later a reply had been sent from the German embassy in Moscow:

> TODMANN
> CUSTOMER NOTIFIED REGARDS FURS. AWAIT RECEIPT.
> SPECIAL SALES #R4-0B3

Thereafter there had been weekly short telegrams, sent in the clear, which were, Zezulin and Pauls both thought, simple confirmations of Todmann's continuing presence.

> TODMANN
> ENTERPRISE CONTINUES. SALES IMMINENT
> SPECIAL SALES #R4-0B3

And the agent's reply:

SPECIAL SALES #R4-0B3
AWAIT CUSTOMERS.
TODMANN

Then nothing at all for a month. Nothing. Not even the confirmation telegrams. When the silence broke it took the form of a warning sent by Todmann, and duly intercepted by the Cheka in the early hours of a late June night:

SPECIAL SALES #R4-0B3
BUSINESS CONDITIONS WORSENING. AWAIT RECEIPT.
TODMANN

It took the German embassy a week to respond with the following set of confusing instructions:

TODMANN
MARKET CLOSING. CUSTOMER WILL PAY AS SOON AS PRACTICAL. OTHER SALES MAY OCCUR. DISTRIBUTOR UNWILLING. RETURN STOCK TO LOCAL MERCHANT IF SAFE. AWAIT RECEIPT. CONFIRM BERLIN SOONEST.
SPECIAL SALES #R4-0B3

Todmann had made a reply, but from the wording it appeared that he must not have received the previous message from Berlin.

SPECIAL SALES #R4-0B3
READY TO PURCHASE SEVEN. ADVISE REGARDS
DELIVERY SOONEST.
TODMANN

By this date, now Zezulin knew, the Czechs had entered the city and the wires had gone down. So the embassy was probably getting nervous. The result was this latest desperate attempt to reach Todmann, sent all the way around the world:

TODMANN

SALES PLANS REVISED. NO FURS REQUIRED. LIQUIDATE ALL STOCK. RETURN OFFICE. URGENT CONFIRM BERLIN SOONEST.

SPECIAL SALES #R4-0B3

Something had changed in Berlin, something that meant that the 'fur market' was collapsing. The telegram may have reached Todmann, but in the chaos that had surrounded Yekaterinburg, probably not. The Whites had pushed through Yekaterinburg, beyond Perm, and were closing on Kazan. It was a military emergency and everyone knew it. To the south the armies of the Whites were converging on Tsaritsyn for a battle that could decide the future of the revolution. A series of battles was looming for control of the Volga.

Now, of course, Zezulin's own special agent, Pyotr Ryzhkov, was lost behind the lines as well. There was no way to warn him about the presence of this 'Todmann', whoever he was. Meanwhile, it had been announced that the entire family had been executed, just a footnote in one of the meetings of the Council of People's Commissars. Zezulin had not been present, of course, but had heard all the details. Was it true? Now more than ever he had to have his ear to the ground.

Zezulin slid the yellow message slips into their folder, walked to the end of the vault, snapped off the lights, levered open the great door and stood there until the clerk came over. The young man reached out to take the folder, but Zezulin pulled it back and held it across his chest.

167

'No, I'm sorry, my boy. Only him,' he said, pointing to Pauls across the room who was busily instructing one of his clerks, pecking away with one bony finger, a weedy rabbi correcting one of his exhausted acolytes.

19

' . . . and then I went to the house of a purported witness, who, as usual turned out not to know anything at all, and they dragged the story out, and tried to get me drunk. I got sick on their food, and stayed the night and couldn't continue. I'm sorry, sir.' Ryzhkov said, making his voice as contrite as he thought was plausible.

'This is your excuse?' said Giustiniani. He was almost reclining in his chair, an amazing device that swivelled and was on rollers so that he could push himself around the office.

'You're right. There's no excuse. Stupid, really. I was working on my own.'

'Everyone does that from time to time, but if we don't know where you are we can't help you if there's some emergency,' Giustiniani said. He looked somewhat red around the eyes himself.

'Yes, Excellency, I understand.'

'You know about proper procedure. You were a real policeman. My God, I shouldn't have to tell you about rules and regulations, eh?'

Ryzhkov nodded and hung his head like a good cop.

Giustiniani shifted position, orbited a half-turn and then back again. 'I hope she was beautiful.'

'Unfortunately . . .'

'Never mind, never mind, never mind. Nothing's going on anyway. Nametkin is going to be fired, so they say. I hate this bloody town. I'd kill for an absinthe.'

'They don't sell that here, I think, sir.'

'No, they don't sell much of anything here. You were once in Paris, correct?'

'After Malancourt, yes.'

'Ahh. Lovely existence. Paris before the war. Exquisite women, the Parisians. Christ! And here we are, now we've come to this! Perhaps this is hell. I think it might be. Have you eaten, Ryzhkov?'

'I don't feel . . .'

'Ah, yes. Well, there's nothing much to eat anyway. Whatever makes it down the railway from Vladivostok, if it manages to get by every starving railroad worker and Czech sergeant-major, then we get the leavings. The peasants are hoarding everything. Do you know what I was charged for a lime the other day? Seventy roubles. Can you believe it? For a fucking lime?' Giustiniani abruptly got up from the chair and stalked out into the centre of the room. Strilchuk was passing the door, saw the sudden movement, stopped and looked in.

'Well, Ryzhkov, now that you're here,' Giustiniani said, drawing himself into a pose of peevish command, 'you might as well make yourself useful. The new military prosecutor, Monsieur Sergeyev, wants to return to the Ipatiev house and re-tally all the bullet holes. He's not satisfied with Nametkin's work. That's the situation we're in now, we're doing each other's jobs two and three times over. Each go round there's a different version.' Giustiniani stood there for a moment, smoothed his jacket and shot his cuffs.

'I'm going to see a friend,' he said with a tight smile and left the room.

Strilchuk moved aside to let him pass, but then hung back by the doorway. 'Have we been learning anything, comrade Ryzhkov?' he said quietly.

Ryzhkov turned and looked at the impassive face. Strilchuk was looking at him steadily, no emotions to read whatsoever. 'I'm sorry?' he said.

'Nothing important. I just wondered if you might have discovered anything on your nocturnal rambles. Clues, odd facts, anything that the rest of us might not yet know? New information? Interesting threads we might pursue . . . comrade.'

Ryzhkov got up and went over to him. 'I don't need any trouble today, Ilya Stepanovich.'

'Trouble? I wasn't giving you any, Pyotr Mikhalovich,' Strilchuk said, not flinching at all, turned out of the door and walked away down the corridor. Ryzhkov stood there watching him go, thinking that sometimes his timing was right, and that today was one of those days. An excellent day to get out of town.

He went back to his desk, where a pile of witness transcripts was waiting for him. He sat there and pretended to read a report on the artefacts collected at the Ganin pit and the Ipatiev house that had been identified as coming from the grand duchesses. He made a few notes, and waited until there was an opportunity to steal a set of transportation orders from the desk of Volkov, the secretary on duty.

By one o'clock Volkov still hadn't left for lunch, so Ryzhkov went over to his desk.

'Anton Petrovich, aren't you hungry?'

The young corporal looked up. Volkov was about twenty-four, with glasses that he was too vain to wear, and a oily white face possessed with acne. 'I've got to get through all these,' he said. There was a pile of paperwork on his desk as well; the typewriter never stopped.

'You know I was sick, I missed a day.'

'Oh God,' Volkov said, thinking of the horror of falling any further behind.

'But I think I'll get through it all. Why don't you take a break, Volkov?'

'Oh, no, sir . . .'

'I'll cover for you. Go on. If you get sick like me we'll have Giustiniani all over us, eh?'

Volkov looked up, big blue eyes blinking beneath the dark brows. 'I'm supposed to lock up.'

'Don't worry. I'm staying right here. If you would be so kind as to pick me up something to eat, a sandwich will be fine, and a couple of bottles of beer at the hotel?' He opened his wallet and extracted a few banknotes.

'Oh, I –'

'Go on. It's going to take all night here for me, too. Get us something sweet for dessert. We deserve a reward, don't you agree?'

'If you say so, sir.' Volkov stood, a smile breaking out for the first time.

Ryzhkov sat down at the young man's desk. 'Tell me what to do. What's all this? I'll finish it for you.'

'It's a transit request. You just fill it in,' Volkov said, heading for the hat rack. 'Thank you, sir. I'll be right back.'

'Take your time, Anton Petrovich. That's an order,' Ryzhkov said as he sat down and began to type.

'I hate flowers, I always have. I don't mind them if they are in the ground, but I always hated them in vases. And they're everywhere, you begin to notice, once you have a fright like that. I can bear them, but mostly it's pure hate. Something about the smell,' Sophie Buxhoeveden said.

172

Her voice came to Giustiniani in the semi-darkness of the rail car. He had propped himself up against the bedroom 'wall', a temporary affair cobbled together by carpenters the Baroness had hired once the Bolsheviks had abandoned the city. It afforded privacy which had been non-existent in the old carriage, a converted second-class coach. Giustiniani wondered why anyone would ever waste a thought for flowers one way or another, but he didn't say so, preferring to simply let her talk.

Their lovemaking had been feverish, owing to his inactivity and frustration. The whole assignment to Siberia was a terrific mistake, and there was no way to rectify it. Oh, he might find himself in at the victory when the monarchy was restored, it would be an amusing story for his friends in Rome, but it was not the Navy. It was not engineering or experimentation. People were not machines, no matter which political system was running things.

'Animals, horses. I can abide horses . . .' her voice continued. From the beginning he had wondered about her. She said she wanted to go to Vladivostok. She had the money to purchase a transportation order. She had requested one from him, and he had agreed to provide it, but had let the actual procuring of it drag on so that he could have her there in the city with him. When she got boring he would write the order and send her on her way.

'Have you ever done anything wrong?' her voice came to him in the gloom. A softer tone this time. The layers of sophistication peeling away.

'Many times.'

'I mean something really wrong, something for which you will be judged?'

'Yes. Many times.'

'Aren't you afraid of the punishment of hell?'

'I don't know.' He inhaled the last of his cigarillo, levered open the window and flicked it outside onto the ballast. 'Besides, it's too late. At least if I'm going to hell I'll have plenty of company. A great many kings and queens, all the best people are billeted there, from what I hear.'

She laughed a little in the darkness. It was mostly pretending, and then she stirred, pulled her leg away. 'Men . . .' she said.

'What?'

'Have you ever betrayed someone, betrayed a friend, a benefactor? Have you ever done something, committed an act so terrible that you were ashamed? Do you know that kind of guilt? The meaning of that? To be truly ashamed?'

He suddenly realized she was crying. What had he done? He moved to embrace her but she only pulled away further. 'And . . . and if I had caused them any . . . and I know that I did, you see? If it was my fault, and I did . . . I did what I had to do . . .' she went on, just babbling.

'Darling, darling.'

'You see, my only excuse is that I was afraid, Tommaso, afraid for my own life. It was a panic. Surely God will understand this, don't you think? Just afraid, like an animal is afraid when the hunters have surrounded it. Terrified.'

'Certainly, my dear. Come here.' He held her for a moment, but then she abruptly got out of the bed and vanished back into the car. He heard her blowing her nose, the clink of glasses, and in a few moments she returned. He saw she had brought back a decanter of liquor and two tiny crystal glasses.

'They had everything with them in the end,' she said. 'They put all the ordinary things in boxes and crates, but with all of their jewels, do you know what they did?'

'I'm sorry, my dear?'

'The Tsaritsa, the girls . . . they sewed them inside their clothing. Into their intimate things, their underwear. They had millions on them the whole time. Everything they would need to give them a start outside Russia. They had to do it.

174

It was the only way. Everything else had been ransacked and confiscated, you see?'

'A portrait of desperation,' he said gravely.

'I just want to leave, Tommaso, to leave everything. To leave it all behind, the memories, this city, Russia. My own . . . It's possible to know too much, to have seen too much, and I need to escape all that, you see?'

'Yes, my dear. Of course,' he said, not really listening or understanding what she was on about now.

She pushed back the curtain; a thin parallelogram of light spilled in across the blankets. She lifted the two little glasses. They had fluted rims and designs carved into the crystal, and she gazed at them with the joy a child might take in a particularly unique toy. 'Alix . . . Empress Alexandra herself gave me these. I've kept them through all this. These two precious, tiny little glasses. Can you believe it?' For a moment her face contracted and Giustiniani thought she was going to break down again, but she gathered herself, pulled the stopper, filled the glasses to overflowing, laughed, tried to mop up the spill with her finger, and handed him his.

They linked arms and drank close, face to face. The air had grown chilly in the car, and he could feel the warmth of her.

'To sinners,' she said, kissing him.

Transportation on the White-held railroads was controlled by a set of orders that were made by every level of the infant Omsk government. Everyone was still learning and there was a language problem. If the orders were written in Czech, no one could read them except other Czechs, and sometimes even they had trouble, since the *Czechs* themselves were a polyglot group made up of Magyars and Slovakians, speakers of various dialects that didn't always harmonize. To make matters worse, neither the Czechs nor the French, who were nominally in command across all of Siberia, could understand orders rendered in Cyrillic.

The solution was to copy everything in two languages, and accordingly Ryzhkov made up a set of transportation orders for five nurses to join the military hospital at Simbirsk. It looked like what it was, a set of documents written by a Russian clerk with a bad grasp of the Slovak tongue. Ryzhkov looked up the unit designation of the military hospital and wrote it in, transferring a section of nurses to the Simbirsk front. He attached a note to the military police of the Czech legions, an authorization for the peasant driver and his son – who would be seen to be ill and resting in the back with the women. No one wanted to poke around in the back and catch the influenza, so no one would check.

From Giustiniani's desk he took a letterhead from the military commission and wrote a two-sentence order for himself and a constable 'Nazarov' who were en route to Simbirsk on the Volga, engaged in conducting a murder investigation associated with members of the White volunteers.

He worked quickly, clearly. He had forged everything but the signatures when he heard the door open and Volkov came bounding up the stairs with a greasy paper parcel under his arm. 'I got six beers with that money,' he exclaimed, all smiles.

They divided the food and Ryzhkov went back to his own desk, forged the signatures and put the orders into two envelopes, ate, and then, taking a sheaf of testimonies as a cover, went on a search through the library for a good map. His plan had them escaping across the Lake Iset, then striking out for the railroad to Simbirsk; it required a map that would cover his route all the way to the Volga.

At the front desk one of the clerks, a young woman, not unattractive, got him the best thing they had. The cartographers had finished their drawing back in 1874, but she opened it to show him that the railroad had been added in with red ink some years later. As a cover he requested other maps surrounding the city, all the routes out, west to Nizhni or east to Omsk and, because he didn't want her to remember anything particular about his travels, tried to act bored and worn down by his job, hoping she'd ignore him.

He was led to a table and given a paper and pen, because the librarian wouldn't let the materials out of her custody. The map might have been old, but it had been glued to a canvas backing and he unrolled it and diagrammed the route they would try to take. They would aim for the town of Pasuts, marked as the place where the river struck the railroad.

He knew that a White army under command of General Denikin was pushing up from the south through the Ukraine. The Red Guards if they wanted to save themselves would have to retreat back across the river. The Czechs were simultaneously pushing westwards towards Kazan. If there was a seam between the armies it might be near Simbirsk. He drew it out, rolled out the other maps, pretended to look at them, rolled them back up, put them on the counter for the girl, and left without comment. By then it was nearly 2.30.

Out in the street he felt he could take a deep breath for a moment. Taking it moment-by-moment, everything was going according to plan. He had passes that might well stand up to inspection; in an effort to confer authenticity he had rummaged through desk drawers and stamped the papers with various official-looking stamps bearing the authority of both Omsk and the Yekaterinburg police department.

He crossed the wide plaza and turned along the wide Glavni Prospekt, wondering if he should push his luck, try to get another pistol that he could hold back and entrust to the Tsar if they ran into an emergency. At the end of the block he saw that the wide doors to the military garage had been thrown open. There was a motley collection of vehicles parked under the canvas awnings. A little yellow runabout, the huge NAG, a collection of wagons and broken-down engines spread out on the bricks or dangling from chains. Propas was there, supervising the changing of a front tyre on one of the armoured vehicles. It was a strange contraption, built for three or four men and mounted with a machine gun, a hybrid with the rear wheels given over to slatted tracks like a tank.

'Odd duck,' Ryzhkov said, watching the men work.

'Oh, yes. Not much good for anything, really,' Propas said, stepping back with a frown. 'What can I help you with today, sir?'

Ryzhkov fished in his pocket, pulled out a warrant, flashed it to Propas and put it back again. Gave him a look. 'I need something big, like a truck. An ambulance would be best.'

'I have an ambulance, sir, that is awaiting a new front fender and door. That is my only lorry, unless you might use one of the big Fiats. It would be ready on Tuesday.'

'I'll take it as it is.'

'No, sir. I'm sorry.'

'Is the engine reliable?'

'Of course, sir.' Propas visibly stiffened.

Ryzhkov tapped the papers in his chest. 'I need it right now, just for tonight, and then you'll get it right back.'

Propas gave him a look that lasted just a fraction of a second too long. 'Yes sir, if you sign for it and say so. Somewhat dangerous without a door.'

'Not dangerous at all. We're not going very far,' Ryzhkov lied, walking deeper into the garage, searching for the battered ambulance.

20

Veni Eikhe found him as he was coming around the wood pile – Yurovsky, who even as a boy had never been a labourer, more the clockmaker type, with finicky hands and an interest in numbers. Pretending to be working at something, stopping to lift some logs and shift them about, cheap role-playing, as if any one of the neighbours seeing him wouldn't know exactly who he was. 'Don't be a fool,' she said to him, picked up the kindling herself and went inside. He followed like a beaten puppy. And this was the kind of man to whom the revolution trusted her most secret tasks? It made her want to retch. He sat down at the table and she went to the stove and dished out something to share with him.

'Yakov, what have you got yourself into now,' she said, not so much a question as an assessment. He looked up and for a moment she thought he was going to burst into tears. She wanted to slap him, but she stopped herself by getting up. And then she turned and actually did slap him, and when he just took it off the back of his head, barely getting his arm up in time, it made her even angrier.

Verena Lichner was from the south-eastern part of Bessarabia, and that's what had attracted Nicholas Eikhe to her – her Germanness. He liked that they had that in common, but his forebears had arrived in the Urals in the early eighteenth century, pushed north along the Volga until they'd traded their farms for new futures in the mines and factories that were beginning to spring up in the Urals. Nicholas so revered his fading Teutonic ancestry, that when he met Veni he was surprised by the unlikely good fortune of it, the discovery of a prospective mate who was more German than he was.

What he loved about his mythic ancestry was what he loved about his own personality. He fancied himself as an intellectual, she remembered, never letting Veni forget that he could read and she could not. So, frequently, he read to her. His showing off was the time he was the kindest, and nearly the only time she had loved Eikhe. Loving mostly that simple act, his pleasure in reading to her. The way his voice would change. The rest of it . . . well . . .

He had a temper the way little men have a temper, the anger of those who have been beaten and kicked all their lives, at home, at school, at work. First it made him political in the factories, then it turned him into a Bolshevik in the bad years. He'd spent a year and a half in a penal camp at Ust Kut in Siberia, and then come back to the city when the Provisional Government took power in February and granted amnesties. He had got back to Yekaterinburg just in time for the October revolution, enough time to sleep together for a few days, coming and going, coming and going. Barely a week – and then he was gone again. The Czechs shot him at Chelyabinsk, the word came back.

'. . . enough for nine people. And clothing, disguises . . .' Yurovsky was saying.

So what was she to do?

'You want this, you want that. You want it by tonight. I can't do it all by myself,' she said.

To avoid fighting with her, he got up and went into the corner room, caught sight of his reflection in the glass over a fading oval photograph of Eikhe's mother.

While she went on complaining, he just stood there, looking at his face layered above the old woman's. He was looking thinner by the day. Well then, they all were. It was the fear, the nerves. The desperation of it. He had been the young hero who had his photograph taken in his revolutionary uniform. Now it was getting dangerous, and he was afraid for himself. Thinking that he was the kind of revolutionary who had believed in a dream, but discovered a nightmare.

'Yakov, I know everything,' she said. 'Everyone knows, Yakov,' she blurted. 'You think it's such a great secret, but people are not stupid, eh?' Then she left, and turned back and hovered just out of the doorway. 'What is happening here? Tell me honestly.'

'It's none of your business.'

'Kill them, is that what it is to be? We'll go back out there and kill them? That's what was voted, that's what we agreed to do. It's not too late.'

'No.'

'The problem is that when something like this goes wrong, it goes terribly wrong, Yakov. You were assigned one thing to do, now it's a wholly different thing. You can't be blamed.'

'No.'

'On behalf of the soviet, I'm ordering you to kill them, comrade,' she said, weakly.

When he didn't move she went on. Her voice was shaking now. Maybe he was lucky she was just an old woman.

'You know I'm right. Everyone knows,' she said.

He turned and walked back into the room. He was tired and needed to sleep. He fell into the chair. 'Veni, everything I am doing is under orders of the Extraordinary Commission and approved through Lenin's secretary, Yakov Sverdlov. It is my assigned revolutionary task. It is yours to help me, to enable me. That is all that matters. Whether you approve or whether you're tired, or afraid –'

'I'm not afraid for myself!' she spat. 'I'm afraid for the success of this revolution, don't you see? We passed a dictat here. We ordered the execution of the Nicholas, the rest of the bloody Romanovs, and their servants. That is the will of the people as represented by the Ural Soviet. There is no higher authority.'

'Oh, so now that's your tune? The Ural Soviet is running the show?'

'You know my opinions. I'll be judged by what I've done. I've helped you. Who do you think is supporting you? I'm just pointing out the dangers, that's all. I –'

'Fine, fine.'

He fell silent and she came back into the room. She had three sprats she'd bought that morning. Even in the heat they were still quite fresh, and she split them and put them on a plate with salt and the remains of a lemon she wrung out to get the last of the juice; took the middle one off the plate and left the rest for him.

'Yes,' he said to her, 'things have changed. We have to improvise and come up with revolutionary ideas to clean up a revolutionary mess. So just help get me what I need, Veni. There is no time to argue theory, eh?'

'Just eat,' she said, walking back out.

He told her what was needed: food and water, blankets enough for a squad to last three days and nights, clothing for the women.

'You wanted nuns' habits last time. Now what?' Eikhe said.

'Nurses. They can wear those bibs that the nurses wear.'

'What about guns?'

He opened his coat to reveal the one Ryzhkov had returned to him.

182

'And you have ammunition for it?' she asked.

'I have seven bullets.'

'Do you think you might need more?' she said with a sneer and a laugh.

'I hope not. Listen to me, Veni. I did not do this on a whim. I did not do this because I needed the adventure. I do not tell you everything not because I think you're a stupid woman, or because I know that you're a compulsive gossip. I am doing this because it is necessary for victory in the revolution. I know this.' He just looked at her for a long time. 'I know this,' he said again.

She put his hand down; he had reached up and taken her elbow while she was standing there. 'What else, then?' she said.

'I need to get a message out.'

'That's an impossibility,' she said flatly.

'No, it's not. Send-this-message,' he said as if he were telling a dog to stay in its place. '"Baggage for nine . . . require assistance . . ."'

'"Baggage for nine . . ."' she repeated, as he made the words on the paper.

'"Arrive Simbirsk soonest. Yurovsky."'

'With your name on it?'

'Yes, my name.'

'Simbirsk?' she said, sniffing at the impossibility of it.

'Yes.' Yurovsky stood up, bent his neck around. Everything felt stiff. His body had grown old, creaky and aching. He might have the influenza. He might die before it was all over. That would be fine, he thought. Fine with him.

He went over to the windows and stared out at the falling light. Not much longer, and then it would be time to leave Yekaterinburg. Probably the last time, he thought, given the odds of Ryzhkov's plan having any success at all. He went through the house and out the back to the privy, emptied

183

himself, and sat in there breathing the sharp stench. Sometimes the worst things were the best, he thought. Sometimes you could go all the way down, and there was still beauty there, still fragrance. Everything in the little privy was real. No lies. No half-truths or promises that men told each other from podiums, or in manifestos or pamphlets. Bullets, blood, shit – that was truth. Everything else was ornamentation, posturing, craven men and women elbowing their way towards better advantage.

He was tired. He knew it. Tired and hazy in his thinking. Prone to making mistakes and other errors, errors in judgement. Prone to giving up, to just sitting there in a shithouse and weeping himself into death.

He hadn't taken a photograph in a very long time, he thought. Art was something he carried with him in a hidden place, carefully stored away. A luxury, to be an artist. Perhaps one day, if everything went right . . .

He finished then, buttoned his clothes, carefully looked out the door to see if anyone was lurking about Eikhe's little house, before he headed back to prepare himself for the evacuation of the Imperial Family. One day it would be a good story, he thought.

If any of them lived through it.

When the sun plummeted behind the low foothills that contained the city, Yurovsky left the house, walking along, climbing another street and edging closer to the forest, making his way across the city to the monastery. Around the area of the old compound the streets were more permanent, cobbled instead of dried mud, and the buildings took on an established tone, brick and plaster, instead of sagging wood and broken ginger-bread. Thus had God attracted riches, which was only natural, since after having thrown the moneylenders out of the temple he had taken over the concession for His own purposes.

He had paid a visit to Father Storozhev in the very beginning, immediately after he was given his instructions in Moscow and returned to the city. It was a perfectly natural visit, since as a boy he had been Storozhev's pet Jew, from a family of free-thinkers, a young person always on the edge of conversion to the Orthodox faith. They had got along, both of them curious about the other; friends across an enormous theological divide. Perhaps it had been because neither of them was particularly devout, or at least because neither of them was afraid of the other.

The monastery was only part of a compound of ancient buildings, starting with a small chapel at its centre, surrounded by more practical buildings, a shingled onion dome the size of a large trunk its only ornamentation. Somehow even now Yurovsky thought it almost shameful that in a mining region where shiny metal was in abundance some philanthropist had never offered funds to gild the dome.

He stopped on the road, turned and listened, heard nothing, and kept on walking until he reached the creaking ironwork gate.

They kept a boy there, an orphaned teenage monk who had heard him and came up, a little nervous. 'Are you here for the Father?' he whispered.

As they went across the courtyard Yurovsky found himself watching the bobbling shadows cast by the boy's kerosene lantern, all the places you could hide a rifleman. It was a large fortified complex and Storozhev's quarters were at the other end of the expanse. Yurovsky could feel them: all the eyes of the nuns, the given-away children, the ones in the asylum, all watching from the buildings, staring out from the shadows. He could almost smell them, like a cat sniffing vermin. Perhaps it was just the incense. Here he was, one of the hated Jew-Bolsheviks, now appearing to them as the Anti-Christ, off on some infernal business right at the heart of their monastery.

Now they would follow him into a courtyard, now to a stairway. Now they would whisper his name: 'Yurovsky. You remember him.' One of the godless ones left behind when the Czechs poured in and rescued the city, one of those who had burned his armbands and banners, scuttled away into an attic or a shed. And now he was back? Back here, seeking favours? Forgiveness?

Once the boy had left Father Storozhev's room he closed the door. 'We need a place for tonight, a safe place. Can you help us?'

'So it's true, then?' The old man was trembling. 'They live?' he said to Yurovsky.

'Yes, Ioann, it's true.'

Storozhev felt his eyes well up with tears, then remembered his hospitality. A few moments later a monk appeared with a dish upon which sat a loaf of black bread, and what Yurovsky was amazed to see was cheese.

'Yakov, tell me, my son. What can we do?'

'Nothing, Father. They are safe,' Yurovsky said, then stood and took in the rest of the tiny room. 'We're taking them out of the city tonight. Tell your boy at the front others will be arriving shortly.'

'May God be praised,' Storozhev finally breathed.

'Yes, yes.'

'We have food. Whatever is required.' Storozhev smiled. Perhaps the world would be saved after all.

'We must hurry, Father. There is no time, you understand?'

'Yes. Yes, my son, of course, of course. Safe! I cannot believe it,' said the cleric, his eyes wide with understanding. He was pacing about the room. 'Here, of course. We have plenty of room, or if it's not suitable there are several empty houses since, of course, a great many people have left the city. I am sure that –'

'No, no. Here will be fine. All we need is the stables. It's

186

just until dawn, then we will be leaving. And, of course, it is of utmost importance that no one must know, Father.' Yurovsky gripped him hard on the shoulder. 'No one must see anything, yes?'

Father Ioann Storozhev turned and saw the hard look in Yurovsky's eyes. The boy had transformed himself, become a true warrior. But from his false Bolshevik gods he had been born again, converted now into a soldier of the true church. To save his soul he was ready to betray the red gods of communism. Now a rescuing angel of Christ, God the Father. A saviour, a saint. The world needed more Jews like him.

'You are here now,' Storozhev smiled beatifically. 'No one will find you. You could keep a circus in here and no one would know. You could stay here with us in safety forever.'

'Only a few hours, and we are gone. Then – none of it never happened.'

They went back out into the shadows, moving from the dormitory wing across the alley, and into kitchens that gave off onto a courtyard. It was where the wagons came in to take the garbage away, and where the carts loaded up the scraps for the pigs and the compost. Storozhev wanted to give the Imperial Family supper while they waited, but Yurovsky stopped him, angled him over to the wall. 'No one must see! No one must know that they live. You understand this?' They just waited there together for a moment. The old man reddened but took it.

'Now we wait for the chauffeur,' Yurovsky said. He found a stool across the room, moved it around so that he could see out the windows. 'Do we need that light out there?' he asked the priest.

'I'll get someone,' Storozhev said. It was an electric bulb that showed the entrance and made a dim and dirty light there at the gate, and Yurovsky suddenly wanted it dark. Wanted to hide.

Storozhev came back. There was another monk with tea. They took glasses and waited. 'Don't worry,' Storozhev said when the young man left. 'We can keep a secret.'

'No . . . I don't doubt it,' Yurovsky said. The church was in the same situation as the Bolsheviks as far as having to keep everything quiet. Even to save the Tsar and the Imperial Family, to collaborate with the Reds was anathema.

'Still, we are doing a good thing. We are helping, you see? It's an act in the name of Christ. In that sense you have me as your hostage, Yakov,' Storozhev said, and even laughed.

'Sometimes you have to compromise,' Yurovsky said. The shadows changed on Storozhev's face and he realized that the electric light had been extinguished.

'So,' Storozhev said, swirling the tea in his glass. He had taken a position against a pantry door. 'We are all grown up now? In charge of our own fate?'

Yurovsky laughed. 'Oh, yes. We're in charge.'

'Difficult times,' Storozhev said.

'Yes. How is your mother?'

'She finally died.'

'Ahh. She was always very kind to me as well.'

'She was very kind, true.'

They watched the entrance for a long time in silence, weighing their consciences in the night.

'If they come, no one must know, Ioann. Everyone will be killed if it gets out. You know that, eh?' Yurovsky said.

Storozhev said nothing, and the two of them kept staring at the darkened gate.

It was the hour when everything was soft and moist, the weather wanting to change back to its colder, more natural state, and doomed to fail with the approach of another hot sunrise. Storozhev was stretched out on the floor, covered with a cook's apron.

He saw her arrive at the gate pushing a barrow, covered

over with vegetable bags, put the burden down and light a match to show her face.

Eikhe.

'Let her in,' he said, reaching out to wake the old priest, but he was already up and heading for the door.

She stood there for a moment, breathing heavily from the work of coming up the long road to the monastery. She picked up the barrow and headed inside, and Yurovsky saw that a boy ran out to escort her. They all met where the boy was unlatching a door to the stables and wheeling the barrow inside.

'I got everything I could,' she said. Her face was red and white from the exertion, a fine sheen of sweat. 'It's the last. They took food out of their own babies' mouths for this.'

She stopped when she saw him looking at her. 'What did you bring?'

'Radishes, potatoes, a bag of salt, tea. Seven loaves of bread. A packet of sausages.'

'Enough, then,' Yurovsky said, nodding.

'Yes, enough.'

Storozhev was heading back to the kitchen, the boy back to his gate. For a moment the two of them stood there in the courtyard. In the background there was a buzzing sound, a rising growl that began to echo against the walls.

At the gates there was a sudden glare and the roaring in his ears resolved itself into the engine of a truck – an ambulance that turned into the gate and stopped with a little skid.

The corners of Eikhe's mouth turned down when she saw him. 'Be careful,' she said, reaching out and tugging on Yurovsky's sleeve. 'Be careful of him. Everyone knows they are out there, hiding somewhere in the woods. So . . .'

'Don't worry, little mother,' Yurovsky said and went to take her in his arms, but she pushed him away.

'You say it's important to save Bloody Nicholas and his

bitch, then I won't disagree. You're Cheka, and we both serve the revolution,' she said and turned away and started walking back down the hill.

'We are not going to let the Tsar fall into White hands,' Yurovsky said.

'Whatever you say. I don't want to know,' she called back over her shoulder. Yurovsky watched her for a moment. Ryzhkov coughed and he climbed onto the running board. Ryzhkov levered the truck into reverse gear and backed the shivering vehicle out of the gates.

21

The road ahead.

They discussed how to get the family to go with them. Sooner or later they would have to make it clear that they were taking them to Moscow, that there would be a trial.

'They are not going to let you, just let you . . .' Yurovsky started.

'Somewhere along the way we might have to separate the women, take them away when we make it to our lines, the Empress, the girls and the boy.'

'Yes. But he's going to have his own ideas and so is she,' Yurovsky said. The ambulance waddled up the rutted road, Ryzhkov trying to drive it smoothly, watching to see if it was going to overheat on the climb.

'We'll have to tell them where we're going.'

'We tell them, Pyotr, then they will try to escape,' Yurovsky said.

'They think they're going to be saved. Sooner or later they'll figure it out. They'll realized they're not being taken out of the country.'

"Are you going to tell them?'

'I can't see any way out of it. Tell them, at some point, I

191

suppose so. Once we're away. I don't know,' Ryzhkov finally said. His mind was all over the place. Some ideas were clear, others were fighting each other. He felt like a man caught in a tidal wave, pushed, pushed wherever it was going to take him. Trying to stay afloat. Alive.

'You can make all the plans you want but she's not going to let him go anywhere by himself,' Yurovsky said. 'She's been like that the entire time. They've always known what might be coming. She's very devoted and she wants to die with him. That's been her idea from the very first,' Yurovsky said. He was leaning in the window, staring ahead a thousand miles.

They drove on like that, speculating, rehearsing, falling silent. Ryzhkov took a breath once the ambulance had climbed the hill and they were easing down the other side. Watching the road, rutted here because of the rains, and trying not to break a wheel. Once the speculation was done, they fell silent.

There was the trail ahead. It had been used, he saw, thinking that there were more tracks since the day before; now the mud seemed turned up a little more as they drove through the tiny village.

He thought maybe it was just his memory playing tricks on him, but then along the road he noticed more marks. They had to go slow and he saw it easily, and Yurovsky saw it too. Ryzhkov slowed and let the ambulance fall into a lower gear, began the climb past the little huts. Yes. Someone had come along the road. A wagon. Come along on some business, then returned along the same route. He could see it in the mud. He pressed on the accelerator.

At the village he began to see the extent of the betrayal. A man was outside his house; he looked up and gave them a toothless wave. Ryzhkov was driving up the hill as quickly as he could.

The wind had come up. It meant rain, more mud, Ryzhkov

was thinking. A hundred metres later came the turn to the mine, a hairpin that went down the bank, the trees growing close there and the track more or less invisible unless you were riding along from the other direction and looking for it. The cart tracks they had been watching also made the turn, the ambulance dropping to cross the low place in the road where rocks had been piled to make a ford, then the last climb to the mineshaft.

There were two horses, silhouetted there in the rising sun. Just standing there.

'Oh, God . . . oh . . .' Yurovsky had begun to chant.

He stopped the ambulance at the bottom of the hill. There were the bodies of Igor and his friend Vassili, the new father who hadn't, after all, deserted. Their throats had been cut. They had been eating, the plates were still in their hands. No sign of a struggle. Yurovsky was out of the cab and running up the hill to the office, and Ryzhkov made himself follow. There was a rustling of cloth as the wind came up, and he saw the flare of one of the grand duchesses' skirts, dressed for travelling – and then undressed. A wide red blood-stain spilled out from her hair. One of the older girls, he couldn't place which. Olga, he thought maybe. Her blouse had been ripped open, breasts exposed. Ahead of her he saw someone else, slumped against the office door – the Empress.

Alexandra, her clothing pulled down around her elbows, shot in the face, the blood pooling in her lap and on the steps there at the entrance.

He saw Yurovsky standing deeper in the entrance. He turned as Ryzhkov walked up.

It was Nicholas. The most powerful man in the world. The man whose word alone meant life and death. The man Ryzhkov had served for most of his adult life, as a subject and as a member of the Okhrana. They had turned him over. He had been shot in the back, and then again in the face.

193

They found another corpse in the shadows, and dragged her out into the light. Her body fell there at his feet and he saw that she'd been stripped as well. Anastasia.

Shot in the back, then shot again, a dark smudge in her golden hair. Around the campfire was her clothing, a hat torn to pieces. A travelling bag ripped open and spilled out.

He looked down in the dust and picked up something shining. A gem of some kind, blinding light smashing into his eyes. A diamond it might be. Big as an acorn.

Yurovsky was looking at him strangely. His hand was on his pistol.

'You didn't come back out here, before, did you?' Yurovsky said, taking a step back.

'No, no. Someone else was on to us. Whoever did it got past the guards pretty easy, don't you think?'

The family had been ready to leave. They were wearing their travelling clothes, and had packed. What was left of the Romanov luggage was spilled around all through the area. Each bag had been ripped through, but hurriedly.

Ryzhkov scanned the mineshaft, looking for the heir and Grand Duchess Marie. At the foot of the hill they found the other older sister, Tatiana.

'They're not here,' he said to Yurovsky.

'Who?'

'They're not here. Alexei and his sister. They're missing.'

'Do you mean whoever did this took hostages?'

'Yes. I think. Did you look in the woods?'

'No.' They turned and headed around to the back of the office building. At the corner, around at the short end wall of the building a window, not very big, had been broken. Through the hole you could see where someone had stood upon the old workman's bench, scrambled out through the broken mullions, run into the woods and then . . . then what?

He turned and went back out the broken door of the

office, stepping over Alexandra's blood that had curdled there into darkness. Flies had already settled in it and begun to colonize the threshold.

He pushed his way through the back into the great cavern where the Imperial Family had made their camp: a little pile of shavings, a samovar overturned, a woman's bag ripped open and dumped out, and there at the entrance the wheelchair that they had been using for the boy.

He walked over to it, stood there looking out towards the entrance to the pit, the long slope to where they would have parked their wagon, or cart, or whatever it was they used, next to the trees where the guards had set up their little kitchen. The guards had been killed close up, their throats slit with calm precision at the end of a meal. The empty glasses. The bottle. If you sniffed it you wouldn't smell anything. Someone just walked right up to Igor and killed him. Vassili hadn't even picked up his rifle. Someone they knew.

Ryzhkov stood there, trying to relive it all . . . Then there would have been a hurried explanation of the killings to the Tsar . . . there would the organizing of the family all in a rush, an improvisation by brave officers ready to die for you, they would have told the family. Let's load the boy in first, they would have said. They would have decided already to take the boy. They would have strapped him in, given him a painkiller. The Tsar would have probably helped them.

And then the betrayal. The killing frenzy, and afterwards they'd taken time enough to ransack the luggage.

But somehow she had got out the window. Escaped, he thought, perhaps in the forest yet.

He walked back now, out and back around the side of the building to where the glass was broken out. Pushed his way through the bushes, trying to follow where she would have run; the grass was all crashed down, and then he and Yurovsky were into the forest itself, and he lost the track.

'Can we follow them? Where would they go?'

'Just wait for a moment.' He walked deeper into the woods. A drop of blood on a birch leaf. Another. They would have taken the boy into town, take him into hiding.

'Ryzhkov, we don't have a lot of time,' Yurovsky was saying behind him.

Ahead the leaves were thrown up and he thought it looked like someone had fallen, perhaps skidded to the ground, to hide. They were right down opposite the place that the wagon would have been drawn up.

There was a little open space there, a riot of berries that grew in a thorny tangle. You could take a little trail through the brambles and make it onto the road there beside the wagon. He walked into the weeds, pushing aside the thorns.

And there on the bank he saw a scuff, a long comma carved out of the bank where someone had climbed up.

Climbed up to save her brother.

'We'd better hurry,' Yurovsky said.

They loaded the bodies into Propas's ambulance, working in their underclothes, because he knew they would have to go back into the city again.

Yurovsky went up to the mine and came back with two shovels, put them in the back with the corpses, pulled the canopy flaps together and laced them closed.

Ryzhkov started the engine and climbed in the driver's seat. He released the brake and they rolled away down the aisle of windy birches, the little ambulance labouring with its ghastly load.

'We'll put their bodies with the others. It's not far,' Yurovsky said. 'When we saw the water in the mine was too shallow we had to move everything. The men were tired. No one wanted to go very far.'

196

'No,' said Ryzhkov. There was no point in talking.

They passed the village and turned out onto the main road, beside the railroad tracks for a few versts. 'Slow down, it's just here.' They turned off the road and through the bushes. They called the place Pig Meadow, he said, but there was nothing there now.

'Slow,' Yurovsky said. 'We got stuck here before.' The ground was muddy, and he stopped.

The grave was hidden under some railway ties they had put down across the wettest part of the road. They came up easily, and the digging went quickly.

They stripped the bodies, and Yurovsky started a fire and stirred the clothing with a stick to keep it burning. Everything was too wet. Still too bloody.

A metre down he came upon the bodies of the servants. There was a stinging smell that grew with each shovel of earth, a mixture of burned flesh and acid that forced him to turn away to take a breath. The acid had burned their skin away in patches and they were bloated; staring at the sky, the leg bone beside them, the mud. Others leered like drunks, or like hideous unfinished sculptures, eyes half closed or burned away.

To make enough room he and Yurovsky dug out around the servants, taking turns as their fatigue grew. Grim work without talking. In the end they both shovelled angrily, until it was big enough.

When there was space one by one the naked Romanovs were piled on top. Everything was there for the viewing – the stiffened, blue-white, bloodstained limbs of the women, their hair shorn, eyes half-opened, mouths agape. The Tsar tossed in at the end.

He and Yurovsky stood there in the glade, looking at the grotesque tangle, then Ryzhkov raised his eyes to the meadow. It was just an irregular little field with a particularly damp patch at one end. Stubble and weeds that gave way to birches and pines. It could be anywhere in Russia. No one would find the place. The trees would reclaim it. The worms would do the rest.

No one would ever know what had been done to them.

22

For months she has prayed for salvation, given herself in promises to all the saints, to God, to the Christ. She has promised from the deepest part of her being. She will gladly trade her life for that of her family.

But mathematics creeps in. After some time there is no answer from God. Nothing from the saints. She sees symbols everywhere. In the moulding that ornaments the corners of the ceiling of the day-room in the Governor's house in Tobolsk. In the number of Alexei's coughs.

She is of this world. That is what she has learned from all her tutors. They have taught her logic, the hard rules. Always something abstract before; now the lessons have all come true.

Each day a repudiation of God, then. Each day a betrayal from God.

She no longer believes.

What kind of God would do all these things, these horrible things? What kind of God would put her, her family, her home and empire through all this? Put the world through it. A test? What kind of God would willingly inflict that much suffering on anyone? Women, children.

And her mother. Her poor mother.

What kind of God would do that?

A test. A test of faith, she thinks.

She thinks it is a test when the sailors and the Red Guards make remarks and push her into the little cabins on the boat, making free with their hands. It's a challenge. A test.

A horrible test, to live in the horrible second floor of the house in Yekaterinburg. To endure it. To watch the people she loves enduring it. And so she begins her promising to God yet again. What else can she do?

And God answers her.

He saves her.

Salvation comes in the form of a tall man, well kept, but obviously in a hurry, dressed like a clerk, who rides up in the most curious vehicle. A little covered wagon with a black curtain all around it, the fabric coated with some sort of shiny oil or tarry paint, that has been towelled on to make a shelter there. From the back a patterned blanket has been pinned up.

She first learns of the man and his cart when she is called by Anya to come and see. In the last few days, as often as possible, one of the children stands watch from the office windows. They carry a book or bit of needlework to cover their presence by the windows; it is like a kind of guard duty, and generally the solitude is comforting. After talking with their father, they have all been granted permission to engage the guards in conversation, even though fraternization has been strictly forbidden by Commissar Yurovsky. Nevertheless she and Anya, for they are the youngest and most innocent, still children in the eyes of many, they take every opportunity to gather gossip, rumours or whatever the boys who are guarding them might let drop, for that is what they are, boys, some of them younger than she is.

'When did he get here?'

'Just a minute ago,' Anya breathes.

'It must have been longer than that.' The man has already stopped his odd little cart and is explaining himself to the guards.

And that is when she begins to dissect his fine looks . . . and comes to find him . . . handsome, yes. In a dark way, an uncomfortable way that makes her nervous the whole time.

Could it be that he is frightened? she wonders. He does not look strong, not like a fighter, and she has seen a great many soldiers and sailors, so she can tell the difference. The guards have stopped him; he waits with his hands up. One of them moves forward, pointing with his long bayonet. She can feel her sister gasp behind her.

'Is he the one?' Anastasia breathes.

'Go tell Papa.'

'You tell him.'

So she does, and then bounds back in from under the great rock overhang at the entrance to the mine, and through the office. A place that she loves, with its racks of raw wooden shelves, little bins containing rusting hooks, screws, hinges, the whole thing smelling of oil when the sun warms it up. Little yellowing labels with numbers and abbreviations that none of them can understand inked there. And when she comes back he is still there.

She can see his feet – they've allowed him to get down and he is showing them something in the back behind the curtain. Just a little wagon, a wagon like a merchant would use to haul . . . something. Vegetables, she imagines. A little cart with its canopy covered in what looks like sewn-together packing bags, painted strangely like that. Something to keep the rain out?

Her father comes through the dusty little entrance and waits behind them, standing in the shadows, since under no circumstance are they ever permitted to show themselves at the head of the mine.

The guards reach in the wagon and take out two large sacks of food, but the man stops them. He has something special. He has brought a hamper. From one side of it she sees two bottles protruding.

'Oh, they are just getting their rations,' her father says.

'Our rations too!' Anya says, too loudly as is her way when she gets enthusiastic about something, and her father puts his hand on her shoulder. 'Come away,' he says, that weary disappointment in his voice, as he takes Anya out, leaving her to watch it all.

Her stomach growls, and she resigns herself to the jealous pain of watching the guards and the messenger eat everything up. No, she thinks, he is not the one. She will wait for Ryzhkov instead, who after all has promised to come, told them to pack, thinking once more that he must really be the one, the mysterious contact Yurovsky and her father have been waiting for, the angel that will take them away.

She looks around at the office, the windows fly-specked, stained with algae that has grown across the glass in green swathes fed by the wet summer. It's better like that, you can hide there, you can see out and not be seen.

A few minutes later Anastasia comes back, having escaped the Tsar's discipline. She is smiling, red-cheeked, and together the two girls watch the guards eating. It's all for the guards, apparently, for the young man doesn't seem to be hungry. He opens both bottles and does the pouring. He smiles. Lights cigars for the guards, cleans up the plates.

'That's supposed to be our food, you know,' Anastasia says, quieter this time. They're all hungry.

'I know,' she says. The young man walks off behind his wagon and from the way he is standing they can tell he is urinating. The guards are seated. One man lifts his cigar to his mouth with a long, contemplative movement. Anya is laughing in her disgust at watching the driver complete his business. He does a curious hopping, busies himself with his button, turns. Cigar still clamped in his teeth.

Now she begins to see it. The guard tries to sit up. The young man has gone over to him. Stands there watching. Both of the guards have fallen asleep. He stands there for a moment longer watching them. Goes back to the rear of the wagon and takes out something; it looks like a short stick, but as he walks back to the two sleeping guards he removes a sheath and she can see it is a knife, a bright shining knife.

'Oh God!' Anastasia says, as the young man kneels and draws the blade across first one, then the other guard's throats. It happens so fast, like stooping to pick up one rock, then another. And she can see the red blood spurting – watching him standing there, watching the sleeping men die. He is the one, she is thinking, as the knife vanishes back into its sheath, and he is walking up the hill towards the office, and Anya has already gone to tell Papa.

He is the one.

She can hear it in the low tones, the words imperceptible, the whole family awake now. See it in the way the two men embrace there at the opening, and him standing there, silhouetted against the sky, with a fringe of birch tops expanding behind him towards the horizon. See that, yes, he is the one, in the way her mother, summoning all her strength, swivels her tired hips out of bed, and Olga struggles with her shoes, and her father tells them all to get ready. Instantly. And she can see it in the way that Alexei puts away his whittling and helps them by pushing the wheels of his chair, until her father and the man lift him out of it and carry him down to the little wagon.

Her heart is pounding. Everything a whirlwind, as she

rushes through the office, grabs her coat, the single bag she will be allowed to take. All that's left, she thinks, looking at it. Now the cave feels like a some comforting fairy-story place from her childhood. Farewell little pillow, farewell rickety table, the crate that holds the samovar that she has come to love.

So lost she is in these reveries that she is late, one last check through of the place where she sleeps, hard in the darkness against the wall of the place where the smell of the earth is strong, and it is cool in these summer nights. Ever prudent Marie making one last pass to see if she has forgotten something.

And that is when she hears the shot that kills her father, and turns to see him standing there, and . . .

And that is when she hears the screams . . .

And taking a step forward, which her body stops her from completing, and Tatiana smashes into her there and her mother is following both of them . . .

And she sees over her shoulder, sees him shoot Anya there, spinning crashing down, and she runs . . .

Is running down the narrow little front of the office there down to the end, and thinking . . . thinking to take the stool and fling it at the windows, for back here, and Tatiana ought to have known this, there is no other way out, no escape, and flinging it at the glass, pulling it back and knocking out a way out, and running away from him.

And into the woods, through tangles that she just rips through, her face and arms scratched and knocking her down when she breaches them into the woods, and turns to see him shooting Tatiana.

And she falls to the ground and hides there, pushes her face into the earth and tries to stop the convulsions that rip through her body causing her to contract, like a worm or some other poor dying insect, stiff and kicking there in the leaves, both her hands crushed against her mouth to silence her sobbing.

When she looks again he has gone inside and she can hear him crashing around. She runs to the wagon and her brother, struggles to climb in the back of the shaking little contrivance, sees him there in the gloom, sleeping. For a moment she is scared to go to him, for fear that she might find his throat has been slashed too, but instead there he is, fast asleep, snoring like the guards.

The man who is not the one has thought of everything. With her father's assistance Alexei has been tied him down and bolsters put around him. A blanket covers everything. He will be comfortable. The women can ride around the side and one in front with you, Excellency, he would have told her father.

She is struggling with the knots, thinking that she will wake him, carry him, escape with him. They will run through the birches, run until she falls. Hide in the darkness. Run again, until they find someone to save both of them. She gets his leg undone and then, always checking behind her, hears it, his footfall on the slope.

In the little space above the flap at the back of the carriage she sees him coming, and her body convulses one time and she frantically digs at the knots.

He is closer now, and she is poised there next to her sleeping brother, with nowhere to go, shrinking back to the corner of the little wagon, trying to stop herself from sobbing when she sees the corsets in his arms, even now as he stuffs them into her father's travelling bag, and then he is at the road and she hides herself under the blanket, pushing right up against Alexei.

On the ride she has a chance to think about salvation. Her fingers explore the knots and she thinks about how she will free her brother. The dark canopy above her is overlaid with all the things she has seen, the sounds that echo through her. On the other side of the bed there is a box rattling about, and in it are the supplies that he had brought. A thermos, some bandages, a bag of what must be radishes, a large bottle of water; a saw, a small kind. She has seen her father use one like it for kindling.

As she has it in her hands, he pulls the wagon over and raises the flap to check on the boy.

And it is that long before he discovers her.

It is too quick then, and she is squealing, and he has come round to the back of the wagon, and all she can do is crouch there with the saw in her hands and wait, and he has the long and shining knife in his hands.

'Come here,' he says, angry now. It only provokes a spasm in her that pushes her even farther back into the vehicle when in one moment he climbs up into the wagon after her.

'Don't,' she says. 'Please, don't.'

'I'm not going to hurt you,' he says.

'Don't.'

'Which one are you?' he asks.

She says her name but it only comes out in a sob. She doesn't worry him at all. The knife is just dangling there. The young man makes a sigh. 'I don't want to hurt you,' he says. There is just the trace of a smile there.

'Please don't hurt us. We'll do anything you say.'

'Will you?'

'He's sick. He can't hurt anybody.'

The man looks at her for a long moment. 'But what good are you?' he says quietly. He's not even looking at her now, and she still has a saw in her hands. 'You know how to take care of him? You know what he needs?'

She nods her head. It's only a sound, a bleat that escapes her now.

'Come here,' he says, holding out his hand. 'Give me that,'

reaching out for the saw. 'I'm going to save him. And you too if you help me take care of him. Come on,' he says, and now the smile finally does emerge, as if he is tired of these childish games. 'Come on, give it to me.'

She does, and he puts it back into the box lashed there against the side of the wagon. Reaches out to take her hand as she crawls back out of the corner, and she give it to him – and the moment he has it he reaches back and smashes her with his fist.

Hard in the face. So that it brings blood and a moment of blackness as the universe rings, and she is knocked back onto Alexei's legs and down into the hard side of the cart, and suddenly his hand is between her legs, in that place, pinching down on her so that when she screams he pinches her into silence.

'You obey me now,' he says, pushing her deeper into the wagon with his hand. 'You do everything I say, or you die and so does he. I can snap my fingers and kill him, but I'll take my time with you,' he says, breathing against her face, and pushing her again, hard back into the bed of the wagon and turning her over, and she can feel him searching for something he can use to tie her up.

And he does.

And he is not the one.

And after he ties her there, no more talking, no more jokes, he steps over her sleeping brother and gropes in the box. Comes out with a green bottle, the kind used for champagne. It has a nipple attached to it like you would use for a baby, and he pushes it into her mouth. When she tries to keep her lips closed, all he does is tweak her nose. The pain causes tears and she gasps and swallows, tears, clots of blood and mucus, and something that tastes like water laced with cloves.

'Good girl,' he says. 'No noise now,' he says, and leaves.

And it goes dark when he pins up the blanket, and she listens to hear him walk around to the front, and she can feel him climb into the driver's seat, and flick the reins to stir the ponies to the task of carrying them down whatever road they are travelling on.

And she cries all alone hopelessly, like an infant.

No one has ever hit her before.

23

The leaves had parted above him as he drove the ponies along the last stretch of long open road approaching the edge of the city. Ahead was a barn, ringed by a too-narrow ditch that had flooded mud across the road. He gave the ponies a flick, looked over at the houses as he passed. All of them built to a nearly common formula, logs and high windows with filigree cut out to make it prettier. When the foundations settled, so did the house – ridge poles bending where they had been spliced, gutters draining to new locations and requiring repair before the snows. All of it twisted and bent, like a home seen through the water or a wasted lens. Ashes dumped, grass uncut, wild flowers growing up around the entrance. It or somewhere like it would do, if he had to go faster than he'd planned. He pulled his eyes away. It wouldn't do to be caught staring.

It was the way his mind worked, like a merchant's adding machine. Always whirring, grinding. Always thinking it out.

The princess was frightened now. Terrorized, her mind in vertigo. He could keep her around, sacrifice her if needed. She was something he could use however he wanted.

He had rehearsed what to say when he came up to the

checkpoint, driving the pony a little harder, calling out to the soldiers standing there beside a lifting gate they'd built in the last few days. There was a little bench there, and they were also working on a roof to make it more comfortable.

This was a test. This was the girl's test. He turned and looked through the flap to the back of the wagon and saw them both sleeping. Quicker now to the checkpoint, standing up at the head of the wagon and waving, calling out in advance to the sergeant. 'It's Dimitri's cousin's son,' he explained to the Czech. 'He's the one who supplies the hotel. The boy's got the fever and I'm taking him to the nuns. His sister too. She's unconscious. Do you want to look?' he said, shaking his head as if this wouldn't be such a good idea.

'You look,' ordered the sergeant, stepping back with a grimace, as if influenza were in bad taste. The second one went back, peered through the flap, saw the two children, and ran back nodding. All of it on the fly, the ponies not even slowing.

And he was through.

Into the city avoiding the centre of the city, avoiding the places where he would see any of the customers from the American. It was almost bound to happen. He was in the town now, coming down into the back of the station. An empty troop train was waiting, the carriages being swept out, the ordnance workers loading ammunition onto a flat car fortified with sandbags and a wedge of steel that guarded the train with a rear-facing heavy machine gun. The troops would arrive in the afternoon, and be fed outside, then they'd board and leave at night for the long pull to Perm.

Sophie's carriage was positioned near the ramps at the back of the yard, resting on the third track distant to afford the Baroness privacy, but able to be approached across the tracks for the convenience of various porters and commercial agents. Quietly as he could he drove the wagon onto the gravel behind the car, checked the ponies and looped the reins over a handhold at the back of the car.

Sophie was waiting at the door. He went around and looked through the flap to see if the children were sleeping, then climbed up to meet her. She made a little gasp and then threw herself at him there in the doorway. She made the big watery eyes that he hated, and they kissed.

'Everything? Were there problems?'

'No, no.' He put a desperate note into his voice. 'It's much worse, darling.' He brushed past her, moving into the car, pulling down shades, peering out underneath to see if he'd been followed. Thinking that the wagon would most likely be taken for a tradesman's, maybe even old Dimitri himself, loading vegetables. 'We have to get out. We have to get out tonight, as soon as possible.'

'Are they –?'

'The rest are dead!' he said, breathing hard. 'It was terrible, horrible. I saved the boy and one of the girls. They were hiding, wounded, near death. She is particularly traumatized. Those Red bastards.'

'Oh my God. Dead!'

'Executed. The Tsar, Alexandra . . .'

'Oh my God,' Sophie said again, reaching out feebly, clutching for the back of the bench seat there, collapsing.

'I'll carry them into your bedroom. And it's very dangerous, darling. Don't look outside. No lights.'

'Oh.' She looked around stupidly.

'And then we leave. All of us, together. We leave tonight.'

He climbed down out of the car and walked the ponies down its length, trying to use the bulk of the rail car to mask the rear of the wagon from view. It was only mid-morning and the light was sharp. So just go about things normally, he was thinking. Just pretend that it's all part of a normal day.

As he persuaded the ponies into place on the gravel, he shook his head in fury. It was almost like a physical revulsion he was beginning to feel about everything that was happening. Now that Germany was losing the war the Reds were growing in confidence every day. He'd poured enough gin down enough English and American throats and listened to their blurry complaints and spittle spraying bellicosity to know which way the wind was blowing.

It was a disaster, he thought, doomed: his mission, his war, his life. Come to a complete cul-de-sac and now he was facing a disastrous return through the gauntlet in order to save himself and get back . . . to get back where? He'd be traded soon, he thought. Sold by whoever was running Germany at the time. Maybe they'd already done him. There would naturally be some kind of deal made when the consulate shut down in Moscow. All the networks would crumble, and eventually someone would be forced into buying favour, and it would have his name on it. When the war was over maybe they would say of him that he was the last German spy to fail. They could chalk that on his headstone, if he was lucky enough to get one. Well, there was no one to grieve anyway, was there?

So now it was a question of getting out. And the girl might make it easier, he thought. Unforeseen, but true. A possibility, only just that. Starting to think the girl might be his way out.

Above him the door opened and Sophie hung in the entrance. She had a blanket in her hands, looked wildly around the yard. The kind of guilty display that was sure to be noticed if anyone was looking in their direction. She was down the step and by his side, hesitating to lift the curtain.

'We'll have to keep them asleep,' he said and reached up to pull the curtain away.

'Oh my God,' when she saw Marie's bloody face.

'Yes.'

'Oh my God. What happened to her?'

He looked at Sophie for a moment, as if speculating if she could take such bitter truths. 'She was beaten, perhaps other things . . .'

'Those bastards,' she said, reaching out to touch Marie's swollen face, the bloody lips, the nose flattened and broken. The eyes swollen, black and teary. 'The poor creature.'

'It's very sad. She's disturbed. Seen too much.' He embraced her, held her by the shoulders and willed his strength into her. 'There's not much time, darling.'

'What?'

'Help me put them inside,' he said, climbing up to the sleeping body of the girl. 'And Sophie, no one must know, eh?'

She looked into his eyes. 'Of course, darling.'

She held the blanket up to protect the entrance, covered the girl with it. Marie's hands were tied in front of her with torn rags. Blood had run from her nostrils and dripped across the bodice of her nurse's uniform. They supported her between them and carried her into the carriage, put her on the large bed. Sophie reached to untie the knots, but he stopped her.

'She's violent. I had to subdue her just to get her to come along.' He guided her out of the compartment.

They were careful with the boy. Thankfully he had not been abused. It would have killed him, Sophie thought. Up in the compartment they put him beside his sister on the bed. His pants were wet with urine, and she rushed to put a towel underneath the two of them.

She turned to see him at the end of the car. He held a travelling bag in his hands. There was a long smear across the leather and she realized it was blood. The bag had been stuffed with what she thought for a moment were bedclothes

213

and then she saw that it was the corsets and underclothes of the Romanov women. He had taken a corner of the material between his fingers and was rolling it over, feeling for the jewels that had been sewn inside. He looked up at her.

'This is a very good job that you did. So,' he held up the corset, 'this is what they were after. Only, because they didn't have you, they didn't know where to look.'

'Thank God,' she said, and suddenly she teared up. It was like a great weight being removed, knowing what it meant, knowing that the jewels were there, and so was their escape. She turned to the sleeping boy and girl, brought her wrist to her nose and tried to stifle a sob. Then he was beside her, thrusting the bag in her hands.

'Listen. There's no time for that,' he said giving her a shake. 'You've got to be hard. There's no hope for any of us if we get caught. When they wake up, give them a swallow or two of this, but hide these.' He pushed the bag into her arms. 'I'll be back and then it will be your turn, darling. We've got to get those passes, eh?' He smiled and kissed her hard. Then he went out to hide the old man's wagon.

She stood there for a moment, and then tried to follow his progress as he crossed the yard by peering out under the shades, moving along from window to window, until he was gone.

She walked back to the bedroom, stood there watching the children for a few moments, tried to recognize the Grand Duchess Marie through the swollen face of the girl on the bed. Alexei looked like a little grandfather starving to death there on the linen. There was a curtain that dangled from the ceiling, woven of fine netting meant to confuse the bugs that swarmed up in the night, and she pulled it around the sleepers and went back to her place by the window. Pulled the shades down on the sunny side of the car, and sat next to the door where at least there was a breeze. Thinking to herself that it would only be until they got to Viatka. In Viatka they could get help for the children. Then together they would be recognized as heroes. He would hate it, of course. He might have to live a clandestine life forever, she realized.

Now she cried again, cursing her fate.

And the horror of it, the murder of the family, the Tsar, the butchery of her closest friend. It was too much to comprehend. She lifted her head and gazed out the narrow doorway towards an array of empty railroad tracks slashing away until there were the backs of fences and the trees beyond.

It might be easier to escape with just the two children, she thought. They could be moved about as two invalids. If necessary she could go out or have someone sent to get more of the drugs. Keep the two of them sedated for the long trip out of Russia. After all, it was dangerous. Anything could happen. They would have a doctor look at Marie's face, someone who wouldn't recognize her. She saw herself standing over the two of them, – she had always been a strict influence on the children. Persuading them that compliance was necessary. 'It's your life, you understand,' she envisioned herself explaining. 'Take your medicine.'

She imagined herself in a few years, the way she would be. In Paris. Coping with it all. Refusing to comment on the past, or at least until the right opportunity was made. Then dictating her reminiscences to a battery of secretaries.

She is standing in front of high and sun-drenched windows, the Seine stretching away into the gathering approach of a dramatic autumn. She is turning to the boy, who is taking down her memories in shorthand; a smile to bestow the appreciation and blessing of a . . . mature woman encountering a beautiful young man at life's threshold, and helping him to understand the passion of it all.

Yes, Conte Giustiniani would let himself be bribed, she thought.

215

24

An emergency in Moscow.

What some were saying was the nadir, perhaps the turning point of the revolution, the crisis when all would be lost.

For Velimir Antonovich Zezulin, hiding behind his alias as Boris Noskov, it was a time of no sleeping, a marathon through which men and women stumbled, gasping, collapsing like tangled marionettes once they had crossed the tape.

Now he had been granted a reprieve and was walking down from Lubyanka Square towards his quarters at Savelovski street. It was the first time he had been outside the building in five days and his steps were loose, his body off balance and nearly defeated, leaving only his curious and threadbare soul. Sinking inevitably towards the river.

A car would be sent around four hours later, and then he would be back into it all again. What fresh hell would await him? More perpetual emergency, more desperate men and women, more blood, more death, more life without sleep?

The most recent crisis started in the morning. Within the Bolshevik world – a world already full with civil war and counter-revolution – the assassination of Petrograd Cheka commander Michael Uritsky panicked the entire security apparatus.

Zezulin had been in the bathroom when it happened. A junior clerk, over-excited, coming through the doors, blabbering in disbelief. In the corridor people were sticking their heads out of the offices to hear the news, everyone telling their neighbour the supposed facts, but except for one alleged telegram no one knew anything. Rumours were the floor upon which they walked.

A man, some clerk he had encountered in the corridors, told him. 'Uritsky's been had,' he said.

Uritsky was one of Lenin's great friends. He wasn't the type who needed to prove himself all the time. Personally he was known to be uncomfortable with the settlement at Brest-Litovsk, and therefore sympathetic to the Right SRs. He had been in the revolution from the start, and he'd been awarded command of the Petrograd Cheka. He'd been on the way to work.

A young student cadet had been arrested. All they had was a name – Leonid Kanegiesser, admitted member of a group called the Union of Regeneration. Neither Zezulin nor anyone else had ever heard of it.

Immediately Zezulin locked away the files he was working on. As he did up the bindings, he reflected on the serendipity in police work. After all the planning, the strategies, the theatre, the cover-stories and rationales, it was the unforeseen that might yield the most benefical opportunity. The trick was in seeing it.

Thus, on a secret note of optimism, began the torment.

A cable reported that the assassin Kanegiesser had been captured trying to hide in the gardens at the Petrograd English Club. That was enough evidence for Jacob Peters, Dzerzhinsky's favourite, who was in charge.

Zezulin had a meeting with Glivenko, his superior, who

wanted to know more about 'Seventeen', Monsieur René Marchand, correspondent for *Le Figaro*. Zezulin told him the man was still working as a Cheka informant and that he had to be protected.

'You realize this is just the beginning of a plot,' Glivenko said to him. 'This is perhaps a plot to decapitate the revolution. We have to look at everyone all over again.'

There would be reprisals for the killing of Uritsky. It was going to be hard and fast, this was certain, and Peters was ready to use his tools. He had a wild head of hair and way of looking in disbelief, always a little cross-eyed with pain. Like a boy on the edge of a tantrum. He so dominated the meeting that Glivenko had to fight for space to deal with 'Seventeen'.

It was a kind of theatre. Peters stormed across the room. 'Just do what you have to do, and then bring them all in. All! All on this list, and any that you want for yourselves. Fucking bring them all in,' Peters was spitting. He shoved a list across Zezulin's desk and left.

It was two typewritten sheets with additions in Dzerzhinsky's hand on the second page and then some other names. The handwriting was Peters', Glivenko's in a place or two, and others.

It was the kind of list that made you want to whistle. Carte blanche to drag in a lot of people who considered themselves important. Only the Americans were absent.

He looked up to see Glivenko walking up the hallway with the commissar of the Latvians assigned to guard the buildings at Lubyanka 11. They were talking about putting a machine-gun emplacement on the third floor.

He put the list in a folder, picked up a clerk and together headed for the dispatching office. The boy was run off his feet already. Scared. Zezulin, feeling charitable for some unknown reason, tried to cheer him up.

'What do you think of the idea of the proposed fortifications?' he asked the boy.

'It seems to be the necessary thing.'

'Could it not be the wrong message?'

'Excuse me, comrade?' the boy said, trailing off.

'Could it not be seen as an act of cowardice? Surely we are not afraid of a riot or demonstration from the people?'

'Not from the people no, but there are the Latvians . . .'

'They are the heroes.'

'Yes, I know, but . . .' the boy trailed off.

'They're elite soldiers, but not really Russians, and therefore . . .'

'Therefore they are suspect. Yes, comrade inspector.'

Zezulin turned to the boy and gave him a pat on the shoulder. 'What you say is true, but if you get rid of the pegs what holds the boat together, eh?'

Victor Mulgounov worked in a large suite of closed offices near the corner of the building with a fine view of the Moskva. The window, a source of paradisiacal daydreams for some clerk before the war, was propped open with a ruler, and the clerk had to put weights on the papers. Together they went over the list.

'This is very interesting, this group,' Zezulin said, reading down the columns. 'This includes the entire French and British legation, everyone who is still in the city, all their operatives. So . . . I think the jaws might be closing, eh, Victor Andreievich?' Everyone laughed, including the clerks.

'Lockhart, Robert . . .' Zezulin began reading the names. 'Reilly, Sidney; Boyce, Ernest. Here's one of our Latvians, artillery regiment commander Colonel Berzin, Eduard; and then a group of French –General Lavergne, Colonel de Vertement, they are both Deuxième Bureau, and Consul-General Grenard . . .' The clerks began writing furiously. In

219

addition to the embassies, there were personal addresses all across the city.

'And this Elizabeta Otten, she is an actress. Did you ever see her, Victor?'

'Otten? No. I don't know. Perhaps.'

'Very attractive girl. Here, this one – have them pick up anyone at No. 3 Sheremetiev Lane.'

'Anyone at all?'

'That's what it says, anyone. Mademoiselle Friede, she is a teacher. Is that a Δ or a Ω?' He swivelled the paper to the clerk so he could read the jottings.

'A Ω, I think,' the boy said.

'Hmm . . . Madame Jeanne Morens, director of the St Peter and Paul School for Girls; Mademoiselle Olsson, also a teacher. This one, Plodski, journalist and a paymaster, it says. He will have some money on him if we're lucky.'

When Zezulin finished he let his clerk go back and waited while Mulgounov sent out the protocols. They were organized by districts, and one by one the flying squads went to work.

The same thing was going on in Petrograd. Everyone was being rounded up. There was a gunfight at the British embassy. The railway stations were shut down to try and cordon off the agents Reilly and de Vertement.

The word came around that Peters had taken charge of the Moscow Cheka. Lenin had ordered Dzerzhinsky to take a special train for Petrograd, the better to defend the revolution against what was now being seen as a coup attempt by a combination of counter-revolutionists and Allied spies. The jaws were closing on all the foreigners and anyone else they could get.

Someone brought tea around.

Word came to remove all objects from the sills of the windows in order to prepare them for soldiers who would be putting sandbag emplacements on the second and third floors. All of Lubyanka Square was being blocked off, and any vehicles were routed through one at a time.

In the afternoon they discussed how to manipulate 'Seventeen's' revelations without revealing Marchand as the source.

Glivenko's strategy was: 'Tell them that he has learned about this fantastic thing, and he has to tell it to someone, anyone. He's a journalist after all, but it will mean death if he speaks out. And because his conscience is troubling him he writes a letter to someone . . . his lover, his mother, his –'

'The President of France.'

'Sure, why not? His priest, and he talks all about the coup, but before he can mail it we discover it in his apartment.'

Zezulin had dozens of agents he was controlling, ten who were important, four who were very important, and most recently Ryzhkov, whom he had kept completely private. Not even an expenditure. All of his agents represented a commitment of money and time. They were livestock, and like livestock they had to be taken care of. But it was different with Ryzhkov. Even though he had been bought cheap, Zezulin still had a faith in him from the old days. Sentimental, true, but at least they understood each other, two *gorokhovniks* who'd managed to keep the noose off their necks.

With Ryzhkov on his mind he made an excuse to go by the cable room. He fretted about Ryzhkov, then told himself not to, that there was very little that could be done.

The wires were down at Kazan.

No one knew if the Fifth Red Army army would fight or run. The only connection was to the military headquarters train occupied by Comrade Trotsky at the station at a little town called Svyazhsk. Military traffic was taking precedence. He would need authorization for any cable they sent to the

221

railhead at Trotsky's headquarters, the man said, face blank with refusal.

'Ahh, well, thank you, comrade.' Zezulin turned away. Kazan was too far away, and he didn't want Glivenko to know anything at all about his interest in Yekaterinburg.

He lingered in the hallway, smoking and looking out to the courtyard where they were beginning the first of the day's executions. He had seen them doing it often enough that he could criticize an individual death squad's technique. In the hot weather the worst were the ones that didn't properly wash down the cobbles.

The results of Jacob Peters's dragnet were obtained piecemeal through the long afternoon. Sandwiches were brought up and placed on the conference table. The clerks went running about serving their masters. There was a giddy democracy of danger spreading around the samovar.

'Seventeen' had been arrested and his apartment had been raided, he'd been delivered to the building and there he was, sweating theatrically. Glivenko sat down to interview him about the coup. It was being blamed on the British military attaché, Robert Lockhart, at present safely locked away in the Kremlin.

Marchand admitted he had been present at a meeting in April. His big revelation was that representatives of all the Allied spy services were there: Reilly, de Vertement, and the even an American named Kalamatiano.

More details came in about the gunfight at the British embassy. The naval attaché was dead. Killed on the stairs in front of his wife because one of the Red Guards had ripped off the Cross of St George he'd been awarded by the Tsar, and he'd resisted. A matter of honour. They'd arrested forty of the embassy staff and were tearing apart the walls of the embassy looking for documents.

When Marchand was done reciting his script, Peters could

hardly help but smile. They sent him back to his cell, the kind with a bed, a desk and reading materials, and had some food brought round.

And then, at the end of a long day of shocks, came the attempt on Lenin.

When the news came, the office paused. As if all the breath had gone out of everyone's lungs. The kind of moment that you remember decades later, the details of the mundane chore you were performing that evening.

Then, as if a tide had begun to turn, he heard the first murmurings and reactions, the sound of the typewriters stuttering with their endless transcriptions, the exclamations of disbelief and the stifling of sobs.

For if Lenin was gone . . . then what?

A moment passed, another. All the phones rang at once. It was the latest reports.

Lenin had been giving a speech at the Michelson factory. They made arms of all kinds there. He had been talking about the need for the proletariat to completely eliminate the bourgeoisie. By that point his audience had learned about the murder of Uritsky and the speech was particularly well received. As he was getting into his car, two women approached him. They were complaining about the attitudes of the searchers and how they stole food from the passengers on the railroad. Then it was reported that three shots were fired, and he had fallen, with one leg in the car and one down in the gutter.

The assassin had fled.

Then more telephones. The assassin was a woman. She had been caught. They'd put her in a car and on her way.

And out the window the sirens growing until they filled the courtyard.

From her photograph, Zezulin thought, she might have been a pretty enough girl. When they found her she'd been

223

leaning against a tree, exhausted from running and from the shock of what she'd done. She had an umbrella and a brief-case with a bottle of water and a half-finished jar of pickles inside.

My name is Fanya Kaplan. Today I shot Lenin. I did it on my own. I will not say from whom I obtained the revolver. I consider him a traitor to the revolution. I will give no details . . .

She was a Jew and a revolutionary who had done eleven years in prison for trying to kill a Tsarist official in Kiev. She'd been a hatmaker when the February revolution came along and changed her life. When the Constituent Assembly was dissolved she blamed Lenin. Another purist SR hothead.

No one touched her. They let her talk and she was eager to say her piece, as if getting it on record might mean something. The kind of woman who was out to change the world and didn't mind throwing her own life into the fire. She was under the impression she'd killed Lenin and they didn't let her know differently. Waiting for her to boast. She did, and they took it all down.

After I was freed I favoured the Constituent Assembly and I still support it. My family are in the United States since 1911. I was educated at home. I shot Lenin . . .

They spent their time trying to establish her relationship to Kanegiesser and his association, but she knew nothing. Glivenko was sure she was one of Lockhart's women. In the end they decided they'd got everything out of her they could and they left her alone for a while.

That next morning they learned the details of Lenin's wounds. She had hit him in the neck and chest, and his lung had been punctured. Still he had tried to climb three floors to his rooms in the Kremlin. They'd taken him there instead of a hospital because they were afraid that the Left SRs would try to murder him.

The executions became wholesale on that second day of the crisis. It was impossible to work in the Lubyanka and avoid the sound of the firing squads. Even refusing to look and with cotton in your ears you could still see the smoke, wafting in on a cloud above the courtyard.

That afternoon Zezulin was present when they gave Fanya Kaplan her last interview. Glivenko asked the same questions all over again, about Kanegiesser, about Lockhart and Sidney Reilly. She just stopped talking, and that was when they decided that they would try and get a reaction out of her by bringing in Lockhart. When they put them together, it didn't work. Either they'd never met or they were good enough actors to suppress any signs of knowing each other.

They shot her in one of the courtyards, and left her body for the rest of the day just in case anyone missed the point. No words, no proclamation.

In the newspapers the next morning there was to be no mistaking the new direction of the people's revolution:

> We will kill our enemies in the scores of hundreds. Let them be thousands, let them drown themselves in their own blood. For the blood of Lenin and Uritsky let there be floods of blood of the bourgeoisie – more blood, as much as possible . . .

They hadn't been hard enough, Jacob Peters was complaining. No longer. Now it was terror unleashed: Death to the bourgeoisie. Mass terror that broke the borders of the imagination. Mass terror as a lesson to the masses. Five hundred and more executions in that first week.

But why talk of numbers? Why take the luxury of even making an accounting in the first place unless it was to inspire even more terror? They were setting a new standard for fear, partially because it was being experienced in a thoroughly modern way – in large scale, and in snatches of statistics that were supposed to make it understandable. The Red Terror, they called it. No empty phrase.

> . . . the least opposition, the least movement among the White Guards, is to be met with wholesale executions. All of the government's efforts are to be directed towards ensuring that there be no hesitation or indecision in carrying out mass terror . . .

So on this day . . . Thursday, or maybe it was the Tuesday, Zezulin's mind no longer had the ability to make the pieces fit, but after the fifth morning, when it was realized that the emergency would never end, and that the revolution would be better served by organizing the work in shifts, after too many gunshots in the courtyard and too many lessons learned and recited, they let him go home for four hours.

He decided to walk through the wakening streets, even as he only wanted to recline against a warm wall, feel the muzzy humidity manufactured from his own body, and snore into the crook of his arm.

Along the route he passed a stamp-collector's shop and noticed the fragments of a great plaster Romanov double eagle that someone had discovered and thrown out. A crack had spread from the bottom and split the face of one of the eagles.

The sight of the relic stopped Zezulin and he stood there swaying for a moment, looking at the plaster fragments arrayed in the cobbles. How impotent it all looked now.

Life was about loyalty, the allegiances that moved ordinary men and women to commit fantastic and terrible deeds. Life was about to whom or what regime that loyalty was owed. Each person had to decide, he thought. Who do you owe it to, the revolution, an idea? The party, the great man? Your friends, your class? And what happens if you have to compromise?

How irrelevant the broken eagles looked! How much had life moved on to other less fanciful things. The Romanovs were no longer intimidating and frightening characters. They only represented a category of human abuse. Association with them was now a taint that could not be washed away.

He turned away from the visions and rocked off down the street, thinking, thinking, thinking. Everything was a blurred Cubist illusion, the face of the Tsar melting in the architecture of a fallen-down building. The sounds colliding in his brain. Everything beginning to go pen-and-ink, like walking through a drawing of himself, caught in a world where dimensions slipped and slid.

At his apartment door he saw that the seal had been broken. Someone had stood on the little mat and crushed the sunflower shells beneath.

A message? Nothing tucked under the threshold. A glance down the short hallway, only two doors, thinking that if they were going to arrest him it was going to come from down the dark little hallway.

Nothing.

The face of the lock looked fine. Of course, he thought. It would look fine.

He had kept nothing incriminating or even interesting in the rooms, but maybe they were planting something. Maybe someone had learned a little too much about comrade Noskov. Maybe they were going to give him ten minutes' rest and then come with a protocol and the evidence cleverly hidden under the bed.

For a long moment he stood there in the hot little hallway wondering if he should just back out of there.

But everything was quiet.

He felt for the pistol that he carried, an inconvenience most of the time, a lump permanently attached to his kidney, something that he had grown around in those most recent days of the emergency.

He sniffed, jiggled the key in the lock, waited to hear a footfall from inside, then turned the lock. The door swung open and he saw the match-end hit the ground. The second seal.

He stepped into the apartment, closed the door and locked it. Went over to the window and suddenly threw it open, fiddled with the revolver. It was impossible for a man of his age and condition to go across the roofs. Absurd.

If they were coming for him there was nothing he could do. Knowing that feeling that way was what you did when you gave up. Your weakened body sent you messages that the most prudent course would be to simply quit. Your weary muscles and aching bones overruled your addled brain and you began to believe that your situation was hopeless, at best a fifty-fifty proposition.

So, he thought, he had a choice. Back out of there, or die.

But it wasn't just lack of sleep and nerves rubbed sharp by the emergency. Now he knew that someone was watching.

It had been smart of whoever had come in, re-sealing the room that way.

Smart, except that he hadn't ever put the match in the jamb in the first place, since the broken bit of match always lived there on the surface of the rug. If it had been repaired and put back in place, it had been disturbed – that was the true seal.

Yes, he thought, struggling with his shoes as he fell back onto the bed. The revolver sliding under the pillow . . .

Be what you are, he reminded himself, to justify his sleep. A man dog tired. A lump of earth. Be a tool of the Cheka.

Be a man who had given up more times than he can remember, and who was someone ordinary, accommodating and invisible.

Sometimes it was best not to do the smart thing.

25

'Hey. Hey you, Moscow stranger.' Someone was calling. A familiar voice . . . Eikhe's woman, he realized. Veni.

'Come on. We've got to move. They're kicking you out, and I'm a woman, they don't want me anyway.' Standing there beside her was a boy, one of the novices. Right. Yes . . . he remembered, after the graves they'd made it back as far as the monastery. She'd come to get them.

He got to his feet and went to wake Yurovsky, but he was already up to a squatting position there on the floor outside the kitchen of the monastery. 'How long have I?' Yurovsky groaned.

'It's almost noon. We've got to get going.'

'Where?'

'In case they decide to move them.'

'Oh, right, yes.' Yurovsky made a kind of spasm with his body and swivelled up, against the wall. 'So you didn't run away?'

'There's no point in it. We either find the two and take them to Sverdlov, or we take ourselves to Sverdlov and beg for mercy. That's the way I see it, eh?'

'There's tea inside, some bread,' Eikhe's woman called to them.

Across the little courtyard the goats had eaten away the grass at the edge of the wall. There was moss growing under the tree. The boy walked away silently and vanished behind a crumbling wall.

'Here.' Eikhe came out of the door. A glass of tea was placed on the stones beside him; she broke a black lump into halves and gave them a portion. Bread. He sniffed it and began to eat.

It was gone in moments. He drained the tea and walked over to the wall and urinated, staring at the tiny creatures living amid the stones – fleeing the flood along nearly invisible crevices that were their neighbourhood byways. An unseen god brings chaos, terror and death on a microscopic scale. Worlds within worlds.

Veni Eikhe escorted them through the monastery gates. She was carrying a carpet rolled up under one arm and didn't want to stop even though she was breathing like a dray horse. Ryzhkov and Yurovsky took it away from her, and she puffed along beside them.

As soon as they were away from all the prying ears and eyes she was suddenly angry. Hissing. '. . . and that's why I'm saying to you, get out now! Get out. Go back. It's your revolutionary duty not to die! To hell with them, to hell with the Romanovs, I say.' She had got out ahead of Yurovsky and was swatting at his chest, as if a fly was stuck on his shirt front.

He batted her hand away. 'Don't, old woman.'

'I realize that I am not supposed to know anything about your secret work, comrades, but this is absolutely absurd. It's so important, these people? To hell with them.'

'We have to do something first,' Ryzhkov said.

'You've tried to keep me out of it. Fine, I appreciate the consideration, comrade. But sometimes a person who is on the outside of things can interpret more clearly. What I interpret

231

is that you're both fools being taken advantage of by other fools.'

'Good, fine. Thank you for your thoughts and comments, comrade. Now this is what you have to do.' Ryzhkov began his list.

They walked up the hill to her house and cut across the grass there, the fence no longer functionally necessary since there was no livestock to pen. They lugged the carpet through her crowded tent-workshop and out to the yard behind her house. Spread it out on the grass to let the sun get at the mildew. Fantastic patterns sewn in some far-off place, shapes in a code that only Moslems could understand. Mysteries. For a long moment he stared at the patterns, hypnotized. When he and Veni went inside Yurovsky was already asleep in her chair.

Eikhe just looked at him and sniffed, shaking her head. Not for the first time she realized the gulf between revolutionary thought and revolutionary action. Peasants, workers, intellectual workers, small producers – they could have all the fine ideas they wanted. They could burn up tons of tobacco and drink vats of tea and fill up every café in Yekaterinburg, but it wouldn't get anything done. Action was required. It required will and persuasion. It required someone to make an example of themselves, to stand in the front lines.

'So,' Ryzhkov said, 'you understand, we're throwing up a cordon. We're making sure they don't leave the city.'

'Fine, then. Don't listen to me.'

'We have to find them. That's our mission. I can't explain it any better than that. I need your help, Madame Eikhe.'

She looked at him. A man who was handsome in a tired way. Face etched with sadness – not unusual in Russia the last few years. He could use a good cleaning, and a visit to a barber. A little on the lean side, not really an ox . . . more of a horse.

Veni Eikhe was a revolutionary, but she had never been one for this type of thing. In truth she was, had always been, a coward. One of the talkers, whom she was fast coming to despise. She had always recoiled from the potential for violence. Hated blood. Hated to kill a chicken. Oh, she'd done it, of course she'd done it.

She'd seen plenty of death. Cleaned and laid out her own father's body. Sewn people up with her own hands. And killed thousands of chickens on the way.

But, truthfully, it wasn't her nature.

So, the alternative? To be a lady?

That was a bad joke. Who was she? A widow of a metal-worker. She wasn't going anywhere. It was time to fight for her own survival. If, in the process, she ended up making the Urals safer for others who had been dealt the short straw, so much the better. To be someone higher, educated, and with a life reading poetry and sniffing exotic blossoms? Well, fuck them, the ones who'd taken it all, and then taken more, and the way they had looked at her, those faces . . .

Life had always equalled work. In her very bones she knew the difference in character between those who made things and who knew how things worked, and the idiots placed above them. She regarded as poor wretches that legion of women who owed their position to an accident of birth, or to money, or beauty. They only existed blindly, precariously up there atop the heap, living in a giddy world behind glass, protected from the elements, not even having an idea of what lay outside.

Now they were hanging from the lampposts, their kind.

And she'd seen those same poor women, eyes wide open for once, lining the streets trying to sell whatever was left, their finest Parisian dresses, their heirlooms, their most precious baubles, that little something special he had given her . . . But there were not enough buyers, and she'd watched

233

all those beautiful women as they started to shrink, day by day, their fine skin growing drier, more wrinkled. Their posture slumping, the smiles erased as the hunger began. Until the Czechs had showed up they were just about gone, seemingly swept away like fine particles of dust.

Well, who needed a ball gown in a revolution, anyway?

But even seeing them, and knowing that they could be, were being beaten, that a Tsar could be brought low and an entire people rise up and take power from nothingness – and even knowing it, and living through it, and even after learning her own strength that she measured against those aristocratic bitches', still she was frightened.

Each time she took a step outside she had begun to tremble. She would stand there at the threshold, her mouth screwed up and her teeth pressed together, unconsciously squaring her shoulders, girding herself to face whatever might come.

Oh, she was probably being watched. She had neighbours who would turn them in for half a potato. And there were others who no doubt remembered Eikhe's activism in the mills. They might already have seen them coming and going – two able-bodied men carrying a rolled-up carpet? You might as well put out a sign. Revolutionary plotters live here, special today, half off.

So . . .

They would catch her eventually. Kill her eventually. She knew it. She knew it in her bones. And maybe that was it, she thought. Maybe she was simply afraid of her own death. Of the pain of it.

She stood there in fear, but in the end she still stepped across the threshold. There was nothing else she could do but say yes to Ryzhkov's big idea.

So she crossed the threshold, she dodged the Czech patrols, although if truth be known they were not so much patrols as collections of idle soldiers, happy to be some several hundred versts behind the so-called lines. The Czech cavalry rode at random around the city, searching for Bolshevik stay-behinds. Frustrated, they had to bring home someone for questioning. It could be a woman as well as a man, and so she took her time on her walk across the city. She was as innocent as one can be. Just an ageing woman, walking the wide streets in her heavy rolling way, humming to herself. On the way to meet another revolutionary, and persuade them that the time for talking was done, now was the time to act.

Svishov is an example.

He is one of those who are always the loudest in a bar. Crippled and angry at the bosses, he nurses his grudges; they multiply like seeds in spring when he drinks, which is quite often. But he can talk, and he can get others going. So for that he is useful. It is always good to have Svishov involved because the others know there will be a party afterwards, and that regardless of what actually happens he is sure to put the touch of victory on it. Any confrontation is a triumph for Svishov, and that, simply, is his value. You won't find that lesson in any of Comrade Lenin's writings, she thinks, knocking on his door.

She is greeted by one of the children, not Svishov's, he is too old, probably his son's, who has gone now for more than a year, vanished in the last great battles that were supposed to save the world for Kerensky's government. Vaporized and part of the soil of Galicia, Eikhe thinks, although Svishov will never admit it; the boy will be coming home one day, he still thinks. Maybe on crutches, maybe with his sleeve pinned up, but coming home down Voznesensky Street, as sure as there is no God.

When the child rouses him, he comes to the door and invites her in. They move though the hideous little rooms, everything stinking that peculiar smell of men and sour milk.

They fetch up at the yard, and for a moment she thinks that Svishov is going to woo her, having been without a wife for some years, and she without a husband. They stand there awkwardly just in the back of his tiny garden, overgrown now except where the children have been digging in the corner. A table surrounded by high grass. They push their way through and sit. He has not thought to ask her to stay for tea.

She begins, using Svishov to practise her spiel, for the day will be given over to mobilizing surviving friends of the Soviet, loyal communists and fellow thinkers, volunteers who have gumption enough to keep their mouths shut, or gossips that she knows, the ones for whom politics is of no importance but who are willing to report on what they have seen from their front window.

'There's no one to turn to for directions or instructions,' Svishov declaims, slapping the table top with his hand for emphasis. It is his rule to live by. Something to stitch onto a pillow and reflect upon for the rest of your life, leave it to your children for their edification: always remember there is no one to turn to.

'Exactly, there is no father. Father is dead. Now we have to think for ourselves. There are no more meetings, there is only action, eh?' That's the way to do it with Svishov. Flatter him into thinking he's a great thinker. Agree with him, then sink the hook.

'Yes, yes. Fine. Anything you need, Veni,' he says, smiling. With the state of his teeth, missing or brindled with tobacco stains and decay, it is a terrible sight. Perhaps he is flirting with her?

'We are looking for two children. A boy and his sister. The boy is younger, perhaps sixteen, the sister a year or so older. We don't know their names, we don't know their importance. They have been stolen away and hidden somewhere in the city.'

'Sure, sure. Whatever you say.'

'No, listen, Svishov. It's very important. Not something that can wait. We are looking for them now.'

He hears her, coughs, straightens in the chair. Her request means he will be forced into activity. He becomes serious. 'Fine,' he says again.

'Thank you so much. I cannot tell you how important it is to have your help.'

He shrugs. 'And you're certain you don't know their names at least?'

'No.'

'Fine, I see.' Then the terrible smile creases his face again and the devious mind takes flight. 'So these two anonymous children are so important that for the past day they have been kept hidden? Why would that be, Veni?'

'We are not told, Mikhal Petrovich,' she tells him firmly. Sometimes you have to be that way with him. If he is going to be one of the inner circle he will have to work a lot harder than he has so far. The rest of us only serve. Now it's his turn to serve.

'I see,' he says, looking at her with his rat-catcher's eyes.

'Right now we are instructed to be organizing a watch on the roads in and out of the city. But we need to watch the lake also.'

'They are trying to take these children away?'

'Perhaps.'

'The lake. That's a good one. They might try to get across it, it is true.'

'So, these children, it is only one day since they were stolen. It might happen tonight that they are escaping. They must not, do you understand?'

'Tonight? So soon?' He looks at her blankly, shrugs. 'I'm free tonight,' he says with another carefree smile. Oh, God, he is flirting with her. Thinking it best that she leaves, she stands, forces a smile of her own.

'If they are spotted, a flying squad will come to rescue them and deliver them into the custody of the Ural Soviet, do you understand?'

'Yes, comrade,' he smiles, making a salute. Everything is a joke to Svishov. 'But how am I to do that? I thought everyone had gone.'

'No, everyone is putting their heads down and hiding. We are stronger, even now, stronger than most people realize,' she says, making her voice sound more confident than she actually is. A revolutionary lie. For a moment he looks at her.

'To whom do I report?'

'You know Kitsovsky at the store, don't you?'

'Yes, of course.'

'He will be at the store or ready for you at his home. Just there.'

'Kitsovsky, of course,' Svishov says, remembering that Kitsovsky too has been a feature at the barricades, and the parties afterwards. 'My cousin will help,' he offers.

'Excellent.' The cousin is an alcoholic and mentally deficient, but a pair of eyes nevertheless. 'With our people on all the exits, there is no other way out of town.' She smiles, glancing at the reddening afternoon sky.

'A real people's opera!' Svishov says and raises an imaginary glass to the pageantry of it all.

'True enough. Many thanks to you, Mikhal Petrovich,' she says, grants him the slightest of touches on his filthy shoulder. If he's flirting she might as well take advantage. Only for the sake of the revolution, of course. With a certain amount of gallantry he rises to see her to the door, and as they go through the darkened interior of the house she can hear the laughter in his voice.

'Two children. Very important. I thought they'd all been killed a couple of weeks ago.'

It causes her to turn on him there at his door, with her eyes gone hard as flint, a hand now on his chest, stopping him. The foul mouth drops open in surprise. For a woman to do something like that, to push a man around, is not done. Not done at all. Still he is propelled backwards a step by her strength.

'We do not know their names, do you understand?'

'Yes . . . I . . .'

'We're not to even ask. It's best not to even think of it.'

'All right, yes, I see.'

'It's for your own good, comrade.' She waits for a moment to see how he will take it, and then leaves, her temper getting the best of her. Her heart flittering away in her chest by the time she has got out onto the street. Suddenly sweating now, exhausted, and it's only the beginning, only the start of her quest to sew the city up, as tightly as she can.

And . . . yes, like a people's opera, it happens.

Stitch by stitch, it closes into a perfect red sack; a worker here, pretending to sleep by the side of the road where it leads to Moscow. Another man and his brother repairing a wheel on their cart on the opposite route out of town. They seem to be taking it leisurely, even thought the day is near ending. A pair of watchful boys sit on the bank and watch their fathers, ready to go running if that's what's required of them.

For everything is suddenly important on this strange high summer day, with rumours flying through the city, and a strange electric buzz that seems to have galvanized the most unlikely people into activity.

The fishermen are very busy seeing to their boats on the docks, and even old Gorgan, who hasn't stirred from his house in days, is surprised to hear the news when his friend tells him.

'Yes, Gorgan, it's true. Your wagon, the one that that fool

239

put tar all over the top of. They found it on the road by the station. The horses baying with hunger. You were robbed, man!'

'No! I didn't even know it was gone!'

'Yes, and do you know what, Gorgan? There was blood in it.'

'No!'

'Yes. I assure you. Blood. And a thick bed, and a pile of bloody rags inside. Come, come and see!' he says, provoking the old man to slip on his shoes and venture outside into the sunset.

26

'Of course,' he told her. 'Everything has changed. The days of Ivanis the bartender are coming to a close.'

'Who shall I play?' asked Sophie.

'We do everything openly. You pose as a rich aristocrat ferrying two wounded children to the custody of special doctors. It's all maintained by relatives. The children's family obviously has money. We're en route to Viatka, then as soon as the tracks open, north to Archangel and into the arms of the British.'

'Who shall I play?' she asked again.

'You are simply yourself. No play-acting needed. We are saving you and the children, and myself in the bargain.'

'You've already done so much.'

He smiled at her for a moment. To give her energy. 'I will become a doctor. We will travel on your special pass, granted from the White government in Omsk, by way of your friend, Signor Giustiniani.'

She sat up in the bed, hugged a pillow to her breast. She liked to play shy; she still thought he liked her that way.

'Anyway, that's the plan,' he told her, and knew she would go with it. After all it was an emergency.

'Everything has changed,' she said. 'In one bloody day . . .'

'Go and get the pass, kitten.'

'Yes, I'll help. You know I'll do whatever you want.'

And she had. She had helped from the moment she'd learned that he was a spy, a German spy dedicated to bringing the family to safety. Told her of his own secret identity, pleaded with her. Another good German, like herself. He needed help, he needed a place to hide, he needed her.

And she had said yes.

As a German, he told her it had long ceased being a question of allegiance. His orders were to ignore the military situation. It was a question of cooperation between empires. Yes, they were fleeing to the British, but all sorts of people were involved. He himself was only a small cog in the machine. The moment the words came out of his mouth she knew it was a lie, and that made her fall in love with him.

It was a modern world that called for practical methods. She knew now that diplomats made their own rules. Get the family out, that was the task. Everything was being prepared. It had to be secret because it was kings helping kings, he had said, knowing she would understand. And she had understood.

And then, in a single day . . .

He had rushed with his team of patriots to the hiding place – of course, without telling her until the last moment, a rescue plan so secret that even she had no inkling, and afterwards coming to her with blood on his hands, in failure. And that was how strong his love was – he refused to tell her everything.

For her own protection.

In return as a sacrifice to this higher love she agreed to abase herself. 'Go and get the pass, kitten,' he'd said.

She smiled and prepared herself to do it. Doing horrible, forbidden things in the service of God, and consoling herself with how wonderful it would be to be the one that saved Alexandra, the Tsar . . . the children. A turning of the tables, and very satisfying. She would be revered as their saviour, her value finally acknowledged. And of course she would continue to serve the Imperial Family as trusted confidante and exemplar. One day princes and princesses would read books about Sophie Buxhoeveden's heroism.

She put out a finger and touched his lower lip, gave a sleepy smile of her own. 'Sleep,' she said, 'because tonight we have to put on a show.'

'Remember,' he said, 'we're doing this for them.' He glanced back towards the rear of the car.

'Oh . . .' she breathed, and pushed her face into his chest.

For God's sake don't do any more crying, he thought. 'You have to be strong,' he said after a moment.

She looked up and smiled at him, eyes filled with tears, then collapsed into his chest again and threw herself upwards to kiss him.

'I'll be strong,' she said. Foul breath. Suddenly he was sick of her. It was everything he could do not to throw himself off the bed and get out of the car. He patted her back down into the covers, sighed. Outside the windows the light had gone rosy with the end of the day. She would have to bathe soon. He decided to get away from her before that.

'You should sleep,' he said. 'I've got some things to do.'

'I have things to do too.'

He heard rather than saw the pout, brushed it aside, walked her through it one more time. 'We're joining with the military train tonight. When you come back –'

'– with the pass –'

'With the pass, we'll be allowed to go, but I want to be ready, with our car made up into the train, so we can get out as soon as possible, you understand? So to do that, I have to pay the man his dues.' He gave her a pat on the rump and swivelled his legs out from the sheets.

She said nothing for a time, then while he was dressing she raised herself on one sleepy elbow and watched him. 'The cruelty of man knows no bounds,' she said.

He looked over at her while he was buttoning his trousers. 'You're right,' he said.

'Please, can you go and find a doctor? I want a doctor to see them.'

'No, no, not now. Tomorrow in Perm we can try for a doctor.'

'She can hardly breathe.'

'We can't risk it. Keep the door shut. Make sure they keep drinking. They will sleep through it all.' He finished with his buttons and knelt beside the bed, took her face in both his hands, gave her the smile. 'I love you,' he said.

'But you saw her, she's hurt.'

'No,' he said firmly. 'We cannot take the chance. Once they're on to us, the best that can happen is that more good men will die. Listen, Sophie, you have to be strong.' He gave her a little shake.

'As strong as you. You are my hero.'

She was not unattractive, he thought. If you didn't really look too closely at what you were doing. 'What time do you see him?'

'I go for drinks at seven at the club, then to this restaurant where he has taken a room. As soon as he gives it to me, then –'

'Then you go into your act.'

'Yes.'

'Promise him the world, but get a headache. The food doesn't agree with you . . . or tell him that you're . . . you know –'

'Bleeding? Ohh . . .' she hissed. She didn't even like to think about it.

'Well, you know what to do,' he said. He went around to

244

her desk and found the envelope he'd made up, tucked it away in his jacket.

'Yes,' she said, rolling over, looking at him speculatively. 'I know what I have to do.'

'It's hard work, but you're good at it,' he said and reached out and pinched one of her nipples.

'You're filthy,' she groaned. 'You're making me into a tart.'

'I bet you like him, don't you? Just a little?' Why wouldn't she? From what he'd seen in the American Hotel he figured the Italian for an aristo with a mind. Trim and tougher than he looked, sharp enough to cut, and as soon as he'd seen that he'd stayed away from him.

'I loathe him.'

'Well, just don't let him know it.' He watched with disgust as she took his hand from her breast and licked his fingers. Where she'd got that from, he had no idea. Something they did in St Petersburg, he decided. He jerked his hand away. 'He's not stupid,' he said, a little too firmly perhaps. Reached down and touched her cheek by way of apology. 'Now listen. I'll come to you once they connect the car. Then you give me the pass and I'll go and fix it with the dispatcher. You won't see me, I'll board the train at the last moment.' He smiled. 'Remember, I'm still a bartender. Probably a bartender without a job.' He turned away from her and straightened his hair in her mirror.

'I'll do anything for you,' she said, reaching out and grabbing at his leg as he walked past her.

'Everything is going to be fine,' he said, pivoting in the doorway. A courageous wave. 'Remember, I love you. I love you and everything you stand for.'

Tears and that thing with her eyes, a kiss blown to him as he turned for the steps, and then . . . thank bloody Christ, he was out of there.

* * *

Walking quickly across the gravel, just another one of the endless stream of tradesmen, journalists and dignitaries that the Baroness had received, his hands in his pockets, fingers patting to make sure the envelope was there.

He crossed to the duckboards at the edge of the track, walked down to the platform, along by the public wash-rooms, and the long house where they stored the freight, and past the entry to the saloon, took the little door and climbed the stairs to the dispatcher's offices.

Varga was there and greeted him with a smile. 'So, is everything arranged for her ladyship?'

'Good evening, Monsieur Varga,' he said, taking off his hat. 'She's asking to leave tonight with the troop train.'

'Ahh . . . just as you said.' Varga made a face, shook his head.

'I know, I know. These people with the blue blood. They have no idea of the problems.'

'Luckily for you she has money, eh?' Varga smiled.

'It's good to have a real job, for a change.'

'It's what I need,' Varga mused, rocking back in his chair. 'To be private secretary to a countess . . .'

'Baroness.'

'Baroness, then. It's all the same to me. As long as I don't have to fight their war, I don't care, friend.'

'Amen.'

'Well, I can probably arrange her for tonight, just as we discussed. Do you have the pass?'

'She's getting it.'

'Can't do anything without a pass.'

'She swears she's getting it. I'm sorry, you know. I have to try and do what she says.'

'Fine. There's also the price,' Varga said. He leaned back in the seat, folded his hands across his belly. Enjoying every minute of it.

246

'She's given me five hundred new roubles.'

'Oh, come on.'

'There's not much left in the larder.'

'There are costs all the way down the line for something like this. Something private. We're in a war, after all.'

'I have this . . .' He reached in his pocket and took out the ruby. It was something one of the Romanov women had sewn into a hat button. Not particularly big, about the size of a little fingernail.

'Hmmm . . .' Varga fished for his spectacles and looked at it under the lamp. 'Well, I don't know, what can I do with something like this?' He shrugged and tossed it back across the desk. 'I need something negotiable. Jewels have lost their lustre, I'm afraid.'

He nodded. 'How much?'

'To go beyond Perm is going to cost you. At least another five hundred for me, and probably some more for the boys down the line. You don't know until you get there, eh?' he said, and then, seeing his expression, 'Sorry, but that's life in these modern times.'

'Are you going to be here later?'

'Certainly, but don't come back unless you have the pass and the rest of it. No pass, we'll have to break the train. Then there will be a report in the log and I'll get in trouble.' Varga held his hands up in a defensive gesture.

'I'll bring everything tonight, just before we go.'

'Well, I suppose I could put her at the back, ahead of the armoured car. There's another car that's carrying supplies between them. At the stations it will be quieter.'

'That would be best. Thank you.' He reached for his wallet.

'No, no.'

'As an instalment, just to get things started. She understands what you're up against. Very difficult times, not without sympathy.'

'Ah, yes.'

'She may have some things delivered. Where shall I tell them?'

'We'll make up the train and she'll be at the very end of the platform.'

He climbed down from the offices and went out onto the platform. For a moment he waited there in the purple dusk. A man lit a cigarette across the tracks and leaned against the wall of a little brick canteen that had recently been built. It was where the firemen and conductors went for their breaks. A quartet of porters waited at far end of the platform, lounging on the baggage wagons that were parked there. The troop train was drawn up on the opposite track, curls of smoke coming from the stoves in the cars. A pair of sentries walking their posts with a sluggish pace.

Everything quiet.

Simple. Pathetically simple, he thought.

27

The jitney honked for access as it shifted into a lower gear
for the climb up the hill to the station. At the stop Ryzhkov
picked up his jacket and made his way down to the street.
On the square in front of the station a White battalion had
formed up. Now the men were collapsed on the sidewalk,
smoking, playing dice, sleeping and clowning around.

There were a few civilians gathered at the entrance, more
lined up at the telegraph kiosk and at the windows where
you arranged to ship parcels to somewhere safer. He went
over to the freight windows. The clerk had come out and
was helping people with their packages. Mostly it was
personal goods, battered trunks, suitcases that had been
wrapped around with rope, paper and glue. Everyone in
Yekaterinburg was still in flux, uncertain about what would
happen next. The Whites had been stopped at Kazan, people
had already heard, even though nothing had been in the
papers about it. Trotsky, they said. Trotsky was coming.

When the clerk was done, Ryzhkov leaned in and asked
him, 'How many trains have left today?'

'None.'

'Nothing? Nothing at all?'

'Tonight is the first.'

'But it's for the troops, isn't it?'

'We can get your packages out as far as Perm but not until tomorrow evening. Everything else has been cancelled.' The man had spotted Ryzhkov as a non-paying pest.

'What about the other way?'

'Eastbound we take parcels in the morning,' the man said, and then moved along, having given Ryzhkov all the information he was entitled to.

Pyotr Ryzhkov suddenly felt as if he stuck out in this little city where everyone knew each other by name. If Giustiniani's men were watching anywhere they would be watching the station. He wanted to make contact, but he didn't want to make a scene. He could see the way it should happen, imagine it like a rehearsal, but as he stepped out into the foyer of the station it still made him uncomfortable.

Eikhe had her own circles she could go to for help, but for Yurovsky, since the flight of the Ural Soviet, it was best if he stayed hidden. If they were going to have a chance of finding the children they needed any help they could get. That was the way the cards were falling. Accordingly he had decided to take advantage of his somewhat slovenly appearance, unshaven, with clothes that were quite filthy now. He could use a haircut. Some sleep. Food. He looked so bad that he figured no one would recognize him.

He walked by the saloon and peered in. A handful of old men perched at a table, and the man behind the counter telling them the truth of the matter, whatever it was. No one he recognized. He walked straight through and looked out the glass doors onto the platforms.

They were making up the military train. There was a crash and a line of grey passenger wagons shivered as the shock moved down the couplers. The man at the bar had fallen silent.

250

No. If they were moving, they wouldn't try and get out by rail, he thought. It was just too difficult, to much attention, surveillance. If they were travelling with two grown children, if they decided to make a run, he decided that they might try to get out the same way he had planned, across the inner pond and onto the big lake, then down to the railhead and then to Simbirsk. If they were making a run, which was by no means certain.

He turned and walked back through the saloon, got to the door and ran right into Ilya Strilchuk. As soon as he saw him he tried to veer away, but it was too late. Strilchuk put out one arm and grabbed him by the bicep. Ryzhkov pulled away and for a moment they both faced each other there at the entrance to the station.

'Where have you been recently, Pyotr Mikhalovich? We've been missing you about the office.'

'I've come here because I wanted to find you.'

Strilchuk laughed. 'Come on, let's go.' He reached out for his arm, and Ryzhkov took a step back. For a moment they did a sort of tango dance there, with Ryzhkov walking back, slowly, just enough to keep out of reach. Looking for somewhere to run if he had to. He'd seen enough to know that Strilchuk was there by himself, but if he had a whistle, if he thought he needed it, he would have used it. If he was going to use his gun, he would have pulled it.

'Don't,' Strilchuk said. 'Don't.' For a moment it sounded like there was genuine sadness in his voice.

'I've got some news for you,' Ryzhkov said.

'Come on now. Don't make this any worse. You're surrounded, in case you haven't noticed.'

'No,' Ryzhkov said, and stopped, looked at him steadily. 'No, I'm not surrounded. You are.'

Strilchuk stopped, reached out and took him by the elbow. Stopped because Ryzhkov was suddenly so calm.

'What are you doing here? You're crazy, you know? I'm taking you in. You're playing both sides. We all know it.'

'That's why it's important that you listen to me, Ilya Stepanovich.'

For a moment Strilchuk looked at him, his expression turning to a cynical smile, a shake of the head. 'All right. What do you have?'

'I know you won't believe this, and I know it sounds like I'm raving, but the Grand Duchess Marie and the Tsarevich are alive.'

'Please, Ryzhkov.'

'Yes, it's true. I swear it. They're being held somewhere in the city.'

'Yes. Come along now.' Strilchuk reached out for his arm. Ryzhkov tore it away roughly and pushed him hard in the chest.

'You have to listen to me,' he hissed. 'You have to help me find them.'

'Why?'

'Because . . .' For a moment he was thrown by the question. 'Because they don't deserve to be abducted and murdered any more than you do.'

'I thought they were all dead already.' Strilchuk was frowning.

'All but two.'

'And you know this because?'

'I saw them, Ilya Stepanovich.'

'You –'

'I saw them. I know.'

Strilchuk took a deep breath. A frown had grown across his brow. An insoluble problem. An unforeseen complication.

'You don't lie to me, Ryzhkov. You tell me a lie and you are dead.'

'I saw it. I know.'

'And you say the two alive. They're being held here?'

'Somewhere in Yekaterinburg. We think so.'

'We?'

'A great many citizens living in the Yekaterinburg area are of the common opinion that they are being held here, Ilya Stepanovich. So. Help me find them.'

'Why? Why should I ? What's the rush? Didn't they kill millions, them and their kind?'

'Their kind?'

'Didn't they? They sent us out there without boots, Ryzhkov. We didn't even have rifles.'

'Killing,' Ryzhkov said. His eyes had hardened, and he began to walk away down the wide entrance towards the steps.

'Wait, wait,' Strilchuk said, and caught up beside him.

'You talk about killing. When it comes to killing, I saw plenty of people doing the killing in France. Rich or poor, you don't seriously think those two children were personally responsible for anything like that?'

Strilchuk had him by the elbow again. 'It's them sure enough. It's their mothers and fathers and aunts. Their blood, which is held to be so much more valuable than our blood. And it's all those like them, their friends. I don't think they'll suddenly convert, instead I think they'll throw off childish things. They'll be just the same when they grow up.'

'So you don't care if they're murdered.'

Strilchuk shrugged. 'Honestly, not much, no. What gets me is their ignorance and yet them thinking they're patriots and the rest of us aren't, the way they think they deserve everything and that their problems are so terrible to bear. I could be their cop for my whole life and if my children died they wouldn't bat an eye. And you, Ryzhkov, you're a cop and it's a measure of what an idiot that you are that you still protect them.'

'Well, that's what cops do, isn't it?'

'Certainly, yeah, yeah. We all know our place. Know our job, maintain order. You don't have to tell me, comrade. I think we know where we stand now, don't we?'

'Not really, Ilya Stepanovich. I'm trying to save two lives, and even my own, if I can. What are you doing? What is your fantasy? That the Bolsheviks are going to let some sort of Social Revolutionary democratic republic flourish here in the Yekaterinburg hills? Are you going to run for office, become chief of police?'

'Yes, I may. I may indeed,' Strilchuk said. He walked a couple of paces away. His hand was still on the butt of his revolver. 'I'm not a Red. I have absolutely no sympathy for those people. I really hate politics, you know?'

Ryzhkov just stood there.

'I expect that they will make a demand of some kind, don't you think?' Strilchuk said.

'I . . . I suppose they must want something. Money. Now they are hiding, and sooner or later they will communicate. I don't know, Ilya, I don't understand any of it. I never dealt with a kidnapping before,' Ryzhkov said, before remembering that he had, but from the other side. 'Well . . . not for ransom anyway.'

'You say they are missing. Why couldn't they be dead, just like the rest of the family?'

'No,' Ryzhkov said quietly. 'No, they're alive.'

'Fine then, Pyotr Mikhalovich, let's say that I believe you. What do you think the local authorities should be doing? Adding some men to the checkpoints?'

'At least.'

'Put a boat on the lake?'

'Yes, that would help. Down at the far end.'

'Then we all search together?'

'We're looking already.'

Strilchuk laughed, took a step or two away from him, turned and looked out over the rooftops, shook his head and ran his hands over his arms like a man washing. He was tired too, Ryzhkov saw.

'Well . . . together, then,' Strilchuk said.

'I'll tell them,' Ryzhkov said.

Strilchuk looked at him for a long moment. His hand had moved to the butt of the pistol again. Finally an expression that fell somewhere between a smile and a sneer crossed his face. 'People would pay a lot for the heir to the Russian throne. Kolchak would love it. He could put the boy up there at the head of his army.'

'He can barely walk.'

For a moment Strilchuk looked at him. The smirk had gone away. 'All right, Ryzhkov, I'll help you. I'll steal your ideas and keep it quiet and start it up, but you'd better keep hidden. I didn't see you tonight, and I'm not going to stick up for you if you get picked up. There's a protocol out for you, I suppose you know?'

'I've been busy, so . . .'

'Ahh, well,' Strilchuk said, and then looked at him. Ryzhkov was shabby, the clothes rumpled and torn, sweat and dirt-stained. He smelled. 'You'd better lose yourself,' Strilchuk said, and stayed to watch after Ryzhkov turned away, headed across the square, and vanished behind the corner of the railroad hotel.

28

The world moves, then moves again. A noise that is familiar yet distant, and the earthquake that comes when they hook the private car up to an engine. For a moment she dreams that she is in her own compartment aboard one of the Imperial trains, heading south for Livadia and a long vacation in the sun. She must have been sleeping for a long time, she can't even remember being driven to the station, or dinner, or kissing her mother good-night, and then she stirs, and feels something against her leg, and then still in sleep she turns her head . . . and then she remembers.

And so horrible is it, so shattering it comes crashing down onto her, that she flinches in her half-sleep, turning her head, and that brings tears, and she tries to breathe, and can't, and then she jerks awake and begins to sob. Because it is still happening, it is all still happening, not merely some hideous dream. And one by one, the pages of the story turn for her; the exile to frigid Tobolsk, the brutal trip to Yekaterinburg, the jeers of the mob, the imprisonment in the stuffy little house, the escape to the mine, and then . . .

The world reels. She is weak, too weak. Just a girl, just a princess after all. And she falls back onto the pillows. Outside

256

the world begins to slowly slide away. She can see through the cracks in the shade.

But . . .

But . . . here she is. In a rail car, she realizes. Here she is. No longer tied up, with her brother beside her. She realizes that the bed is damp. One of them, maybe both of them have wet the bed in the night. She groans . . . and can hear someone coming down the aisle towards their room.

And then, miracle of miracles, the little door opens and Aunt Sophie is there, putting on a smile.

'Oh, my little girl,' she says, and the smile immediately turns to one of pity as the cool fingers reach out to touch her cheek. 'Oh, my poor, poor child.' And it reduces her to tears once more. 'I wish we had some ice,' Sophie says, still caressing her cheek.

In all the commotion, Alexei begins to wake. Still everything is dizzy, confusing. Her strength is gone. He looks up at her, blinks. 'Hello, Auntie,' he says, making his impish smile. Trying to rise. He can't muster the strength either.

'Oh, my,' Sophie says, touching the sheets and then recoiling. 'All these will have to be changed, and I don't think we have any others.'

'I have to go wees,' says Alexei in a tone that suggests the wonder a child would have when looking at the moon. He tries to get up to one elbow, but can't manage it. Sophie pulls the blanket off, and suddenly it is cool. She falls back against the pillows and waits her turn while Alexei struggles to sit up, Sophie muttering under her breath. Never good at housework, Sophie. Not surprisingly, since it had always been something for the servants to do. Now everyone will have to learn new tricks, Marie thinks with a tinge of quiet satisfaction.

The door closes. Alexei is sitting there, steadying himself with one hand against the wall. He smells, smells like a boy, salty and musky. Reflecting on it, she supposes they both smell; the compartment smells of piss, and something metallic, the way it does when they've put you to bed against the influenza and given you the latest potion.

'So we're free,' Alexei says. 'We've been saved. We're free, Mima.' His head turns. She can't quite focus on him, but sees the smile. He needs a haircut. It's all grown out shaggy since the last time.

'God,' he says, frowning. 'What in hell happened to you?' She only looks at him, raises her hand to her face. It feels like a second skin, something hot and stretched, a blister ready to explode. Her fingers stray across her cheek until they find her nose; gone is the pert little ridge, now it is a fiery flattened swollen prow that blocks her vision and brings tears if anything touches it. He doesn't know, she thinks. He doesn't know anything at all.

'There was some trouble,' she says.

'Where's Papa? I want to see Papa,' he says, struggling to get up. Slides his rump off the bed and begins to stagger towards the door just as Sophie opens it.

'No, no,' Sophie says. 'Here, use this. I'll wait outside.' She hands him a bowl to do his business in. Marie obediently turns away and looks out the window. The door closes and she knows, knows without seeing or hearing it that Sophie is blocking it with her back.

Outside, through the crack in the shade, she sees railroad tracks, lots of them. They are in a marshalling yard. In the distance is a line of bushes, a fence. The backs of buildings. Behind her is the rippling sound of Alexei urinating into the bowl.

'How are you coming along in there?' Sophie calls through the door. Not even an answering grunt from her brother, the prince. The tinkling sound stops, the door opens. Sophie takes the bowl away. Alexei abandons his attempt to leave the compartment, falls back on the wet bed beside her, rolls over and pushes himself against her side.

'Don't worry, Mima,' he says. 'I'll keep you safe.' His hand crosses her breast and ends up next to her face. It hurts and she flinches away. 'Oh, God, I'm sorry,' he says, and moves his hand to her shoulder and pats her. The way you would soothe a kitten.

'Something terrible happened,' she begins.

'Yes, yes,' he murmurs into her shoulder.

'Something terrible.'

'It's over now,' he says.

Sophie comes back in. 'Take all those clothes off now, you two. You can wear these.' She gives a pair of her own pyjamas to her brother, a Chinese silk robe for her. 'We have to do the sheets. I'm going to have to get someone to get blankets. And there's not all that much time.' She helps Alexei tug off his clothes, stuffs it all into a suitcase that she'd dragged down the corridor. Marie woozily undresses while lying down, shivering, as Sophie strips the sheets off the bed around her. Struggling into the robe. 'If you bleed on it, it doesn't matter,' Sophie says, as if this is a good thing.

'He was the Devil,' Marie says. It's all she can remember, all she can compose of the story to tell Auntie. Somehow it's all whirled around and she's been rescued from the Devil.

'Here. Come and clean up. Help me get you clean and then you must sleep.'

Marie begins to sob. A wet cloth, something warm and lemony, but it hurts too much and she pushes it away. Sophie delicately moves the robe aside to see if they hurt her down there. No, and Marie shakes her head, jerks the robe away out of Sophie's fingers, turns her face to the window. Now outside they have reached the start of an empty platform, and she clutches the robe around herself in case anyone is there to see, but there isn't.

259

Sophie is wheezing with the effort of stuffing all the laundry into the suitcase. 'There,' she says triumphantly. She's accomplished something.

Marie looks over at her standing in the doorway, one long strand of her fine hair gone awry. 'Something terrible has happened,' she manages to say again, and Sophie looks up at her and for a moment Marie thinks that she too is going to cry. 'It was awful.'

'Yes, darling.'

'No. He was the Devil, the real Devil.'

'Where are we?' Alexei groans.

'On our way home.'

Outside Marie can see the edge of the buildings, the checkerboard roof tiles of the main station, remembers it from when they arrived in wintry April. Still in Yekaterinburg, but leaving. Leaving.

'Don't worry, darlings. Don't worry. Everything will be all right. You have to sleep now.'

'I want to see Papa,' Alexei says, even as he lets her push him back down onto the bed.

Sophie hesitates for just a moment, and Marie realizes that she knows. It's going to be their little secret they keep from Alexei, a little secret to keep him quiet and help him get through the rest of it.

'Here,' she says. Drink this. It will help you get better. Sleep, my darlings.' A crystal tumbler of water is passed to each of them. Alexei drinks like a man in a desert. When it gets to her she does the same, and then recognizes . . . something. Something from her memory, her childhood . . . from before.

'Something terrible,' she says. Her tongue is thick and she's not even sure if she made a sound. Anyway, no one will listen to her. It is always the way. No one has ever listened to her.

260

Too late, she understands. The taste of cloves. Closes her lips. Too late.

'Peace above all . . . still and quiet, still and quiet . . .' Sophie says. She reaches out into the corridor and comes back with a blanket, something grey and scratchy that the soldiers use, puts it over both of them. Marie can feel Sophie's cool fingers touch her forehead, the only part of her that doesn't sting. 'We'll take care of your face when we get to Perm. Both of you. We are going to be getting you a doctor, all right?'

'Yes,' she says, and her voice seems like it comes from a distant place. The light from the window is hazy, rippled and shot through with rainbows, but it might just be her tears. She experimentally tries to breathe through her nose. It only makes a sucking sound and a pain that turns everything white for a moment.

'Don't lock this,' Sophie says, as she goes.

Alexei stirs beside her, looks up to the window, and then falls back, coughs. 'I want to see Papa' he says again.

Sophie reaches back inside. She has a handful of sticks, his little whittling knife, the half of a tin soldier that he kept as a charm. A rock. He'd taken to keeping talismans in all his pockets. 'Here, these are all your things. They're all up here.' She dumps them onto the little shelf built into the wall. The door closes. She's gone to do laundry.

Still restless, he moves his bad leg against her. She slips over against the edge of the bed to accommodate him.

The car is gliding along and he wants to see. He pulls the shade back and gazes out the dirty glass as they roll past a signal switch. Standing there beside it is a signalman.

'Hello. Hello, idiot,' Alexei says. They roll on a few more metres. There must be others on the platform that Alexei can see.

'Hello to you, mentally defective Jew.' She hears the laughter in his voice.

Everything is dissolving, everything . . .

'Hello, stinking half-wit.'

The sound of the door opening and she opens her eyes and sees the blur of Sophie reaching across both of them to pull the shade back across the glass.

'Hello, Auntie,' Alexei says.

'Hello,' Marie croons softly as she falls, falls away into darkness.

'Keep this closed. We're still in danger, children.'

29

'What do you think you're doing here, Ivanis? I can't have help that comes and goes as they please!' Pavel Florinsky, the manager of the newly renovated Hotel American bar glowered at him in the darkened light of the storeroom. He had entered the hotel from off the alley, hoping to avoid exactly this kind of thing.

'I was sick. I thought I had the flu.'

'Sure, sure. Just get out. I can find a hundred more bartenders who know the latest drinks in Paris.'

'I doubt that, Pavel Egoriovich. Honestly. I was flat on my back. Ask my landlady. I was shitting blood.'

'Ach . . .'

'It wasn't very nice.'

'If you're sick, I don't want you around here.'

'That's right. I knew that so I stayed away.'

'Well, how was I to know about your health? Why didn't you send someone?'

'I sent the boy. The little one. Manda's cousin.'

'Who?'

'They live down there just below me. I sent him. I dropped a rouble out the window to him, told him to tell you.'

'You should box his ears, then, because he never showed.'

'He might have told Giesa or Loman.'

'I'll find out if that's the case.'

'Well, I'm here, and it looks like you're busy.'

'We're always busy lately,' Florinsky said, his mood changing. Everything was fine; there were plenty of customers rolling in.

'So, look. Why don't I put on my uniform and get to work, eh?'

For a long moment Florinsky glowered at him still. Idiot Slav, he was thinking. Always pretending to be tougher than they were. That was the great Russian failing, the pretence of strength when the true qualities were lacking. Bluff and bluster; all you had to do was push them and they collapsed, just like at Tannenberg, he thought, smiling.

'All right, what the hell,' Florinsky said, slapping him on the shoulder. 'I admit it, when you're around you're a sophisticated fellow, but let me know next time, eh? There's a lot of planning that goes into an operation like this.'

'Of course, Pavel Egoriovich. My apologies.'

'Apologies don't sell bread,' he said, and vanished into the shadows. Now that he was here, maybe Florinsky would take off early, get back to his young bride. An addled girl that he had taken, a trophy of his new good fortune as a hotelier in the revitalized, White-controlled Yekaterinburg.

He watched Florinsky go, then moved through the storeroom and into the large saloon. Loman was there behind the bar, doing his job, and laughed, glad to see him.

'There's no more schnapps,' he said. 'And we're out of the British whisky,' by which he meant Scotch. The girls were moving trays filled with glasses of *konyak* out to the customers. Almost all the tables were full, and there was a wall of men and women clustered at the bar shouting, screaming, laughing. It looked like one of the outer rings of hell: civilians mingling with soldiers and embassy personnel, a scene of madness and hysteria, political arguments, seductions, and the boozy recollections of soldiers who'd been shot at in dozens of conflicts ranging across Europe. Admiral Aleksandr Kolchak's day certainly had arrived, he thought. Congratulations to the Supreme Ruler of the new Russia, *varieté blanc*, he thought, looking at them all. Ignorant, oblivious. Like lemmings.

He put on his waistcoat, draped a towel over his shoulder and moved into the fray alongside Loman. He poured a dozen drinks or so, repeated his excuse about the influenza to Loman, who went white at the thought of catching it. His sister had died and his uncle too, he said, backing away.

He had a good hour or two before he had to be back at the station, and he took the time to watch Giesa manning the register. There was plenty of money already mounting up there. He waited until a customer passed him a large bill, a hundred rouble note, and moved over to the register to change it and top up his float of another hundred from her.

'Where have you been?' Giesa asked. She was nothing like Sophie. A hot little number that he would be happy to try on for size if she wasn't already spoken for by Brune who kept the restaurant across the foyer, a big bruiser and smart too, who knew the value of what he had, didn't leave any marks, and kept her happy.

'In bed. Sick as a dog.' He sighed, trying to give the impression that his return to the job had been an act of selfless heroism.

'Poor little thing,' she pouted and smiled, slipping him the bills, and taking his receipt for the float.

For another hour it was just one drunk after another. He poured generously, enjoying the chaos of the room, gave a few complimentary drinks when Loman wasn't standing too close, and pocketed at least another two hundred in tips.

At quarter to eleven he shouted an excuse to Loman, made a frown and circular motion with his hand, and moved back through the storeroom to the toilet, stuffed his tips into his back pocket, took his jacket and cap and placed it next to the storeroom door where he could get it later, and then looked out into the lane. Giesa was helping to load a fresh block of ice into the cabinet, and Kristo was chipping it on one end. It was the kind of frigid, boring job that went on all night long and was the permanent property of a dullard like Kristo who could lose himself in the shattered crystalline world of cracked ice. He flashed another hundred in Giesa's face and moved to the register. 'Your husband wants you,' he called to her. 'Pavel Egoriovich told me.'

'Oh.' A frown crossed her lovely brow.

'I don't think it's an emergency, but I'll gladly cover for you,' he said, continuing to the register. She had locked it, like a good girl, while she did the ice, but now, eager to hear what was the matter with her man, she tossed him the key, undid her apron and began to try and push her way out of the room.

By the time she had got to the doorway he'd lifted half the stack of the big notes that were kept under the tray, replaced it with his tips so it would bulk up about the same, re-locked the drawer and given the key to Loman for safe-keeping, which was, he thought, about the same as flushing it down the gutter.

Another few steps and he was at the door, checking to see that none of the waiters or busboys were smoking outside. They weren't, it was much too busy a night, and then he was out in the alley, moving quickly now, before she returned to her register.

It was too bad, he thought. A real waste to be taking advantage of a nice girl like Giesa, but that was the new world for you, people were temporary and he was never coming back this way again.

* * *

266

Standing there at the corner of the Yekaterinburg station platform, Ilya Stepanovich Strilchuk decided that it really wasn't a problem of regret. For himself, he had no regrets. He could not have been risen much higher than to be an ordinary policeman.

He was smart enough, smarter than most. He could read. Liked to read. And liked numbers and the impulse there was behind them, as if discovering numbers was a way to discover a secret source of money and power. And in each aspect of life wasn't there always an investment? Didn't everything require the addition of human energy to make it work? Wasn't that what capitalism was, what it meant? You borrow, you buy, you own, you extract, you put something in, and it pays off. So coming up through the ranks he had applied himself rigorously enough. Even if he'd admitted that he had no power to change anything, still he'd gone along with the flow of things, and waited for his opportunities, and then he'd put in his energy when he got the chance. And he'd always played it fair, he'd held on to his ethics. All the way. The only ones he ever stuck it to had deserved it every time, that was one thing he could always say.

So he was thinking that it wasn't really regret. It was a simpler proposition, a question of choices and the paths not taken. Still, he had managed. Always managed. It was a matter of labels. He'd been a cop, tried to do some good where a cop could do good. Provided for his wife while it lasted. Then he'd sent the boy to his mother because it would have been impossible for him to take care of him. Stanislaus, she'd wanted to name him. He'd seen him every year since.

Yes, he'd put in his energy.

And now what he was stuck with was a parlour rat, an Italian submariner – if there even was such a thing – ordering him to follow his mistress around the city. All on his own time, of course, after everything else that he was required to

267

do. Find the bones of the goddamn Tsar and his children, round up Red terrorists still hiding in the city, keep the Czech soldiers from shooting anyone who beat them at cards or simply rubbed them the wrong way. But now here he was, doing his job. He was going to follow, and pursue, and arrest, and report – yes, Excellency, my regrets, Excellency, but your whore is fucking some other whore . . .

It made him spit, and he did, into the gutter at the corner of the platform. The soldiers were sleepily moving into their compartments and he saw the Baroness's car a hundred metres down the yard.

He stood there on the platform for a moment and lit a cigarette, pulled his watch out and checked the time. Two hours, he'd been told. At least two hours from the time they'd arrived at the restaurant. It might be longer, Giustiniani had suggested. After all, who knew about women? Two hours was fine, he thought. He could do it. He would look around, and he would report, and if Giustiniani didn't like what he heard, he'd be fired or sent to do something even worse.

Or he could just keep walking, he was thinking. He could go to any of the mills and work the security there, but . . . those were all different circles, new men brought from outside a lot of times, and it was dirty work for a Yekaterinburg boy who still had friends in town.

So if he was going to keep walking, it would be a long, long distance.

Perhaps his only choice was to finish up, go visit his mother and retrieve his son. They could pick up a pass and move, east to Omsk, he was thinking, and then if Ryzhkov was right, well, he and the boy could just keep going. Trying to stick it out here was no good. If the Whites failed, just like Ryzhkov had said, there was a good chance that he and the rest of the Yekaterinburg police force would be shot. Stanislaus would never know him.

Maybe it was better that way, he was thinking. And, yes . . . maybe that counted as a regret.

He saw Vladimir Popov up the tracks. They had grown up at the same end of town and played together as children. He was a slow-moving bear, limping along, a lot heaver now than he had been.

'Do you know about that car, Valya?'

'What car?'

'That one, the one that belongs to the Baroness.'

'Oh, is that hers?'

'She's been living in it just down at the other end of the yard for three months, and you didn't know about it?'

'So that's her car. I never get down that end.'

'No?'

'No. They had the army boys down there. They have sentries all around, that's their look-out, not ours. So that's her car, eh?'

'They made it up into the army train, so she must be leaving town.'

'No, see? That's not hers, that's got a cross on it, that's a hospital car,' Popov said. They had walked up to the platform, and three tracks over they could see the side of the car. A circle with a white cross had been hastily painted on the siding of the car, the paint running down off one side of the curve so that it looked like a four-spoked wheel in the rain.

'I'm sure that's her car. I'm supposed to take her a message,' Strilchuk said to him.

'Oh, ho! Who is the dog now!'

'So give us a little privacy, eh?' he said, and cut across the tracks, careful to step over the tarry sleepers, moving up the long gravelled roadbeds to come around behind the armoured car.

'Alt!' came a shout, a sentry that the Czechs had posted back there, barking out a challenge.

'He's OK,' Popov shouted from the platform.

'Police,' Strilchuk announced, clamping the cigarette between his lips and holding his hands out where the boy could see them. Getting shot by a Czech teenager, now that would be a regret. 'I just have a message for the Baroness.' For a moment the boy-soldier looked at him oddly. 'Baroness,' Strilchuk said distinctly and pointed.

They walked around the length of the huge armoured car. It blocked out the light from the station. He waved the boy away and kept on walking. When he got to the end of the car he looked back to see if the boy was watching. It was dark and he wasn't sure, so he just mounted the stairs as if he was supposed to be there.

It took about two breaths to pick the lock on the carriage and he slipped into the short corridor and waited to let his eyes adjust.

The light came slivered through the shades on the station side. He could see the soft curves of the furniture that had been brought into the front portion of the car. It was a second-class car that had been converted. Carpets had been thrown across the places where they had knocked the partitions out to make a living room. At one end was a low divider with an open bed, a chaise big enough to sleep on. There was a pillow there, and blankets. A tray with the remains of some black bread, and a tiny square of butter. He put his finger down and slipped the butter off the plate and ate it. Salty and rich. Sucked his finger and reached for his torch. Across from the chaise was a rolltop desk and he tested the top and opened it. Unlocked. Tried the drawers. Bundles of letters tied together. An album of photographs. The rest of the drawers were empty.

There was a long counter, a set of shelves that had been nailed on the wall, and several piles of personal clothing had been folded. Beside the counter on the floor was what looked like a leather travel bag. It had underclothes stuffed into it, dirty laundry, he thought.

He opened one of the drawers and the scent of lavender washed over him from a sachet that had been placed in there to guard the Baroness's underwear. He tapped it and found a necklace underneath. Lifted up the cloths and found a rope of pearls. He didn't bother pulling them out, they coiled around and filled the entire bottom of the drawer. He dangled them back into place and covered them up.

In the rear of the car was a large compartment walled off, and a curtain hung over the entrance to the corridor. He pushed his face through the curtain, and then the torch, flicking it on for a second. Nothing. A bag of potatoes that had been hoarded there. A travelling trunk, the open door to the toilet.

He tried the door to the bedroom and opened it easily. There was a good-sized bed folded down and two people sleeping there.

It stopped him for a moment and he froze there until, listening, he realized they were both sleeping soundly.

He stared at the two sleepers for a moment, and was thinking about turning on the torch, when he heard steps on the gravel outside.

He let the door shut but did not latch it for fear of making a noise, stepped to the edge of the curtain and peered through. A shadow of someone walking cut across the windows.

He stepped out into the centre of the car to give himself room, felt for the revolver at his hip, unsnapped the holster.

There was a clicking in the lock, a sudden stillness and then, 'You're back already?' a man's voice called as he climbed the stairs. 'You're asleep already?' he said, quieter now as he came into the darkened room.

A match flared, and the man jumped back when he saw

271

Strilchuk there, the little flame spending itself as it plummeted to the carpet.

'I'm police,' Strilchuk said.

'Wha–aat!' the man gasped. Strilchuk took a step forward and grabbed him by the shoulder.

'Just be calm. Who are you?'

'What's happened? I'm the doctor. Doctor Anishev,' the man said. 'Please don't hurt me. We don't have any money.'

'I don't want money. I told you I'm with the police.'

'All right, fine. Good.'

'We got a message that someone had broken into this car. They sent me round to check.' They were still sitting there in the dark.

'Was anything taken?' the man asked. His voice had calmed but still sounded fearful.

'I don't know, we'll have to check. Put on the lights.'

'Oh, certainly. Let me . . .' Strilchuk felt him on the couch beside him, groping for a match, standing up and fumbling for the lamp.

'You're leaving the city?'

'Ah . . . Yes, yes. The Baroness, she is donating her car as a mobile hospital. We're going to Perm.'

'Very good of her,' Strilchuk said. The match flared and the man moved towards the lanterns. An orange glow silhouetted him there against the shades.

'Wait a minute,' Strilchuk said. 'I know you. You're no doctor, you're Ivanis. You work at the hotel.'

The man turned, extended his hands. Smiled helplessly. 'I've been sleeping with her. She's taking me along as her doctor, you see?'

'To tend the wounded?'

'Well, yes. I know a little medicine. I can get by better than most.'

'What about those two in the back?'

For a moment the bartender looked stunned, then he darted forward. 'They're not awake, are they? The girl is very ill,' he said worriedly.

'Girl?' Strilchuk said. He'd seen two people under the blankets; he hadn't realized one of them was a girl.

'I don't know if she will make it.' He had moved past Strilchuk into the little office, taken a porcelain bowl off the counter, reached into a cupboard, taken out a bottle of alcohol and poured some of it into the basin. 'Everything has to be clean,' he said.

Strilchuk came into that part of the car and watched him work. 'If it's not clean, you can die,' the bartender said. He was stepping forward and reaching past Strilchuk and wiping his hands on a towel as he did it. And Strilchuk was thinking that it was very narrow in that part of the rebuilt car, thinking that he was just in the way. He tried to step aside, and that was when the bartender put the knife in.

Low in his stomach, just above the belt, and jabbing up at the same time, so that Strilchuk knew immediately it was fatal. He staggered away, pushing Ivanis back against the wall, and crashed backwards along the counter trying to get away.

Ivanis blocked the door and Strilchuk plunged towards the rear of the car, falling through the curtain and pulling on the handle to the rear exit –

Locked.

And then – spinning to see Ivanis behind him, and feeling his hand move back and this time it was like a punch to the centre of his chest and he could feel the blade skid along his breastbone and puncture the top of his lung.

He fell back, and his only chance was to kick, and he grappled there and flung his knee up, hard and sharp and angry at the unfairness of it –

And missing –

The two of them were wedged in the little doorway to the compartment, turning around there, and Ivanis held him. Strong for a thin man. Too strong, he knew. Over his shoulder Strilchuk could see a girl waking up now, trying to sit up, clutching herself . . . as he kept trying to run, his feet waggling on the slippery flooring –

And Ivanis thrust the knife in once more, this time between the ribs, and all the life began to leave Strilchuk as he coughed away his blood.

In fading fragments his last sight was the girl's reflection in the mirror on the door as it banged back and forth: a broken purple mask, her mouth opened in a silent scream, the terrible visage of some gremlin from Hell who'd finally been snared by the Devil.

30

It had only been coincidence, she knew.

Exhausted, heart alternately pounding like a drum and flittering away like a butterfly in her chest, dizzy, Eikhe had climbed the rising Voznesensky Prospekt towards the Yekaterinburg railroad station. She had pushed herself too near to collapse, only stopping to rest when she saw the spots before her eyes.

Her work for this long day had nearly been completed; a network of volunteers had been dragged away from other pressing duties and stitched together to form a cordon that now ringed the city to block the escape of the Romanov hostages. She had finished with all her lists and was now improvising with the last bit of her strength. Her intention was to pay a visit to the station and try to find Vladimir Popov, whom she knew well as a quiet revolutionary, a prudent man who'd had kept his head down but could still be counted on if you didn't exhaust him with busy work. And everyone knew the railway workers were the most militant. They knew about machines and engineering and also understood the mysteries of communication. Many of them travelled hundreds of versts each day, and if they were sympathetic, messages, packages, all sorts of items could be couriered safely by these highly skilled and very mobile workers, in many cases far faster than by any other means.

As she had climbed the hill, her clothing sodden with perspiration, using a hand against the wall to steady herself and her weak rolling ankles, each step sending a spike of pain through her foot and knees, she vowed to stop. She was too old, too frail, especially in her legs; each year they got worse, more inflexible, harder to do up her shoes on the left leg. Soon she would be a real *babushka* unable to dress herself, and in her empty household there was no one to help.

She'd been thinking these morbid, self-pitying thoughts as she struggled up the deserted street, only an occasional drunkard reeling past her, heading downhill. Who was better, she'd wondered, a man killing himself with drink or a woman killing herself to save the life of parasites?

And with that thought, ahead of her had occurred the co-incidence – a shaft of light spilled out onto the cobbles, and she realized it was coming from her acquaintance Magda Borkewicz's house. She was a Hungarian who'd found herself abandoned in the city by her criminal-minded husband some years before. The two women had been drawn to each other's anger, and during the bitter war years, husbandless, had become something like friends, although Magda was religious and superstitious, worried constantly about her children and didn't have a true revolutionary bone in her body.

Perhaps, she thought, she could get some water there, catch her breath before the final climb to the station, and when she got to the door she saw Magda bending over a steaming tub of water, wringing out laundry. 'Ho, Magda,' she wheezed, and held a hand up to stop the excitable woman in her mid-whirl to see who was at her door.

'Oh!' she said, jumping. She was nervous, Magda was.

'Oh, Veni, it's you. I was afraid they were coming to get me. This is so . . . crazy.'

'What are you doing working at this time of night?' she'd gasped.

'Emergency, they said. They brought me this from the station. Some aristocrat has to have her washing done before the midnight train leaves.'

'Ahh.'

'And of course it's going to be wet. Can you imagine, travelling with a pile of wet laundry? It will mildew. Serve her right for waiting until the last minute, but the money is good.' She patted her pocket with a wet hand that left its imprint, and continued with her work, turning a long bed sheet through the wringer.

Eikhe hung there in the doorway, still out of breath. Too out of breath to ask for water. After a moment Magda looked over her shoulder and saw her. 'Are you all right?'

'I'm beat, comrade.'

'Come in, sit down. Do you need some tea?'

'Water would be good. I can't come in.'

'Yes, yes . . . you're too busy. You're not a girl any more, young lady.'

Eikhe had laughed. 'No . . . no . . . I don't think I ever was, really.'

'Here.' Magda handed her a tumbler of water. It was warm, but it felt like life itself as she drank it down.

'At least there's not much of it, but the stains . . .'

'Ahh,' Eikhe had said, the spots fading from her eyes as the tumbler of water vanished down her gullet. Her mind was still on what she was going to say to Popov to get him to help her out.

'I've never seen anything like this. Rich people. They said they were wounded soldiers, and I suppose that would explain the blood, but I never saw a uniform like this.' She had held

277

up a pair of soldier's uniform trousers. The fabric was exceptional, nothing like the ordinary rough wool. Magda rolled up the cuff and displayed a silk lining. 'Have you ever seen such a thing?' she shrugged.

'No,' Eikhe had said.

'And of course we have to do her underwear, and there's this shift. And there's bloodstains all over the bodice . . . see? They left it too long and it'll never come out,' Magda had said, shaking her head.

By that time Eikhe had risen from her stool, come over to the wringer and run her hands over the cloth, and looked over the rest of the pile.

'It's wet, but I'd still better fold it, otherwise they'll have a fit,' Magda said.

'I'm going to the station right now. I can take them up for you if you want.'

'Oh, my God, you've saved me again,' Magda had said, but then her face had darkened, she'd reached out and put a steadying hand on Eikhe's shoulder. 'But only if you're able. I can do it, and you look all in to me.'

'No,' Eikhe had said, 'no, it's nothing. Nothing at all.'

And, it seemed, coincidences had multiplied with other coincidences, because as soon as she had left with the hamper, just a few steps up the street she ran into young Kyril, her friend Geni's second son. Maybe there was a God for revolutionaries after all, she thought, as she reached in under the towels that covered the damp laundry, fished around for one of the exotic underthings, and with an iron claw dug her fingers into the child's shoulder, so he would remember that it was a matter of life and death to run, to run as fast as he could to the lake at the edge of the park and show this to Comrade Yurovsky, and made him repeat the name and message, so that there would be no mistake.

31

'You have done everything you could, comrade. If they're gone, they're gone,' Yurovsky said.

'If they're gone, we're dead. We might as well head for Vladivostok ourselves,' Ryzhkov retorted. They were at the lake, the place where he had selected for their evening's 'headquarters', close enough to the rope loft to retreat in case the Czechs came around, secluded enough that they could gather without causing much suspicion.

'Not me, comrade. I'll make my way back to Moscow. When I make my report, I'll explain carefully . . .'

'I don't think you'll be given that much time, to be honest.'

Yurovsky turned and looked at him. 'You're not really a true revolutionary, are you, Pyotr Mikhalovich? Your grasp of theory is somewhat wanting. We don't exist to serve anything but the true idea of the liberation of the proletariat.'

'Yes, yes, I know all about it, Yakov. I'm trying to be realistic, that's all.'

He left Yurovsky by a little campfire they had built beside the lake, tired of the boastful talk of the revolutionaries, and the endless loops of theory and posturing that each and every discussion always seemed to devolve into these days. He walked off into the cool night and stood there in the rushes, looking out over the surface of the water – completely still, as placid as a marble table-top. Across the larger of the lakes, another darker fringe of trees, the occasional light. He should try to relax. This was the calm before the storm and there was no way to know what would be required later.

Yurovsky was right. He had done everything he could. Their people were alerted and posted out there in boats. Comrades loyal to the fugitive Ural Soviet would eagerly stop anyone moving on the inner pond or trying to cross Lake Iset tonight. For the abductors there would be no escape. The whole city was shut down tight. As well, he knew that Strilchuk and his White policemen, on their side of the divide, were also on the job.

So why was he worried? Why couldn't he relax and just sit there, enjoy the fire, accept a friendly drink of home-made vodka, or whatever it was being called? Plan how he was going to explain everything to Zezulin? It was his curse, his personal curse. Never to be able to stop, to stop thinking, to stop worrying. To always look for the mistake being made, where the carpet was coming up, the paint flaking, the edge of the stamp ungluing itself when you weren't paying attention. A failed cop, a failed spy and, if truth was to be told, an anxiety-ridden little boy. He could almost hear his mother's voice: 'Go to sleep. Please, just go to sleep, can't you?'

Someone moved beside him and he turned and saw that a woman had walked over into the bushes. She had brought him a glass, held it out for him to take. They had warmed some of the vodka over the coals and he could smell it, floating above the rim, sweet and flavoured with pepper.

'I saw you before, I think,' she said.

'Oh,' he said. He couldn't remember. He'd gone all over the city with Yurovsky and down at the lake they had been spending a lot of time with the more radically minded fishermen in all the various gypsy camps they had around the lake.

'It's a beautiful night,' she said.

'Yes. We have a little moon. That's good.'

'You're looking for someone, someone trying to escape?'

'Yes.'

She was still for a moment. 'People say it's two of the Romanov children. Is that so?'

He shrugged in the darkness. 'I'm not in charge,' he said, not wanting to lie to her. It wasn't a lie really, he decided.

'Well, they can rot in hell if you ask me,' she said petulantly. He looked at her, at the firm uptilted chin, and suddenly recognized her as the girl he had made love to in the hotel corridor when he had first come into the city. It seemed like aeons ago.

She glanced over and saw his look. 'I remember you,' she said softly. It came out like a simple fact, not really much sentiment in the tone of her voice. Just an encounter, a moment that had come and gone.

'How are you?' he asked, reached out for a moment to just touch her arm, but she pulled back from him and the corners of her mouth turned down.

'It depends on who you're talking to, or how you want to think about it, I suppose. I guess I'm better. My brother came and got me, sent me to live down here. I don't remember much about it. I'm with my uncle now. He's helping me to dry out, you see.'

'Ahh . . .'

'It was pretty bad there for a while.'

They looked at the lake a little longer. He took a long sip from the vodka and then poured the remainder out into the reeds. 'I have to be ready,' he explained to the girl.

'I don't mind watching people drink. I just tell myself that it's not for me any more, that's all,' she said. And then after a moment she went on, quieter. 'He says I'm a whore. He says

281

I'm going to hell. He won't let me show my hair in public. That's why I'm wearing this. He makes me. Even at night.' She pulled the scarf off, and he could see that her hair was longer now by at least an inch, dark roots that showed up against the blonde fringe in the moonlight. She was still pretty, even with the bizarre haircut. Thin and serious, but pretty.

'I have to work for him, clean up, do everything. So, that's how I am.' She smiled tightly, reached out and took his glass away. Someone was calling from the fire, and she turned to go.

'He's a bastard, my uncle. A real shit,' she said and melted into the darkness.

He watched her silhouette as she went back towards the fire, retying the scarf around her newly shameful hair, a low growl as the man berated her, reaching out to slap at her as she moved past the others gathered there. A moment later when she was gone they were laughing about it.

Hearing their laughter made him angry, and Ryzhkov went back to the fire and glared at the men, who shut up, having all heard from the rumours that he was Cheka, the special man from Moscow, someone not to be trifled with.

'Aren't you supposed to be on guard?' he said to the man who he supposed to be her uncle.

'We're taking it in shifts, comrade.'

'Well, take an additional shift. This is an emergency, comrade,' he said, dismissing the man, letting his eyes rest on the fire. The uncle didn't reply, he simply stood and walked away and the circle fell silent.

'In fact why don't all of you take an additional shift. I want to speak to Comrade Yurovsky in private,' he said. There was a pause and after one or two grumbled assents the men got up, stretched themselves and, their party spoiled, moved away into the darkness, spreading themselves out around that section of the lake.

'You certainly know how to speak to the masses,' Yurovsky said.

'Something's wrong, Yakov. We're in the wrong place. They're not trying to escape this way. If they were leaving they should have made an attempt by now.' He was suddenly filled with the need to do something. Anything. To walk, to run. To go out and find the girl's uncle and slap him senseless, to steal a boat and try to escape himself. It was a terrible urge that was almost animalistic, to flee, to bite himself in frustration. Instead he kicked the ground, unconsciously felt for the pistol in his belt.

'You'd better get used to this. If they're still in town we'll have to do this several nights in a row, Pyotr Mikhalovich.'

'No.' Ryzhkov shook his head. None of it quite made sense, but he couldn't find the solution.

'What's wrong?' Yurovsky asked. He was sitting by the fire, twirling a stick in his hands, one direction and then the other.

'We've guessed wrong, somehow. I don't know. They didn't ask for any money.'

'Oh? How do you know?'

'I spoke to someone. The cops didn't even know about it.'

Yurovsky made a face, scratched his beard that he was sprouting in an effort to further his disguise as a priest. 'Speaking to the cops? That's somewhat odd, I'd say.'

'We do whatever is necessary, yes? So, we know it's not something they're doing for ransom. It's some other motivation. More for . . . protection. For . . .'

'It's only the first night.'

'No,' Ryzhkov said. 'Something's gone wrong.'

'OK, OK. Just calm down.' Yurovsky had stood up now. There were voices coming from the head of the lake, in the direction that the girl had gone, and he wondered if the uncle had found her and was going to beat her. That's what was in store. She'd get a beating just for handing him a glass and speaking a few sentences. What kind of a revolution was it when a woman couldn't wear her hair the way she wanted?

The voices were continuing, louder, and they both turned to see a boy running along the path that wound by the lake. It was the kind of place where in normal times couples would stroll, athletes would do their running and old people would sit and remember a life less frantic. Now from out of the gloom the boy arrived, all out of breath, his face a mask of emergency, trying, too quickly, to gasp out his message.

'Madame Eikhe sent me!' the boy blurted to Yurovsky. She wanted him and comrade Ryzhkov to meet her at the station right away. He dug in his pocket, came out with a white square of cloth that he held out to them, like an offering.

'She said you'd know what it was,' the boy gasped.

When Ryzhkov reached out and felt the fabric he realized he was holding a pair of women's silk underpants. The cloth was as fine as air, and he fumbled, nearly letting them slip from his fingers into the fire.

'What the hell is she on about now?' Yurovsky said. Ryzhkov turned the panties over in his hand. There was a label stitched on the inside below the band, and he bent down closer to the fire to read it.

'My God!' said Yurovsky, peering over his shoulder.

Perfect script stitched in gold gave the name of the couturier. Below that was an embroidered golden double eagle and the single shining initial:

m

'Fetch a carriage, boy,' Ryzhkov said. Yurovsky had started stepping on the fire, like a demented folk dancer, trying to put it out.

'Go, go! Right now! Now! We have to get to the station,' he said, pushing the boy in the back to get him off the mark.

And then the three of them were running through the darkness.

32

Conte Captain Tommaso di Giustiniani was not a stupid man. He had fenced with the best, had moved through his life holding to a strategy designed to produce the greatest benefits with the least effort, and in every crisis he had encountered so far it had always worked. He had avoided death, a certainty on a few occasions, and serious injury. Had avoided entanglements, legal, marital, and as far as he knew had fathered no children that might burden his estate. He was, in the popular vernacular, slippery, and he was quite proud of it.

So, it made him happy – he was surprised at how much it actually relieved him – to be done with Baroness Sophie von Buxhoeveden, a scatterbrained aristocrat down to her last assets, and to have come away with an evening's erotic pleasure that, truthfully, he had been counting on for some days.

So, poof! Let her go. She hadn't wanted to linger. A headache, she had claimed. Which only displayed how airheaded she was, to come up with a trite excuse like that. The evening had not been without cost. Dinner at Yekaterinburg's best, Limon the restaurant attached to the

Metropole Hotel, had cost him nearly four pounds sterling, not counting the champagne (real champagne!) which he had purchased and then had couriered all the way from Vladivostok under armed guard in a diplomatic box, altogether totalling another six pounds. And now he would have to ration himself for the rest of the month. Bitch.

She hadn't been that wonderful. They had eaten, he had flattered her. All the while searching for signs of betrayal. He had his suspicions, of course, and in truth in this modern age there was no sense in getting oneself worked up over fidelity, but they had met at least a half-dozen times in the past few weeks, she had made all the right noises, revealed herself to be, beneath the mask of *faux* school-girlish *naïveté*, to be a wanton, somewhat experienced and inventive companion in the bedroom. Or on the sofa, or upon one delightful occasion, the chair. Yes, well . . .

And in the end, when she wanted to leave, he gave her the precious transit pass. She could go and now he could look for her replacement. The evening had been pleasurable enough in its own way, and had given Inspector Strilchuk time to search her railway carriage for proof of his suspicions – evidence of another lover, one whom he had long suspected. It made him smile, this odd peculiarity of his personality. Very curious, he reflected: even though he really didn't want her, he didn't want anyone else in the game.

In the end he had been forced to escort her to the station in the Renault that he had signed out from the motor pool; he had had to book it in advance, now he owed favours to de Heuzy and to the sergeant who ran the garage. He fancied that everyone, particularly the men, were looking at him as he led her through the foyer of the Yekaterinburg station, arm in arm, privately envious, holding their comments until they had passed.

She begged off his offer to see her to her carriage, and

honestly he was glad to go. She was playing some sort of goodbye scene; her fingers fluttered to her forehead, he made a gallant kiss on the hand while glancing over her shoulder to see if Strilchuk was hanging about in the lounge. Then, with a sharp click of his heels, and the softest of caresses from her fingers on his cheek, she was gone, and he was left with the vision of her entirely adequate hips as she walked out across the platform.

He immediately headed for the American Hotel to get drunk, silent through the entire drive, then ordered the chauffeur to return the ridiculous automobile to the motor pool. He moved through the lobby into the smoky bar with the weight coming off his shoulders. Here he didn't have to pretend, here there was no courtship dance, unless he decided to choose a prostitute. Here he could be himself, lose his desire in simple conversation with other men, and drink, drink, drink to his heart's content.

He pushed his way to a place at the bar. Two men, civilians in suits, moved aside for him and Loman took his order and filled it smartly. The three of them toasted each other and the death of Lenin, and he ordered another right away. As far as he was concerned Sophie Buxhoeveden was a thief and a whore whom he was already starting to forget, and, let's face it, she had given as much as she'd got. For wasn't it just a great multifaceted game, something like tridimensional chess, that men and women played? Only using emotions instead of rooks and pawns. Men wanted something, it was the game for the women to outwit them, preserve their queen until the ultimate moment, then when there was no opportunity but checkmate, well . . . in a perfect game no one knew exactly who had won, yes?

Oh, when he coughed up the pass she'd thanked him profusely. Expressed, once more, her loathing for the Urals and for her imprisonment in the rebuilt second-class carriage

287

that had been assigned to her. It was one thing they agreed upon, their hatred of Siberia, a useful conversation filler. She had blown him a kiss, they had lifted a glass to each other's generosity. Two grown-up modern people, getting what they each wanted at a price that each could bear.

As he drained off his third *konyak* the civilians thanked him, tipping their hats. He stood there looking at his reflection in the mirror above the row of bottles, mostly containing the same mixture of fiery home-made vodka flavoured with various coloured ingredients to imitate other brands which had long been out of stock.

It was Ivanis, he knew. His suspicions had been aroused when he ran into him in the lounge at the station. Coming out just as he was heading in. The particular smell of the man's cologne. Noticed it again inside her carriage, her face flushed, and the excitation of her love-making – truly, truly enthusiastic in a way that she had never been before – should have tipped him off immediately. But he had been in a hurry himself, full of pride.

Perhaps he would wait until Ivanis came in and confront him. Have a little discussion. He rejected the thought almost immediately as being beneath him. There was no way that he, after all a man of somewhat noble birth, was going to share a lover with a common bartender. Besides, it was over. But what on earth did she see in him? The bartender had nothing, he was nothing, but . . . Giustiniani shook his head, cursing in self-loathing. Vanity, vanity, wasn't it always vanity? He absently genuflected to his image in the mirror, and, tired of himself, turned from the bar. What he needed tonight was real companionship.

At the end of the bar the writer, the Englishman named . . . Wilton, was loudly going on about the most absurd things. Another idiot – a red-faced, ink-stained wretch on an expense account who produced more talk than writing. He had long before had enough of the man, who could always be trusted to spin a mystical interpretation out of any set of facts that were presented to him. The Tsar was alive, he was now proclaiming; he himself had seen Alexei and was leaving that very night to interview him. His listeners were hanging on every word. Yes, he was sure it was Alexei, dammit, and yes, he had a pass to travel, not only signed by the Czech military authority but countersigned by the American consul himself, Wilton shouted as he downed another pseudo-Scotch. Absurdities.

Surely Yekaterinburg was hell. Giustiniani scanned the room, looking for someone sane to talk to. He was lonely and he needed someone he could really converse with. Ryzhkov would be good but he had vanished, gone back to whatever clandestine Russian faction he was affiliated with, who knew, it didn't matter.

The whole damn thing was crumbling. The Bolsheviks were improving their forces with each battle, and the Czechs were getting tired of doing the Allies' dirty work. The White Russians were poseurs and dilettantes, and he decided right there and then that it was time to get out, to get back to Italy and a sun-baked piazza where he could have some real coffee, and women who knew their place, and the many other subtle improvements that Italian culture had made upon civilization.

He saw that the sweet little barmaid, Giesa, was in tears and Loman was doing his best to comfort her. A fight with her man, perhaps? More romantic melodrama, the last thing he wanted to think about, but he saw they were standing by the register, opening and closing the drawer, fiddling with the mechanism, and that the girl, really she was very nice, was quite disturbed, gesticulating with her helpless hands. Florinsky, not a very pleasant person at the best of times, growled something at her, and stormed out, and when Loman made it back down to his end of the bar he asked him what was wrong.

'Ahh. Tonight we have been the victim of a robbery, monsieur. Someone has relieved us of quite a considerable sum.'

'Catastrophe!'

'Absolument, monsieur. We are looking for him at this moment.'

'Who was the culprit?'

Loman looked pained. 'I'd rather not speculate, monsieur.'

'Ahh.' Giustiniani took this in, nodded sagely while Loman poured him another drink. 'When do you think Ivanis might come in? I need to speak with him,' he said, and noticed the funny look in Loman's eye when he said it.

'I doubt he will be in this evening, monsieur.'

'Really.'

'I very much doubt it.'

'Sick?' Giustiniani probed, and Loman only returned a strange expression, sort of a wince, a frown and a shrug all mixed together, and then fled to another customer.

There was no one very interesting in the room, and Giustiniani made up his mind to call it a night. He let the drink slide down his throat and began to manoeuvre his way across the room, through the tangle of tables and chairs – Florinsky had packed the room with them in an effort to squeeze every last rouble out of the White occupation – when he saw Volkov, one of his junior investigators, standing there at the door. He tried to put on a stern face to mask his retreat out of the room, as if he were recommending an early night since there was so much work to do the next day.

'What a crazy night,' Volkov gushed to him. He was smiling, his face lit up like a boy at an amusement park. 'A robbery, all sorts of things going on.'

'It is a wide, wide world,' Giustiniani intoned with a patronizing smile, and began to walk away.

'It was someone who works here. That's what they're saying,' Volkov said. He was staring straight ahead. Drunk already. It was only a little after eleven. He must have just come over from the office.

'Really?'

'That's what they're saying,' Volkov repeated, nodding his head.

For a moment Giustiniani looked at him. The look lasted so long that Volkov lost his smile, went to take a drink from his glass, and then stopped, paralysed by Giustiniani's stare.

'Tell me, have you seen Inspector Strilchuk this evening?'

'No, sir.'

'Not at all?'

'No sir. He left at, oh . . . about eight thirty, something like that.' There was a bustling as Wilton moved behind him through the door.

'Say.' He reached out and grabbed Wilton by the shoulder of his jacket. 'You're leaving now, leaving the city, I mean?'

'Getting out of this hell-hole tonight,' Wilton said with a bleary-eyed smile, patting his pocket where presumably he'd tucked his pass.

'Good luck to you then, sir.'

'And to you, mon capitaine.' Wilton made an intoxicated salaaming motion with his finger, tipped his fedora back on his head, turned again for the door.

'Have you heard about the robbery?' Volkov called to him, the smile now back in place. Wilton stopped, turned on them with a garish smirk.

'Yes, and honestly, it just goes to show you. Obviously an inside job! These fucking bloody people, they'll steal from their own mothers!' he screamed into the room, smiled cruelly at Volkov, and then bulled his way out the door.

Giustiniani watched him go. He was suddenly cold sober. He turned back to his young investigator and regarded him for a long moment. 'Volkov,' he said, 'go and ask Loman to give us the address where the bartender Ivanis keeps his rooms, and then get out on the street and find us a cab.'

'Now, sir?'

'Yes, now. Our day is not yet done,' Giustiniani said to the young man, who had so much more to learn.

33

'Where is she?' Ryzhkov said. 'She's supposed to be here, isn't she?'

'I don't know, comrade, but I do know we can't get in this way.' The mouth of the station was clotted with soldiers, and uniformed railway officials consulting their watches. He and Yurovsky abruptly turned off the wide street; Yurovsky maintained his hold on Ryzhkov's elbow – the picture they'd been making was that of a kindly priest helping a drunken parishioner back to the safety of his rooms, the two of them staggering slowly along the street, one a sinner, one a confessor. Immediately they turned the corner they felt safer in the darkness along the back street that paralleled the tracks.

'I know a way into the yard, just up here. If they haven't patched the fence. And why would they? These are Czechs, after all,' Yurovsky said.

'Fine, but once we're inside we still have to find her, don't we?'

'You have a better plan?'

'Unfortunately, no.'

'So maybe we die here, then, eh?' Yurovsky said. And a few steps later, 'Here.' He pointed, and they crossed the street

293

and slipped into the bushes. Behind was a low wall topped with a barbed-wire fence.

'This wire is new. We'll have to go along further,' Yurovsky said.

They began pushing their way along the wall, brushing back the bushes; at least they weren't thorns, just something that had been planted years before in a futile attempt to dampen the sound of the rail yard from the surrounding district, unpruned from decades and overgrown. In only a few metres they came to the end of the wall. Where the wire stepped down at the end of the masonry there was a gap that they had to get down on their hands and knees to push apart and crawl through.

Immediately on the other side the ground descended sharply, and Yurovsky had to reach back and hold onto the wire before he slid away into the darkness. 'Be careful,' Ryzhkov heard him call just before he sank away.

He waited a moment and then followed, slipping down a bank, bashing his bad knee on the rocks, and coming to rest on his behind. They were on more or less level ground beside the tracks at the western end of the yard. To his right, about a hundred metres away, were the lights of the station building. Much closer he could see a locomotive engine drawn up, the length of the train made up behind it, the engineer and firemen working in the cabin, preparing to depart.

'That's the military train,' Ryzhkov said. 'It's supposed to leave at midnight, isn't it?'

'I wouldn't know. The authorities don't usually advise me of these things. I don't know why not – for fear of espionage, I suppose.'

'Come on,' Ryzhkov said, angry now and tired of dealing with Yurovsky's wit. He started back along the tracks towards the station, anxious to be doing something, anything. He warned himself that it was dangerous to be so impetuous, but it didn't stop him.

'Wait, wait, wait! You can't go there. There are soldiers all over the place.'

'Come on. There's no time. They're trying to get out on that train, I'm sure of it.'

'But it's a military train.'

'I know, but they're using it somehow.'

In the gloom they could see the railwaymen working on the locomotive, walking around checking for oil leaks, fiddling with valves, their torches playing about the articulated wheels, performing the myriad exotic tasks that elevated them above the common proletariat in the new workers' hierarchy. He and Yurovsky tried to walk on the grassy verge to keep the noise of their feet on the gravel down, but the breathing of the engine was loud enough to mask everything. Ahead of them, at the end of the platform, a sentry idled. A few soldiers were standing around at the entrance to their carriages, urinating on the ballast, smoking and joking, waiting. Between them and the platform was a closed switchman's hut and Ryzhkov angled across the rails towards it, putting it between the two of them and the sentry's point of view. They opened the door and slipped inside. It was about the size of a large closet with a tiny stove in one corner and windows on three sides. From there they could see the main platform and the entire length of the train.

'They can't be with the soldiers.'

'I know, I know, I know, but why did she send us –' Ryzhkov's eyes went down the length of the train, a row of ordinary carriages for the soldiers, armoured flatcars at either end of the train, and then, almost at the rear, he saw it. 'There!'

'Where?' Yurovsky leaned around, trying to see because of the sharp angle.

'Just there, see? The carriage next to last before the big gun at the end.'

'That's an ambulance, Pyotr.'

'Wait,' he said. They watched the activity around the station for a few more moments. A brace of Czech officers with clipboards comparing notes. Another officer ascertaining that all his men were aboard. A sergeant saluting. A railroad gendarme walking pensively back and forth at the entrance to the saloon, pipe in his mouth, hands clasped behind his back. Soon the soldiers would be gone and he could go back to doing nothing.

'Isn't that her?' At the corner he saw a woman step out from the saloon. A railway policeman handed her a large basket covered with a towel. She stood there looking weary for a moment, and when she turned he saw her face.

'Yes!' Yurovsky breathed behind him.

Eikhe stopped for a moment and made conversation with the gendarme; he gestured to the train. It looked like she was just taking her time, engaging in small talk, shifting the basket to her other hip, and Ryzhkov realized that she was waiting for them.

'Well, there she is. Now we just have to get to her.' He reached out to open the door.

'Take this,' Yurovsky said. A grease-smeared topcoat hung on a peg behind the door, and Ryzhkov slipped it on. As he turned to push his arms down the sleeves, he looked out the window and saw the sentry pacing along. He had moved along and was heading down the platform towards their hut.

'You'd better go into your act,' Ryzhkov said and slipped out the door, walked along, head down, straight over to the military train, and down the length of the cars, pretending to check the wheels. It was all theatre; he had no idea what he was doing. At the end of one of the cars the soldiers had to move out of his way while he took his time, getting down on his knees, pretending to inspect things in the dark. Behind him he saw Yurovsky walking back up towards the locomotive, ostentatiously blessing each and every car, stopping to give each knot of Czechs a few lucky words from God. When he stood up from the trucks, he saw Eikhe making her way across the tracks, heading towards the 'ambulance' at the end of the train.

One of the Czech soldiers said something to him as he was walking past. The accent was bad, and Ryzhkov froze, thinking that his time was up, then turned, tried to look innocent, stupid, whatever they expected of him. The man had to say it again, and this time Ryzhkov realized it was a harmless request. 'What are you looking for?' the man had asked.

'Sabotage,' Ryzhkov said, and then when the Czech frowned, not knowing the Russian word for it, he made a big gesture with his hands and made a 'boom' and a smile.

The Czechs laughed.

'It's very dangerous,' Ryzhkov said overly clearly and with a smile, and the young soldiers laughed again.

'Danger. Yes, it can be,' the soldier said with a slight bow.

When Ryzhkov turned away from them, and started along the line of cars, he saw that Eikhe had disappeared.

That bloody boy Kyril, she thought. When she saw him she'd kick him across the moon. Idiot offspring of a long family of idiots . . . In such fashion she walked into the foyer of the Yekaterinburg station. The basket of wet laundry was heavy and she stopped frequently, to get her breathing back, and to look quietly around to see if she could see either Comrade Ryzhkov or Comrade Yurovsky. But nothing. Nothing! She moved into the waiting room; it was empty since there were no passengers travelling on the army's train at this hour, and into the lounge. Popov was there, and she held the basket out so he could see it.

'I'm delivering this, Valya, but I don't know where to go.'

'Ask Osorgin at the window,' he said. Always gruff. A useless man, the kind who always thought he was right.

She struggled through the door, Popov not bothering to rise to help her, and back out onto the platform. There was a counter and a wicket there that was pulled down half way so that only a small rectangle of light came out of it.

'I've got laundry from Magda's,' she said to the shutters.

There was a rustling in the back and Osorgin opened the grille, wiping his mouth. She could smell the reek of schnapps. He had decided to quit early this evening, do his drinking in his little office instead of at home. She heard more movements. There was someone else in there with him. 'What he hell do I know about your laundry?' Osorgin said, but not angrily, more out of confusion.

'Someone sent it out to Magda, and it's supposed to come back for the midnight train. It's women's things, most of it.'

'This is an army train. There are no women on it.'

'I'm just doing a favour for Magda.'

'Ask upstairs. They know everything,' Popov said. He had come up behind her to help.

'Yes, and don't bother me when we're closing,' Osorgin said, and slid the wicket all the way closed this time.

She made her way out onto the platform. Popov took the basket through the foyer for her, following behind like a penitent, measuring his steps, concentrating on the concrete walkway, lost in his thoughts.

'I was hoping I'd find you, Valya,' she said, putting on a smile.

'And how are you, Veni?'

'Quite out of sorts, to be honest. Where is this supposed to go? This is just the army, I see.'

'Someone sent these things to Magda.'

'Ah . . . that must be the Baroness's things.'

'Yes? The Baroness?'

'That car, you see the one, just before the rearmost on the train?'

She peered through the gloom. A man was walking towards them; it looked like he had just stepped down from the car, as if he were in a hurry, clutching a piece of paper in his hands. He was wearing a white coat, the kind that doctors dressed in when they examined you.

'The hospital car, you mean?' she asked.

'Yes, she's transporting some wounded soldiers in there.' Popov contemplated the car with its hastily painted cross on the side for a moment. 'Charitable act,' he said with a sigh.

Their attention was drawn by the man. As he got to the main platform he looked over at Popov and nodded. Didn't even glance at her; brushed past the two of them and attacked the stairs to the dispatcher's office two at a time.

'Just there. You'd better hurry Veni,' Popov said, checking his pocket watch.

'Many thanks to you, Valya. And how's your wife?' she said, taking the opportunity to step out a little on the platform and look around for Yurovsky and Ryzhkov. Nothing.

'She's fine. There's the coughing, however. It keeps her up at night and she takes it out on me.' Popov smiled. He used to be fun, she remembered. Then he got old. Like an old horse that followed the same route every day.

'Be safe, Valasha,' she said, turned towards the crossover, and made her way to the third track and towards the hospital car. She knocked on the door and heard someone moving about; after a moment the door opened and she saw a woman standing at the top of the steps. She looked as if she had been crying. For a moment the woman just stared at her. 'Oh,' was all she could manage to say.

'My friend sent me with your things, mademoiselle,' Eikhe said. The words had the effect of jarring her out of her trance,

299

and she stepped back and realized that she would have to go inside to get her purse.

'Yes, yes . . . just a moment,' she said in a rather clipped and nervous tone, a voice that said that in a confused world such as hers even this one last thing was just too much, too much to bear.

When she stepped back into the compartment Eikhe took the opportunity to climb the stairs, the laundry still propped against her hip. She wanted to get into the car, see everything she could see.

It didn't look much like a hospital car. There were no beds that she could see, the front of the carriage looked like it had been converted into a parlour, and there might have been an adjoining room. She couldn't see around the edge of the little partition. Something had spilled there, she saw, and there were towels on the floor, to soak up the mess. The woman moved back around the partition, carefully stepping over the towels, and Eikhe took another step into the room. The lights from the station were only partially damped by the shades that were pulled down throughout the carriage. She put the basket on the carpeted floor and, looking to steal some minutes, began to take the clothes out.

'One moment,' she heard the aristocrat call out.

'These are still wet, mademoiselle. Do you want me to hang them up for you?'

'Oh . . . oh, no. It's fine. Just a moment.'

Then Eikhe heard her moving and turned her head to see her coming back to the front. She had put on a nurse's white apron for her entrance, and as she came in she accidentally stepped on the towels, slipped on the floor, which forced her to grab the edge of the counter with a look of distress, then she shook it off. Eikhe went over to her as she fumbled with the catch on her purse, dug for coins and found none, looked up at her with a pathetic expression. Then she opened the second compartment of the purse and pulled out a ten-rouble note. 'This should do,' she said, regaining her clipped manner, although her hands were shaking, Eikhe could see.

'Oh, please, no, mademoiselle. That's much too much.'

'It's fine, it's fine. Go on. Take it.'

'Here,' she said. 'You just need a little light.' She reached across and raised the shade; a shaft of light shone through the carriage. The woman almost flinched at the sudden illumination. She reacted immediately, pulled the shade down abruptly, forced the banknote into her hands, tossed the purse onto the sofa. Eikhe felt the woman's hand on her shoulder turning her back towards the steps.

'Thank you so much, thank you, madam. It's most generous,' she said, going on in this way and letting the woman guide her back to the entrance. And that was fine with Eikhe. She wanted to get out of there, so she stepped along with the Baroness's hand on her shoulder, a little weight there that she could feel through he fabric of her clothing, burning like a blessing or a curse – yes, fine to be getting out of there because in the light she had seen the blood on the floor.

She rolled her way down the stairs, gripping the steel banister and turning to give her thanks to the woman, but the door was already closing, even as she was in the middle of a theatrical bow, and saying something syrupy – 'May God bless you, my little sweet one' – still thinking that she needed to buy some time, and then turning to run right into the man who was there, the one dressed like a doctor, his face tight with anger.

'What are you doing here, little mother?' he said. It was a quiet voice. The kind of voice you would use to lull someone to sleep. The voice didn't match the face. The face looked at her with hard eyes. She could see the set of the jaw, the hand in his pocket. 'I asked, what are you doing here?' the doctor said, and this time the voice was even quieter, sweeter, and he had moved closer.

She stood there on the platform, her mouth moving but unable to form words, not even able to explain that she was simply a peasant woman who'd brought back the laundry, because now she knew, and he did too . . .

He had worked his way down the train in his unlikely guise as some sort of railway inspector. He'd stopped a few cars ahead of the ambulance at the moment that he caught sight of Eikhe. She was on the elbow of a doctor, and he was helping her climb laboriously up to the car. It was a high step to the entrance and it was awkward for her. Once she was up he followed and closed the door behind them.

Ryzhkov turned to find Yurovsky, and at that same moment there was a double scream from the locomotive's whistle. Almost in answer a conductor began walking towards him, doubtless wondering why he was standing dangerously in the tracks as the train was about to pull away. He waved to Yurovsky, but he was three cars away, and then Ryzhkov stepped up onto the platform and started towards the ambulance. The conductor changed direction to meet him. 'What are you about?' he said.

Ryzhkov could see the man tighten his grip on his lamp. There was no time to talk his way out of the situation. He was moving forward quickly now.

'I'm hunting a saboteur! Come on! He's this way,' he said to the man, brushing past. He reached out to grab his arm, but Ryzhkov pulled away. It was getting desperate and going all wrong now. They were standing there, only a few feet apart, and the conductor dug for his whistle.

'Come on!' Ryzhkov hissed to the man, but he knew that the bluff had failed. He turned and ran directly for the carriage as there came the heavy ripple of the slack being taken out of the couplers, and he could see the carriage wheels slowly beginning to gather speed. Out of the corner of his eye he saw Yurovsky running down the platform.

'Wait! Stand still!' the conductor was shouting behind him. Across the platform he saw a large man turning – one of the railway detectives. A group of yardmen were emptying out of the lounge, and the air was filled with whistles.

It was impossible.

He skidded to a top and turned, his arms out from his sides. The soldiers posted on the armoured car had been roused by the cacophony and woke up from behind the sand-bags and steel plates, peeping over to see what was the matter.

Yurovsky had ran along the platform, timed his lunge and jumped for the handrail at the door to the ambulance carriage. Suddenly Ryzhkov was aware that no one was looking at him. The conductor's attention had been pulled around to the station house. There was a pillar of smoke coming from the grille at the mouth of the station.

'He's on the train,' Ryzhkov said to the man, and ran past him.

The yardmen had unpacked a hose from a large cabinet on the ground; another man was screwing it onto a stand-pipe as they began opening the valve. A civilian had run out from the office and was retching there on the platform; behind him Ryzhkov could see flames through a window. No one was watching him now, they were all fighting the fire in the telegrapher's kiosk.

He ran along, stumbling in the ballast beside the armoured car, trying to catch up to the rear of the carriage. He thought he heard a gunshot, then another. It made him run faster. He saw the door where Yurovsky had vanished into the car, and he leaped up and caught the handrail to the rear doors and hung, his feet swaying in mid-air. Someone was shouting, and he looked back over his shoulder. Two soldiers were on top of the armoured car; one was laughing at him, the other was lifting his rifle and working the bolt into position.

The train had gathered speed. They were nearly at the end of the platform when the door suddenly opened in his face. Yurovsky stumbled backwards, forced down the steps by someone on the threshold. He had a moment to see the man clearly, recognizing the familiar face: the bartender. The bartender at the American Hotel, Ryzhkov realized. Ivanis was the name. But now he was dressed in a medical smock, and in his hands was an automatic pistol, his finger slowly slipping off the safety.

Yurovsky was trying to talk to him, babbling some nonsense. 'Look,' Yurovsky was saying, 'we're all brothers in Christ,' but Ryzhkov knew it wasn't going to work and he lunged and grabbed Yurovsky by the back of his cassock and jerked him away as Ivanis pulled the trigger –

And then they were falling. Falling out of the car, a dark moment in mid-air, and collapsing onto the hard gravel, knocking the wind out of both of them, the world heaving with the weight of the armoured car rolling over the sleepers just by their heads –

A hastily fired shot from the rifleman on the armoured car buzzed towards them and sparked off the rails, and then the dark behemoth was past them and gone.

Only a moment and Yurovsky was on his feet and running back towards the station. He turned and saw that they were an unbelievable distance away. It seemed like it had all happened in just seconds, but they had travelled down the tracks past their original entrance through the barbed wire.

And then he was up and following Yurovsky back towards something –

At first he couldn't recognize it, only a kind of pile there beside the rails . . . and when he got closer he recognized the basket, one side broken and caved in, and Veni Eikhe seated awkwardly beside the tracks. There was a dark circle of blood swelling from her stomach and her eyes were rolling up. Yurovsky fell to his knees beside her.

'Go,' she said, meaning to say it urgently, but her voice's weakness betrayed how badly she'd been shot.

'Do you have any water?' Yurovsky turned to him.

'Water will kill her,' he said, having seen it scores of times in France, and besides they hadn't brought any from the lake.

'Go, Yakov,' she said.

'They're gone. We can't, Veni.'

Looking past the two of them Ryzhkov saw the policemen were still fighting the fire in the station. Smart of him, he thought, to do that. Now there would be no telegraph communication from the city for at least an hour or two until the damage was repaired.

He stood and took a few steps down the tracks. He could see two men walking their way. Police.

Eikhe's face was rimed with perspiration, and her skin showed grey even in the dim light. Her eyes were rolling up in her head. It was over for her, he knew. 'We have to go,' he said to Yurovsky, and reached out to put a hand on his shoulder. Yurovsky shook him off angrily.

'Go,' she said again, and sank back onto the gravel. 'Go. Get away. Make a better world.' She was looking up at the night sky now, seeing more than just their faces, looking inwards to her life and all that she had become, looking outwards to the future that might still yet be.

'Yakov,' Ryzhkov said. Realizing that Yurovsky wouldn't abandon her until she was finally gone, he took out his pistol, turned and shot twice down towards the guards. They flinched and split apart and dove for cover beside the tracks. It would buy them a minute, he thought.

'Oh, poor, poor . . .,' Yurovsky said. He had cradled her

305

head in his lap, and he put his hand on her cheek. She blinked at his touch, looked over to him, tried to focus on his face.

'Go,' she said.

He grabbed Yurovsky hard now, lifting him up. There was the snap of a gunshot from one of the guards, missing since they had nothing to sight against in the gloom.

'Come on, Yakov. You can't help her now. She knows it.'

'Save yourself, comrade.' Eikhe's voice was soft, like a girl's.

Yurovsky pulled away from him again, dug under his cassock for his own pistol and began walking away towards the guards, firing directly at them. One, two, three . . . firing at a steady rate. Ryzhkov followed him for a few steps and then knelt, braced his arm on his knee and squeezed off three shots of his own. After the second, the men got up and fled down the tracks.

He caught up to Yurovsky, who was standing there looking at the gun in his hand. He'd used all his bullets. For a moment they just looked at each other, then he saw Yurovsky's eyes travel to Ryzhkov's gun. 'One for you and one for me?' he said calmly.

'No, no, brother. It's not over yet. We go and we catch them.' For a moment Yurovsky's expression changed. Ryzhkov could see the tears in his eyes. It had been a long and futile chase already. A tremor ran through his body. He made a sound like a little cough, a sob of desperation.

'We go. I have a way, Yakov,' Ryzhkov said.

'You're insane.'

'I think I have a way.'

Down the tracks the guards had recovered and gathered two fresh recruits to take up their pursuit.

'We have to go now, comrade,' Ryzhkov said. For a moment Yurovsky just stood there calmly watching the policemen creeping towards them. If they got within shooting range he might have to give up on Yurovsky, he thought.

'I'm not going to let you die here, Yakov. Come on now,' Ryzhkov said. And he took him by the hand and began leading him obediently towards the shadows, past the crumpled body of Verena Eikhe, hero of the people's revolution.

34

'This is the place, Excellency,' Volkov said to Giustiniani.

For a moment they stood outside the tall building. It was less than a block from the main plaza at the centre of the city. They had dragooned a section of five Czech soldiers from a checkpoint at the confluence of the two largest streets just in front of the Municipal Hall, and they had sent a runner back for more help.

'There isn't time to wait for the others, but send someone around the back, there might be a stairway. Quickly!' Giustiniani said.

Volkov and two of the soldiers broke off and made their way through the foyer to the rear of the building. They found the *dvornik*, who like all such janitors was drunk, addled, and fit only to empty the night-soil buckets when the carts came around each week.

Giustiniani's Russian was too grammatically sophisticated for the man's hopeless ear. They were wasting precious minutes trying to find the exact room number of Ivanis's flat.

It was on the third floor, at the back, number 34, and they climbed the stairs quietly, guns drawn. Giustiniani was in the lead, hating that he was wearing his best pair of boots, which creaked. The building was neither rich nor poor, there was carpet, a little soiled and threadbare in places, laid along the corridors. They didn't switch on the lights on the landings.

When they got to the third floor they made sure the bathroom and the water closets were vacant. As they were moving towards number 34 an old man popped his head out of his apartment, but fell silent when he saw the guns and the look in their eyes.

The key went in softly and the lock turned with a barely audible snap.

Giustiniani waited a bare half-second, waiting for a gunshot if Ivanis had heard them coming, and when it didn't come he and the corporal jumped through the doorway.

The shades were drawn, the room lit only by a long rectangle of light that filtered through the paper. The window was open. The sergeant flicked on the lights and the room was suddenly lit with a dim rosy light from the overhead chandelier.

An unmade bed. A table. A chest of drawers with one open drawer. A chair. Some clothing strewn across the floor. Another chair in the corner with a pair of boots underneath. And that was all. Nothing.

They all relaxed for a moment.

The corporal looked over at him, waiting.

'Search,' he said.

Demtschenko and the soldiers started going through everything, looking under the mattress, the empty chest. There was a cupboard on one side of the room, some uneaten food. A bottle of schnapps. They found magazines, a copy of *Figaro* that was more than two months out of date.

'When did he take these rooms?' he asked the *dvornik*, who frowned, shrugged, wrung his hands and gazed around the ceiling as if inspecting for leaks. Giustiniani walked over

309

and slapped the man hard twice. All the others stopped and looked at the two of them, then Demtschenko started trying to translate. It took a few minutes to learn that Ivanis had moved into the building in July.

'The Bolsheviks were in town then,' Giustiniani said to no one in particular.

The *dvornik* obediently hovered in the doorway, doubtless hoping there would be no more questions in Italian-inflected Russian, mopped his brow and wetted his lips.

It only took a few minutes to search the room, but Giustiniani made them do it all again, turning the drawers over and looking at their bottoms, pulling the furniture away from the walls, climbing on a chair so that he could inspect the light socket, making one of the men go down the hall and check inside the toilet tank. At each request the soldiers looked at him wonderingly.

Something had been glued to the bottom of one of the cupboard drawers; the marks still remained. The tiny bookcase had been emptied out before they arrived, and something taken away from the back of it. Why would anyone spill out their shelf of cheap paperback novels on the floor, then go out stealing from their employer, and then abandon their rooms?

His heart was racing, and he was struck by the foolhardiness he'd displayed by procuring the transit pass for Sophie. He'd had to cadge it from de Heuzy, and now he began to put it together with his suspicions of the man.

When they'd met the Czechs he sent word the station with orders to stop the train and remove Sophie Buxhoeveden and anyone that answered Ivanis's description.

A soldier came in from the bathroom. 'I found this, Excellency,' the young man said. He was holding a wastebasket in his hand. When Giustiniani looked he saw it was full of shards of broken wood and glass, and bits of copper wire.

'Ahh,' he said quietly, turned the contents out on the table and began moving them about with his finger.

'What is it?' the sergeant asked.

He turned over a few more of the bits without answering, and then went over to the window, rolled up the shade. It was the usual double-glazed window with a central pane for ventilation in winter. Giustiniani pushed it open and leaned out into the darkness. Below him two infantrymen were idling in the courtyard, smoking.

He ran his hands out the window and felt along the sides of the wall. After a moment he found the nail and the thin wire attached to it; a tail hung from it, long enough to feed back up through the window.

'It's a wireless. Put the pieces in a bag and take them to the station, would you, Volkov?'

'Yes, sir.'

'I've never seen one of those, sir,' the corporal said.

'We have them on submarines. But this is something special, and we only have just a little part of it. He smashed it, you see? Dumped the pieces here and there.'

There was the sound of boots running up the stairs, and the *dvornik* shrank nervously away when Giustiniani appeared at the threshold. A young infantryman turned at the stair and ran down the corridor followed by a squad of soldiers, rifles at the ready. Too late, he was thinking.

The sweating infantryman snapped to attention. 'The station telegraph has been destroyed by fire, Excellency!'

'What?'

'Tonight, Excellency. Only minutes ago. They say it's impossible to contact Perm until morning.'

'Bloody Christ in hell!' Giustiniani hissed. The *dvornik* reflexively put his arms up to block the blow.

'There was an attack on the train as well. There was shooting and a man answering the description sent this out

311

just before the fire broke out,' the boy bowed and stiffly extended a telegraph form for Giustiniani's appraisal.

He took it and moved into the light:

SPECIAL SALES #R4-0B3

NO RECEIPT. STOCK LIQUIDATED. TWO PIECES REMAIN. REQUIRE INSURANCE EN ROUTE OR WILL DISCARD. REPLY PERM SOONEST.

TODMANN.

He read the paper and then read it again. The room seemed to slowly whirl, the way it felt when a small boat was held in a current so powerful that it couldn't be seen, only felt, a dizzying feeling that threatened to make him nauseous.

He was a creature of the water, not of this land of steppes and forests without limit. He was supposed to be fighting a war with torpedoes and deck guns, not subterfuge and bedroom betrayals. Did she know what she was doing to him? He had let a woman make a fool of him, he realized. He should have realized all along, realized when Ivanis mixed him a Sambo. A drink like that? How would a Russian bartender know about something like that?

He should have seen Ryzhkov for whatever he was, interrogated him until he coughed up everything he knew; instead he'd trusted him, given him latitude. He felt a fresh wave of nausea, combined with shame at how greatly he'd failed.

'Has anyone seen Inspector Strilchuk?' he asked the young soldier who'd run back from the station.

But the only answer was silence.

35

'Quiet,' he commanded her from out of the darkness.

A few minutes before one of the officers had come back down the train, knocked on their door, and the Baroness had been ordered to extinguish all the lights. It was regrettable, but there were still Bolshevik patrols in the forests along the tracks, he explained. 'Of course,' Sophie had said in her little girl's voice, waiting for him to leave and stop staring at her.

'Quiet. Stop your tears, damn it,' he said to her. She stood up and started back to the rear of the car, more to get away from him than anything else.

'Leave them alone. There's nothing you can do. I took care of them myself.' Now his voice was like ice, utterly frozen against her. She came back and settled into her place on the sofa. After a moment she asked, 'Could you close the windows? There's a draught.'

'Close them yourself.' Just surly ice. She only sat there, the tears welling up again, trying to stifle a sob that wouldn't stay down.

'You know nothing of necessity, Sophie,' he said. Now the ice was calmer but the weight just as heavy. A glacier. 'You know nothing of the way the world works. You've led a privileged life.'

'I . . . I've led a life of . . . sacrifice.'

She was unprepared for his slap when it came in the darkness. How could he even see her in the gloom? But it knocked her sideways on the sofa, and she flinched away and drew her legs up.

'You've sacrificed exactly nothing!' He was on top of her now, holding her down on the torn sofa. A little spray of horsehair had poked its way through the brocade and pricked her cheek. She was too terrified to do more than whimper. 'You've been a child of privilege all your life. You've been given everything you wanted by your royal pals.'

'You killed them, didn't you?' she said.

She hadn't meant to actually say it. She was shocked when the words came out of her mouth. She hadn't even really thought it out, clearly. It had only been a suspicion in her mind, a fearful fantasy. But the words had leapt out. He too was surprised by her declaration and for a moment he drew away, and she tensed, waiting for him to hit her again.

'I told you what happened,' he said.

'Yes, you did.'

'You've been a part of this from the beginning, don't forget. We were together in the whole thing. We are partners. Collaborators. One day, when this is all over, you're going to tell our grandchildren how you helped save the heir to the throne of Russia. You'll be a great heroine. But you've got to be strong. You can't be a girl any more. You have to find your killer, the killer deep inside you, Sophie.' He was sitting up beside her now, his hand on her knee.

'I'm not a collaborator. You lied to me.'

'Be quiet. Stop it.'

'You killed that man.'

'He was a thief. He was sent by the wop to spy on us.'

314

'You . . . you . . .' she could only bleat.

'Later, when the soldiers back there are asleep, I'll throw him out,' he said. She felt him rubbing her knee, stroking it, back and forth, the kind of motion you'd use to quiet an infant. 'And I'll clean up everything, you don't need to worry about that. Just be quiet and go to sleep. Don't worry so much. We're going to make it, Sophie. You have to believe. I keep telling you that, but it's true. You have to believe.'

'I don't understand you . I don't know you. I don't know why you're doing this, any of it.'

'I'm doing it – I *was* doing it – for the Fatherland,' he said, his voice low, humorous and ironic. 'I was doing it for a lot of reasons, a lot of other people's reasons. I might still be doing it for them. I haven't decided yet, to be honest.'

'I thought we were doing it because it was the right thing to do.'

He laughed, just a little sniff in the darkness. 'Sure it was,' he said. 'The right thing.'

'You don't have to tell me about it. I don't want to know. You can't bring the dead back to life,' she said. She wanted to lock her suspicions away and never take them out again. Somewhere safe where they would stay a secret, even to her. But Alexandra had been her friend, she told herself. She had.

'You talk too much,' he said.

'I'm sorry.'

'We've got something good back there. We've got something valuable that other people want. That's power, Sophie. More powerful than a title or a crown on your head. We're going to use that power however we need to. We're going to come out on top. Don't worry about it. My mother had gypsy blood, I can see the future, you know.'

They had travelled slowly up the rising ground out of Yekaterinburg, stopping only briefly at the freight station on the outsirts of the city. He had taken out his pistol – she had

315

only seen it once before – and waited with his back pressed against the door. Ready to kill, she thought. Or run. But in the end no one came to bother them, and after only a few moments, since there were no soldiers getting on or off at the tiny station, they began moving again, rolling slowly through the dark forests.

'I can't stop shaking,' she said. 'It's all too horrible.'

His laugh was just as much as surprise as his slap. 'It's not very bad at all. This is nothing.' She thought he was going to tell her about the war again. Whenever he wanted to impress her, he told her about the war.

'Maybe not for you, but –'

'It's only because you've had a privileged life. That's what I mean.' The hand on the knee again. 'Look, we are different. The two of us, we are a different type of creature entirely, you and I. You're not just a daft aristocratic bitch, Sophie. You're a queen in your own way. You're better than either of those two back there. You're entitled to use them, or kill them, or sell them, or make what you will of your opportunity to be their guardian. That's because you're better than them. You're made of better stuff. You deserve more than they gave you. "Lady in waiting"!' he said, his voice full of contempt.

They travelled on for a while.

'Should I check on them?'

'I tied her up. The boy is still asleep. Check on them if you want.'

'Are you tired? You must be tired.'

'Yes.' He had slipped his hand under her skirt. His hand was on her thigh now. Kneading her like bread.

'Don't,' she said.

'What?'

'Don't. Not now.'

'What's wrong? You should be happy. I saved your life back there, you know.'

'Just don't.' She pushed his hand away. Now he loomed over her.

'I don't understand you,' he said. 'I give you everything. I put my life in the fire for you. For them. I've done it all. You wanted to get out of Russia, and now you're going to get the chance, but –' His hand was up her skirts again, and she tried to push him away, but he only leaned on her with his weight. 'Don't start crying,' he said. 'Don't start again, or I'll give you something to really cry about.'

And then he was kissing her. She felt his hand, and his tongue filling her mouth; after a long moment she brought the kiss to an end, her hands on his cheeks, resisting the urge to push him away because he wouldn't like it, instead made her voice as sweet as she could, begging him to let her go. 'You're tired, baby. You should rest.'

'I'm never that tired,' he said.

She waited until he slept, and then she made her way back to the bedroom compartment, absurdly knocking with one knuckle before she opened the door, and in defiance of the Czech army snapped on the lights. It cast a dim glow down the side of the wall of the stinking little room. Marie looked up at her. The swelling had gone down but her face was purple and yellow, with bruises that fanned out from her nose. It had been flattened horribly. My God, Sophie thought with a shudder, what the poor child has been through.

She put one finger to her lips, reached over to untie her wrists. The girl began to cry, dry sobs that convulsed her body so that she was rocking back and forth. It woke Alexei.

'Are we at the hotel yet?' he muttered.

'There's no hotel,' Sophie shushed him, it coming out a little harder than she meant. 'There's nothing like that.'

Alexei rolled over and looked at her. 'My knee hurts,' he said.

'Listen,' she said to them. 'Listen to me. We're in trouble. I tried but I . . . I didn't mean . . . I made a mistake.' She had started to cry herself, tears pouring out of her eyes. Marie snuffled and was just looking at her, rubbing her wrists. They were bruised where he had done them up too tight. 'I love you,' Sophie said to the children. 'I love you both. You have to believe me.'

'Is he still here?' the girl said, staring straight at her. For a moment they just looked into each other's eyes. 'He is here, isn't he?' Marie said.

'It's very dangerous,' she said.

'Is there anything to eat?' Alexei said. Marie looked over at him and hissed him into silence.

'Be ready,' Sophie said. 'When I say, be ready to run, both of you.'

'What's this all about? Can't you tell them we need to eat?' Alexei said. He was up on one elbow, and then rolled half sideways and noisily farted.

'Stop it, barbarian,' Marie said, pushing him back down onto the pillows. She looked up at Sophie. 'We're ready,' she said.

'You'd better sleep, you need your rest,' she said, but Marie was quicker. She reached the bottle first and poured it out on the floor.

'We're ready,' she said.

36

So secure were the Czech forces that there were no sentries to guard the entrance to the motor pool garage. Ryzhkov and Yurovsky were cautious at first. Yurovsky groused the entire time while they stood in the shadows watching the place, but then Ryzhkov stormed into the place, Yurovsky tugging at his sleeve, beginning to panic, acutely aware of his status as the most wanted Bolshevik behind White lines.

Propas's quarters were above the motor pool office; clearly he was a man who loved his work. He sat up in his bed and stared at the two men standing in his doorway, probably wondering if the whole thing was a dream.

'I'm very sorry to wake you, Propas.'

'Oh, it's you, sir. I'm sorry, my eyes aren't what they used to be, especially when I first wake up,' Propas said, swinging his legs out of the bed. Ryzhkov and Yurovsky stepped into the room and Ryzhkov lit the lantern. When Propas pushed back the sheets Yurovsky could see the wide scar that covered one side of his torso and shoulder. Propas caught the direction of his look.

'A burn, Father,' he said. 'Very dangerous collision when I was driving for Monsieur Lemmers in France.' He blinked and rubbed his eyes, then focused on Yurovsky for another moment, then frowned. 'Is there some sort of problem?'

'Unfortunately we're pressed for time, Propas. Do you have something fast, like the little yellow one I saw?'

'Oh yes. That's the Talbot. British built. Very quick. Everyone wants it, but Prince Riza-Kuli-Mirza is at the top of the list. I take it out every week, just to keep it limber, you know.'

'How far can it go?'

'Around the world if your bladder can hold out that long, sir.'

'I mean, before you need to get more petrol?'

'It has a large tank. Perhaps two hundred miles. Let's see, that's three hundred and fifty versts.'

'We would like to borrow it for a while.'

'Oh, no, sir. As I explained, everyone is coveting that little piece. They had a meeting just the other night completely devoted to the disposition of the car. De Heuzy came up with the idea of auctioning it off. You might be able to bid on it.'

'No, you see –'

'We're not bidding on anything,' Yurovsky said, reaching under his cassock and taking out his pistol.

'No, no,' Ryzhkov said, pushing the gun back down and standing in front of him. Propas had got to his feet now, a big man who'd seen a lot and come out of it not possessed with an abundance of fear.

'Excuse him, Propas, he's just excited.'

'Did you bring back my ambulance?' Propas asked. His voice was level now; the warmth had gone out of it.

'Ahh . . .'

Yurovsky stepped out from behind Ryzhkov and pointed the pistol at Propas. 'Take us to this car. We have to catch someone,' he said.

Propas didn't react at all. His eyes just narrowed and he

crossed his thick arms across the ravaged chest. 'Do you know how to drive, Excellency?' he asked calmly.

'Not something like that,' Ryzhkov said. 'We need your help, Propas. My friend, he –'

'You know they are looking for you, sir. I'll have to report the ambulance, or at least send someone to get it.'

'You'll find it down by the lake, Propas,' he said and, turning to Yurovsky, reached out and grabbed the pistol by the barrel, twisted it so that Yurovsky's fingers were caught in the guard, and pulled it out of his hand. He held the gun out to show Propas. 'I don't have time to explain. We need your help. You can tell them we stole the car, you can tell them whatever you want, but we need the car, and we need you to drive it, and we have no time,' he said.

Yurovsky paced back and forth, shaking the pain out of his hand. 'This is turning out to be a brilliant idea,' he muttered.

'Where do you want me to go, sir?'

'Perm.'

'Now, tonight?'

'We should have left ten minutes ago. It's a race, Propas. We're trying to beat the train.'

For a moment the chauffeur's eyes narrowed. He let his arms fall away, rolled the stiffness out of his shoulders. 'I suppose I could say you forced me,' he mused.

'We are. We're forcing you,' Ryzhkov said, smiling.

'Drive all night? Not exactly comfortable, and it is a very small cockpit.'

'We'll fit.'

'And directions? These Russian maps, I don't mean to be harsh, but we might be better off without one.'

'I know the way,' Yurovsky said. 'There's only one real road anyway.'

Propas looked at him for a moment and then smiled. 'All

right, gentlemen,' he said, reaching for his clothes. 'Some men are addicted to morphine, some to women. For me it's the challenge, and if truth be told I've been looking for a chance to get that thing out on an open road.'

The Talbot was protected by an embroidered bed sheet, and for a moment when Ryzhkov saw it he had doubts. The cockpit was a bench seat with a protrusion in the middle that effectively divided it into seating for only two persons. Propas had dug out a pair of mechanic's overalls for Yurovsky and had put him to work. They rolled the car out into the yard and over to the pumps. Ryzhkov was given the job of fuelling it, straining the petrol through a clean handkerchief that Propas gave him. A few minutes later he gave him a can and instructed him to fill that as well.

Ryzhkov held his breath against the fumes, worked the pump with his other hand and then capped the can and set it on the running board. Now that he could see it, he could understand why Prince Riza-Kuli-Mirza would fall in love with the little car. It looked fast even standing still. The windshield could be folded down for less resistance to the wind, the long bonnet tapered to a compact radiator, flanked by two large headlamps, and there were long sloping fenders to protect against stones and spray, all of it painted a butter-yellow.

'It's a lovely little thing, isn't it, sir?'

'What do you think it will it fetch at auction?'

'Oh, they don't know what they've got. Maybe fifty pounds, something like that. You could sell it for four times that easily if you could get it back to Britain.'

Yurovsky came back from the garage, buttoning his overalls. He had a set of goggles on his forehead, and a cap that he'd turned around backwards.

'You'd better put this on,' Propas said to Ryzhkov, handing

him a leather jacket. 'I know it's high summer, but once we get out there it will be chilly enough. Sorry, I don't have one for you, Father,' he said to Yurovsky.

'That's all right. I'm Russian, I'm used to the cold, and I'm not a Father.'

'Whatever you say, sir.'

They lashed the extra petrol can onto the rear spare tyre and rolled the car out onto the street; Propas climbed in and set the spark, and Yurovsky was given the job of turning the crank. The Talbot started immediately and they all piled in, Ryzhkov climbing over the side and wedging himself against the door, but Yurovsky was punished by having to arrange his legs around the gear shift and brake levers and perching on the little island between the seats. For all of them it was the opposite of comfortable.

It was not a roaring sound that the Talbot made as it sped through the plaza and along Glavni Prospekt, instead it was more like the sound of tearing fabric, a smooth series of growls that changed in pitch at Propas's whim. They climbed past the Ipatiev house, where for unknown reasons the palisade still remained in place. A lone sentry stepped out of his box to watch them pass. Ryzhkov gave him a wave. The city of Yekaterinburg vanished in moments.

At the intersection of the Moscow road Propas shouted to the sergeant, who recognized him, and Ryzhkov and Yurovsky, masked by their goggles, were not even questioned. The little car accelerated up the hill. There were no lights, only the gleam from the Talbot's headlamps, which shuddered and flickered so that the road and birch trees seemed to flicker as they bore on through the night.

After another few hundred metres they came upon a cart that blocked the road, and Propas abruptly slowed. 'Looks like some trouble, gentlemen,' Ryzhkov heard him say, but Yurovsky had already started to stand up in the car, and tearing off his goggles he showed his face to the men who had been guarding the road all night long.

'We're chasing the train, brothers. Let us through!' he shouted, and the volunteers immediately sprang to work. The cart magically turned to clear the path, and Propas released the brake. From out of the woods another four men had emerged at Yurovsky's appearance. They had a motley collection of rifles, and one had brought an axe that he held over his shoulder. Propas just stared at them as they approached the car.

'They passed by the tracks less than a half-hour ago! Go, commissar!' one man said as he leaped onto the fender, thrusting a package and a bottle into Yurovsky's hands. 'All power to the Ural Soviet, comrades!' the man shouted with a great laugh, finished off by slapping Propas on the back, then jumped down as the car rolled through the blockade.

Yurovsky sat down. 'They gave us their food,' he said, marvelling. Propas shifted up the gears and looked over at the parcel: bread, a large block of cheese, a long cylinder of sausage. A feast by most peasants' standards. For a moment he and Yurovsky looked at each other.

'I'll just say you forced me, eh?' Propas said.

'That's right, comrade. We're forcing you.' Yurovsky laughed, tearing the bread into three portions and doling it out as they accelerated along the road into the night.

When Yurovsky had said there was only one road, it was a lie.

There were a great many roads, but most were simple cart tracks that broke away from the wider, more travelled Moscow road; still, many of the intersections were confusing, and Yurovsky and Propas communicated with a series of hand signals, finger-pointing the way across the mountains.

The magic of it quickly wore off. The road was rutted

and dusty, and soon their faces were encrusted with insects that crashed into their skin sharp as gravel . . . well, maybe not, because if a piece of gravel had hit you at that speed it would have put out an eye. Ryzhkov tried to imagine what it would be like to be racing, following or trying to overtake another car through a spray of rocks – like being shot at repeatedly, he thought. When Yurovsky shouted for Propas to put up the windshield he shook him off, explaining that it would only cut their speed. Ryzhkov slumped down and held his hand over his face to cut the sting of it.

They climbed higher out of the birches and into the great dark fir forest. The road had long since diverted from the railroad line, and become a series of switchbacks Propas took at speed, sliding the rear of the car around in a way that made Ryzhkov want to retch.

At times the speed was unbelievable. He had never travelled so fast, he thought. He found himself tensing his fingers, his own foot working a phantom break pedal dozens of metres before Propas made the same movement and the little car slowed. It was like being on the end of an elastic band that was being stretched out and then drawn in, over and over and over.

The madness never ceased. At one point after a particularly straight stretch, then a hard braking where all the tyres actually locked up and skidded in the dirt as they plunged into a stomach-churning curve, he turned to see Yurovsky looking at him and slowly shaking his head, in a gesture of mute disbelief.

He realized that he was smiling.

Well, it was a matter of being killed in a road accident, or shot by a firing squad if the Whites took them, or, if they turned up in Moscow empty-handed, taken out to a quick death in a Lubyanka courtyard. Pick your poison, he thought, slumping even lower beneath the cowl of the little Talbot.

There was the occasional instantaneous emergency. Flying along one particularly rutted stretch of road, a creature suddenly appeared before them, lit by the beams of the head-lamps. Propas spotted it only at the last moment, and swerved the car desperately, barely missing the shape – the statue-like form of a stag, gigantic, towering above them, rooted to the middle of the road, and then it was gone, vanished behind them in the dusty dark.

At the first station where the road converged with the tracks, a single building with one long roof and a clearing piled with cut logs awaiting peace and the restarting of the Russian lumber industry, they finally stopped.

An ancient *dvornik* came out of the office. A single light-bulb burned above the door. The military train had come through, yes. How long? Oh, nearly an hour, Excellencies, nearly an hour. They had lost time coming over the moun-tains. The old man spent the entire time looking at the vehicle, which even set at idle trembled and shook like some angry dragon. Propas got out and checked the tyres, shook out his hands and pumped his legs up and down.

The old man gave them water to drink, and they all cleaned their goggles, wiped their faces and took a few moments to urinate beside the road, then Propas ushered them back into the car.

'I could sit over on this side, why not?' Yurovsky said, his voice starting to creep up in pitch towards a whine.

'No, no, I need you beside me, comrade. You're acting as my navigator,' Propas said, smiling. And when Yurovsky looked helplessly towards Ryzhkov he only got a shrug.

'You'd probably best do what he says. After all he's the driver.'

'And you did pull a gun on me, don't forget,' Propas said, shoving him into the car.

'But I didn't mean it –' Yurovsky began, but his words were lost as they turned out onto the road.

'Don't worry, we'll go faster on the downhill!' Propas shouted across to him, and Ryzhkov nodded and stuck his thumb in the air as if that would be just fine.

They plunged through the darkness, and he could indeed feel the road sloping down, then it would level and climb again. He had no idea exactly where they were, and probably neither did Propas. They were depending on Yurovsky's hand signals to guide them through the abyss.

Somewhere in the night they stopped and refilled from the petrol can they'd lashed to the back of the car. Occasionally they would slow at a washout, or creep around boulders blocking the road.

The sound of the motor had somehow vanished; Ryzhkov no longer heard it. Similarly his body had grown numb to the hard seat and the rigid edge of the door where he clung to keep his body from being slung from side to side in the corners. He heard Propas yelling to Yurovsky; they were talking about the car, he realized. He could only pick up snatches of their conversation . . . the stiffer the springs, the better the car took the corners . . . this model had something called an L-head, yes, a great advantage . . . four gears and one reverse . . . the sister model had 75 horsepower and could make 80 miles an hour, and before the war a cut-down version had set the one-hour record . . . All the while Propas's hands and feet never stopped moving, twisting the wheel about its steering shaft, working the levers that controlled the gears, throwing his weight against the brakes . . . and never ceasing to shout the little car's praises.

Climbing down through the passes heading for Perm, Ryzhkov realized the sky was a deep blue above him. The long night was over. Now he could see things alongside the road: a woodcutter's cottage, a thin stream of smoke coming from the chimney; a solitary man walking along the road who stopped and turned, then leaped onto the verge as they rocketed past; the birds of the morning, confused as they darted out of the trees to take the insects that hovered in the first rays of the dawn.

And, far below, as they crested a hill, the silver ribbon of the railroad tracks, and in the very far distance a plume of smoke.

He saw it and recognized that it could only be one thing: the locomotive of the military train bound for the battle west of Perm.

And as they all saw it Yurovsky was slapping the metal body of the little car, and slapping Propas on the back too. They had unshackled themselves from the chains of space and time, they were hurling themselves forward, three avenging angels of the new army of heaven on earth, coming with ungodly swiftness to claim back their own.

37

What defeated them was the traffic, the narrow streets and the carts and wagons, the fact that no one would move out of the way, no matter how many times Ryzhkov squeezed the silly rubber bulb that merely produced a bleat meant to alert those in your way. Compared to crossing the Urals, entering Perm was a nightmare of frustration.

The last hundred metres were covered in one long ascending burst through the gears, and they rounded the corner to discover the façade of the station in a cloud of fine yellow dust. Ryzhkov was immediately out of the car. He could see the military train stationed several tracks over, but the ambulance car was missing.

Yurovsky hung back and said his goodbyes for him. The last thing he saw of Propas was a raised hand; the man hadn't even taken time to clean his goggles.

'He's driving back today,' Yurovsky said behind him. 'He says he wants to see the countryside.'

'It's gone,' he said. Together they walked out onto the platform, a strange pair, dust and insect covered, their goggles draped about their necks, cloaked now in motley – dirty mechanic's overalls, an ill-fitting leather jacket, Yurovsky with his cap reversed. Dressed like clowns, they drew attention right away. Ryzhkov noticed it first and took his goggles off, jamming them into his pocket. 'Fix yourself,' he said, and they walked along, adjusting their clothing as best as they could, over the crossover towards the military train.

There was a boy posted there as a cadet sentry, leaning against a lamp standard. When he saw them approach he put out his cigarette, picked up his rifle and dutifully blocked their way.

'You can't come here,' the boy said. He sounded scared.

'What happened to the car that was there?'

The boy frowned, turned towards the train. 'Which one?'

'The hospital car. It was hooked up just in front of the monster.' The boy frowned and turned again. They could have taken the rifle away from him and given him a spanking, but it would have been too easy. Instead Ryzhkov took out a cigarette and gave it to him. He tucked it in his uniform pocket with a smile.

'I don't know. They must have taken it away.'

'We have to find out about that car.' Ryzhkov reached into his pocket and pulled out his papers. The boy looked at them blankly. 'We're with military intelligence in Yekaterinburg. We think there were fugitives in that car.'

'Oh, yes. We heard about that,' the boy said, gripping his rifle tighter. 'We're supposed to be on watch for a man who bombed the station last night.'

'Show us the way,' Yurovsky growled at the boy, and they headed out towards the tracks. The soldiers had spilled out of the cars and were lounging in the stairwells, strolling up and down along the tracks smoking. There were a couple of quick comments in Czech between the boy and his sergeant; he peeled off back to his post, and Ryzhkov and Yurovsky were taken to the train commandant, a sleepy man burdened with a sheaf of papers.

'I can't help you, I'm afraid,' he started right off. 'I know

330

nothing about this medical carriage,' he said in passable Russian. 'It was removed from our train less than a half-hour ago. It's probably still in the yard somewhere.'

'Do you know their destination?'

'They were originally, from the authorizations –' He took a moment to leaf through the papers on his clipboard. '– supposed to be leaving for Viatka, but I don't think that's possible any longer.'

'What about you?' Yurovsky said. The train commander's face darkened.

'It looks like Kazan for us. Trotsky is about to take the city. We'll probably be too late.' The commander's face had taken on the weary expression of a man who was mourning his defeat in advance. Ryzhkov had seen it far too often. 'Something about the locomotive, technical things. It's not up to me,' the Czech officer shrugged.

'Thank you. We have to find that car.'

'So they sent you to look for the bomber they warned us about?'

'We're police, yes,' Ryzhkov said.

'Well, they took the ambulance off and put it on that track there. Where it went after that is none of my concern. It was a private car anyway. Some sort of charity.' Ryzhkov saw that a boy was running up with a telegram in his hands. Behind him followed a cadaverous clerk in a railwayman's uniform with a sheaf of papers.

'Finally,' said the commander. 'Sergeant!' he called, and Ryzhkov saw the unmistakable signs written in the body language of the men gathered there along the tracks. They were getting their movement orders.

'Good luck to you,' Ryzhkov said to the commander, whose attention was on the telegram, took Yurovsky by the sleeve, and together they began briskly walking towards the head of the train.

The engineer was climbing back into the cabin and the fireman was already hard at work, standing on top of the tender, shovelling coal along the chute that carried it to the firebox. They shouted up to the man and asked about who had moved the ambulance car.

'Oh, that's that rat-arsed Torko and his brother. They've gone already,' the fireman said. He stood up high on the mountain of coal and peered down the tracks, shook his head. 'I thought you might be able to see it, but it's just gone. Why they'd be so eager to get to Kazan, I don't know.' But Ryzhkov and Yurovsky were already running around the front of the locomotive, surveying the yard.

There was nothing. The summer sun slammed down across the empty tracks and the air was still. Passenger and refugee trains had long gone. If you were in Perm now, you weren't getting out.

'What about that?' Yurovsky said. The tone of his voice was doubtful. Coming in their direction two tracks away was a shuttle engine. A beat-up antique. A face had been painted on the front of the boiler with chalk. The rain had made it look like it was crying white tears.

'Why not?' Ryzhkov said, and together they began to run towards the engine, waving their hands. The driver saw them, woke from his reverie at the last moment, reached up, pulled a lever and braked to a stop.

'How fast is this thing?' Ryzhkov said.

'Who wants to know?'

'Police.'

'You don't look like police to me.'

'Don't play with us. How fast can you go?' Ryzhkov said.

'It's fast enough. Why?'

'Did you see that train that just left?'

The man's face was all the answer they needed. 'That's Torko,' he said with a little smile.

'Go then,' said Yurovsky, climbing aboard. 'We're after them.'

'Hey, wait a minute, I can't just take off –' But by then Yurovsky was up the ladder and had his gun in the man's side.

'Get moving,' Ryzhkov said.

'We have to go to the roundhouse and turn around.'

'You can go backwards, can't you?' Yurovsky said, shoving the gun hard into the man's round back.

'Reverse, yes, of course, but the strain will kill her.'

'There's no time to turn around.' Now Ryzhkov was on board. On the other side of the cabin was a young boy, his features flattened and crushed by some sort of defect of birth. He stood looking from one to the other. The driver reached out and motioned to him.

'Why don't we all stay calm,' said the driver. He was a man who liked his food, liked his drink; it showed in the placid rolls of fat that encased his body. He said something to the boy – a private language – and in response he levered open the firebox and began to shovel.

'It'll be hard catching them, Excellency. They've a much bigger engine.'

Ryzhkov just looked at him, flashed the gun, and then put it away. 'Just do your best, that's all we ask,' he said.

'I don't understand why so many people want to go to Kazan today,' the driver said. They were gathering speed now, the train clattering over the points, angling towards the track that would take them over the Kama river and the route west to the city of the Tatars, the great historic high-tide mark of the Mongol hordes – Kazan, city of the Golden East.

Robert Wilton heaved a great sigh, straightened his shoulders, decided that he ought to repair to the bar, order something cool and spend the afternoon reassessing his next move. Kazan and the Volga was obviously where the action was; he should file something about the battle. It was obviously going to be a turning point – you could read it in the faces of the White Guards; everyone had begun to wear grim expressions, and no one would say much. He really should be there. Probably time to reach into the old wallet again and bribe his way down the tracks. He had just pushed his way through the wide glass-paned doors when he saw the woman, obviously in distress.

Something about her was familiar. She was weeping, sitting alone, quite well dressed, attractive, but a little unkempt – her hair had come slightly awry, and her dress could do with a steam. But he recognized her, or at least he thought he did.

'Excuse me,' he said, doffing the fedora, resisting the urge to smooth his own hair. He was a little travel worn himself, but why call attention? 'Excuse me, but I believe we have met. I'm Robert Wilton of *The Times*,' he said, putting on his best smile, a little bow from the hips. 'I don't wish to intrude, but I wonder if I might be of some assistance?'

'Oh, no, no. Thank you, Mr . . .'

'Wilton. Oh my! Yes, now I recognize you,' he said, slipping into the chair across from her, simultaneously waving at the waiter. 'You're Baroness von Buxhoeveden.'

'Ahh.' She suddenly teared up again and clutched at her sodden handkerchief. He reached for his own automatically. It wasn't fresh, but it would serve. 'Dear lady,' he said.

'I'm so very sorry, Mr . . .'

'Wilton, Robert. Back in Tyumen I had an interview scheduled with you. I knew I remembered. I never forget a face, especially such a lovely one,' he said tapping his temple with one finger. He thought about moving closer to her, but next to her chair was parked a porter's handcart piled with boxes and topped with a barely concealed wreath of sausages covered with oily paper.

'Might I offer you something? Tea? Something a little stiffer? I'm having a lemonade myself. Moscow style.' He winked and looked up at the waiter, who smiled beatifically down on them. 'Might I recommend one? Just a little kick in it. You look as if you could use a pick-me-up, eh? They serve it cold. Perfection on a day like this.'

She smiled. Nodded her acceptance.

'I say, that wasn't your carriage that was outfitted as a hospice?'

She hesitated, looked out towards the yard. 'Yes, they've gone on without me. I went for provisions, you see.'

'Everything is an emergency, this close to the fighting,' he murmured. 'And most gallant of you, but now you're stranded, eh? It's bloody hell, these wars. It damages us all.' He took the risk and reached out and patted her hand. In response she placed her other hand on top of his, gave a little squeeze and then retracted them both.

'Thank you so much, Mr Wilton. You're so very kind. Yes. I am stranded here. They have . . . requisitioned my car, and . . .' She suddenly looked absolutely stricken, staring out at the empty yard as if she had the ability to see beyond it somehow, as if there was a solution waiting on the tracks. It was the end of an era for people like her, Wilton thought.

'You know, I happened to be walking through the station at Yekaterinburg the other night and I had the most curious experience. I looked up into the windows of your car – of course I didn't know it was yours at the time, I didn't recognize it – and I saw this wounded soldier's face. Just a boy. And y'know he looked exactly like the Tsarevich.'

She turned to him now. Her mouth was open, the sweet little chin trembling, and the tears again beginning to start. He just smiled at her, a man who'd been around.

'The last time we spoke we were cut short. You were required elsewhere, I believe. Something about –'

'I . . . I was called to give testimony.'

'Yes, that's right, for Conte Giustiniani's inquiry. I was so sorry about that, since I desperately wanted to hear a bit more from you. After all, you were the Empress's closest friend.'

'Yes, her friend,' she said. And there was that look again. Straight on to him. Open as a child. He'd seen it a thousand times, that look. A secret on the verge of being transformed into a confession. The waiter appeared with the Moscow lemonades.

'You know, Baroness, you're a very interesting person. A real character. And you have seen many things. Things unexpected. Horrible, life-altering events, and, well . . . Sometimes the simple act, just the simple act of talking about your troubles to a willing ear can have the greatest benefit, my dear.' He reached out and took her hand again, just a little squeeze and a retreat. 'Oh, it goes without saying that my newspaper would be interested in your story. But, if you ask me, that's far too common for you. They wrap fish with newspapers, but have you ever thought about a book?'

'Oh, I'm not a writer.'

'But I am, dear lady. And I have been, as they say, around the pitch a time or three, and I've learned that everyone has a story. I know 'em when I see 'em, and more than that, I know what they will fetch on the open market,' he said, looking kindly into her eyes.

And he raised his glass, and she did the same.

336

38

'Pretty simple, eh?' Torko spun from the cabin and shot him a look. He had his hand on a highly burnished lever. 'You pull this way, you go faster, you let it go, you slow down.' He shrugged and laughed. 'You pull it out, clip this over, and it leaves your hands free for other things.' At which Torko's brother mimed masturbating, and they all laughed.

'A cretin could do it. That's why I have him,' Torko said, and the other brother reached out and pushed him in reply. They were both happy to make a little money on the side. A simple trip to Kazan with nothing much to pull behind them; if they were lucky they'd be back by morning. And it wasn't even so bad to be going into the teeth of battle: at Kazan they would be picking up; certainly there would be cars of wounded or refugees to bring back to Perm. So, with a pocketful of jewels to ease the way, the plan had worked for everyone.

As they crossed the hills and climbed out of Perm, he sat and listened to their stories and took an interest in how they manipulated the great machine. The levers could be set by stops and ratchets, the fire was stoked regularly, based on dials that indicated the pressure in the boiler. There were other gauges and dials, but it seemed that the principal job was to regulate the speed and manage the steam. After all, you couldn't take a wrong turn. He noticed that both men alternated looking ahead to keep an eye on the tracks ahead, depending on the direction of the curve, and more attentively when they approached the smaller stations. Checking for signals, undoubtedly, since this was an unscheduled run.

For an hour or so he watched them, helped them, without getting himself too filthy, by shovelling coal down closer to the chute so that it would be ready when Torko's brother needed to load the firebox. When he felt his stomach growl he made an excuse to climb back. He would get something to eat, and check on the two Romanovs. He wouldn't need them much longer, he thought.

Once in Kazan he could have his pick of at least three escape routes. He could push through the lines there, infiltrate himself into Bolshevik-controlled Russia, make contact with someone from the embassy, and get out overland across Europe; he could bribe his way up the Volga as far as possible, heading for St Petersburg, and get out via Finland; or, depending on the progress of the southern White armies, he could set off to the south, down the Volga, with a goal of the Black Sea. The last route was the most dangerous, and the longest. It would be used only as a last resort.

These thoughts occupied his mind as he climbed carefully across the top of the tender, with Torko calling out cautionary instructions to him that he couldn't hear, and having to turn his back on the man, gripping the low rail tightly and sidling along the little ledge surrounding the mountain of coal, walking like a bent-over vegetable picker until he reached the ladder at the very back of the tender, reverse himself again, and then carefully climb down. The rungs were made of small-diameter steel rods, rubbed into shining slipperiness. At the bottom he hung for a moment and then reached down and put his foot on the end of the ramp that spanned from the tender to the buffer of Sophie's carriage. It could be raised and lowered from the tender, and it jittered constantly with a high-pitched clanking. He balanced his way across it and into the buffer. He had not locked the door to the car; he clawed the handle down, pulled the heavy door back and moved into the car –

And saw the two of them there.

Alexei saw him first. He was sitting on the sofa, looking deathly pale, his fine features like a translucent mask, the blue, tired eyes looking up at once.

Marie reacted to her brother's look. She was dressing him, helping him with his socks. He must have had some sort of relapse. Sophie had mentioned that he had a disease, something rare that was never spoken of, that required special handling. It was the root of it all, she said, beginning to cry. She was always crying, as if that would do any good. The root of it all, she told him: Rasputin, Alexandra's own illnesses, the family's mania for privacy. The root of it all.

For a moment the three of them just stood there staring at each other.

He could see from the boy's expression that Marie had told him everything she knew: who he really was, what had happened to the rest of his kin.

He smiled. It was amusing really. Right in front of him he had the perfect exhibit of the uselessness of the noble classes – a young, foolish boy. A scared, angry invalid. Too proud for his own good and anxious to survive and avenge the death of his father, the Tsar. An angry child with absurd ideas who had jacked himself up with hate and was now committed to some desperate and idiotic gesture.

'Since you're getting dressed, I assume you are thinking of going somewhere?'

Marie broke first, rushing to the counter and grasping for

339

a pair of scissors that she had found, and put there for that specific purpose.

Once she had them in her hand she whirled to face him, crouched like the little tigress she was. He was coming to like her in spite of her pushiness, even to admire her. Perhaps in Germany she might have made something of herself, but it was too late. You had to take girls like her and train them from childhood. Not unattractive, and her face would heal.

He took a step towards her and she began her rush as the boy was struggling to get up from the sofa. He grabbed her hand, bent the scissors out of it and threw her down to the floor, and when she scrambled back up to her knees he simply leaned down and swatted her, hard on the top of her head, and she fell down and began to cry.

'I don't want to hurt you. Didn't I explain that already?' he said, pushing Alexei back down onto the sofa. Even that little movement hurt him; he winced and made a little groaning sound. He hauled Marie into position beside the boy.

'Try anything like that again,' he said to her, 'and I'll kill your little brother. Do you understand?'

She looked up at him through the tears, not even nodding. Stubborn little bitch. He reached down and took her chin between his thumb and forefinger, pushed her face from one side to the other. It really was too bad about the nose. Maybe they could get it fixed in Germany. She was dressed in a chemise, and she had put on a nurse's uniform, but the buttons were undone. It hung about her like a raincoat, and he could see the swell of her breasts.

'I'm going to tie you up,' he said, smiling, 'until you decide to cooperate a little more.' The boy was just looking up at him with those flat blue eyes.

To demonstrate his power he walked away from them, back into the bedroom, and pulled the top sheet off the bed, dragged it out behind him and, using the scissors, made a

340

series of cuts and then ripped long strips out of the fabric. The boy was leaning over, still trying to get his socks on.

'I told you that I was going to help you. I gave you my word. That's something I don't do very lightly,' he said to them.

'The word of a murderer? What good is that?' the boy said, and it stopped him for a moment. He could kill him right now, toss him out the back of the car. What good was he any more? Why not? The girl was slumped beside her brother, whimpering. And, standing there, he made his plan. Kill the boy and dump him before they reached Kazan, and then he could take his time with the girl.

He began by tying the boy's hands with the strips of sheet.

'You know, for a Tsar you haven't been educated very well, have you?' he said, jerking the knots tight. The boy squirmed against the pain, but said nothing. 'Someone told you a fairy tale a long time ago, a mythic legend that people of royal blood were all very special, yes? Someone told you that the Kaiser was your great cousin in the sky, and that whatever happened, whatever politics might come into play, you'd always be safe, didn't they?'

'You're the one who's uneducated,' the boy said to him quietly, watching as he began working on his feet. Just moving them together must have hurt him; the knee was swollen. Maybe it was some kind of gout, he thought as he tied the ankles together.

'You're a beast,' the girl said. 'You're mad!' she said louder, as if it was the worst insult she could imagine.

He smiled at her. 'Perhaps I am. But how does that make me different to anyone else, eh?' he said, reaching over and taking her hands to lash them together. As he did it he looked into her eyes.

'Don't hurt her,' the boy said. He had caught the look; he knew what was coming.

'Oh, don't worry, Your Majesty, I'll be very nice to your sister,' he said. She had started to cry again. He raised her skirts, to tie her legs together, and there was something about the touch of the hairs on her legs that aroused him. He pulled her to her feet.

'Don't you hurt her!' the boy cried louder, squirmed against the sofa and only succeeded in falling over.

'If you're planning on going somewhere, you won't need these, will you,' he said, reaching down and grabbing the boy's shoes. They were walking shoes, of excellent quality, soft leather. They would bring a fortune on the street, he thought.

He pulled Marie along by one elbow back to the bedroom. He could open a window and get rid of the smell. He tossed her inside. She was sobbing now. He reached down and caressed her ankle for a moment, and then decided to take off her shoes as well.

'You think you're going somewhere, thinking about making an escape?' he said loudly so that the boy would hear him from the front of the car. 'You won't get very far without these,' he called, stepping back into the corridor and opening the rear door to toss them out.

And that was when he saw a yard engine, chugging along backwards, coming up behind them. There were four men in the cabin and two of them were looking in his direction. He recognized one as the White cop he'd served in the hotel. The other dug in his pants and pulled out a revolver.

He was so shocked that he just stood there with his mouth open while the man aimed and fired. Beside him there was the snap and spray of splinters as the bullet punctured the rear wall of the carriage.

It catalysed him into action, and he slammed the door, snapped over the lock and began running back through the carriage, past Alexei flailing away on the sofa, shouting curses at him in three languages – all of his elaborate plans for the girl forgotten.

'Good shooting!' the engineer shouted to Yurovsky, but at the same time he pushed his son down into shelter behind the tender. It was a low one, not meant to carry very much coal, and they were almost completely exposed.

They had been gaining on the ambulance car by inches, helped by the fact that they had crept up behind them in surprise.

'Come on,' said Ryzhkov as he climbed over the coal towards the coupler that extended off the rear of the little engine.

'What?'

'Come on! If we don't get on board now, they'll outrun us!'

'It's just a little too far, don't you think,' said Yurovsky as he followed.

Ryzhkov turned and waved at their pilot; he, in turn, rechecked his levers and gauges, then turned and shrugged. The gap between the two trains was maddeningly close now . . . a matter of perhaps only three metres and a long jump from one train to another.

'I wouldn't do that if I were you.'

'Yes, yes,' Ryzhkov said, thinking that, yes, he was crazy, it was too far, that he would never make it, all his last thoughts rushing through his mind. Thinking that it was just because of the thrill of being in combat again, the sound of the gunshot, and knowing inside himself what it could do to men, not just to him in particular – to be shot at and the surge of energy that made him see everything in a clear, straight line.

They had reached a slight grade in the line, the momentum of the two trains changed almost imperceptibly, and the yard engine was closing the gap.

'Oh . . . oh . . .' he heard Yurovsky say behind him as he jumped.

He almost made it, and would have, had not the coupler been oily, and his foot, clad in leather-bottomed street shoes, slipped, so that he was hanging from the narrow railing by the door.

There was the immediate squealing of the shuttle engine's driving wheels as the brakes were set. Ryzhkov felt his hand too weak to grip and began sliding down the narrow hand rail. And then he was clawing, first against the coupler, and then at the hoses that hung loose beneath it . . . And then he lost his grip.

He dangled for a moment, his feet knocking painfully against the sleepers, losing one of his inadequate shoes and then, with the switching engine skidding on the rails above him, fell under.

There was a moment when he knew he was certainly dead, lying there with the wind knocked out of him, looking up at the sky above, the last thing he would ever glimpse – and then it was eclipsed by the darkness of the tender rolling over him . . . and stopping, so that the sky was blacked out by the iron bottom of the tender, and he was suddenly aware of the heat and smell of burning steel radiating from the rails where the little engine had ground to a halt.

Then Yurovsky was down under the back of the train, dragging him out from under the tender, whirling him about and shouting in his face, '– your revolutionary duty! Your job is to survive, not to waste your effectiveness on romantic heroics! If you ever do something like that again I will kill you! Do you understand! I'll kill you myself, with my own hands.'

'You're entirely correct, comrade,' he said a little shakily.

'My God!' Yurovsky looked at him for a moment, then ran his hands around the waistband of his trousers. 'At least you didn't lose your pistol,' he said, and then whirled him round and took him by the arm back to the steps where they climbed back up onto the little engine. The boy was furiously shovelling coal into the firebox. He stopped when Ryzhkov came up and collapsed against the coal chute, shook his head and laughed at him. The old man laughed too, and reached down and cupped his balls. They were moving again. Yurovsky took a step up onto the tender.

'They're gone now,' he said.

They began climbing; the engine was powerful and accelerated well up to a certain point. They rounded a long curve, descending this time, and Ryzhkov got to his knees to watch. In the distance they could see a tall plume of smoke issuing from the Torko brothers' locomotive. The trees parted and they had reached a patchwork of fields. There were a few houses sprinkled out among dry stalks, cut back to stubble, their grain long ago requisitioned by the Red Army to feed its retreat back across the Volga.

The engineer had come to stand beside them. He was looking intently down the tracks.

'Now we will see,' he said, and reached down and put a comforting hand on Ryzhkov's shoulder. And then a moment later, he laughed. 'Ah-ha!' he said, making a little dance. When the boy turned and tried to decipher his father's mood, in response he made some gestures, and the boy threw down the shovel and sprang to the controls.

'You,' said the old man to Ryzhkov, 'get ready to jump out and turn the switch to white, eh? Just grab the lever and give it a kick. And when we stop, you run ahead to the next switch and do the same,' he said to Yurovsky.

Ryzhkov and Yurovsky looked at each other doubtfully.

'Christ, just give it a kick and make it white, that's all. A child could do it.'

'But they're gone,' Ryzhkov said.

'Oh, no, Excellency. Not gone. Not at all. Here we go then.' Ahead they saw a small station. The tracks veered off to a siding that made a T-shaped intersection leading to a business. At the entrance was a hoarding – a woman's smiling face, much faded with the lettering in English and Cyrillic, 'Diadem Coke-Terminal 3'. He felt someone push him in the back as the engine slowed to a halt, and he jumped down the steps and started running. At the switching point was a long iron bar with rusted tabs, much painted over. He grabbed the bar and kicked it; he had to do it twice before it moved. Yurovsky had jumped down and was helping him. The bar seemed to twist and swivel at the same time, the leverage was unusual, and then ahead of him the rails shifted, even as Ryzhkov fell back onto the gravel ballast. Yurovsky was running, leaping across the tracks, even as the tender began rolling across the newly set switch. Ryzhkov saw that the old driver had leaped out and was running ahead. The boy piloted the engine along until he could stop past the second switch. Yurovsky had already set it, there was a squeal from the braking wheels, and then a furious snort of steam as the tender, now pointed forwards, began heading up the stem of the T.

He ran forward and climbed up into the engine as it reached the third switch that would return it to the main line. The boy was surprised, turned and frowned and waved his finger at him. Across the cabin, first Yurovsky and then the old driver clambered aboard. The boy made sounds and the old man frowned.

'You can lose a leg like that, Excellency. This is not some adventure. The railroad can kill you.'

No sooner were they on the main line than they just as quickly stopped again. Yurovsky stood there, out of breath from his exertions. The boy had climbed out of the cabin and lowered the water spout down above the boiler, swivelled it into place and opened it up. A flood of water poured into the little engine.

'They're gone, I think,' Yurovsky said, kicking at the coal pile. 'Gone for good. So it's either die here or die in Moscow, eh? Dammit.'

'Oh, no, Excellency,' said the old man. He was watching the water pouring from the tower. The boy looked up at him. 'Drink, my little darling. She only needs a little more, and we're turned around, which is only good form after all.'

'What do you mean? They're nowhere in sight.'

'But we took water, Excellency, and Torko ran right through. You see? We have them now,' the driver said. He turned and waved at his son, who was running along the top of the boiler like a monkey, a huge smile on his face, making sounds that Ryzhkov realized were laughter.

The driver began setting the levers and then called the boy over. There was a moment, so different from anything they had seen before, between the two of them. The boy looked around suddenly, his face blank, almost fearful, and Ryzhkov was suddenly aware that the old man was telling him to get off, to wait there at the station.

He turned and saw Ryzhkov's look. 'It's too dangerous, Excellency,' the old man said, and then to the boy, who still had not moved, he raised his voice for the first time. 'Go on!' he said, and the boy cowered, slid past him and began to climb down the ladder.

'You too,' Ryzhkov said.

'But –'

'Just set it up for us, then get off.' He pulled his pistol out and pointed it at the man. 'Come on, set it up. What's his life worth without yours, eh?'

The old man hesitated for a moment, then set the levers and gauges. The yard engine answered with a chorus of hisses and knocks. The driver let the brake off and they began to

347

ease ahead. He moved to the ladder, looked back at Ryzhkov. The boy was running along the track below his father. 'Thank you, Excellency,' the old man said, and jumped off.

As they gained speed, the little station falling away in the distance, Ryzhkov could see them standing there waving.

'You're a sentimental fellow, aren't you, Ryzhkov?' Yurovsky said.

He didn't reply, just turned and tried to make sense of the maze of levers, toggles and gauges that spanned the cockpit, shook his head. Sometimes he didn't know what he was doing.

'I don't know if there's a place for sentimentality in a revolution, but . . .'

'But what?'

Yurovsky wasn't looking at him, he was leaning out of the cockpit, staring ahead into the wind, thinking about it.

'But, on balance, I think you did the right thing, comrade.'

For a moment Yurovsky continued to stare ahead, then, turning and catching Ryzhkov's look, he pumped one fist in the air, and yelled a cheer. A wild yell, something a child or a cossack might come out with in a moment of irrational exuberance.

39

They caught the Torko brothers on the upslope along the river. They had been drawing closer throughout the afternoon and now, as the skies were beginning to redden and the shadows lengthened across the fields, they were as close as they had been when Ryzhkov had tried his suicidal leap.

'Wait a little longer this time, eh?'

He nodded to Yurovsky. They had checked their pistols and set the controls. Nothing could be seen of the train ahead of them except when they arrived at a curve, then to look out would risk a shot.

Ryzhkov peered forward, measured the distance, and then waited behind the shield of the boiler. Looking behind him the rails stretched . . . all the way to Vladivostok. Thousands of kilometres of possibilities, thousands of little towns where you could start all over again, thousands, millions . . . an infinity of possibilities, and instead his life had come to this – two scared men preparing to assault a moving train, more afraid of failure than the task itself. Men acted that way, he had seen it; terrified of things they could not understand and forces that were about to overwhelm them, they attacked each other, dragged their friends down with them in their desperation to survive. He looked over at Yurovsky, and suddenly he saw him – the terrorist Bolshevik killer, an absolutely deadly expression on his face, eyes flat and dark as the abyss.

The Torko engine was labouring, the rhythm of its pistons noticeably less frequent. There simply wasn't enough water to make the steam. Ryzhkov leaned out as they went around a long curve; the track was climbing slightly and they had inched closer. The curve was a long one; if they crawled out along the outside of the tender they would be shielded.

'It's time,' he shouted to Yurovsky, who was pulled out of his reverie, and nodded his assent.

They swung out over the tracks and walked along the narrow ledge, crouching behind the boiler. If the man who had called himself Ivanis was waiting inside the ambulance car, he would be able to see them in only a few feet. There was a handrail fixed to the side of the boiler. It was scalding hot, and Ryzhkov realized that a railwayman would have been wearing gloves; he pulled his sleeve down over his hand and used it to guide himself along. It was only a few more feet.

There was the sharp report of a gunshot and simultaneously a bullet ricocheted off the boiler as he reached the front of the engine. Below he could see that the couplers were almost touching. It was only a matter of a few feet. He put two bullets into the wall beside the carriage door, clambered down and jumped.

He hung there in the doorway with Yurovsky standing at the front of the engine, his pistol at the ready. The couplers were knocking together, then suddenly locked, with a lurch that nearly threw Yurovsky off the front of the little switcher.

Ryzhkov tried the door but it would not give. He turned away and was preparing to attempt to crash through when there was an explosion and he realized he had been shot through the door. His fingers went numb, and a dreadful heat filled his arm. He dropped his pistol on the step and instantaneously bent to grab it before it slid off the step onto the tracks, and as he did a spent bullet fell out of his sleeve, clattered across the metal plates for a moment and then fell away onto the blur of the tracks. He sheltered against the other side of the door and shook his arm, trying to get the feeling to return. There was a hole in his jacket sleeve, but no blood. Just lucky, he thought. Just lucky.

Yurovsky had seen and had squirmed around and crouched on the other side of the boiler now, his gun poised for a shot. There was a ladder there on Ryzhkov's side of the ambulance and he shook his arm again, stuffed the pistol in his pocket and began to climb it. Yurovsky saw what he was doing and came to the front of the tender and jumped across the couplers to the back of the ambulance.

Yurovsky waited for a moment and then put his eye to the bullet hole in the door, trying to see inside. It was just a blur; the wood was shattered into too many splinters to get a good sighting. As Ryzhkov climbed up to the roof, he examined the locks. The whole thing looked pretty flimsy, he thought. He counted his bullets, four shots left, and wondered how well armed the man inside was.

He thought he heard someone shouting, and decided that to give Ryzhkov better cover he should attack the door. He swung back, holding the thin steel handrail, and kicked at the mechanism. The door sprung inwards and rebounded again. He was about to kick it again when a shot came through the door, blowing out a fist-sized sliver of wood. He reached across, put the muzzle of his pistol through the hole and pulled the trigger, then retracted the gun and kicked at the lock again. The door sprung off its lock and he kicked it again to free it completely.

There was shouting from someone inside and a gunshot

and splinters burst out of the side of the door jamb, so close that he could feel them flying into the skin of his cheek.

For a moment he felt like laughing at the absurd heroics of his situation. Here he was, the great realist, the scientist of human motivations, a clockmaker, a photographer, a man who worshipped only what he could see, getting ready to . . .

And then the threw himself through the door. It was everything he could do not to pull the trigger, but he only had two . . . two? Shots left. Not time enough to look at the pistol. He crashed into an area at the steps that was covered with a cloth. It was a sort of closet that had been cobbled together where passengers would have stowed their excess baggage. The floor was sticky and he saw that there was blood there, that someone had tried to mop it up in a hurry, leaving footprints.

There was a thin wall, and a curtain; that was all that was protecting him. In the crease he could see a sliver of mirror and a gleam from the window. Someone was standing there in the centre of the car, crouched behind what looked like a miniature parlour complete with furniture.

'I'll kill them, do you understand?' the man was shouting. 'I'll kill them if you try anything more. Put your gun down and we can start dealing, eh?' the man said, but the voice was nervous, high pitched and frenzied. Underneath the sound of the voice Yurovsky could hear the sobbing.

She told herself not to be weak, that this was the trial, the final trial, that God did everything for a reason, and that she was being tested. She told herself that in nature, as in poetry, some little ones were destined to only live for a day, to fly towards the sun, and that these paradoxically were the ones that were God's favourites, that he was bringing them home to be with him as quickly as possible, out of love. She told herself that life, even in its torments, was still a special kind of temporary bliss and that she, a princess, had had more than most, and so she should be thankful.

But the Devil had moved them to the centre of the carriage. His back was pressed up against a half-wall, and a sofa that he now sat in, clutching her around the breast, with her brother wedged tightly between them. He was nervous, shouting at someone who had broken in through the back door. He reached out beside her with his gun and waved it around. When he shot it deafened her and the world went white. She realized that no matter what she had commanded herself she was sobbing. Alexei was holding her hand, and muttering to her. 'Calma, calma.' Something he had learned from one of his nurses.

There was a sudden shriek, a whistle that pierced the car, and she turned and saw through the windows that they were entering some kind of station, that the train had not slowed at all, that outside were soldiers, looking their way, waving and running in panic, and that they were ploughing through it all. The shriek was another train's whistling, a kind of alarm, she realized in that instant . . . and then she saw out of the corner of her eye the man leaping across the little corridor to the bedroom, and behind her the Devil made a huge contortion and threw her aside.

'I told you!' he screamed as he jumped up from the sofa. 'I told you!' His gun suddenly exploded and she realized he was shooting blind through the wall, and had walked away from them.

There was an explosion from behind her and she turned to see another man. She suddenly recognized him – the one who had come to visit them at the mines, the one she had talked with. The good one.

He was standing in the corridor now, having somehow contrived to enter from the front of the train, and his gun was belching fire. The room was full of smoke, and the Devil had crouched, surprised by the advent of her angel. She could feel it, the powers of the universe starting to swirl around her.

But the Devil was not done.

In the bedroom Yurovsky realized he had made a terrible mistake. For a moment he thought of throwing himself out the window. Bullets were smashing through the thin wall, and it was just a matter of time. He had trapped himself. There was nowhere to go in the tiny bedroom, and at that very moment one of the bullets tore into his face. He felt it, hot along his cheek, like being smashed in the jaw, and he tasted his own blood.

There was more firing, and somewhere in the deepest part of his brain he realized it was Ryzhkov, and he pushed himself off the bed into he corridor, falling low and seeing his target standing there. He pulled the trigger and shot him with his last bullet, high in the chest.

The impact of it knocked him spinning backwards against the girl, both of them falling back onto the sofa, and then he slipped off. Ryzhkov was standing there, smoke pouring out of the muzzle of his weapon. There was a sudden lurch, and the carriage was filled with dust, as if they had collided with something. There were other gunshots and the sound of bullets crashing into the carriage. The windows shattered and he saw Ryzhkov flinch and look his way.

Suddenly shaky, Yurovsky stood and walked along the corridor. Outside he could see soldiers and barricades made from freshly cut logs. More bullets smashed into the carriage, but it all seemed unreal. Ryzhkov was beginning to straighten from his crouch; he was saying something, but Yurovsky could not hear it. A girl screamed at the same moment that he saw the boy – the Tsarevich – leaping from the sofa, something in his hand. He turned now, and seeing Ryzhkov's face he realized that it was too late . . .

Ivanis was there – come back from the dead, jumping back up with a smile. Yes, a hole smashed into his chest where he had just shot him, but where he should have been bleeding there was only a trickle of what looked like bits of glass.

And then Alexei was between them, and Yurovsky saw he was stabbing upwards from his low position, a pocket knife in his hand, and connecting with the man's thigh, so that he flinched and crouched over to protect his privates, too late, and wincing in pain as he jerked backwards from the boy's attack and reflexively pulled the trigger.

Yurovsky felt the bullet take him. He fell back with its force, his head hitting something, stunning him on the way down. And then everything was different somehow. A whirling chaos of dust and dirt . . . the shattering glass. A girl's scream and then the girl herself, leaping across to shield her brother; Ryzhkov bulling ahead and fighting to get a clear shot, and the other, his face twisted in anger, shouting his wrath at the Romanovs, and his gun, firing, firing, firing . . .

And this is the way it ends, he thought.

Ryzhkov saw his first shot hit Ivanis in the back, just under the shoulder; the force of it spun him around and he stood up from his crouch, a terrible expression on his face, meeting his eyes, and just as he was about to fire, Yurovsky at the end of the carriage shot him, and he collapsed behind the wall.

Marie was looking up at him in shocked amazement, her hair gone awry in a long cascade that blew behind her in the wind from the shattered windows. Ryzhkov lowered his gun and took a step towards her; beyond her he saw that Yurovsky had been hit in the fight – there was a smear of blood down his face and neck and he was staggering, bracing himself along a counter top that had been built along that side of the carriage.

Gunshots were crashing into the car and he saw they had driven themselves right through the front lines where the White Armies had thrown up emplacements, sandbags and barricades to protect their retreat from Kazan. They must have hit something, and the entire train shook like some great animal; their speed had slowed, but not by much, and he was thinking that he should get back to the tender and take off the throttle when he saw Ivanis moving out of the corner of his eye.

Yurovsky was looking in the wrong direction, saying something to him that came out in a garbled spray of blood, his hand reaching out for help.

And suddenly Ivanis was up and shooting at them. Ryzhkov saw Alexei down on the floor, clutching at his knees, and Ivanis screaming. He had pushed backwards unsteadily and had lowered his aim to fire down into the boy's back. At the same moment Marie leaped across to protect him, and Ivanis raising his gun to fire at Yurovsky.

And then Ryzhkov was up, scrambling, knowing that he'd been too slow, and he reached out with his pistol and shot the man, once in the chest, and then realizing that he should have aimed at the head, and raising his pistol so that the sights covered his laughing face, and pulling the trigger –

And that, he realized much later, was when they had the collision.

40

Ryzhkov found himself outside, remembering nothing. Somehow he was walking along, not making much progress. His leg, the bad one, was hurt again. It was always the left leg, he thought, as if God had given him one limb that was destined to always fail him, one leg that was in the way of German shrapnel, one leg that broke when he was escaping from a window, one leg slower than the other. He tried not to limp, conscious of the looks of the pedestrians, and then he realized that there were no pedestrians, that he was walking alongside a derailed locomotive, and that people were shooting at him. It all came back with a snap.

He saw Yurovsky standing over the body of Ivanis, ripping at his clothes, cursing his dead body. A great smear of blood had flowed down the bartender's face and soaked his chest, and beside him in the rubble the boy was gasping for breath, and Ryzhkov, as bad as the leg was, ran towards him. The world seemed tilted, and it came to his fogged mind that the railcar was turned over on its side, and that the furniture had spilled out onto the roadbed.

Then he realized that he too had fallen. Marie was sitting amid the splintered planking of the railroad car. He saw they must have collided with a barricade; there were logs and sandbags that had been ripped apart by the crash. She was there in the dust, face pale, staring at Yurovsky above her, one hand reaching out to him when she saw him. There was blood on her dress, and she seemed to lose consciousness for a moment and then woke up again, looked over to him and smiled. She was leaning against a slab of metal sheeting, a tent-like projection that he realized was one of the chimneys from the little stove that had been built into the car. In effect she was leaning against the roof, a shard of the same roof he had climbed along. She reached out her hand to him again. It was bloody. She looked like she was falling asleep.

Yurovsky stood up, jerking Ivanis's clothing away, and for the first time Ryzhkov saw the crazy markings in the sky. A lattice of girders. They were on a bridge, he realized.

'Good afternoon,' he heard Marie say. Yurovsky turned and looked down on her. She was trying to get to her feet but couldn't make it. Ryzhkov began to crawl over towards her.

Yurovsky was holding strung-together bloody corsets in his hands. 'This was how he did it,' he said, and then looked down and kicked Ivanis in the face. 'Fucking bastard.' The head rocked back and then fell forward again. The eyes didn't even close.

'She needs help,' Ryzhkov heard himself saying. 'She needs a doctor.'

Yurovsky stood there looking out at the bridge. 'This is a little treacherous,' he said. At that moment a bullet shattered one of the windows and a cascade of glass fragments slid down the floor. 'We're on a bridge,' he said to Ryzhkov wonderingly.

The girl was leaning back against the torn roof of the car, falling asleep. He felt along her dress, trying to see where she'd been injured. It might be something inside. She opened her eyes.

'I'm not going to marry a prince. I hate princes.' Her voice had a lilt to it, as if she were reciting a singsong rhyme she'd learned to skip rope to. 'Except my brother, but he's very agreeable. He's going to come along with me.'

Ryzhkov reached up and pulled the corsets out of Yurovsky's hands, covered the girl with them, looked around for something else. It was important to stay warm, he knew.

'Is there some water?' she said.

'I'll try and get it,' he said, knowing that if she was hurt inside it would only churn through her insides, leak through her torn intestines, carry the poisons into places no surgeon could ever find.

'It's certainly a lovely day,' she said. 'Everything one could ask for.'

'Yes.'

He was on his feet now. For a moment he had to remember where he was and why he was stumbling through the wreckage. He found a mattress that had been flung out of the destruction, bent to pull it from under the pile and saw through the plating the river below. The bridge was an open lattice of steel, a great arch above them. All along the tracks they had dragged fragments of the barricades. Somewhere there was a bugle blowing. Underneath the wheels, pinned and dead, he saw the blue uniform of one of the Czechs who must have been manning the barricade they'd ploughed through.

He ripped the mattress away; all that came loose in his hands was a long strip of cloth. It was something, he thought, something to cover her. He walked along the rungs of the bridge now. You have to be careful, he told himself; if you stepped aside from the centre of the tracks you could fall right through. He covered her with the rag. She looked up and smiled. 'Thank you. Has the car been waiting long?'

'I'm going to get you to a doctor,' he said, kneeling beside her. She smiled and closed her eyes, as if what he had said was too childish to be taken seriously.

'Do you know the secret of life?' she asked him.

'No, not really. I want you to relax, it's best if you rest.'

'The secret of life is to live each day as if it were your last. You make every moment count,' she said.

'Yes. I try and do that myself.'

'And always remember that you're loved,' she said with just a trace of admonition, as if she were coaching one of her naughty cousins. 'A lie can be expensive, but forgiveness is cheap. Promise me you'll remember.'

'I promise,' he said.

Yurovsky walked by them. He had the body of Alexei in his arms. The boy's head hung back over his elbow, the mouth open. His shirt front was soaked red, and Yurovsky's grip was slipping in the gore. Rather than drop him, he knelt and put the boy down on the rails for a moment. He gave the girl a long look. 'How are you feeling, miss?' he asked.

'Not so bad,' she said, trying to raise her hand to shade her eyes.

Yurovsky looked at Ryzhkov, then his gaze went down to the dead Tsarevich. 'No one must know, Pyotr. Understand?'

For a long moment they just looked at each other. 'No one can be allowed to find him, or to find . . . any of them.' His eyes travelled over to the girl, and he blushed.

'I'm just a simple maiden,' she said, sliding back into her singsong.

'Yes, that's right,' he said, looking at Yurovsky.

'They'll kill us, Ryzhkov.' Simultaneously a spray of bullets slapped into the metal roof behind them, sending up dust and splinters. 'Those are Red Guards!' Yurovsky said angrily. 'Down there at the other end of the bridge. Hey! Stop shooting! We're on your side!' Immediately another volley cascaded into the rubble all around them.

'I love this music,' the girl said. Ryzhkov pushed himself against her, trying to keep her warm. Her lips were going blue now, and he was afraid that it would not be long.

'Would you honour me with this dance?' he said to her, and she smiled.

Yurovsky watched them for a moment and then began crawling around the shelter of the torn-off roof, alternately dragging and pushing the corpse of Alexei Romanov ahead of him along the rails. There was a gap there and he finally got the boy's body far enough along so that it hung for a moment – and then fell through down into the river. The noise from the shooting was so great that he heard nothing when the body hit. It was a narrow river, rocky, with fast-moving water. For a moment he tried to follow the movement of the body, but the boy was gone. The boy that had saved his life, he realized.

He began to tremble, and for a moment panic seized him. He thought he would run towards the Red Guards' emplacements, and he tried to get to his knees, but his legs would not obey, and instead he began to slither backwards. He wanted to hide. There was an explosion and he realized that someone, White or Red, he could not tell, had brought up an artillery piece. Something small, a little trench howitzer, and they had begun shelling the wreckage.

'They're fighting right on top of us,' Yurovsky yelled at him. The girl was looking up at him with a dreamy expression, eyes half-closed like a dope addict.

'Hey, we have to go, eh?' he heard Yurovsky yelling.

'Yes,' Ryzhkov said, but he hadn't taken his eyes away from her. They were just looking at each other. Yurovsky stood up and poked his head out, looking back down the tracks, reached for his pistol, and then looked down when he realized it was gone.

'Will you help me with her?' he said to Yurovsky.

'She's gone.'

'Will you just help me?' Ryzhkov knelt on the sharp iron decking and lifted her into his arms, stepped on the mattress ticking, stumbled backwards and almost fell through the bridge. Yurovsky reached and grabbed his sleeve to stop him, and his hands travelled to the blood-soaked corsets.

'Come on then,' he said. He stepped out into the tracks and waved the bloody corset over his head, and together they began running down the plated-over centre of the tracks toward the Bolshevik end of the bridge, Yurovsky holding the corsets over his head like a bloody flag, and Ryzhkov limping along behind, the girl in his arms.

A second artillery shell crashed into the wreckage behind them. The train was on fire now, and the air was full of smoke. The Whites had stopped firing because they couldn't see, and Yurovsky's flag trick seemed to be working.

Ryzhkov ran along, not taking his eyes from hers, trying to give her the same smile she was giving him. Trying to convince her that everything was going to turn out, that her dreams had a chance of coming true.

'It's going to be all right,' he said to her, and his voice caught and he found himself holding back his tears. 'You'll see, it's going to be really good,' he said to the girl in his arms, meaning every syllable of it. Because he knew now that he was the only one she had, that he had to believe for her, if only to help her through the last. And so he stumbled along the tracks with the bullets zipping through the smoke, and his leg sending jolts of pain with every step, and believing . . .

'Drop your weapons! Put your hands in the air!' came the voices. He looked up dumbly, exhausted. In front of him was a knot of Red Guards, crouched behind their barricades. In ones and twos, each of them eager to prove themselves as brave as their comrades, they emerged from the sandbags and bullet-marked logs. He stood there, arms trembling with the weight of her. Yurovsky stood there with a terrible expression on his face.

'I am Commissar Yakov Yurovsky, this is Inspector Pyotr Mikhalovich Ryzhkov. We are both Cheka! I demand to speak to –'

It didn't keep them from spinning him around and ripping the corsets out of his hands. When they did, there was a tinkling of gemstones hitting the steel plating on the bridge. The soldiers knelt in amazement. Someone snapped a rifle bolt, chambering a round, and Ryzhkov looked up to see a bayonet inches away from his face.

'She needs a doctor,' he said. But the boy with the rifle only put on a snarling expression.

A bullet rang in the girders and they all suddenly realized that they were standing around exposed in front of the barricades. Someone pushed him through the narrow entrance. He turned to see that they had taken the bloody corsets away from Yurovsky and that he was being prodded down the tracks at bayonet point. He turned, trying to argue until one of the soldiers gave him a jab, high in the chest, just a prick that would hurt and bring blood, and he flinched away and did what they said.

Down the tracks there was a bridge-keeper's hut that had been taken over as the temporary headquarters for the soldiers who were holding that side of the ravine. Alongside it were several tents pitched to provide shelter and shade. They had a mess set up there, sheltered by barricades from any marksmen that might be aiming at them from the trees opposite. The smoke from the burning train wafted over the little camp. It smelled sickly, reminiscent of the gas chemicals he'd encountered in the trenches.

They took her away from him and put her on a stretcher,

and when he tried to follow they made him sit down on a stump with his hands clasped over his head. When he lost the strength to do that they screamed at him until he made the effort to do it again.

They had taken Yurovsky into the tent. Ryzhkov could hear him shouting that he would have them all executed as soon as his story was verified. If hot air could save them, Yurovsky was going to do it easily. A great fatigue overcame him. In front of him he saw the trampled grass and mud where the soldiers had occupied the area around the hut. He lifted his eyes to watch the train burn. The heat in the metal made strange groans and squeals and he wondered if the fire would actually melt the bridge somehow, and maybe give the Czechs all the breathing room they needed to retreat.

When he woke up he was on the ground. He realized that he had passed out and fallen off the stump. He got to his knees and climbed back on and a voice behind him told him to put his hands back on his head, and he did.

A few minutes later he saw a commissar, unmistakable in his bearing, with a closely shaven head and a uniform that he had somehow managed to keep immaculate through the mud and the fighting coming over towards him. He was wearing expensive boots that he had taken off a cavalry officer, and he was carrying a flour sack in one hand.

'Your name is Pyotr Mikhalovich Ryzhkov?'

'Yes.'

'You are claiming also to be Cheka?'

'Yes.'

'That is a lie.'

'If you say so.'

'It is a lie. You are lying and so is your friend. You are both under arrest,' he said, shaking his head with disgust. Unable to believe that the two vermin in custody were guardians of the new people's empire.

'I assumed so.'

'When you were searched your credentials as a member of the White police were discovered together with the booty you stole. Taken as a whole this is conclusive evidence, therefore you will be executed.'

Ryzhkov tried to say something, but nothing formed itself in his mouth. He ended up by nodding and looking away. He had dodged death many times, now it had come around again. He wondered if the laughing guard back in the Lubyanka would be happier. If his death would even register. Perhaps the boy would find himself walking through the corridor and would be suddenly, unaccountably struck with a ray of joy, never knowing that it was his distant death that had caused it. Maybe it would make the world a better place, if only microscopically.

'How is the girl?' he asked the commissar.

'What girl?'

'She came in with me. She was wounded. They were taking to a doctor.'

'I know nothing of this girl. There are more important things,' the commissar said. He held up the bag.

'Where did you get these?'

'It is part of our mission. We are in custody of all of it.'

'These are jewels. Valuables you have stolen.'

'We are to return them to Moscow. The girl is part of our mission too,' he said.

'Mission? You still maintain this? You are truly addled.'

'It is a secret, comrade.'

The commissar slapped him and he fell off the stump. His ears were ringing and all he could see were the expensive boots. 'You people are such fools,' the commissar said. 'No wonder you are afraid. Comrade Trotsky has been victorious in Kazan. The tide is turning. It's the biggest Red victory of the revolution so far.'

'Ahh.'

Another pair of boots, far worse – muddy and wrapped in puttees – ran up beside the commissar. It was a courier.

'The wires are back up,' a voice said. The courier held out a slip of paper. The commissar looked at it, frowned and they both walked away to the hut.

He climbed back up onto the stump. The ringing in his ears had faded, and the guard behind him had forgotten to order him to keep his hands on his head. Across the yard there was firing; some of the men had spied a sniper in the trees and were trying to pick him off. He could smell cooking, potatoes and something richer, some kind of meat. His stomach rolled over, and he was suddenly aware of all his bruises, the throbbing in his leg.

A young soldier, a shock of fine blond hair that had thinned all around the crown of his head, so that he looked like a monk in a brown uniform, came running over. He had a glass of kvass that he handed Ryzhkov, with the slightest of deferential bows. At the entrance to the hut Yurovsky walked out. There was a great bandage on the side of his face that wrapped all the way around his neck but he was smiling. There was another guard behind him, but they were both smoking cigarettes.

Yurovsky looked over, raised the flour sack in his hand, high so that Ryzhkov could see it.

It will all be fine, he had told her.

41

According to everyone Ryzhkov spoke to, Kazan had been a big victory. Trotsky had rushed to the front, rallied the vanquished Bolsheviks at the little town of Shivyask, a few kilometres west of the city. There had been all the elements of a good story: a young hero named Raskolnikov, a navy lieutenant who had brought his gunboats down the canals into the Volga and made it to the battle in time; a hero on the White side, one Colonel Kappel and his cavalry, who had nearly captured Trotsky and his headquarters, a troupe of secretaries and actors billeted on an agit train at the station; the fortunes of battle had swung wildly, there was an artillery duel across the river, a Red mutiny and executions aboard a barge by Trotsky's flying squad of Chekists. Finally the Bolsheviks took the bridge to the city, and the 'privileged classes' were seen carrying their prized possessions out of town.

He and Yurovsky were still under arrest, if not close custody. Telegrams had flown back and forth. He thought about it, but did not try to send anything to Zezulin, worried that it would only get them both in worse trouble.

In the evening, after he awoke from a sleep that felt

drugged, he stumbled around the encampment until he found the medical station. No one remembered a girl who had been brought out of the train wreck on the bridge.

'Besides, comrade, the wounded are evacuated to the rear immediately. She might be in the hospital in Kazan by now. It's a very efficient process.'

'But there is no record.'

'We keep no records here, comrade. We are much too busy. Most of the men cannot read, so what use are records?'

He and Yurovsky were summoned to the commissar in the afternoon and ordered to board the next train, soon to arrive bringing supplies and evacuating the wounded to the rear.

He managed to have a bath, and accepted the loan of a razor; stood in the steamy bathhouse, a series of canvas tents strung around a fire pit upon which hot water was poured to create a kind of sauna there beside the river, and tried to shave. If he didn't look himself in the eye he could almost manage. He emerged after an hour in the little tented labyrinth with his face pink and raw, the air cool on his cheeks, which he kept touching with wonder that anything could be so smooth. Up on the bank he saw there was sporadic gunfire coming from the trees. It was still considered great sport on the White side to sneak up into the woods and snipe at the Bolshevik encampment. But it would get them nothing in the end, and everyone knew it.

The commissar asked them to account for their time after the Bolsheviks had fled Yekaterinburg and Yurovsky refused immediately, insisting that they both were in no way obliged to talk about their mission until they reached Moscow. The young commissar just looked at them, ran a finger across his moustache, and grumbled for them to get out.

Their clothes had been washed and were still damp by the time they were escorted to the train. Just climbing on the train gave Ryzhkov pause. He took a breath and hung in the door for a long moment before entering the car, but made himself walk through into the darkness, picked his way down the nearly empty car and found a seat.

There was a section of bookkeepers going over some sort of voluminous report, four young men who kept to themselves and made abbreviated conversation. He and Yurovsky took seats across from each other as far away as possible, and stared out the window.

Once they were en route the car was noisy and Yurovsky leaned forward and tapped him on the knee to get his attention. 'We should get our story straight,' he said.

'Is such a thing possible?' Everything he heard now seemed like a joke, some sort of humorous condition brought on by a cynical God. What was the point in a story?

'I'm serious. We both have to make a report, yes?'

'I suppose.'

'All right, comrade. It's your life.'

Ryzhkov laughed again, and fell to staring out the window.

They slowed outside of the city, rolling into the centre of Kazan. It was all different there, everything more Russian in architecture and decoration. The domes on the mosques, the streets that twisted their way up the bluff that overlooked the river, the Tatars walking along the streets dressed in their native costumes, the red banners hanging from the windows. Along the riverside there was damage from the shelling.

He limped off to the hospital while waiting for the next train. Yurovsky, who was growing worried about his state of mind, went with him.

'A woman?' the supervisor said. There were lots of women.

'She would have been brought in yesterday,' Ryzhkov said. 'Young, barely in her twenties,' he told the man.

The man shrugged and went away to check. He returned

a quarter of an hour later with a nurse. She remembered her, she said.

'Where is she? Can I see her?' Ryzhkov asked, practically jumping on the woman.

'Dead. With a wound like that, what could you expect? After all, most of her head was gone.'

'No!' Ryzhkov began screaming at her. Yurovsky had to hold him back. The supervisor looked at them nervously.

'Sorry,' the woman said. 'Wrong patient.'

A doctor, a thin man with yellow skin and a cigarette that spilled ashes down the front of his smock, clearly remembered her. The entire experience had been remarkable. First, her wounds had been only superficial; the girl was chattering and wide awake all through the procedure. And to top it off she had walked out of the hospital on her own volition just moments after he'd sewn her up. Quite amazing, really.

He left them and only a few minutes later they met a different doctor who admitted she'd caught his eye when she first came in; yes, a pretty girl with a wound in the abdomen, just a splinter, you couldn't even see it. Sadly the bleeding internally was too much for her. She had succumbed, and, having no papers, had been delivered to the morgue for the unknowns. Would they volunteer to walk the ranks of the corpses and identify her?

Yurovsky shook his head. It was madness. They paced the hallway, Yurovsky following while Ryzhkov limped along trying to figure out a course of action. When he finally decided to go and visit the morgue, Yurovsky refused, pointing out that they had to be on the next train, but Ryzhkov tore away and climbed through the hot streets. Everyone else was inside escaping the late summer heat, but Ryzhkov tore along, rushing the sweating orderly towards the morgue. The boy had trouble finding the place; the regular morgue had been overrun with bodies from the fighting and they had expanded into the refrigeration room of a meat-packer's. There was no electricity but it was the coolest place they could come up with.

The orderly delivered him to Zlatek, who had been there working for both sides throughout the fighting. If she was there he would know about it, the orderly said, as he saluted and left the room, not wanting to linger.

Zlatek was a hard man, an ex-convict, in his thirties, and strong from carrying stretchers around all day. He was dark, from somewhere near Georgia but not quite Georgian to hear his accent. Short black hair and a beard that never went away no matter how often he shaved. Lucky, and he knew it. He'd got the job in the hospital because he had been wounded in the head, he said, tapping the place, and Ryzhkov could see the saw cuts in his scalp.

The refrigeration room was large and extremely clean, Ryzhkov thought. Cool, but not cool enough to stop the decomposition. Ryzhkov found himself stopping for a moment. Zlatek looked back and smiled.

'It's only started to get bad in the last week,' he said. Against one wall was a rack stacked with bodies of all types, for the fighting had thrown government into such turmoil that they had housed both military and civilian dead in the one room, with space out on the floor for the overflow.

It took him twenty minutes to walk the ranks of the bodies, a series of portraits of lives ended. Some looked like they had simply gone asleep, others were blown apart, surprised, eyes opened, arms clutched over their chests, shoes missing, clothing awry. Men, women, children; all ages and all classes, death had taken them indiscriminately.

'Did you find the one you want?' Zlatek came up behind him at the end of his tour. He looked up at the man, a little surprised.

'No.'

'If she's not here, maybe they've already taken her outside to the courtyard,' he said, pushing past him and throwing open a wide door. When he did it, the air was so fresh that the fragrance nearly overwhelmed Ryzhkov.

The courtyard was a large open space where in the past wagons must have driven up. Now, across its expanse a series of long trenches had been dug, the earth piled along one side, and the corpses had been removed and buried there en mass. Half of the first trench had already been filled and there was a stack of wooden crosses piled at the head of the trench waiting for new arrivals.

'She might be in there somewhere,' Zlatek said helpfully. 'But, to be honest, she might be anywhere.'

When he got back to the station Yurovsky was asleep on one of the benches. A nervous Red Guard hovered above him, but would not wake him. They had missed the train, he whispered to Ryzhkov. He had been assigned as their escort, and now they were all in trouble. There were already telegrams querying their whereabouts. Obviously someone in Moscow was upset and their presence was urgently required.

Yurovsky woke up and made the guard fetch them some tea. The boy returned in minutes with two steaming glasses. They sat there in the foul-smelling station. It was crowded with soldiers and refugees. 'There is another train in forty minutes,' the boy said hesitantly, as if he was worried what they might think of such a fact.

'You can leave us now. We'll be on it,' Yurovsky growled at him. The boy nodded, almost clicking his heels, and retreated a few metres, but wouldn't leave the station lobby.

'Do you know what he told me?' Yurovsky said. 'He said that the Empress and her daughters were seen right here at the station.'

Ryzhkov looked up at him, trying to decide if he was making a joke.

'They apparently had their own private railway car in which they had been living for some months.'

'Where are they now?' Ryzhkov said dryly. The tea was good. He hadn't eaten all day, and was suddenly aware of his hunger.

'Who knows, but just before we retook the city Grand Duchess Olga was seen climbing into an aeroplane piloted by a tall, dark man with an English accent.'

'Ahh,' he said.

'Did you find her?' Yurovsky said after a moment.

'No.'

'Maybe she recovered, maybe she . . . got on an aeroplane.'

'Maybe.'

Their train arrived and the boy dutifully escorted them out to their carriage. A Cheka officer was waiting for them. He was small, with thick glasses, a wispy beard and a leather coat that he obviously found far too hot, but nevertheless wore to demonstrate his authority. He led them to their compartment and locked them in. 'For your protection,' he explained.

They were late leaving and didn't get away until dusk. The air over the river was thick, the whole city humid and smelling of fires and garbage that had been rotting in the streets since the beginning of the siege. Ryzhkov was glad to see it go.

They rolled along at a snail's pace over the broken and newly repaired tracks. Trotsky's agit train had rushed ahead with its staff of projectionists, actors, singers and writers. Taken its colourfully painted cars to some other front where the vanguard of the people's revolution needed fresh inspiration.

The Cheka officer returned to their compartment and sat

down across from them and questioned them closely. It was the same routine. They refused to tell him any details of their work in Yekaterinburg, and he played his part of the game, trying to discover what they preferred to keep hidden.

After an hour of fruitless interrogation the Chekist took off his glasses and massaged the creases on the bridge of his nose. His name was Stein and he was no cop, that much was obvious.

'I suppose you've heard the news about the Tsar?' he said.

They both contrived to look at him with blank expressions.

'He's been killed.'

'Really?' said Yurovsky.

Stein looked at him with eyes that tried to focus without the benefit of lenses. He looked even more childlike that way.

'Some members of the Ural Soviet have escaped and given a report.'

'Ahh,' said Yurovsky. He looked over to Ryzhkov and nodded.

'Your names, both of you, were prominent in the report. That's why I was sent to meet you. It's just luck that you missed your train.'

'A civil war can often lead to coincidence,' said Ryzhkov.

'The, ah, various members of the Ural Soviet were interviewed, as far as I have been informed, separately. Although I have not been given access to any of these reports, I am reliably informed that the details of the various testimonies differ widely. There are some who are clearly seeking to bolster their participation in the matter of the family's demise, others who say they know little or nothing. Their accounts differ on matters of substance and detail,' Stein said, and then carefully placed his spectacles on his nose in the pink slots. 'There are a great many discrepancies.'

'I see,' said Ryzhkov. Yurovsky nodded and scratched his bandage innocently.

'When we arrive in Moscow I will escort you to your . . . quarters in the Kremlin. But before anything else happens you will be allowed to consult with your attorney.'

Yurovsky sat forward. 'Our –?'

'Yes,' Stein said. 'Yes, comrades, there will be a trial,' he said as if the troublesome fact gave him great personal sadness. Then he closed his ledger and stood up to leave the compartment, turned at the door and gave them a tight little smile. 'I rather think that the verdict has already been decided,' Stein said. And then, with an imperceptible bow, he left, remembering, of course, to lock the door.

42

When she woke the first thing she saw was a dense canopy of birch leaves, a thick green barrier between her and the heavens. A breeze stirring them, then everything falling still until the next breeze. Little keyholes of sky opening and closing. She fell to watching it, over and over.

She was on a bed that had been put out under the trees; a tent was on the other side; it was a kind of open-air hospital and operating theatre. Everything was quiet except for the groaning of the wounded men. A magpie flew across her vision right between her bed and the tent, landed on the grass, looked around and left again.

There was a young man standing there, an orderly of some kind. He was wearing a long stained apron, and a white linen cap to keep the hair our of his eyes. He had seen her moving and now he came over. 'How are you feeling?'

'I'm fine. Sleepy, but I think I'm fine.'

'That's good. Can you move everything?' He smiled. She held her hands up and wiggled her fingers as if she were playing the piano in the air. He laughed and then she did too. 'What about your legs?' She raised one up, and then the other. 'That's excellent,' she heard him say. 'Try sitting up then.'

Sitting was harder. She reached over until she found the edge of the bed and swung her legs around. For a moment she felt faint. He reached out and steadied her until she got all the way round. It took an enormous effort. There were spots in front of her eyes, as if someone was flicking raindrops onto her field of vision. She realized she was looking right at the smiling face of the orderly.

'I think you're going to be fine. Try turning your head. How's your neck? Does anything hurt?'

She followed all his instructions, like a puppet. At the end of it she was pronounced whole. No strings broken. 'No, no, stay here. I'll get you something. When is the last time you ate?'

She just looked at him. The calculation was too difficult for her to come up with an answer.

A few moments later he came back with a bowl of soup. It was an enamelled cup with a great chip out of the rim. The soup was a yellow broth with something green floating in it. No spoon. He held the cup for her so that she could take a drink.

'Do you remember what happened?' he asked after she had taken a second gulp of the soup, and then quickly polished off the entire cup.

She looked at him for a moment; a kind face, big eyes that were made bigger by his glasses, a scraggly beard. Just a boy. She turned and stared out at the forest. Except for the tent it was all she could see. 'Where am I?'

'You were in the train that crashed. Don't you remember?' He looked over his shoulder, back in the direction where the wreck must have occurred. All she could see was birch woods. An unending forest; who knew, maybe it went on forever.

'I remember,' she said.

'I think you should rest. I'll get some more,' the young doctor said. He took the cup and stepped back and looked at her for a long moment. 'People can die from shock, you know. You're a very lucky girl,' he said.

'I am. I know.'

'What's your name?'

'Marie,' she said softly.

'Marie?'

'Marina, actually. I'm just an ordinary girl.'

'Not all that ordinary,' he said. She realized he was flirting with her. She smiled.

'You can get up and walk around as soon as you feel like it, all right, Marina?' he said and then left to find her some more soup.

As soon as he had gone she struggled to her feet. Took a few steps towards the tent. There were rows of beds inside. Most of them were empty. A few men, just lumps beneath the sheets. One man groaning in his sleep.

She turned carefully, walking in a slow procession like an old woman. Soon the medical tent went out from her view and was replaced by the vast yellow-green forest, the white spires of the birch trees reaching up towards the canopy. She walked from tree to tree, bracing herself by grasping the smooth papery bark.

Everything was gone now. Her family, her poor beautiful brother who had died fighting for both of them. Washed away in blood and inconceivable violence. She couldn't think about it, about everything that was lost. Wallowing in it wouldn't bring anything back. What was her future now? Should she walk out of Russia, make her way to Europe, live a life as Empress in exile? Hanging onto the arms of people she hated, begging distant relatives so she could pay the rent and update her trousseau? What was the point of that? It hurt too much to think about. And she shouldn't think of it; after all, people could die from shock.

'I am free now,' she said to the forest. And she was. True,

it was a terrible freedom to be washed clean of the past, to be reborn out of such violence. But, nevertheless, she was. Free.

And a breeze came up, swaying the branches and riffling through the leaves as if to answer her. Below, her hesitant feet picked a route through the rocks and rotten limbs, the tangle of berries and the thorns that sought to trap her but scratchily gave way, as with each step she walked deeper into the woods.

'Don't go too far!' She turned and saw the young attendant standing there with her soup.

'Don't worry,' she called back to him. 'I'm not afraid.'

43

The Kazan station in the rain. An escort through the chaos by four waiting Chekisti. A dash through the storm and piling into a motor car. Stony-faced escorts, younger than they deserved to be. The car showed that they were serious about things, but it broke down before they had gone three blocks. Stein had vanished after their interview and they hadn't seen him when the train unloaded. The breaking down of the car – it was a sleek Renault with a separate compartment for the driver and passengers, a vehicle that had once been owned by someone with money, with a rosewood interior and velvet cushions – threw the Chekists into disarray. Not being responsible, Yurovsky and Ryzhkov stayed inside out of the wet and laughed at the men fighting among themselves. After only a few minutes of looking under the hood, one of the Chekists stepped out into the street and commandeered a cab, and they were ordered into it. The others were to follow presumably when they had repaired the fantastic vehicle.

Moscow hadn't changed much, Ryzhkov thought. The weather had cooled and the trees had gone yellow and gold, the rain was knocking the leaves off and the streets were slippery and clotted up with their debris. There were fewer people out and about. A great many shops were closed. But not many idlers, or wounded standing around. The weather was too bad to be outside anyway, and the Bolsheviks had everyone back to work.

They followed the boulevard past the Lubyanka and down Nikolskaya, across the wide plaza bounded by St Basil's, and entered the Kremlin from the high side, through the Spasskiya gate, all the time guarded by at least a dozen Red Guards and a quartet of Cheka to keep them on their toes. The leather overcoat had by now become the *de facto* uniform of a Chekist. To Ryzhkov's eyes it looked absurd, a little more expensive a solution to the problem of inclemency than the old raincoat he had carried as a *gorokhovnik* when he had laboured for the Okhrana. A long, long time ago, he thought. A lifetime spent in only four years. He heaved a sigh and Yurovsky looked over at him.

'There are no deals between us. I just want you to know that, Ryzhkov.'

'You said as much on the train.'

'As long as we're clear.'

'We're clear.'

'I had a job, you had a job. We each did what we did. So it goes.'

He didn't answer. The car rolled past the huge broken Tsar's bell. It was too big to move, and the Bolsheviks probably enjoyed the symbolism of its cracked bulk. They continued through the palaces and dormitories, and along beside the warrens of offices, the quarters for the priests who had kept the cathedrals, servants who dusted off the artworks in the cellars. Now the Bolsheviks had moved in and the priests had been moved out. Now there were cells within cells, and arts of a different kind were being practised in the interrogation and torture chambers beneath the great buildings.

They rolled to a stop and a fresh contingent of Red Guards scampered out into the rain to take charge of them.

'Good luck, comrade,' he said to Yurovsky. And then they were led off in their separate directions.

Another measure of how important it all was showed in their punctuality. He didn't have time to wait or slumber with his head on the hard table. It was a small room. He was directed to a chair, and a few minutes later someone brought him a glass of tea. It wasn't even real tea. That was another way you measured the civil war: broken cars, ersatz tea. A man came in the room, a stenographer in tow. No greetings, no names exchanged. He was as blank as a human could be, military tunic buttoned up to the neck, a smooth head and features that managed to fade into its surface – a face painted onto a ball. A voice that was flat and uninflected, insinuated nothing whatsoever.

Ryzhkov pre-empted the man's questions by saying that he was Cheka, assigned to a secret mission, and had not been given the opportunity to report to his controller.

'The name of your controller?'

For a moment he stopped. Staring at the flat eyes. 'I don't think I am allowed.'

'This is an authorized inquiry comrade. You have nothing to fear.'

'Yes, I realize.'

'The name of your controller.'

'I am not allowed.' And then after a moment where the man just stared at him he said, 'I'm sure you understand.'

The man glanced at the stenographer, who turned a page and began again. He reported on his movements, the train to Yekaterinburg, his contact with the counter-revolutionary White forces.

'You worked for them?'

'I had little choice.'

'You worked for them.'

'Yes.'

'And your mission?'

'An investigation into the fate of the Imperial Family.'

A trace of a smile from the red-faced man. They continued. He was asked for details, the names of his White superiors, and he gave them all – Giustiniani, de Heuzy. Nothing new there.

'And state for me what you eventually discovered about the Romanovs, their fate exactly?'

Before he could answer there was a tap at the door. A clerk came in and handed the interrogator a yellow slip of paper, and the interview was abruptly concluded.

'Your name?' the man asks.

'Yakov Yurovsky. You already have my name.'

'This is an interview to determine your responsibility for events in Yekaterinburg.'

'I am not permitted to speak on such topics.'

'You will answer the questions put to you.'

'Unfortunately –'

'Never mind. Why were you sent to Yekaterinburg?'

'I was to head the execution squad.'

'And you performed this duty.'

'I did.'

'You will describe the events of the night of 16–17 June.'

'A great deal went on. It is very difficult.'

'We have plenty of time. Continue.'

'It was a chaotic situation. The Czech counter-revolutionary forces were at the outskirts of the city. It is unclear –'

'You will describe for me –'

'I am not permitted –'

The man opposite him suddenly stands from the table. Perhaps it has been a long day. Perhaps he is under too much stress. Red faced, begins to scream about Yurovsky's revolutionary commitment.

Yurovsky stands and screams back, 'No one is more committed to the revolution than I. No one,' and for a stretch they both stand there yelling accusations at each other. A guard comes into the room and holds him down in the seat. They threaten to shackle him, and he in turn threatens them one more time with his rank, with his privileged position in the secret political police.

The interrogator leaves the room for a moment, gathers himself, returns. Now he wants to know about the Ural Soviet.

'Beloborodov, Goloschkin . . .' he recites the names.

'And what was your relationship to these men?'

'I was a member of the Ural Soviet, but I was not under their direction.'

'Explain.'

'I am not allowed.'

For a long moment the interrogator just looks at him. Everything is contained within his gaze: hatred, frustration, a notion of the scientific principles of history, an awareness of class conflict, and the correct way to deal with the enemies of the people.

'You will tell me about your colleague, Pyotr Mikhalovich Ryzhkov.'

For a moment Yurovsky only sits there; he has known that this would come up sooner or later. 'Comrade Ryzhkov was sent to report on my mission. I had been unable to communicate. We were trapped behind the White frontier, and he helped –'

'How do you know this? How do you know he was sent?'

And now it begins to crumble. Yurovsky shrugs, spreads his hands on the table. He has lost, and both of them know it.

'He said he had been sent. He identified himself as Cheka.'

'Ahh . . . but you didn't know, did you? You had no proof.'

And the two men just look at each other, for there is nothing he can say.

On the third day, of which he was certain because his 'cell' had a window and his meals had been regular, Ryzhkov was moved. This time there was no window. And the transfer, coming as it did in the morning, meant that he missed breakfast. The cell was cold, down the stairs in the basement. There was a bed, a military bunk made of metal legs with wires strung across it to support the mattress, a relic, thin and, as he realized after sitting on it, flea infested.

The fleas took him back to the trenches, to the years of accommodation between man and vermin, to the constant wearying war within a greater war that he had waged to keep himself clean. And now, he knew, it was all undone in a few moments.

As proof of his unimportance no one entered the room for what he guessed were several hours.

Eventually there were footsteps in the hall which woke him. He had moved to the floor and wrapped himself in the single blanket he had been provided. He was sitting up and knuckling his eyes open when the door opened, and two strong young guards lifted him into the air and transported him down the corridor to where they had made a little interrogation room.

Inside was Stein. He stood up when Ryzhkov was brought in. The guards cuffed his hands and jammed him down into the chair.

'We'll try to do something about this,' Stein said, indicating the cuffs.

'Thank you. That would be fine.'

'There are some irregularities.'

'It's a very difficult position.'

385

'Yes, it is. You probably should just tell everything and let the chips fall where they may, don't you think? Are you protecting someone?'

'I really don't know. I was on a secret assignment. If I talk about it it's not secret any more, is it?'

Stein looked at him for a moment, nodded. 'Yes, I see,' he said, in a tone that carried overtones of inevitability and fatalism. 'I think,' Stein said slowly, choosing his words with care, 'that they want a full report . . . a full report on your activities regarding the former Tsar and his family. If you gave them that much they might be satisfied.'

'I think if I do that I'll be executed, comrade.'

'Why?'

'Because clearly there was something going on in Yekaterinburg. Something working at cross purposes. I don't know who was responsible, I don't know who had the big idea, but there were players working behind the curtains. I don't really think it's to my advantage to admit that I got a peek behind those curtains. I think that would mean the end.'

'This is paranoia, my friend.'

'You're not my friend.'

'No, but I'm now your attorney.' For a moment Stein looked at him, then took his spectacles off and stared at the table top. 'You see, Ryzhkov, there are many varieties of revolution,' he said quietly. 'Many varieties of political thought, of theory and of practice. Let us suppose that you are correct, that everything that went on in Yekaterinburg was not as it appeared. Surely if you possess . . . a certain special knowledge of these circumstances, that knowledge could be valuable. One might, if one was, let's say, nervous about one's chances, use that special knowledge as a lever.'

'Fine. If you want that, get Yakov in here. We'll tell you what happened, but no one else. Just us three. And bring some paper. We'll put it all down and then you can decide how to use it.'

'I don't know if I can arrange –'

'We have one story, and that's it. If they don't like it, well . . .'

'Then you will be executed.'

'I think it all depends on whom we expose. On what we saw when we looked behind those curtains, eh?'

Stein looked at him for a long moment. 'I have some friends,' he said. People who think . . .' He didn't elaborate, only waggled his hand through the air. 'They might see the wisdom in your idea. You would have to tell the truth. Any errors or omissions . . .'

'Get Yakov, and he and I will tell you what we saw and what we did. Everything we know. Then, how it's used is up to you. But I'm not going to let them pick us apart.'

Stein said nothing, only went to the door and knocked. A few moments later the guards came and took him away.

Yurovsky, despite living in a suite of rooms, which are locked for his inconvenience, and having a volume of Pushkin to read, is on edge. Outside the window all he can see is the yellow bulk of the Senate building. Periodically Red Guards march past. Beyond is the crenellated wall of the Kremlin. He leans at the window on his elbows watching the soldiers, the clerks, the knots of higher-ranking Bolsheviks – once he sees Stalin walking along laughing and chatting with his wife. They all live here, he realizes, the innermost circle of the revolution, here in these great Tsarist buildings. Sharing their meals, having entertainment brought in, going from meeting to meeting, to plenary session, to conclave. All together behind the same walls.

There is a noise, and guards unlock the door. He turns from the window to see Stein and a second man, shorter, with unruly hair and frowzy whiskers, a stained waistcoat beneath a shabby suit. Stein smiles, the other man grimaces. Greetings are exchanged, and they take their places around a small table in the upholstered chairs, and a settee that have been left by some Tsarist factotum, long gone to the wall, he supposes.

'They will bring us something to eat,' Stein says. A moment later a stenographer comes in. He has a thick pad, pulls up a chair and gets ready to work.

'How is your wound?' Stein says gesturing to his neck.

'Healing nicely, thank you.'

'Excellent. There has been a development,' Stein says, with a quick glance to the man sitting beside him. 'Pyotr Ryzhkov has suggested, well, he wishes to, ah . . .'

'Let me try to put it clearly,' says the unidentified man. 'What happened to the two of you in Yekaterinburg affects not only yourselves, but others, do you understand?'

'I think so, yes.'

'Your testimony, yours and Ryzhkov's, can be –'

'Will be,' interjects Stein.

'Used against you, and used against others, used in any number of ways. So . . .'

'So?'

'We must not let that happen,' the man says.

'I don't believe I have had the pleasure,' Yurovsky says, and reaches out to shake his hand.

'My apologies. I am Boris Maximovich Noskov. I was Pyotr Ryzhkov's controller, and together we are going to, ah . . .'

'Harmonize,' says Stein.

'Coordinate your recollections of Yekaterinburg.'

'What is in this for me, comrades?'

For a moment both men look at him. The older man, Noskov, shakes his head in an expression of mirth tinged with exasperation.

'Life, for beginners,' says Stein.

'So . . . we are agreed?' Noskov asks, the little eyes giving away nothing.

'For life,' Yurovsky says with a sigh. 'For life, we are agreed.'

'Good,' Noskov says, and stands up. He surveys the suite of rooms, runs one hand over the back of the settee. 'This place is terrible. We can't do anything here,' he says.

'No,' Stein says, mouth arcing downwards.

'We need a place less . . .'

'Regimented.'

'Yes, a place where we can create,' Noskov says. He has walked all the way around the settee, and now he lays one heavy hand on Yurovsky's shoulder.

'We need to relocate to somewhere a little more bucolic, where bodies can mend and the memory can be stimulated, eh? A place where we aren't surrounded all the time by all these guards and bureaucrats, where there's a little serenity, eh? Where we can talk –'

'Freely,' says Stein. And Yurovsky sees that he is smiling.

44

They do it in a dacha a few miles outside of Moscow, a rambling wooden summer place once owned by a man named Warmkessel, who had something to do with linen mills. Fortunes and biographies long gone. But the pictures are still on the wall, the books still in the book case, and most of the better furniture still serviceable.

Zezulin has contrived to bring along a brace of young Chekist apprentices to do the cooking and watch the driveway, leaving the principals free to wander around in the breaks; they can choose to do their work on the terrace when the sun shines, or inside when the rains resume.

The effect is absurd. Ryzhkov is humbled by the surroundings. It all brings back painful memories of his lost childhood, paths not taken; a dacha like this is all that his father ever wanted, and never achieved. The photographs of the smiling family arrayed on the walls are just depressing ghosts.

From the start Zezulin is in control. 'We write two documents,' Zezulin declares, and then goes on to explain. 'Let me put it this way, gentlemen. You are victims, you were manipulated and used; of course you didn't know it at the time. You thought you were serving the people's revolution.

You did what you were told. You were playing one game; someone else was playing another. Let's get down to the basics. Tell me about the night of the murders.'

'Executions,' Stein says, shooting a meaningful look towards the stenographers.

'First the guards were all sent away,' Yurovsky starts.

'Where?'

'Across the street to the temporary barracks.'

'All right, then what?'

'We rounded everyone up,' Yurovsky says in a rather tired voice. 'We led them through the top rooms, down the back stairs, to a storeroom in the cellars.'

'Everyone? Just what do you mean by everyone, Comrade Yurovsky?'

'Just the servants, Demidova, Botkin, the doctor, Kharitonov, their chef, and Trupp, the old footman.'

'What about the Tsar, the others?'

'They were made to wait in their quarters, and after the servants were inside the storeroom they were brought down a few minutes later.'

'And put into the second truck?'

'Yes.'

'The motors were running on both of the trucks, you said.'

'Yes, to cover the noise of the shooting.'

'This was a measure designed to increase the ah . . . privacy.'

'For the secrecy of it, yes.'

'Then what happened?'

'Once the Tsar and the Imperial Family had been driven away, the first set of guards were recalled and the shooting began.'

'And these were guards who had been purposely kept away.'

'None of them had been used before. They were unfamiliar

with the family. We had taken the servants' clothing. They were naked.'

'Hmmm,' says Zezulin, sitting back and crossing his arms. 'Well . . . we can't use very much of that, can we?'

'No,' says Stein sadly, shaking his head.

'So, then what happened?'

'Well, the truck with Citizen Romanov and his family went to the mine location, and after the shooting the bodies of the others were loaded into the second truck and taken out to the Four Brothers site.'

'That is the Ganin pit that this fellow, what's his name . . . ?'

'Ermakov,' Yurovsky says dully.

'Yes, this 'Ermakov', another one of the Ural Soviet. The pit, was that he place he had chosen?'

'Yes. He had been assigned that task. He had been drinking and he did it very poorly.'

'Because as it turned out they could not be buried in the, ah . . .' Zezulin checks his papers.

'That is correct. It is a type of mine, an open shaft, a hole in the ground. There are dozens in the area. We threw the bodies in but the water was too shallow.'

'Shallow, yes. Which meant they had to be moved to another location.'

'They attempted to burn the corpses and failed in that, too. So then they decided to move them.'

'Where?'

'I'm not even sure. Some distance,' Yurovsky says, glancing down at his feet.

'Who selected this location?'

'I have no idea, someone in the Ural Soviet. They just found it.'

'Hmm.'

'That's not so good. That makes it look like you weren't doing your job,' Stein says.

'But I was! My job was to make sure the Imperial Family was taken to a safe –'

'Ah, ah, ah,' says Zezulin and waves to the stenographer to stop.

'Well, it *was*,' says Yurovsky, humbly.

Stein looks over at Zezulin. 'We might as well tell them.'

'Fine.' Zezulin looks over at the stenographer.

'Why don't you go for dinner. And close the doors behind you.' The young apprentice nods his assent and does what he is told. When the door is closed, Zezulin puts his papers aside, eases himself into the big chair and begins, like a favourite uncle telling a ghost story.

'You see, there was a plot,' Zezulin begins.

'You might call it an arrangement.'

'An agreement. An offer was made –'

'From the Kaiser,' says Ryzhkov. So far he has been sitting over by the window slowly drinking a full glass of schnapps. The whole thing is thoroughly depressing, lies upon lies. Whose knife is in whose back.

'Very good, Pyotr Mikhalovich, very astute. Yes, an offer from Kaiser Wilhelm, who after all was cousin to the Tsar. He wanted to be a hero. He contacted –'

'It doesn't matter who,' Stein interjects.

'Yes, yes. At any rate, contact was made with someone in the highest circles.'

'I'd put my roubles on Lenin,' Ryzhkov says. Zezulin just turns and looks at him for a long moment. Ryzhkov lifts his glass in acknowledgement.

'It really doesn't matter who was contacted. All that matters is that for a certain sum of money –'

'How much, no one knows,' says Stein.

'– the plan was set in motion to help the Tsar, his wife and children escape.'

'And the money?' Ryzhkov puts in.

'The money would be for the revolution. Everyone knows we are short of money. We need to buy things, guns, bullets, food . . .' Zezulin threatens to begin a tirade.

'I was only directed to remove them to a place of safety, that I was to do it in secret, and wait for the contact,' Yurovsky says. His voice is taking on a higher pitch, the sound of a man who has lost his place in the book of life.

'Of course, of course. That was for your own protection.'

'And a good job you did of it too.'

'Of course,' says Ryzhkov. Zezulin gets up from his chair and in two strides crosses to Ryzhkov, takes the glass out of his hand and tosses it out onto the veranda where it shatters. In a moment they see one of the young men running out from the kitchen entrance to see what's the matter. Zezulin waves him away.

'Let's try to give our best efforts, eh? Let's try to not lose our way by falling into the slough of despond, eh, Pyotr Mikhalovich?'

'Back to the story,' Stein prods.

'Yes. So what happened, we think –'

'It's all speculation. We surmise, we assume from fragmentary evidence –'

'What happened is that the Kaiser changed his plans.'

'They started losing the war, is what happened.'

'Once again you have put your finger on it, Pyotr. You can imagine the scene. Someone comes into the Kaiser's palace. They have the bad news from the western front. "You can't bring the Romanovs here for safekeeping. At the very least you will have to hide them in some neutral country. They will have to change their identity and if it ever comes out" . . . and so on and so forth. Something along those lines.'

'So he reluctantly –'

'Reluctantly? Well, let's give him the benefit of the doubt.

394

It's family, it's blue blood, not very nice, but still he did it. He gave the order, or he allowed someone else to give it.'

'The Germans cut them loose,' says Yurovsky.

'Yes. We infer from this telegram sent to . . .' Once more he fishes in his papers. 'We don't know for sure, but it must be this man you reported. Todmann?'

'He called himself Ivanis,' says Ryzhkov.

'Well, he was sending messages as Todmann.' Zezulin finds the slip of paper. Shows it to him. 'It's not very sophisticated. They had to send it as if it were a normal business code, all this pretence about furs and sales. Boys' games, if you ask me.'

'So that's the reason for the delay?' asks Yurovsky.

'Sure. And in the aftermath this Todmann contact doesn't know what to do. He's waiting for instructions. The Czechs have taken the town and now he's in hiding. He doesn't know you, he doesn't know where your mineshaft is. He is growing more desperate.'

'They cut him loose too, Boris,' says Ryzhkov from his dark corner.

'So he's thinking –'

'He is thinking about himself for once, I am imagining. He is suddenly aware that he is expendable,' says Ryzhkov.

'Yes.'

'And when he learns about your mineshaft, Yakov, he goes out there. He follows his instincts, but then he is thinking –'

'Thinking, thinking, always thinking.'

'Yes, very much so, and so he steals Alexei and the girl.'

'Sure,' says Stein. 'And he has already has made a way to get them out. It's desperate, but it almost works.'

'But thanks to you,' Zezulin nods and smiles to Yurovsky, 'and to you,' he throws a glance to Ryzhkov, 'they all end up dead.'

'But what about the girl?' Stein says a little hesitantly. 'What about her? Grand Duchess Marie?'

'She's gone,' says Ryzhkov.

Zezulin turns and walks over to the window where Ryzhkov slumps. He stands for a long moment, hands in his pockets, rocking back and forth. 'Gone? What does that mean, Pyotr Mikhalovich? Gone where, exactly?'

'I don't know.'

'Dead? Alive?'

And all Ryzhkov can do is turn away to stare out the window where the trees are swirling around, and the first large drops are crashing onto the walk.

'"Gone." I suppose we can use that, can't we?'

'Sure,' says Stein. 'A little disinformation always works.'

Zezulin goes away for three days. No one knows where. Ryzhkov begins to think that he's taken up his old alcoholic habit again. Stein has begun to drink himself. They all have. Meeting around the table, saying nothing, then drinking too much and falling into arguments about Todmann's motivation. The incredible cynicism of emperors and spies.

What does it matter? Ryzhkov screams at them. They just watch him, glasses in hand. He stalks outside, perches in the collapsed seat of a wicker chair and sulks in the rain. Chills himself to the bone, tries to die out there in the linen tycoon's overgrown garden. Gets a head cold and collapses in the bed he's been given. No fleas, he thinks, thanking all the gods. At least no fleas.

When Zezulin returns he has brought a man named Mirvis with him. When he is out of the room Stein describes him as Sverdlov's hand-picked delegate. So . . .

Together, working as a collective, they create Yurovsky's personal report. It will be a note, a memorandum. Something that he has jotted down while the memories are fresh. The requirements of the note are by now obvious to them all: it must both hide the truth and hide the horror, explain the missing bodies and the newly discovered jewels. Most importantly, there must be no whiff of complicity between the Bolshevik leadership and the Kaiser. The various errors and chaos of the night of 16–17 June will be blamed on the amateurish guards recruited from the Verkh-Isetsk factory and the over-zealous actions of the Ural Soviet. The barbarity of it will be laid at the feet of men and women hungry for revenge.

Creating the note is accomplished in the same manner as a team of playwrights around a table might rush a drama into production. Zezulin begins the recitation, but soon everyone is chiming in as they rewrite history. Ryzhkov sits in his accustomed place, now with his own tumbler of schnapps that Zezulin tolerates as long as he doesn't get too sarcastic. The game, the psychological part of it, as Mirvis explains, is to have Yurovsky put it all in his own words.

'Just as you would if you were writing a letter to your mother,' Mirvis says, waving his hands around as if he were conjuring a spell. 'Now,' he says, 'begin!'

They work from a pastiche of statements: their own, which the stenographers have dutifully typed up in the evenings, and others. Similar interrogations have been conducted on the other characters in the farce: leaders of the Ural Soviet who have washed up in Bolshevik-held territory – Beloborodov, Goloshchokin and Peter Ermakov himself, whose braggadocio has already got him more lines than he deserves.

They take breaks to smoke outside under the eaves of the house, sheltering from the rain and the occasional snow that is starting early this year. Inside it is too noisy because Zezulin has found a guitar and has begun a serenade. Yurovsky laughs about thinking he had been shot more times than in reality, about mistaking the train wreck for a bullet's impact.

Mirvis admits after a few drinks that the threat of death is hanging over all of them so that the stakes are very high, very high indeed, and for this reason, once completed, the note will not be made public. Obviously nothing will be said about Todmann and their wild train ride, still even Grand Duchess Marie Nikolaievna's disappearance can be used, Mirvis explains to Ryzhkov as they smoke out on the terrace.

'Yes, disinformation and keeping all the various conspiracy theories alive is a useful component of the plan, my dear Ryzhkov. It's vital. You give people something to believe in, and then you watch them carefully to see exactly what part of it they do believe in. Take some away, maybe. See what they do. Then your enemies are revealed and it's suddenly very simple to pick your allies.'

'I think I see.'

'It is a sort of . . . what is it called? Ah, yes, a litmus test, comrade. Only those who are being tested, they don't even know it, they're not even aware that we are measuring them for a new suit of clothes. If they fit, then we know what to do with them.'

'Yes, I do see.'

'Its only one tool, this kind of propaganda. We don't really have a name for what we do, not yet. No, we don't! These techniques are all just being born. We'll understand what we're doing, but that will be in the future. Right now, we don't yet.'

Mirvis is the most enthusiastic Bolshevik he has ever met, Ryzhkov thinks.

'We are as children.'

'Yes.'

'It's diabolical isn't it?'

'Very clever.'

'Were you fooled?'

'I just answered the questions that were put to me.'

'Of course, of course. And you see we know that. You

were conscientious, trying to save those children. All right, forget that they were parasites, class enemies and potential banners for all the various counter-revolutionary blah-blah-blahs. You were a good Bolshevik. You tried to do the right thing. A man with a conscience.'

'So I was.'

'Some would say that having a conscience is a weakness, but I would never, ever say such a thing. What's the point of a revolution if we can't be human beings with human feelings and human emotions? Then it's only a revolution of, what? Machines? I'm not a machine, neither are you. My actions are predictable, but that's based on my class, how I've been raised, what I've been taught. It's very hard to shed your stripes, Ryzhkov.'

'Yes, I know.'

'What's important is that you're seen to be making the effort, and as far as that goes your conduct has been . . .'

'Exemplary?'

'Exactly. You, Yurovsky in there? You're men we can point to, leaders, icons of the new order. We need more people like you. They're giving you an award, did you know that? Oops! I wasn't supposed to say that. Pretend you didn't hear, eh? I'll just get in trouble.'

'Is that part of the test?'

'Oh . . . Oh! Ha, ha, ha. Very clever. You've got a real future here. Well, it's starting to get a little cold out here, eh? My apologies for the rigour of the entire process. Let's get something to eat. After this is all done you can go into the city, fit yourself out with some better clothes. You have some unfinished business, as I understand it.'

'If you say so.'

'Like everyone I only know part of the picture. It can be very confusing.' Mirvis puts his arm around him. 'I have blinkers on, Pyotr Mikhalovich. So do you. Invisible blinkers, eh? We look ahead. And that's what we see, whatever's in front of us. That's all we have to see, eh?'

'You have to learn to love the blinkers, I am thinking.'

'After a while you don't even notice they are on. That's the best way.'

The note, when it is finished, rests there on the low table, a document of some twenty pages, with handwritten additions. Hands are shaken. Glasses are raised. Creative flourishes are praised. Particularly appreciated is the thread that depicts the discovery of the jewels sewn into the grand duchesses' corsets, and the heightened drama of the scene: the terror of the superstitious guards – simple proletarians, after all – as their bullets ricochet off the corsets, the terrorized girls careening around the tiny storeroom like wraiths, and the gemstones only discovered out at the Ganin pit when the corpses are stripped for burning. 'That touch ties up everything,' Zezulin says with a smile and a laugh.

'Oh, by the way, your trial has been cancelled,' says Mirvis. 'But you're still under arrest.'

And everyone laughs and retires to the various corners of the dacha to sleep it off.

In the morning a sleepy-eyed Stein stumbles out to heat up the samovar, and notices that the final draft of the note and the papers they'd collated on the table are missing.

And so is Ryzhkov.

45

He spent the night hiding. Moving from workers' café to workers' café to get out of the cold, sleeping in workers' libraries, and endlessly on the trams, now free to anyone who wanted to ride them. He didn't stand out.

The plan, such as it was, had come to him as an impulse in the midst of Zezulin's gypsy singing. He had seen the way the cards were falling, seen a way to change things. Change things, protect himself, or at least strike back. A lever.

The danger – well, it was suicidal, but what did he have to lose? They might be having parties at the dacha and slapping each other on the back, but he knew that they would probably shoot him and Yurovsky in the morning. So when the idea came to him, even though it was a crazy thing to do, it lit him up enough to cause him to run out of the dacha with the drafts of Yurovsky's note stuffed under his jacket.

The problem was, it was a lever, but where was the rock? Who to take it to? He finally decided on Sverdlov. He was secretary to the Central Committee, the gatekeeper for Lenin, Trotsky and the inner circle. If an approach had been made from the Kaiser, it would have come from the German ambassador. It would have occured at the highest levels, and everything would have gone through Sverdlov. And besides, Sverdlov was from Yekaterinburg. So was Yurovsky. So was the first interrogator he'd stonewalled as soon as they'd brought him back and installed him in his cell in the Kremlin. He couldn't spend the rest of his life sleeping in trams and eating from the workers' soup lines off the Arbat, so he'd decided to put his lever under Sverdlov.

It meant going to the Kremlin.

He went through with a knot of pilgrims, nodding and genuflecting, who were being allowed to approach but not actually visit the Assumption Cathedral. He separated himself, put a few sheets of the papers in his hand and started walking across the wide plaza, staring at the ground, like an emerging Bolshevik bureaucrat travelling between offices on the people's business.

All across the city there had been no manhunt. Not that he could see. He flashed his Cheka identification and walked right into the Senate building.

It looked like they were playing it quiet. They had to play it quiet. Then he told himself not to get confident, to stay scared. Certainly Zezulin was at the head of efforts to find him quietly and with as little fuss as possible. They'd eventually capture him, then they'd spend a while talking to him, take the drafts and all the notes back, and then they'd torture and kill him once they had everything.

Sverdlov's office was a huge anteroom to the suite of offices that Lenin used. He waited until the door was open and he walked in. Sverdlov was on the telephone, frowning. He looked up for a moment. There was a battery of wireless printers in one of the adjacent rooms that stuttered and popped. 'Just a moment,' Sverdlov said to Ryzhkov, putting his hand over the receiver, and listened a moment more.

'Tell them it is allowed,' he said to the person on the end of the line, and then, 'You're welcome.'

'This is what's going to happen,' Ryzhkov said when he hung up.

At the entrance to the room one of Sverdlov's assistants hovered, a younger, thicker man than Ryzhkov. He had a revolver in a holster and his hand was on the flap. Sverdlov waved him away.

Yakov Sverdlov stood, one hand poised on the edge of his desk. At one time it must have been owned by a banker or some industrial magnate. It was ornate and carved in the flamboyant style favoured by Tsarist-era generals or country gentlemen. One of the legs was scuffed and a portion of the carved grapes had been broken away. It would have happened recently, judging by the difference in colour of the wood.

'Close the door, Kowalski,' he said to the assistant, then cocked his head and peered at Ryzhkov, as if he might discover something important by prolonging his gaze.

'Yes. Here's the way it's going to be,' Ryzhkov said as Sverdlov regained his composure and moved back to his place behind the great desk. 'I have everything.' He fumbled for the papers; some he had tied with string; they were warm from his body and he held them aloft, as if they were something given to him on the Mount. 'It's the story of the murder of the Tsar and his family. It's all here, just the way you want it,' he said and tossed the sheaf onto Sverdlov's desk where it landed with a slapping sound, Sverdlov flinching and reaching out to catch it before it upset the inkwell. 'It's the cleaned-up version. The version that you've already started to tell the world.'

'All right. Fine. I understood it had gone missing. Thank you for recovering it.'

'You're most welcome, comrade secretary. But there's also another version.'

'I'm afraid I don't understand.'

The smoothness of his reply infuriated Ryzhkov. His face

403

grew hot; it was the same way he had felt climbing through the wreckage in Verdun, a charge of energy that erased his fatigue. Now he had begun to shout. He saw droplets of his own spittle flying out across the desk. His vision had narrowed and for a moment he saw himself from within, like the pilot of a dirigible watching his ship going down, down . . .

'Yes, you do understand! You understand! There's the real version, the truth. I have the truth!' he said, and then stopped, realizing that he was raving and that he was tired. Very tired.

'Comrade, I think you could use a meal. Some tea, perhaps?'

'I don't want your food. I want you to know that I have the truth about the Romanovs, about what happened to them. If you don't do what I say I'll make sure everyone finds out.'

'Oh? How will you do that?'

'I have the notes.' He leaned over the desk and tapped the sheaf of papers. 'I have all the testimony, everything we used to create this – this piece of shit. It's in a safe place.'

'A safe place? Really? And what is it that you want, Comrade Ryzhkov? Put simply, I mean?'

'Nothing will happen to Yurovsky. Take your cleaned-up story, tell it to the world if you want, but nothing happens to him. And nothing happens to me. We get to go on.'

'Well, of course you will,' Sverdlov said. He was leaning back in his chair now. Smiling, fingers laced behind his skull, completely at ease. 'Did you have doubts on that score?'

'I know everything. I know how the Kaiser paid money to save his cousins, and how you took it. You don't think the SRs will enjoy reading about that? How long do you think the revolution will last once the people learn about a betrayal like that?'

'Calm down. You've done the right thing. You certainly don't have to worry. You're not a criminal.'

'Put it in writing. Nothing happens to us. To any of us. To me, to him, or to our families.'

Now Sverdlov began to laugh. He shook his head the way you might react to a puppy that simply could not learn to go on the newspaper. 'All right, fine. If you're so terrified I'll put it in writing if you want, although writing never stopped anything.'

'Don't think I'm not serious.'

'I know, I know. You're a very bold fellow. The revolution has lots of ways to put bold fellows like you to very good use. But please, believe me, you have nothing to worry about at all.'

'Sure.'

'That's all you wanted?'

Ryzhkov reached forward, tapped the papers again. 'Listen, the real version of this will bring you down. It will kill the revolution.'

'I think I disagree, but go ahead.'

'If they find out about this deal, they'll drag you and the entire committee through the streets. It'll be you they hang from the lampposts. You will make what excuse you want – you needed to buy time, or guns, or breathing space – but they won't care about that. They won't understand whatever it was you were trying to do.'

Sverdlov unlaced his fingers, sat forward and pressed a button on his desk. The assistant was already waiting at the door. He came in a few steps and made a little arc around to have a better angle if he had to shoot Ryzhkov down right there in the office. Sverdlov picked up the bundle of papers and handed it to him.

'This has to be transcribed. Room fourteen, right away.'

'Yes, Comrade Secretary. Is there anything –'

'No, no, no, everything's fine,' Sverdlov said. 'Have someone bring a plate up for Comrade Ryzhkov here. He's performed a valuable service for the revolution and he's hungry and a little disturbed.'

'Yes, Comrade Secretary. Right away,' the assistant said, and backed out of the room.

Ryzhkov's face was hot. He was sweating and out of breath. Crazy, he thought. He'd finally gone crazy with his schemes worked out in a vodka haze after days of interrogation, his refinements made on endless tram rides across Moscow. What an idiot! 'I don't think you're taking this as seriously as you should,' he managed to say.

'Oh, I'm taking you very seriously.' Sverdlov reached into a drawer and came out with a bottle of schnapps, poured and pushed a glass across the desk to him. Made another one for himself. 'You've got the power of knowledge and, yes, you could do something brave and honourable and foolish. A misguided gesture, and perhaps cause a lot of damage. And, I admit it, you're correct, more or less, in your assessment of the threat to the revolution. No, if I seem a little casual about things, perhaps you could put it down to a kind of . . .' Sverdlov knocked back his glass, and then got up and went over to the window. 'You could put it down to shell shock, I suppose. Take another if you want, Pyotr Mikhalovich.'

'Thank you.' He refilled the two glasses and took them over to the window. They stood there looking out at the Kremlin wall, the curve of the Moskva river, the grey clouds in the sky, the coming winter.

'You see, I deal in death every day, Ryzhkov. All day long. I see it in numbers. Numbers of poods of grain that we've confiscated from peasant producers versus the much larger numbers of poods that we need to feed the Red Army; numbers of hectares of land destroyed by the capitalists and their hired armies; numbers of bullets we need to manufacture but can't. The amount of rainfall. The falling temperature, the number of wounded, number of bandages, gallons of petrol. Collaborators executed, the percentage points the rouble has fallen against the dollar, the pound, the peso. It's all numbers, but it's death just the same.' He raised his drink. 'To the revolution,' he said, turning to look at Ryzhkov. They touched glasses.

'You don't have to worry, Ryzhkov. We know about power here, the heads that have to roll and the deals that have to be made. We know about truth and we know about lies. We know all about that sort of thing. I wouldn't recommend publishing your theories, but nevertheless you're safe. You're quite safe, just as long as we are.'

There was a ring from the telephone on the desk, and Sverdlov crossed back to it, leaving him there at the window. His hands were shaking. Maybe they would bring the food soon.

'Yes, in fact he's right here,' Sverdlov was saying. Ryzhkov turned and looked at him. Sverdlov looked up and, smiling, nodded. 'Yes, yes . . . Well, yes, I do think you should meet him,' he said and hung up.

For a moment the two of them just looked at each other.

'Sometimes,' Sverdlov said, giving him a patient smile, 'sometimes everything comes together. It's a combination of things, usually: the forces of history, injustices that have festered for far too long, shortages. People reach the breaking point and they collapse, or they rise to the occasion. This is one of those times, Ryzhkov. I congratulate you.'

At the opposite end of the room a door opened. Ryzhkov could see the back of a military uniform as a man backed in through the door. He was pulling a wheelchair through the narrow door and over the raised jamb. The sound of the wheels made rhythmic little clickings on the parquet. Once he was through the door he swung the wheelchair around and Ryzhkov saw that Vladimir Ilyich Lenin was seated there, his legs covered by a blanket.

He looked thinner than his pictures; his skin was pale and

stretched over the cheekbones. He raised his hand to Ryzhkov and waved as if from a great distance.

'Look at him, Vladimir Ilyich,' Sverdlov said, taking over the wheelchair from the guard. 'He's dumbfounded!' He was laughing as he pushed Lenin across the room.

'And here he is,' Lenin said in a voice that was surprisingly loud. 'Here he is, our hero!'

46

He walked through the crowds of people all heading down towards St Basil's Square, the only free man in the city.

There were the uniforms of Red Guards, soldiers and sailors, proletarian workers with flags to wave or a bit of red fabric pinned to their lapels. Even in the chill with the wet snow starting again there was an atmosphere of electric energy. Snatches of revolutionary songs came to him as he passed through the shopping district that followed the perimeter of the old city wall. All across the city the citizens of Moscow were gathering, their energy coalescing into something much greater – the newly created animal they were going to celebrate on this night, the first anniversary of the Bolshevik revolution.

'You have defied them all. How very brave of you,' Zezulin said. He was wearing a long overcoat and a thick cossack's hat to shelter his balding head against the cold.

'It was never defiance. Just logic. You would have done the same.'

'But not like you, nothing like you,' Zezulin said, and Ryzhkov thought he could hear a laugh in his voice. 'I honestly don't think I would have made the tactical choice to go into the Central Committee Secretary's office and start making demands.'

'Well . . .'

'Very foolhardy, if you ask me.'

'I didn't ask you.'

'But you should have. I would have given you good advice, and you know in your heart I would have never let anything happen to you. We had an agreement, remember? You did your job. A bloody good job. Above and beyond. You think I couldn't see that?'

'It doesn't matter now.'

'No, you're right, Pyotr. Against all odds, against all logic, everything's worked out just fine,' Zezulin said. He took Ryzhkov by the arm. It would look to anyone watching them like a friendly gesture. Two pals walking along towards the celebrations.

'What will happen to Yurovsky?'

'Oh, just like you, he's set for life. He's going to be given a job, a good job out of the way. A position where he can organize things. Don't worry about him.'

'I didn't get a chance to say goodbye.'

'You're not getting sentimental on me, are you?'

'If you are ever in touch with him, give him my regards. I owe him, eh? He saved my life.'

'And you saved his, so you're even. Just forget all about it, Pyotr Mikhalovich. Don't send him any birthday cards, or else someone might put two and two together. Officially you're not even in the record.'

'If that's the way they want it, all right.'

'And regarding the note for which you were so willing to lay down your life, yes, it's going to be filed. At the very back of some vault probably, as soon as it's finished, of course.'

'We finished it.' He stopped and looked at Zezulin.

410

'You did indeed. But various accounts from all sources are still being harmonized. The story of the killings has made the international news, and sooner or later something official must be said.'

'Something more than just admitting that they're dead?'

'Obviously our version must come out. Everyone is blaming us. We're being called barbarians. Much ado over a little bit of royal blood, if you ask me, but who am I to have an opinion? As far as we are concerned the over-zealousness of the Ural Soviet is the culprit. Comrade Trotsky is obviously very upset since, as everyone knows, he had his heart set on putting the Tsar on trial here in Moscow with himself as prosecutor, another chance to show off his oratorical skills. It would have been a grand show, I admit.'

'It would have been,' Ryzhkov said. He suddenly had a flash of memory: the Tsar with his newly shaven face, stoking the breakfast fire while his family waited in the dank mineshaft; the look of the girl after she'd washed her face with rainwater.

'No, no, it's all very plausible. Tell it like this: some very angry metal workers just got a little out of control. You know how men can get under the pressure of combat, eh? It's understandable the way these passions build and build to the breaking point. The abuses accumulate and they have to take it out on someone. Even if the victim never hurt a fly. It's symbolic. When you think about it like that, you can see that it's actually the Tsar's fault, all that happened to his family. "Live by the sword . . ."'

Ahead of them the gate loomed. There was a band playing inside, a revolutionary anthem. He'd even learned the words – not intentionally, they'd just seeped in from repetition. Prisoners, chains, destiny and the inevitable victory of the people. 'Aren't you tired of this, Velimir?'

'No, strangely enough I find it invigorating. And you know,

honestly, the absurdity continues to amaze me. Those above us actually welcome the fact that everyone thinks that the Romanovs escaped and are in hiding. Mexico is the favoured location in the last few weeks. Mexico, Greece. Fine, whatever comes up. If enough people are ready to swallow that, then it just makes it easier for us to further obscure whatever we decide has to be obscured.'

'The truth, for example.'

'"Truth." That's really very funny.'

'I suppose it is.'

Ahead of them the streets were curving and the crowds were slowing down and backing up as they all tried to get through the narrow entry of the street onto the square. They had blocked things off for the parades.

'I hate it when it gets dark like this.'

'Winter. Our curse and our saviour.'

'How soon can I go back to France?'

'I didn't say anything about that.'

'Somewhere else then. Somewhere warm.'

'Every Russian wants to die in warmth.'

They walked on in silence, came up onto the back of the crowds. There was a lot of drinking, bottles were being passed along through the crowd, one came their way and they both drank and let the bottle continue on its voyage. Zezulin started humming a tune. One of his gypsy melodies. Ryzhkov remembered it, something he'd first heard years before, something from back in their days together in Petersburg. He supposed they had both come a long way. Well . . . so had Russia.

'There is going to be a trial, of course.'

For a moment Ryzhkov stopped. Turned to Zezulin, pulled his arm away in a reflex.

'Oh, no, no, no, not you!' Zezulin cried, reaching out and actually pulling him back into a fraternal embrace. 'No, no, it's going to be those other members of the Ural Soviet. They're the ones we've identified as the people who got carried away in the heat of the thing, deviated from the correct line by defying the orders of the committee, and illegally and brutally murdered the Romanov family. They are going to hold it in Perm, so I am given to know.'

'My God!' Ryzhkov said. 'None of them did it. None of them did anything. They are all innocent. You know that, Velimir.' It was like swimming in an ocean of cynicism.

Zezulin saw his expression, and took him by the arm again. 'Innocent. A very hard quality to nail down, eh? Anyhow, there will be a trial, and thus will the Bolshevik regime show the world its concern for justice and its abhorrence of brutality.'

'Please, please . . . It doesn't have to be France. Send me to China, Mexico, anywhere at all.'

'They've done all the planning. It's quite a concept. As soon as they retake Yekaterinburg they're going to call Glavni Prospekt "Lenin Street" and the plaza outside the Ipatiev house the "Square of the People's Revenge". I guess that says it all, eh?'

Ryzhkov took a deep breath. Ahead the great square had been divided off into areas for the audience to stand, tiers of seating for those who required to sit, a stage with a curtained wall beneath which an orchestra sawed away to fight off the cold. Loudspeakers with great horns had been set up and an announcer was describing the wonderful evening that had been planned for them all.

'Oh, yes . . . one last thing, Pyotr Mikhalovich. Do you want this? As a keepsake? I know, I know. You keep claiming that you don't know her, but . . .' Zezulin was holding out the photograph of Vera, the same one he'd slid across the table when he'd interrogated him in the basement of the Lubyanka.

He stood there for a moment and then looked up into the man's cold eyes.

The band was playing. A parade had begun. They pushed their way close to the front and he could see the marchers, a regiment of horribly thin adolescents striding along in step, wooden rifles on their shoulders, each rank of the serious-faced boys preceded by equally serious girls waving banners. A torrent of red blotting out the domes of the cathedral and the skies above them all.

There were pasteboard shingles of food being passed out through the crowd, as much as could be eaten combined with exhortations to conserve as much as possible. To each according to his hunger.

Heroes of the revolution were being acknowledged on the stand, filing across to be given the newly created Order of the Red Banner, the first decoration of the infant regime, to have the story of their individual heroism depicted for the crowd. A file of wounded soldiers and sailors, ordinary men and women who had been put through hell and managed to somehow shrug it off and do something selfless.

And then she came onto the stage.

The press of bodies held him in place when he tried to move closer, but it was her. Unmistakable, even bundled into her long overcoat that just brushed the tops of her boots. Only her hair had changed, back to its natural brown. She took the stage hand in hand with a man who was announced as her husband. Tall, a little older, thin with a smile that he tried to hold back. A doctor.

Now she was Vera Musatova, he learned from the announcer. It was a dramatic story: they had met at the front at the start of the war, fallen in love while up to their elbows in surgery; appalled by the carnage brought on by the warring empires, the two of them had been among the first to lead the Tsarist military hospitals to overthrow their commanders

414

and come over to the revolution. Now that the revolution was under attack from all sides by the Whites and Allied capitalist forces the two had continued their struggle to improve the efficiency with which soldiers of the Red Army received emergency care. Heroic doctor, heroic nurse.

Musatov had his arm around her waist as they gratefully accepted their awards, promising to heal all those wounded in the future.

There was a cheer and a fanfare from the orchestra; on their heels other heroes were announced, and he watched her walking off the stage with her husband. Smiles in place. He must have made a remark to her because she looked over and smiled at him as they made their exit. At the steps he paused and let her go down first.

Ryzhkov turned to speak to him but Zezulin had slipped away without notice. He craned his neck to find the man, but it was no use.

He still had the portrait in his hand, and for a moment he bent his hands around the pasteboard frame and was about to tear it into pieces, but he hesitated and after that could not make his fingers obey and finish the task. He couldn't harm her by loving her any more. If anyone was safe, she was. He had given her everything he could. It would have to be enough.

He tucked the photograph in his jacket and pushed his way out of the crowd. The torches and electric searchlights that fanned the sky bounced off the Kremlin wall and made it appear as if something behind him was burning. Silhouettes whipped across the masonry; the celebrating proletariat continued to cheer. The fanfares echoed over one another in the great square. Amid the verses of the songs were shouted slogans, threats and promises of a better world to come. He wanted to run but made himself resist the urge. Men were dancing in the firelight.

A new era had swallowed them all.

Sources and acknowledgements

A debt of gratitude to Suzie Payne for being completely involved in this novel and for her advice and confidence. In Mexico: the perceptive comments of Spencer Miller; to Suzanne Walker for the shoes and more, and Miles for the margaritas. To my fantastic agent and Russophile Helen Heller, as always. To Brenda Leadlay for discussions in the early stages. To the staffs of the various museums and galleries of La Spezia, especially the Museo Navale della Marina Militare; in Trieste, most particularly La Riseria concentration camp; and in Turin the Museo Nazionale del Risorgimento Italiano, for inspirations which were the genesis of Giustiniani. For her excellent guidance in St Petersburg and Moscow, Ms Katya Mourer.

Last Train to Kazan is fiction. Historical characters that I have included (Yurovsky, Grand Duchess Marie, Goloschokin, Wilton, Lenin, etc.) are not portrayed as accurate representations of the real persons. This is especially true in the case of Sophie Buxhoeveden; my fictional creation should in no way be confused with the real woman. Similarly, a great many events have been compressed, rearranged and reimagined for dramatic purposes.

As historians continue to warn us, truth is an elusive commodity; this is especially true in the case of the fate of the Romanov family. Minds more noble than mine have been irretrievably lured into the dramatic gravity of their tragedy. Throughout the last century a wealth of testimony, speculation, obfuscation, hallucination, litigation and propaganda has engulfed the subject. Just as with the events at Sarajevo in 1914, much should be taken with a grain of salt. At present, after sifting through the bones, ashes and DNA, there remain two bodies unaccounted for – Alexei and one of his sisters, almost certainly Marie. The search for forensic closure has been truncated by the interment of the bones in the Romanov vault in St Petersburg.

If you wish to read one book about the events that took place in Yekaterinburg in July 1918 it should be Greg King and Penny Wilson's *The Fate of the Romanovs* (John Wiley & Sons, Hoboken, NJ, 2003). It is very clear, extremely well researched and objective to a fault; the current truth.

On the Romanovs generally: Of the masses of histories and biographies that are widely available one of my favourites is the beautifully produced *Nicholas and Alexandra: The Last Imperial Family of Tsarist Russia* by the State Hermitage Museum and the State Archive of the Russian Federation (Booth-Clibborn, London, 1998).

In addition to those sources consulted for *A Game of Soldiers*, and in no particular order, particularly helpful were:

Brook-Shepherd, Gordon, *Ironmaze: The Western Secret Services and the Bolsheviks* (Macmillan, London, 1998), and Michael Kettle's *The Road to Intervention* (Routledge, London, 1988), were both very helpful for the machinations of the Lockhart plot.

Clarke, William, *The Lost Fortune of the Tsars* (St Martin's Press, New York, 1994). A detailed review of the disposition of Romanov personal effects, fortunes, jewels, estates and relics.

Lincoln, W. Bruce, *Red Victory* (Simon & Schuster, New York, 1989). My chapter on Uritsky's murder and Fanya Kaplan's attempt on Lenin is largely derived from Lincoln's excellent book. Like all of Lincoln's *œuvre* this book is highly recommended.

Massie, Robert K., *The Romanovs: The Final Chapter* (Random House, New York, 1995). Written after the various DNA tests.

For an early Soviet adventure-novel point of view see *The Commissar of the Gold Express* by V. Matveyev, with illustrations by Ernst (published by New York International Publishers and originally by the Co-operative Publishing Society of Foreign Workers, Moscow, in 1933).

McNeal, Shay, *The Secret Plot to Save the Tsar* (William Morrow, New York, 2001). The most recent survival-theory proponent, this very interesting book speculates on the veracity of *Rescuing the Czar*, a book published in San Francisco in 1920, and further suggests that various analyses of Romanov DNA evidence are faulty.

Nicholson, T.R, *Sports Cars 1907–1927* (Blandford Press, London, 1970) for details of the motor cars.

O'Conor, John F., *The Sokolov Investigation* (Robert Speller & Sons, New York, 1971). In 1918 Sokolov was appointed by the Whites to investigate the Romanov murders. From the beginning his report was the subject of controversy. There is an original French edition of Sokolov's work that is more complete, and held to be 'better'.

For an example of the black hole into which one can be drawn while researching the last days of the Romanovs, see Occleshaw, Michael, *The Romanov Conspiracies: The Romanovs and the House of Windsor* (Chapmans, London, 1993). I admit to being nearly completely persuaded by Occleshaw when I first read him. An example of a seductively plausible addition to the Romanov survival legends.

Radzinsky, Edvard, *The Last Tsar: The Life and Death of Nicholas II* (Doubleday, New York, 1992). Depicts the pre-DNA discovery of bones and the creation of the Yurovsky note. Excellent book.

Serge, Victor, *Year One of the Russian Revolution*, translated by Peter Sedgwick, photographic research by Celestine Dars (Holt, Rinehart & Winston, New York, 1972).

Summers, Anthony and Tom Mangold, *The File on the Tsar* (Harper & Row, New York, 1976). Upon publication this book turned Romanov speculation into an industry. Fascinating, but written before the Pig Meadow site was discovered and, being pre-DNA, is obsolete. Includes much about the supposed Perm escape route.

Trewin, J.C., *The House of Special Purpose: An Intimate Portrait of the Last Days of the Russian Imperial Family*, from the papers of Charles Sydney Gibbes (Stein & Day, New York, 1975).

For details of the Civil War around Kazan: Leon Trotsky's *My Life*, Chapter 33, and *Svyazhsk*, by Larissa Reisner, contained in Hansen, Joseph, *et al.*, *Leon Trotsky: The Man and His Work* (Merit Publishers, New York, 1969). If you want Trotsky all the time, this is the book. For more on Larissa Reisner, see Porter, Cathy, *Larissa Reisner* (Virago Press, London, 1988).

On the internet; of great interest and much help is the Alexander Palace Discussion Forum, and for an excellent tour, plus archival photographs of the Ipatiev house, see www.romanov-memorial.com

And finally . . . this book is dedicated to my mother, Laura Miller, a truly amazing Southern woman who overcame many challenges in her life, showed me the meaning of courage and persistence, and gave me my appreciation of drama, many of my dreams, my pride, my anger and my spine.